MARY BALOGH, who won the *Romantic Times* Award for Best New Regency Writer in 1985, has since become the genre's most popular and bestselling author. She has won four Waldenbook Awards and a B. Dalton Award for bestselling Regencies, and a *Romantic Times* Lifetime Achievement Award in 1989. Her newest Regency is *Courting Julia*.

GAYLE BUCK has freelanced for regional publications, worked for a radio station, and as a secretary. Until recently, she was involved in public relations for a major Texas university. Her latest Regency is *Miss Dower's Paragon*.

SANDRA HEATH, the daughter of an officer in the Royal Air Force, spent most of her life traveling to various European posts. She now resides in Gloucester, England, together with her husband and young daughter. Her newest Regency is *Cruel Lord Cranham*.

EMILY HENDRICKSON lives in Incline Village, Nevada, with her retired airline pilot husband. Of all the many places she has visited around the world, England is her favorite and the most natural choice as the setting for her novels. Her latest Regencies include *The Gallant Lord Ives* and *Julia's Spirit*.

LAURA MATTHEWS lives with her architect husband, Paul in San Francisco. Ms. Matthews' favorite pursuits are traveling and scrounging in old book stores for research material. Her newest Regency is *The Village Spinster*.

A Regency Christmas

Mary Balogh • Gayle Buck
Sandra Heath • Emily Hendrickson
Laura Matthews

A SIGNET BOOK

SIGNET
Published by the Penguin Group
Penguin Books USA Inc., 375 Hudson Street,
New York, New York 10014, U.S.A.
Penguin Books Ltd, 27 Wrights Lane,
London W8 5TZ, England
Penguin Books Australia Ltd, Ringwood,
Victoria, Australia
Penguin Books Canada Ltd, 10 Alcorn Avenue,
Toronto, Ontario, Canada M4V 3B2
Penguin Books (N.Z.) Ltd, 182–190 Wairau Road,
Auckland 10, New Zealand

Penguin Books Ltd, Registered Offices:
Harmondsworth, Middlesex, England

First published by Signet,
an imprint of Dutton Signet, a division of Penguin Books USA Inc.

First Printing, November, 1993
10 9 8 7 6 5 4 3 2 1

 REGISTERED TRADEMARK—MARCA REGISTRADA

Printed in the United States of America

Contents

Under the
Kissing Bough
by
Sandra Heath

IT WAS a wet and windswept morning eight days before Christmas as the traveling carriage drove in through the gates of Fairhill Park, high on the wooded cliffs above the seaside town of Lyme Regis. The carriage conveyed a solitary gentleman passenger whose interest in the property should have been much greater, for he had been its owner for eleven months now, but this was the first time he had come anywhere near.

Sir Philip Levington was handsome to a fault, and very much a dashing man of fashion, from his black greatcoat with its astrakhan collar, to his gleaming top boots with their shining gilt spurs, but at that moment there was nothing dashing about the way he felt. His tall hat was tipped back wearily upon his dark curls, and his striking blue eyes were tired and unhappy. His complexion was still tanned from the summer, but if he'd stayed much longer in the heated drawing rooms and smoke of London, he knew he would soon have looked as jaded and done in as he felt.

He was twenty-nine years old, a member of London's *beau monde*, and was usually completely taken up in the capital's social whirl. He was also charming, sought-after, and eligible in the extreme, but at the moment he was exceedingly frustrated with his existence, because his private life was a very unsatisfactory tangle. Hence this long overdue visit to the wilds of Dorset, where he intended to see if country diversions were more to his liking. Anything had to be better than the catastrophe of his ill-judged love for Lady Delia Fitzroy, the beautiful willful widow who had played the flirt once too often, and finally destroyed any lingering illusions he had about her.

Reaching inside his coat, he took out a small silver-framed miniature, and gazed at the lovely painted face of the woman who'd toyed so carelessly with his heart. Delia Fitzroy. The name would always cause him pain. He studied the little portrait, taking in the subject's tawny hair, heart-shaped face, and magnificent gray eyes. It was hard to believe that such an angelic creature was really a *chienne* of the highest order, but now he was forced to wonder if there was any eligible gentleman in London at whom she hadn't set her scheming cap. What a fool he'd been to ever ask her to marry him. Well, she was in the past now. Lowering the window, he tossed the miniature out of the carriage, and then raised the glass again.

Then he leaned his head back against the brown leather seat and gazed out through the rain-washed window toward the house as it came into view along the curve of the drive. He'd bought the property on a whim, without knowing anything about it beyond the fact that it dated back to the Tudor period, and had to be sold because its previous owner, an unfortunate gentleman by the name of Charlton, had fallen upon hard times. But as he looked at it now, he knew that at last Dame Fortune had smiled upon him. Maybe this odious year of 1820 would end agreeably after all.

Fairhill Park was an exquisite Elizabethan mansion built of stone that had mellowed over the centuries, so that the house appeared to have almost grown out of the ground, rather than been placed there by man. It had a rambling lichen-covered roof, gables, finials, tall twined chimneys, and mullioned windows, some of which boasted exquisite stained glass. No doubt many would regard it to be in need of improvement, but it pleased him greatly. He was suffering from a surfeit of all that was novel and new, and found comfort in that which was traditional and timeless. This place was both of these latter things, and he had a notion he would like it here.

The carriage drew up before the heavy stone porch with its column supports and guardian lions, the emblem of the Charlton family. As Philip alighted, he had to hold on to the brim of his hat as the wind snatched at it. He turned to the cold, wet coachman and raised his voice above the bluster of the weather.

"From what I remember of the plans, the stables are to be found around that corner. I know I'm a few days early, and that most of the servants have been given some days off before my Christmas guests arrive, but there should be someone in the kitchens to attend to our requirements. Go there as soon as you've made the horses comfortable."

"Sir." The coachman touched his dripping hat, and then stirred the team into action again.

As the carriage drove away toward the corner, Philip searched in his greatcoat pocket for the key. A moment later he had opened the studded door and entered a baronial hall that was dark with shadows. It had a high hammerbeam ceiling where wheel-rimmed chandeliers were suspended on heavy iron chains, a minstrels' gallery, an immense stone fireplace, and a long refectory table made of ancient English oak. A grand staircase rose to one side of a dais where once the lords of the manor had presided over feasts and banquets, and the paneled walls were adorned with paintings, tapestries, and a collection of sixteenth-century weapons. There was a tall and elegant stained-glass oriel window through which he could see a sunken garden that was filled with lovingly tended topiary trees and shrubs. Beyond the garden the park stretched to the clifftop, and then there were the gray storm-tossed waters of Lyme Bay.

His spurs jingled on the uneven stone floor as he crossed toward the staircase and made his way up to the gallery, from where he could gaze down over everything. Taking off his greatcoat and resting it over the balustrade, he then placed his hat and gloves on top of it before allowing his appreciative eyes to wander. Yes, he would like it here. Suddenly he found himself looking forward to the Yuletide arrival of his sister and a large gathering of friends. He could only feel sympathy for the luckless Mr. Charlton, whose disastrous financial ventures had brought him to ruin, and who was now obliged to live with his wife and daughters in severely reduced circumstances in Lyme Regis, barely half a mile away from all he had lost.

* * *

As fate would have it, the two Misses Charlton were at that very moment engaged upon a conversation that concerned Fairhill Park.

"Madeleine, if you still intend to be wicked enough to scrump the fir cones from the park, you had best do so before Sunday." Margaret Charlton glanced up from embroidering the cambric shirt she was giving her betrothed for Christmas.

She was pale because she was still recuperating after the influenza that had subsequently struck their mother. There was a thick white cashmere shawl around her shoulders to keep out the winter drafts, and she wore a long-sleeved aquamarine merino gown with a belt high beneath her breasts. It was the warmest gown remaining in her gravely reduced wardrobe. Her long chestnut hair was pinned up beneath a lace cap with frilled lappets tied beneath her chin. She looked across the cottage parlor at her elder sister, who sat dreamily upon the chintz window seat.

Madeleine's dark crimson velvet gown was burnished by the dancing firelight as she gazed down the steep Lyme Regis street toward the narrow strip of sea glimpsed between the buildings around the small harbor. The little town was fashionable during the summer, but just before Christmas it was quite empty of society. "One scrumps apples, not cones," she replied, not looking around.

"Whatever the name, the crime is the same. You mean to sneak on to someone else's property and steal from their trees."

"They used to be our trees."

Margaret lowered her needle. "Yes, but they aren't now, no matter how much we wish they were. I know that the grounds at Fairhill mean much more to you than they ever did to me, and that you can give every tree and shrub its Latin name, but they all belong to Sir Philip now."

"I know." Madeleine turned her head and smiled sadly at her.

Both sisters had rich chestnut hair and vivid green eyes, but where Margaret was striking, Madeleine was truly beautiful. They were aged nineteen and twenty-one respectively, and their high-waisted clinging gowns were all that had still been the mode in the previous year of 1819. The new year had seen the advent of natural waistlines and wide stiffened hems, but there was nothing new in either of their wardrobes, nor had there been since they had been forced to quit Fairhill Park.

Madeleine got up from the window seat, and shook out the folds of her gown. She wore her long hair twisted up into a loose knot on top of her head, and like Margaret, she had no jewelry, for everything had had to be sold to meet the family's debts.

Thinking about it again, she was more than a little puzzled by her sister's original observation. "Why must the theft be accomplished before Sunday?" she asked curiously.

"Because Sir Philip is at last coming to stay, and intends to be in residence from then until well into the New Year. And because there won't be any servants for the next few days as they've been given time off in lieu due to Sir Philip's plans to have a large party of Christmas guests."

"How on earth do you know all this?"

"Because when Father went out for his usual constitutional along the sea front earlier this morning, he encountered Mrs. Crayforth. She told him all about it, and listed all the wonderful provisions she has had to purchase in readiness. I vow there will be feasting a-plenty up there this Christmas."

"You're probably right." Madeleine looked down. Mrs. Crayforth had been their housekeeper at Fairhill Park; now she was Sir Philip's.

Margaret went on with her embroidery. "According to Mrs. Crayforth, Sir Philip is intending to arrive very late on Sunday, and his guests begin to arrive in time for Christmas Eve. That's why I think you should go before Sunday if you are set upon stealing those wretched cones."

"They aren't wretched, they look excellent with all the other greenery, especially when I decorate them with flour and water so that they look frosty."

Margaret smiled. "True, they do look excellent. I must pay close attention to how you do it, for I intend to do the same this time next year."

"When you are William's bride," Madeleine murmured, smiling as well.

"Mrs. William Hancock," Margaret breathed, pausing in her work once again as she contemplated her adored husband-to-be. He was from Ireland and had originally been one of their tenant farmers, but then he had come into an inheritance and had bought his farm, which was one of the finest in the area, and which had become the envy of the county because of its very modern methods and machinery. There was no doubt that William's enterprise and ambition would one day make him a very wealthy and influential man.

Margaret sighed. "I do hope he returns from Ireland in time for us to spend at least part of Christmas together."

"I'm sure he will, for the sort of family affairs that have called him back there do not take all that long to deal with. Oh, I'm so glad that you and he are to marry. It was clear from the outset that you were made for each other," Madeleine replied.

"He would never have dared to pay court to me if Father's affairs had not tumbled."

"Oh, I don't know. He's a very forceful person, and has always been greatly smitten with you. I lost count of the days he came to discuss unimportant agricultural matters with Father, simply so that he could see you. I know you're both going to be very happy."

Margaret looked a little sadly at her. "I wish you had someone too, Madeleine."

"You've snapped up the only eligible man in Lyme Regis, unless one counts the fat curate or the lecherous lawyer, which God forbid." Madeleine gave a brief laugh and then looked out of the window again. It was still raining, and the wind blustered down the street, catching the women's skirts and making the men hold tightly to their hats. "I think I'll go to get those cones now," she said with sudden decision.

Margaret was horrified. "In this weather? You can't possibly!"

"I feel like it. Besides, if I wrap up well in my cloak . . ."

"There are two more days to go before Sunday, and it will probably stop raining in that time," Margaret pointed out sensibly.

"I'd prefer to go now." Madeleine looked around the little parlor with its low beams and inglenook fireplace. "Maybe I won't be able to make this cottage look quite like Fairhill Park, but I mean to do the best I can."

Margaret followed her glance around the simply furnished room. "I fear that this will be the worst Christmas ever," she declared unhappily.

"I grant that it will be more modest than we've been used to in the past, but it won't be the worst ever, I'm set upon that!" Madeleine replied briskly. "And if I have to steal Sir Philip Levington's fir cones in the meantime, then so be it.

"I'll come with you," Margaret decided, beginning to set the shirt aside.

"You most certainly will not. You've only just recovered from being so ill, and with Mother still very poorly of the same influenza, Father would be justified in boxing my foolish ears if I permitted you to come out in the rain for something as inconsequential as cone gathering!"

"But—"

"Don't argue. You must put up with being an invalid for the time being. If it were a fine day it would be different, but definitely not today."

Margaret sighed. "I'm tired of being unwell. These past weeks have been the most tedious ever. I'm always horridly pale, but now I look positively ghostly!"

"You'll be better soon, and by your wedding in the spring you'll be glowing again." Madeleine went to kiss her on the cheek. "Besides, it was your interesting pallor that first tugged William's heart. So you stay here to lovingly embroider his initials, while I go about my criminal business."

"Do you promise that we'll *both* collect greenery soon?"

"On the first fine day."

"Then that will have to suffice, I suppose." Margaret looked earnestly at her. "I'm not sure Father would approve of this if he knew. He thinks it's best that we should stay well away from Fairhill."

"He isn't likely to find out. To him a fir cone is a fir cone, and he won't know whether it came from Fairhill Park or under the gooseberry bush. I will be very discreet, and anyway, from what you say, there isn't anyone up there at the moment to catch me in the act."

"True."

"I'll go then."

"Just remember that as soon as it's fine, we're going together for the greenery."

"I won't forget." Madeleine gathered her skirts to hurry from the room.

Several minutes later, wearing ankle boots and a full-length brown velvet Witchoura mantle which had a hood to raise over her head, she left Ferncombe Cottage, stepping out into the wind and rain to turn the corner from the street into the narrow path that led up out of Lyme Regis toward the clifftops through the tree-choked dell known as Fern Combe. For the cones, she carried the larger of the two wicker baskets kept at the cottage.

The wildness of the weather excited the gulls, and their screams could be heard all around, as could the distant crashing of the waves upon the shore. There was a taste of salt upon her lips as she made her way up the steep path, which in summer was lined with ferns and foxgloves, but which was now bare and unfriendly. The wind soughed through the leafless trees overhead, and the branches swayed against lowering skies that raced inland across the bay.

At the top of the combe, where the woodland trees ended and the cultivated specimens in the park began, was the high stone boundary wall of her former home, and the wrought iron postern gate still used by the servants on their way to and from the town to see their families. It was never locked, and she knew she would gain easy access. The hinges groaned rustily as she opened it, but before stepping through into the park, she turned to look at the stormy sea, where the white-capped waves heaved and boiled as the storm blew its course. Far out toward the spumy horizon she could see two frigates, their sails full and their pennants and ensigns streaming as they fled before the strong wind.

Turning her back on the sea, she gazed at last at the house where she had been born, and where, until the beginning of this ill-fated year, she had spent her whole life. It presided over grounds where native evergreens flourished among those from foreign lands, and where winter foliage of every shade could be admired. Facing over the sunken topiary garden that was as intricately laid out as a half-finished chess game, it was the most peerless house in all England, at least, it was in her prejudiced eyes. Now it was Sir Philip Levington's home. Would he be good to it? Would he love it as she did? Or would he continue to be a careless owner, mostly absent, who thought more of his Mayfair residence and St. James's club than he ever did of this precious corner of Dorset? She wished she knew more about him, but she knew nothing, not even his age or whether or not there was a Lady Levington.

Her glance moved back to the wonderful collection of trees planted by her grandfather. She remembered her contented childhood, when she had walked hand-in-hand with him and he had pointed out each tree, telling her its Latin name and where it had come from. There was *Cedrus libani*, the Cedar of Lebanon, which had come to England from Turkey in the seventeenth century, *Picea mariana*, the black spruce from North America, *Abies alba*, the common silver fir that was to be found all over Europe, and many many more.

She pulled her thoughts back to the present, and the reason she had ventured here. Knowing which trees provided which cones, from the long pendulous cones of the spruces, to the variety of different shapes and sizes found on the pines, she decided to commence by gathering those that had fallen from the three black spruces planted by the west wing.

The wind rushed through the trees as she hurried across the park and began to gather fallen cones. There was a smell of resin all around. It was a remembered smell, redolent of times gone by, when she and her family had been happy. Blinking back tears, she moved on to the silver firs, and then the spruces. Her basket was almost full as she paused to see which tree to select next. Her unwilling gaze was drawn to one quite young tree, which was planted all alone close to the sunken garden, and which she had been trying not to look at at all because it meant more to her than any of the others. It was a Norway spruce, planted just for her. More tears stung her eyes as she remembered how overjoyed she had been.

As she looked at it, her glance moved beyond, to the house itself. It was then that she noticed that the curtains had been drawn back. Until now each time she'd secretly come up here from the town, the curtains had all been drawn, not allowing anyone to look inside, but now that Sir Philip was expected, the house was being aired in readiness.

This might be her only chance to ever see inside again. Still carrying the basket of cones, she hurried down the steps into the sunken garden. For a while she was sheltered from the wind and rain, but then she ascended the other steps to the terrace immediately in front of the house, and her mantle fluttered again, sometimes billowing, sometimes pressing against her legs as she crossed to the window of the library.

A fire flickered inside, safe behind its wire screen. Her father's books were as they always had been, each one bound in his own personal green-and-gold leather. The paneled walls were warm and dark, and the firelight flickered over everything, including the intricate plasterwork on the low coffered ceiling. She moved on toward the adjacent oriel window of the great hall. Peeping through the small stained-glass panes, she saw the vast chamber where so many grand occasions had been held in the past. The stained glass was distorting, but still it was as she remembered, the high hammerbeam ceiling, paneled walls, minstrels' gallery, and fine tapestries . . .

She walked on along the terrace, peeping into each window as she went, and then she moved around the side of the house to the front, and the view down the drive toward the main highway from Lyme Regis to Bridport. She made her way to the stone porch, and before she knew it she'd reached out to turn the heavy ring handle on the iron-studded door. It was an instinctive action, and the last thing she expected was for the door to open, but it did, swinging slowly before her to reveal the hall, so warm and welcoming in the gloom of the dark winter afternoon.

Philip had observed her gathering the cones and watched curiously as she came to the house to eventually look through the oriel window. Given her obvious intense interest, it had come as no surprise to him when she opened the front door and stepped inside. He straightened and drew back slightly from the edge of the gallery, so that she couldn't see him, but he could still see her. He watched as she slowly crossed the stone-flagged floor to place the basket of cones on the table, before removing her mantle and draping it carefully over the back of a chair. His approving gaze took in her rich russet hair and the trim figure outlined by her crimson velvet gown. Who was she? Not a maid, she was too elegant and well dressed for that, but then neither was she quite a lady, for her high-waisted gown was a little out of date. Whoever she was, she was entrancingly beautiful . . .

Unaware of the surveillance she was under from the gallery, Madeleine turned to feast her eyes upon the hall. The happy past was with her now, especially the Christmasses, when this place had been filled with Dorset society for the Yuletide balls. Every corner, mantelshelf, table and window had been adorned with the greenery she had always so enjoyed gathering and arranging, and the atmosphere had been joyous. Perhaps the year she remembered best of all had been 1815, the year of Waterloo, when she had been sixteen and allowed to dance her first waltz—the wicked, exciting waltz. She'd been partnered by dashing Commander Venables, captain of HMS *Belvedere*, for whom she had briefly entertained a secret affection, before he'd disappointed her by offering for her cousin Hester. That waltz had been magical, however, for she'd worn a new lemon silk gown and her mother's diamonds, and she'd known how very lovely she looked.

She closed her eyes for a moment, immersing herself in her memories. Suddenly she was at the ball again, with music and laughter all around, and a throng of guests dancing beneath the bright chandeliers. She could hear the orchestra playing, and see Commander Venables as he bowed over her hand and asked her to honor him with the waltz. She was dancing on air, whirling dizzily around the floor with his arm around her waist. Past and present swam together, and before she knew it she had begun to dance around the empty floor just as she had done that magical night five years before.

From the gallery Philip watched with increasing fascination. Who could this fair stranger be? And what sweet memories were in the ascendant for her now? She intrigued him beyond endurance, and slowly he went down the staircase, still watching her as she danced unknowingly around the floor. She came closer, unconscious of his presence, and as she whirled within reach, suddenly he could no longer resist. Stepping out before her, he caught her hand and pulled her close enough to put his arm around her slender waist and begin to dance with her.

She gasped and the past fled, leaving only the present. She was beset with embarrassment and confusion, but he smiled into her wide green eyes and held her firmly as he continued with the silent waltz. She followed his lead, unable to help herself, and for a spellbound minute they danced together without a word being uttered. But then she was overcome with mortification at being discovered in such foolishness, especially as she guessed who he must be. Suddenly it was too much to bear, and she pulled sharply out of his arms.

As she ran to collect her mantle, he called after her. "Please don't go! I must at least know who you are!"

The last thing she wished was for him to learn her

identity, and without replying she hurried outside, leaving the basket of cones behind in her haste to escape. As she fled past the front of the house, she was further dismayed to catch a glimpse of a pony and trap coming up the drive, conveying Mrs. Crayforth and her husband, the head gardener, back from Lyme Regis.

The startled housekeeper recognized her, and called out a greeting, but Madeleine continued to flee, pulling her hood over her head as she dashed around the corner of the house and then across the park toward the postern gate and the sanctuary of the combe.

Philip emerged from the porch behind her, and halted as he too saw the astonished housekeeper and her husband. The pony and trap came to a halt by the porch, and Mrs. Crayforth alighted, her scarlet country cloak billowing. She guessed who Philip was by his looks, manner, and clothes.

"Sir Philip?" she asked in her soft Dorset accent. She was a plump body, with a rosy face and graying hair she wore tied back in a bun.

"Er, yes. Mrs. Crayforth, I presume?"

"Yes, sir." She curtsied, only just resisting the temptation to glance after Madeleine. Her curiosity was tremendous as she wondered what had happened to make Miss Madeleine flee so from him. She looked at him again. "We weren't expecting you just yet, sir."

"I decided to come early," he replied, his thoughts returning briefly to Delia, whose wanton flirtations had driven him away.

The housekeeper followed him back into the house. He could sense her intense interest in the odd scene she had seen a moment before, and he knew he had to say something to explain it away, but first he wished to find out about his mysterious dancing partner.

"Did I hear you call out to the lady who left a moment ago?" he asked.

"Miss Madeleine? Yes, sir, you did."

"Miss Madeleine, er . . . ?"

"Why, Charlton, sir. She used to live here." Mrs. Crayforth's curiosity deepened. Didn't he know who he'd been with?

His blue eyes cleared. "Ah, yes, of course. I'm afraid I didn't have time to introduce myself. I startled her. She thought she was alone in the hall, and then I appeared from nowhere." It was the truth, as far as it went. There was no need to mention a soundless waltz on a deserted floor . . .

Mrs. Crayforth noticed the forgotten basket, and she smiled a little. "So that was why she ventured up here," she murmured.

He went to pick up one of the cones. "What on earth does she require these for?"

"Why, for Christmas garlands and such like, Sir Philip. She's very clever with things like that, and always did this whole house each year, she and her sister, Miss Margaret. It looked wonderful when they'd finished."

He studied the cone in his hand. "I wish to return the basket in person, to assure Miss Charlton that she is welcome to take as many of these or anything else she may wish to gather. Where may I find her?"

"I will gladly return it for you, Sir Philip."

He glanced at her. "I wish to return it myself."

The housekeeper smiled a little. "I see, sir. Well, she and her family live at Ferncombe Cottage down in Lyme, sir. If you go by the road, it's the whitewashed cottage with the thatched roof on the left almost at the bottom of the hill."

"And if I don't go by road?" he asked, thinking of the direction in which Madeleine had run.

"Then you use the postern gate across the park, sir. It leads into Fern Combe itself, which comes out right by the cottage."

"Thank you, Mrs. Crayforth."

"Not at all, sir," the housekeeper replied, knowing there was no idleness to his interest. Miss Madeleine would appear to have made an impression on him. She cleared her throat a little. "Sir, now that I'm here, do you require some refreshment? I had no idea you'd arrive today, so there is nothing especially prepared, but I can soon attend to that failing, for I've laid in everything you ordered, and the larder and pantry are stocked to overflowing. I promise your guests won't lack for anything while they're here," she added quickly, hoping that she hadn't given him the idea she was inefficient.

"Thank you, Mrs. Crayforth. I confess to feeling quite hungry."

"Would a nice piece of beefsteak suit?"

"Excellently."

The housekeeper began to cross the hall in the direction of the door to the kitchens, then she halted to look back at him. "Miss Charlton can be found at home most days, sir."

"Can she indeed? Thank you, Mrs. Crayforth." He smiled at the woman's transparency.

"Sir." Bobbing brief curtsy, she hurried on.

Philip replaced the cone in the basket, his thoughts returning to the intriguing Miss Madeleine Charlton. If this was a sample of life in the country, he wasn't going to be in the least bored, and it was going to be easier than expected to put behind him the pain of his dealings with Lady Delia Fitzroy.

He would call upon Miss Charlton in the morning, for he wished to know her more. Much more.

Madeleine paused in the combe to regain her breath after her headlong flight from Philip's arms. Her cheeks were still crimson with embarrassment, and she realized to her dismay that she'd left the basket behind. She leaned against the trunk of an immense beech tree, her eyes closed as the wind and rain cooled her hot face. What on earth had possessed her to behave like that? To dance by oneself was bad enough, but to have been caught doing it was humiliating in the extreme. And what was worse, Mrs. Crayforth was almost bound to identify her to Sir Philip! Oh, if only she hadn't come up here today, if only she'd never decided to gather those thrice-cursed cones!

Composing herself, she at last went on down toward the town. She had no intention of saying anything to anyone, not even to Margaret, and she hoped that the basket's disappearance would not be noticed. But in this last she was to be swiftly disappointed, however, for on her return she entered the cottage by the back door and found Peg, their only remaining servant, grumbling as she searched the kitchen high and low for the missing item.

Peg had been with the family for many years, commencing as a kitchenmaid, and when disaster had struck, she had loyally decided to stay with them and leave Fairhill Park for the lesser surroundings of Ferncombe Cottage. She was forty years old now, and as thin and wiry as she had been at sixteen. Her hair was that strange salt-and-pepper color that is halfway between brown and gray, and her eyes were hazel. She liked to wear very crisply starched aprons, and so always seemed to rustle when she walked. She was rustling with a vengeance now as she looked in every corner and cupboard for the basket.

"What is it, Peg?" Madeleine asked as she entered.

"The best basket's gone and hid itself somewhere, darned thing."

Madeleine's heart sank. "Why do you need it?"

"Because Mrs. Charlton wishes me to take some preserves to Biddy Trench, on account of her being taken with the 'flu as well now, and there's enough jars for me to need the basket. Only I can't find it anywhere."

"Can't you take the other basket instead?" Madeleine suggested hopefully.

"That battered thing? Mrs. Charlton would skin me alive if I went out with that on my arm!" Peg sighed crossly and stood in the middle of the low-beamed kitchen with her hands on her hips. "Still, reckon I've got no choice. Skin me she'll have to."

Madeleine said nothing more, but hurried guiltily into the hall to hang her mantle on the hook. Then she went up to her room to take off her ankle boots. She heard the murmur of voices from her mother's room, and after straightening her hair and making sure she didn't look flustered anymore, she went across the wooden landing to lift the latch and look inside.

The bedroom was up in the roof, with a sloping ceiling and dormer windows that in summer let in the scent of the rambling rose growing against the wall. It was at the back of the house, facing the hillside and Fern Combe, but it gave no view of Fairhill Park. The wooden floor boasted two rugs, and the tester bed was hung with faded blue damask.

Her mother was propped up on four pillows, and Margaret and her father were seated on either side of the bed. Mrs. Charlton was still a very elegant woman, and her chestnut hair, so like her daughters', had only gone gray at the temples. She had patrician features, and her eyes were the softest of browns. She wore a nightgown that was lavishly trimmed with lace and a warm shawl around her shoulders. She was very pale and unwell, with dark shadows beneath her eyes, but the worst of the influenza was behind her now, and in another week she would leave her bed and be able to sit downstairs with them. Another week after that would find her as much on the road to recovery as Margaret, who improved daily now.

She smiled fondly at her elder daughter. "Ah, there you are, my dear. We've just been discussing poor Biddy Trench, who now has the influenza as well. Do you remember Biddy?"

"Yes, of course. She was married to our head groom. How could I not remember her?" Madeleine stood at the foot of the bed, one arm linked around a post in an endeavor to look casual.

Margaret glanced curiously at her, detecting that all was not well. Instead of looking conspiratorially triumphant after the expedition to Fairhill Park, there was no mistaking Madeleine's not-quite-concealed unease. Margaret wondered what had happened, but said nothing in front of their parents.

Mr. Charlton did not notice anything amiss as he, too, smiled up at his elder daughter. "And how was your perambulation, my dear?" he asked. He wore a green coat and beige breeches, and there was a tasseled hat on his head. The trials of the past year were very evident upon his once robust face, which was now care-worn and drawn, for he had never stopped blaming himself for the unwise financial dealings that had led to ruin. And things had not been made any easier for him by the recent grave illnesses of both his wife and younger daughter.

"My perambulation? Oh, wet, I suppose," Madeleine replied, trying to sound lighthearted.

Her mother gave her a cross look. "It was very unwise of you to go out in such conditions, Madeleine."

"I wore my mantle and am quite all right."

"I trust so," Mr. Charlton observed.

Margaret continued to thoughtfully survey her sister, noting the very deliberate way Madeleine avoided her eyes. Something was up. But what?

There was a tap at the door. It was Peg, now wrapped up in her cloak, with the old basket over her arm. "I'm just off then, ma'am. Is there anything you require from the shops?"

"No, nothing, thank you, Peg." Mrs. Charlton's disapproving glance went to the basket. "Must you use that disreputable thing?"

"I can't find the other one, ma'am."

Madeleine stared out of the window, and Margaret's curiosity intensified, for she knew her sister would have taken it for the cones.

Mrs. Charlton's brows drew together. "Can't find it?"

Peg shook her head. "No, ma'am, and I've looked absolutely everywhere. It was there this morning, I'm sure of that."

"Oh, well, I suppose you must take that horrid object then," Mrs. Charlton declared with a sigh.

Peg withdrew, and a moment later they heard the front door open and close. Mrs. Charlton was a little cross. "I suppose Peg left the kitchen door open again, and someone saw their opportunity. Really, one cannot trust anyone these days, and to think that there is such dishonesty even here in Lyme. Oh, well, to better things. I must be on the mend because I am actually interested in our plans for Christmas. Margaret, I trust that Mr. Hancock will return in time to join us for dinner?"

Margaret nodded. "He intends to, but even if he can't, he has left instructions at the farm that we are to have the largest turkey there. He has also managed to secure us some bottles of good French wine, although I suspect they have not been through Excise warehouses."

Mrs. Charlton shrugged. "I have no conscience about that. There is too much duty on everything."

Her husband looked wryly at her. "Tut, tut, my dear, and to think there is such dishonesty here in Lyme," he murmured, echoing her own observation of a moment before.

She was offended. "That wasn't called for, sir."

He smiled fondly at her. "Forgive me, Constance, but I simply couldn't resist it. Now, where were we? Christmas Day? I take it we will be decorating the cottage with greenery and so on?" He turned his attention to Madeleine.

She colored. "Er, yes, Father. I will begin soon. Margaret and I will go gathering as soon as the weather changes." She felt her sister's scrutiny, but refused to look at her.

"Well, one thing is certain, you won't require anywhere near the cartloads needed for Fairhill Park. Several armfuls should suffice here," he reflected sadly.

It was much later that evening Margaret at last found herself alone with Madeleine and was able to question her about her mysterious reticence regarding the visit to Fairhill Park.

"Well, sister mine, since you have declined to tell me anything, I am obliged to ask outright. What happened?"

Telltale color warmed Madeleine's cheeks. "I don't know what you mean."

"No? Oh, come on. You went out with the famous basket and apparently returned without it. You also returned in a mood that is reserved, to say the least. I would almost go so far as to say you wish to forget you ever left the cottage today."

Madeleine shifted uncomfortably. "You're right about that," she muttered with feeling.

"Oh?"

Madeleine gave in. "Very well, I'll tell you, but if you ever breathe a word, I'll never forgive you."

Seeing her obvious embarrassment, Margaret become concerned. "Whatever happened, Madeleine?" she asked gently, reaching across to put her hand on her sister's.

"I gathered the cones as I set out to, but then I was tempted to look in through the windows of the house. The curtains were drawn back, you see, and I wanted to look in for a last time." She then proceeded to relate in detail everything that had happened, and Margaret's eyes widened more with each sentence, until at last she gave a gasp.

"Sir Philip actually took you in his arms and danced with you?"

Madeleine squirmed self-consciously. "Yes."

Margaret stared.

"Oh, do stop looking at me like that; it's bad enough already without you letting me know how scandalized you are." Madeleine got up agitatedly and went to the window, holding the chintz curtain aside and looking out into the darkness. It was still raining, and the wind blustered down the street, where candles burned in windows, and a lantern swung to and fro on a corner.

Margaret studied her. "I'm not scandalized, you goose, I'm just taken aback. I can understand him saying something to you, but to go so far as to join in by dancing as well . . . What is he like? Is he young and handsome? Or old and stout?"

"Young and exceedingly handsome," Madeleine replied, remembering.

"Really? Describe him."

"He is tall and slender, with black curly hair and blue eyes. His complexion is tanned and clear, and his clothes are all that you would expect of a titled gentleman with a Mayfair address. I suppose he is about thirty years old, give or take a year."

Margaret smiled. "Well, *I* wouldn't mind dancing a waltz with such a paragon."

"You would, you'd hate it as much as I did. I don't know why I let him persist for so long, it was as if I were spellbound. Anyway, at last I *did* find my wits, and I fled, leaving the wretched basket behind. Almost the worst thing of all was that Mrs. Crayforth saw me and called out! She's bound to tell him who I am. Oh, it's all so mortifying, and I feel unspeakably foolish."

"Madeleine, it doesn't seem to me that he thought you were in the least foolish," Margaret pointed out.

"No, he thought me all that was amusing. I can imagine that my antics are going to entertain his guests at dinner the first night they arrive!"

"I don't think he will do that, Madeleine."

"No? What do we know of him? He might think it the end in hilarity to regale his family and friends with the cavortings of a local rustic!" Unable to bear the thought any longer, Madeleine hurried out and up to her room.

The truth about the missing basket was destined to come fully to light the following morning, which dawned bright and sunny, in complete contrast to the previous day.

Mr. Charlton, about to set off on his customary daily walk around the town, was in the kitchen with his daughters and Peg as they prepared to make the Christmas plum puddings. The kitchen was warm, for the fire in the inglenook had been stoked up, and the wall oven was still hot after the bread Peg had baked earlier. A very large pot of boiling water steamed in readiness for the puddings, and the December sunlight streamed in through the window, making everything even warmer.

The sisters were wearing aprons and mobcaps, and were just waiting for their father to leave before the pudding making began in earnest. Peg was weighing the flour, and there was a great deal of chattering when suddenly there was the knock of a gentleman's cane upon the front door. Surprised, everyone fell silent. Peg wiped her hands on a damp cloth and smoothed her apron and brown woolen gown, before hastening to see who it was.

Madeleine's heart almost stopped within her as a well-spoken male voice was heard inquiring if she was at home. Oh, no! Please don't let it be what she feared most! She closed her eyes as she felt the familiar giveaway blush begin to warm her cheeks again.

Peg returned, a bemused expression on her face as she placed the basket of cones on the newly scrubbed table. She looked at Madeleine. "Sir Philip Levington has returned the basket you left at Fairhill Park yesterday, Miss Madeleine, and he requests to speak to you for a moment."

Margaret gazed at the beams on the ceiling, and Mr. Charlton, who recalled the mystery of the missing basket, stared at the elusive item as if it had walked in of its own accord. Madeleine wished she were dead.

Peg cleared her throat. "It's Sir Philip Levington, Miss Madeleine," she said again. "He's waiting in the hall. Shall I show him in here? Only, the parlor fire has smoked and made it quite nasty in there. I've opened the windows to let the smoke out, but . . ."

Mr. Charlton nodded. "Yes, yes, show him in here, Peg. What place is there for pride and etiquette in our present circumstances?" But as Peg hurried out again, he subjected his elder daughter to a reproving look. "It seems to me that you have some explaining to do, missy."

"Yes, Father." Madeleine couldn't meet his eyes.

Then Peg was showing their unexpected visitor into the kitchen. His spurs jingled as he bowed his head beneath the low doorway. He wore his black greatcoat over a sky blue coat and cream cord trousers, and his dark hair shone in the sunlight coming in so strongly through the window.

His blue eyes went directly to Madeleine, and then to her father. "Mr. Charlton?"

"We meet at last, Sir Philip. I confess I had no idea you were acquainted with my daughter."

"We, er, met briefly yesterday afternoon."

"At Fairhill Park, I understand?"

Philip was belatedly beginning to realize that Madeleine hadn't told her father about the visit to their former home, but it was too late now. "Yes, at Fairhill Park. She, er, left this behind," he said reluctantly, indicating the basket.

Madeleine wished the floor would open up and swallow her, and suddenly all she wanted to do was to cut and run. Snatching off her mobcap and apron, she gathered the skirts of her crimson velvet gown and dashed from the kitchen. In the hall she paused long enough to take her mantle from the peg, and then hurried out of the cottage and down the street toward the harbor.

In the kitchen everyone was startled by her precipitate action. Philip didn't quite know what to do, but then he gave the others an apologetic smile. "I, er, have things to attend to, and so will not detain you in idle chatter," he murmured, bowing to them and then withdrawing. He picked up his top hat and gloves from the little table by the door, and then walked swiftly out into the street, where he paused to see which way Madeleine had gone. He saw her hurrying in the direction of the harbor, and without a moment's hesitation he followed.

In the kitchen Mr. Charlton gave Margaret a baleful look. "I see from your face that you know about this. I trust you mean to share it with the rest of us?"

Margaret gazed unhappily at the basket of cones and then nodded.

Madeleine didn't realize that Philip was pursuing her. She'd skirted the harbor to reach the sea front and was now walking along the narrow promenade that led toward the great sweeping arm of the Cobb, the fourteenth-century stone breakwater that protected the town from the worst of the weather from Lyme Bay. There were cottages, houses, and villas to her right, some of them seeming in imminent danger of toppling over into the water, and some fishing boats were sailing out on the high tide to her left. The weather was completely different today, the wind and rain had gone, and the air was almost warm in the sunshine. There were no waves, just a gentle lapping of water against the shore.

The change in the weather had brought many people out, both those who simply wished to take the air, and those who wished to buy and sell Christmas fare of every kind. There was a mistletoe man with a huge basket on his back, and a boy with a donkey cart laden with holly. A small flock of geese was being driven along the front, and some mummers were rehearsing their seasonal play, *St. George*. Some boys, evidently from the church choir, were seated at the edge of the front with their legs dangling six feet above the narrow beach as they went over and over a portion of "Good King Wenceslaus," and then argued as to precisely how a certain sequence of notes should be sung. They were very fractious, and displayed little Christmas joy or bonhomie. It seemed that the vicar was a perfectionist, and the boys felt that at least two of their number were letting the others down.

A number of people had already decked their houses in readiness, with holly boughs in the windows and Christmas wreaths upon the doors, but Madeleine hardly glanced at all the signs of approaching festivity as she struggled to regain what she could of her severely shaken composure. If she had dreamed it up in a nightmare, she could not have envisaged a worse way for her previous day's activities to come to light. How she was going to face them all at home, she didn't know.

"Miss Charlton?"

She stopped, and for the second time that morning her heart did, too. Reluctantly she turned and saw Philip standing there. Her mouth went dry, and she couldn't do anything except stare foolishly at him.

He removed his hat. "Forgive me, I didn't mean to cause you any embarrassment in front of your family. It didn't occur to me that you hadn't mentioned coming up to Fairhill Park."

"There was no reason why it should have occurred to you. Besides, any embarrassment I've experienced of late has been caused entirely by my own foolishness."

"Everyone is entitled to a little daydreaming, Miss Charlton, and it wasn't your fault that I happened to be there to see you dancing."

Her cheeks were aflame. "I was trespassing on your land, Sir Philip, and I'd stolen the cones, to say nothing of then trespassing in the house itself. It was reprehensible conduct on my part, and I trust that you will at least endeavor to forget it."

"Forget the most agreeable waltz I've had in ages?" He smiled.

Her face felt hotter than ever. "Please don't mention the waltz," she begged.

"Miss Charlton, if you are alarmed that I intend to poke fun at you, please put such a fear from your head. I thought you were all that was enchanting yesterday, and if you succumbed to the moment, then so did I. I enjoyed being Prince Charming to your Cinderella, even if you left a basket of cones behind instead of a glass slipper." He smiled again, his blue eyes warm and direct.

In spite of her embarrassment, she found herself returning the smile. "You are very kind, Sir Philip."

"I trust that in future you will not feel obliged to flee from me?"

"I will endeavor not to, sir."

"Would you mind if I walked with you now?" he asked suddenly.

"I . . ."

"Such a prospect displeases you?"

"No, of course not. I was merely going to say that I was about to return home, to explain my misdemeanors to my parents. You see, I'm not really supposed to go to Fairhill at all; my father thinks it's better not to."

"I see. Well, at least allow me to walk you to your door, for it is on my way, is it not?" He turned to glance up at the headland and the chimneys of Fairhill Park emerging above the trees.

She followed his glance. "Do you like your new residence, Sir Philip?"

"Yes, very much."

"Do you really mean that?"

He searched her face. "Why do you ask?"

"Because I love it and would like to feel that its new owner loves it, too."

"I think you may be sure that I will, Miss Charlton. Granted I have only spent one night there so far, but I know it will be very much to my liking." He offered her his arm, and they began to walk back the way they'd come. "What can you tell me about Lyme Regis, Miss Charlton, for I confess to shameful ignorance? For instance, where did it acquire the 'Regis'?"

"From King Edward I, who used its harbor in the thirteenth century in one of our various wars against the French."

"The hereditary enemy, if our allies at the moment," he murmured.

"So it would seem."

"I understand that the Duke of Monmouth landed here?"

She nodded. "In 1685, in what is now called Monmouth Beach to the west of the harbor." She pointed behind, past the Cobb.

He turned to look. "And that is the famous Cobb, as described by Miss Austen?"

"It is, and the lady herself stayed at one of these houses here." Madeleine glanced up at the properties immediately by the sea front.

She was conscious of his closeness, and of the feel of his arm beneath her fingers. He was the sort of man she'd always dreamed of; and the sort of man who was now far beyond her reach. Besides, he was probably already married, or at the very least spoken for. . . . The path her thoughts were taking caught her by surprise, and she swiftly lowered her eyes.

Soon they were walking up from the harbor toward Ferncombe Cottage, and in what seemed far too short a time they were at the door. Before taking his leave, he turned to face her. "Miss Charlton, about yesterday. I don't wish you to feel you are trespassing if you come to Fairhill Park again. Please feel at liberty to come whenever you choose, and to take whatever greenery and so on it pleases you to take. I trust you will convey my feelings on this to your father?"

"You are generous, sir."

"No, just aware of how I would feel if I were you. It must be hard to live here, when once you lived up there."

"It isn't the easiest of situations," she admitted.

"Then come whenever you wish."

"Actually . . ."

"Yes?"

"I was hoping that my sister and I could gather greenery from the combe in the next day or so, but there are some better trees in the park." She was surprised at her sudden boldness.

"The weather would seem perfect today, Miss Charlton. You and your sister could come this afternoon, if you wish."

"It's most kind of you. Thank you."

He smiled. "Until this afternoon, then," he murmured, inclining his head and then replacing his hat before walking away toward the corner of the cottage, and the path up through the combe.

She gazed after him for a long moment, and then tried to put him from her mind for the time being as she went into the cottage to face the parental wrath she knew would be waiting, for by now her father was bound to have wrung the full story out of Margaret. Well, perhaps not the full story, for the shocking waltz would have remained unmentioned!

When he returned to Fairhill Park, Philip adjourned to the library, where he poured himself a generous measure of cognac and then sat by the fire, gazing out past the sunken garden toward the trees where first he had observed Miss Madeleine Charlton.

He swirled the glass thoughtfully. She was all that Lady Delia Fitzroy was not, for where Delia was a confident, rather affected tease who was far too much a woman-of-the-world, Madeleine Charlton was refreshingly *un*affected and most definitely not a tease. But Delia was also fascinating in the extreme, the belle of every occasion she attended, and she'd found her way into his blood. At least she had until he'd discovered all her other amours. From knowing nothing, suddenly it had seemed he was hearing whispers at every turn. He'd been the last to learn the truth. Well, perhaps not the last, for his sister Elizabeth was Delia's best friend and certainly had not yet become acquainted with all her indiscretions. Poor Elizabeth—she was far too trusting and kind-hearted, and probably wouldn't believe the gossip if she heard it.

He drained the glass and then placed it on the table beside his chair. Leaning his head back, he contemplated the enigmatic Miss Madeleine Charlton. Who had she been dancing with in her dreams the day before? Was she too beset by unrequited love? He wanted to know. He opened his eyes and looked out at the park again, hoping that she and her sister would indeed come that afternoon.

The wrought iron of the postern gate felt very cold to the touch as Madeleine pushed it open and she and Margaret went through. The park stretched gloriously before them, drenched in the peculiarly clear but pale sunshine of December. Behind them the water of Lyme Bay sparkled deep blue, and overhead the sky was devoid of even the smallest cloud.

For a moment Madeleine almost turned away because she knew she did herself no favors by coming here again. This was her past, and that was where it should remain. Ferncombe Cottage was her home now, and her future lay down in the town, not up here on the hill. Then she hesitated, for if she was honest with herself, there was another reason why she'd come up here again today. That reason was Sir Philip Levington.

Margaret made the decision for her by linking her arm and beginning to walk across the grass toward some red-berried holly trees by the sunken garden. But Christmas greenery was the last thing on Madeleine's mind, for with each step she was conscious of going closer to the folly of being attracted to Sir Philip Levington.

They began their pleasant task, and after a while Margaret smiled at her. "I suppose you don't regard this as mere holly, but rather as *Ilex aquithingummy?*"

"*Aquifolium*, and you can stop teasing me right now, for I'll have you know that I don't go around thinking of every tree by its Latin name."

"No, just the trees up here." Margaret placed a spray in her basket and then looked at her sister. "I used to be quite jealous of you, you know."

"Whatever for?"

"Because you and Grandfather were so interested in trees and other things botanical. I felt left out."

"We tried to make you interested as well, but you said trees bored you," Madeleine protested.

"I know, they did, and they still do, but that didn't stop me being jealous. I was an odious brat at times. Do you know, I nearly tried to spoil your tree by chopping off some of its branches." Margaret's guilty glance went to the little Norway spruce.

Madeleine stared at her. "Did you really?"

"Yes. I crept out here late one night. It was cloudy and dark, and I was sure no one would see me, but just as I was poised to do the evil deed, the moon came out, and I felt as if it was trying to show everyone how wicked I was. I ran back to the house and felt wretchedly guilty for days afterward. It cured me of my jealousy, though, and after that I decided that you and Grandfather were welcome to your horrid trees."

"I had no idea."

Margaret smiled. "I don't know why I told you now. I'd forgotten all about it."

Madeleine smiled as well. "I suppose I was fairly insufferable at times, wasn't I? Most little girls would embroider alphabet samplers, but I had to embroider Latin plant names!"

"And spell them correctly! Yes, you *were* insufferable."

They gathered some more holly and were about to move on to a border of periwinkle down in the garden, when Madeleine's pulse quickened as she heard the jingle of Philip's spurs on the steps opposite. Turning, she looked at him. He wore the sky blue coat and cream trousers he'd had on that morning, and his hair was a little tousled, as if he'd run his fingers through it a moment before.

He smiled as he came over to them. "Good afternoon," he said, his glance encompassing Madeleine for a moment before going to Margaret, whom he had seen in the kitchen at the cottage, but to whom he hadn't actually been introduced.

Madeleine quickly corrected the omission. "Sir Philip, this is my sister, Miss Margaret Charlton. Margaret, may I present Sir Philip Levington?"

He bowed over Margaret's hand. "I'm delighted to make your acquaintance, Miss Charlton."

"And I yours, sir," she replied.

He smiled at Madeleine. "I hope you do not mind, but I've taken the liberty of instructing Crayforth to have the pony and trap waiting to take you and your gatherings back to Ferncombe Cottage."

"Oh, there is no need—" she began.

"On the contrary, for it seems to me that what you've already gathered is awkward to carry, and that by the time you've finished, you will find it all immensely difficult to manage. We can leave everything in piles on the steps, and Crayforth will collect it all. At the moment he's been despatched to the orchard for some mistletoe."

"You are very thoughtful, sir."

Their eyes met for a moment, and then she had to look quickly away because she was afraid the blush on her cheeks would give her secret thoughts away.

He assisted them after that, helping to pick sprays that were just a little too high to reach. Soon the garden steps were littered with small heaps of holly, box, sweet bay, Chinese privet, periwinkle, ivy, pine, fir, and, lastly, Norway spruce from Madeleine's tree.

Margaret teased her a little. "I am astonished you can bring yourself to pluck these precious branches," she said.

Madeleine gave her a cross look, and Philip turned inquiringly. "These precious branches?"

Margaret nodded. "It's Madeleine's tree." She explained all about it and was sufficiently unsparing of herself to again reveal the childishly jealous deed of which she had once almost been guilty.

Philip smiled a little, and then returned his attention to the tree, running his fingertips over the scented needles. "An important tree indeed," he murmured.

Madeleine noticed a spray that boasted three handsome cones. It was several feet above her head, but very tempting, and she stretched up to try to pick it. But it was a little too high, and she almost lost her balance.

"Take care!" Philip caught her swiftly around the waist to steady her.

His hands were firm, and the intimacy of the contact

brought the color back to her cheeks, but if he noticed he gave no sign. Releasing her, he turned to Margaret. "Actually, I have an ulterior motive in asking you both here today. I wish to beg a great favor."

"A favor, sir?" Margaret looked inquiringly at him.

"You may be aware that I'm having my sister and a large party of friends to stay here over Christmas, and it has occurred to me that the house is far from seasonal inside, nor is it likely to become so if left to me. I'm reliably informed by Mrs. Crayforth that you are both exceedingly clever at . . ." His voice died away on a note of vague embarrassment. "On reflection, I think perhaps I should not ask, for such a request might be construed as a little improper."

"Improper?" Margaret was taken aback, wondering what on earth he had in mind.

He smiled then. "Well, perhaps not improper exactly, but nevertheless not quite within the rules. It concerns your talent for decorating houses at this time of the year."

Margaret laughed. "I'm not in the least clever with such things, sir, but Madeleine certainly is. I am merely her underling."

Madeleine colored. "I *like* to decorate houses at Christmas, Sir Philip, but I certainly cannot lay claim to having a talent," she said self-consciously.

"That isn't what I've been hearing from the inestimable Mrs. Crayforth. According to her you are a positive genius with holly, mistletoe, *et al.*, and that has prompted me to wonder if you can be prevailed upon to decorate Fairhill Park again this year. At least, it was my intention to ask, but if I'm honest, etiquette really does preclude such a request."

Madeleine didn't know what to say, for the suggestion took her by surprise.

Margaret was curious. "But, sir, if your sister is coming to stay, surely she will wish to perform such a duty for you?"

"Elizabeth hasn't an artistic bone in her body, except when it comes to matters of fashion." He paused and then smiled a little ruefully. "No doubt you are somewhat dismayed to discover that a gentleman with whom you are barely acquainted should have entertained thoughts of such a request. I'm sure your father would be justifiably incensed if he knew."

Margaret glanced at her sister from beneath lowered lashes, guessing that nothing would delight her more than such an undertaking. Madeleine might not have said outright that she was drawn to Sir Philip Levington like a pin to a magnet, but it was plain enough to someone who knew her really well.

Madeleine was indeed torn both ways. Half of her wished to oblige him, but the other half was fearful of gossip and parental disapproval.

Margaret prompted her slightly. "I'm willing if you are, Madeleine," she murmured.

"It would be very agreeable, but—"

"What is there to 'but' about? It isn't as if you will be here alone, for I will be with you. What could be more proper than that? Father and Mother will approve, I'm sure."

The temptation was suddenly too much for Madeleine. She wanted to decorate Fairhill Park again, and she wanted to be as much in Sir Philip Levington's company as possible. All niggling reservations were suddenly cast aside. "My sister is right, Sir Philip."

He gave a quick smile. "You mean you'll come to my assistance?"

"Yes, Sir Philip, for I would love to decorate Fairhill Park again, sir," she replied truthfully.

He took her hand and kissed it. "I will be forever in your debt, Miss Charlton."

His lips seemed to sear her skin, and she knew that she was close to a precipice that might soon claim her, heart and soul. But she did not want to draw back from the brink; she wanted to tumble headlong over the edge into the folly of love. She, Madeleine Charlton, who was usually so sensible and levelheaded, seemed to have taken leave of her senses. Or to have found new senses she'd never known before . . .

She swallowed. "When would you like me to start, Sir Philip?"

"I leave that entirely to you, Miss Charlton. My sister arrives here on the twenty-third, and the rest of the guests on Christmas Eve."

"Then all must be done by the twenty-third, must it not? I fear it will take several days to accomplish everything satisfactorily, for there is much to do."

"I am at your command."

"Then we will begin the day after tomorrow. Perhaps you could instruct Crayforth? I'm sure he will remember which trees to gather from, and how much is required. If he and some of the men pick the greenery tomorrow, Margaret and I can commence immediately we arrive."

"Consider it done, Miss Charlton. I will send my carriage for you, and it will take you home again each day as well." He smiled at Margaret. "I understand that you haven't been well, Miss Charlton, so I will make sure that every room in the house is heated."

"I appreciate your kindness, Sir Philip," she replied.

He turned back to Madeleine, taking her hand and raising it to his lips again. "And I appreciate *your* kindness, Miss Charlton, for without it Fairhill Park would look very bare this Christmas."

She looked up into his clear blue eyes, and the precipice claimed her.

The scene in the great hall was still one of sublime chaos, even though the decorations in the rest of the house were complete. It was the twenty-third, the day Philip's sister Elizabeth was due to arrive, and the hall was in the final throes of acquiring its seasonal adornment. Heaps of holly, ivy, mistletoe, pine, and various other evergreens lay strewn all over the floor, together with bunches of dried but colorful everlasting flowers, and bowls of camellias and roses that had arrived by carrier from Exeter.

The refectory table had been moved to the side of the hall so that dancing could take place in the coming days, and it was laden with scarlet satin ribbons, rose-red apples, oranges, and golden ropes of varying lengths and thicknesses. The chandler in Lyme had supplied virtually his entire stock of candles, and two maids were engaged upon cutting paper to be folded into stars and rosettes before being painted with gold or silver. Servants dashed hither and thither at Madeleine's command, just as they had in the past, and leafy garlands were beginning to form as some more maids sat in groups stringing all the festive leaves together.

The Yule log had been dragged in in readiness. It had come from an ancient but rather unsafe oak tree on the edge of the park, and had been brought into the house to the accompaniment of much merriment among the servants. Those garlands that had been finished lay waiting to be draped around the walls, doors, mantelpiece, and staircase, and some had already been placed on the balustrade of the minstrels' gallery. As the paper stars and rosettes were finished, and their paint considered dry enough, they were threaded on string and suspended from the hammerbeams far above, and all but the central chandelier had acquired adornments of holly, ivy, and fir. This place of honor was reserved for the most magnificent decoration of all, the kissing bough.

A delicious smell of baking permeated the whole house, for a great many mince pies were needed, to say nothing of plum puddings and rich spiced fruit bread. All was set for a magnificent Christmas, and the mummers and church choir from Lyme Regis had been engaged to perform the following night, Christmas Eve. There was wine in plenty, and several seasonal punches had already been prepared and left in the cellars to come to perfection for the next day.

Wearing her crimson velvet dress, with her russet hair twisted up into a knot on top of her head, Madeleine enjoyed the diversion to the full, as did Margaret, who had always been her lieutenant at this time of year, and who fell back into the role with ease. Margaret still looked a little pale and wan, a fact not entirely helped by her dimity gown's particular shade of emerald. She felt well enough, but was careful to keep warm at all times and was never to be found without her thick cashmere shawl. Aside from enjoying the excitement of decorating their old home, she was actually a little low-spirited, for she hadn't heard anything from William and still did not know if he would return from Ireland

in time. Christmas without him wouldn't be Christmas
at all.

As the afternoon began to draw in, all was at last
accomplished, with the exception of the kissing bough,
which Madeleine had made herself. It had taken some
time, but to her relief Philip's sister had still not arrived
when it was ready. She stepped back to admire it.
Formed of two large wheel rims placed at right angles,
one within the other, and wrapped with moss, holly,
and ivy, it was adorned with candles, apples, and
countless ribbons. From beneath it was suspended a
ball of mistletoe.

It was was so large and heavy that two men were
required to haul it into place on its sturdy golden ropes,
and a hush fell over the hall as the men took up their
positions. With the first strong pull, a spontaneous
chant broke out over the hall. "Heave, heave, heave . . ."
Then, when the bough had been made fast, and its
scarlet ribbons trembled softly in the rising heat from
the fire, a great cheer broke out.

Madeleine's eyes shone as she gazed up at her *pièce
de résistance*. Of all the Christmas decorations, she liked
making the kissing bough the most.

Philip had entered the hall in time to witness the
raising of the bough, and he came over to Madeleine
with an appreciative smile. "Exquisite, Miss Charlton.
I vow you are the Michelangelo of Christmas decorations."

"Why, thank you, sir," she replied, laughing a little
as she sank into a curtsy.

"I trust that you and your sister will help me to toast
your efforts with a glass of Chablis from the bottle I
have set aside in the coldest place that could be found."
He nodded at Mrs. Crayforth, who immediately hur-

ried away and returned with a tray upon which stood the bottle in question and three crystal glasses.

Philip smiled at the housekeeper as she placed the tray on the refectory table. "The sterling effort shown by you and all the servants requires rewarding as well, Mrs. Crayforth, so you may all adjourn to the kitchens to enjoy whatever drink and refreshment you deem to be appropriate."

A stir of anticipation went through the gathering, and the housekeeper beamed. "Thank you, Sir Philip," she said, ushering everyone away toward the kitchens, not that they needed much ushering, for they all moved eagerly before her.

Philip went to pour the wine for himself, Madeleine, and Margaret, and then realized that the latter had fallen asleep in the chair by the fire after all the exertions of the past few days. Madeleine went to awaken her, but he shook his head.

"Leave her for a few moments more. My carriage will be at the door in a while, and we will arouse her then. In the meantime let us drink a toast." He poured two glasses from the bottle, and then pressed one into her hand.

"What shall we drink to, sir?" she asked.

"Why, to Christmas, of course."

"To Christmas."

Their glasses chinked together, and she sipped the deliciously cold, dry wine.

He looked around. "You have transformed this house, Miss Charlton."

"I have to admit to years of practice," she reminded him.

"True, but nevertheless you do indeed have a great talent for such things, no matter what you may say to the contrary."

"Thank you, Sir Philip."

He glanced at her. "Would you regard it as impertinent if I asked you to dispense with formality and address me without my title? I would much prefer it if you felt at liberty to call me by my first name only."

"Oh, I . . ."

"Please, Madeleine, for I would regard it as an honor."

She felt her face warming, for it was more than pleasing to hear such words on his lips. It was also very pleasing indeed to hear him use her own first name . . . "If you wish, then of course."

He smiled. "You are quite delightful when you blush, Madeleine, indeed I have to confess that I find everything about you quite delightful."

"You are practiced with your compliments."

"Is that what you think?"

"If you were me, it's what you would think," she pointed out.

"Ah, but I'm not you, I'm me, and I know exactly what I'm thinking when I compliment you. There is nothing practiced about it, just a simple statement of fact. You've been like a breath of fresh air to me, Madeleine, and I would not be lying if I said you'd changed my life."

She knew that if she looked into his eyes in that moment, he would read the truth in her glance, but she had to meet his gaze. "For the better, I trust?" she inquired hesitantly.

"Oh, yes, very much for the better," he murmured, his blue eyes so steady and compelling it was as if he could see into her very soul. For a long moment he did not look away, and when he did, it was up at the kissing bough, which still turned slowly high above the center of the hall.

Those heartstopping moments had covered her with confusion, and she strove to sound normal and unaffected. "Is . . . is there something amiss with the bough?"

"No, nothing at all. If the truth be known I was being base enough to contemplate what might happen if you and I were at this moment standing beneath that wickedly pagan emblem. Would you surrender a kiss, Madeleine?" This last was uttered very softly.

She stared at him.

"Would you, Madeleine?" he asked again, his voice low and caressing.

"Please . . ." Her glance fled toward Margaret, who still slept in the fireside chair.

"Would you surrender a kiss, Madeleine?" he asked a third time, suddenly putting his hand to her cheek.

Her whole body trembled at the touch of his fingers. "But we aren't beneath the kissing bough," she breathed.

"No, but that can swiftly be remedied," he replied, firmly taking her glass and placing it with his own on the table. Then he caught her hand and led her across the floor until they were directly under the bough, with its inviting ball of mistletoe.

She was completely at sixes and sevens as he made her face him and then put his hand to her cheek again. "Will you favor me with a seasonal kiss, Madeleine?" he requested gently. .

"Kissing boughs are for Christmas Eve, Sir Philip," she whispered.

"I thought we had agreed to be less formal. As for kissing boughs and Christmas Eve . . . Madam, methinks you try to fob me off, for I perceive the bough above us now, and I feel obliged to obey its command." He smiled and then bent forward to brush his lips softly over hers.

She closed her eyes and could not prevent her breath escaping on a sigh.

He drew her nearer then, slipping his arm around her waist and kissing her once more. This time it was no brush of the lips, but the skilled and passionate act of a man who knew how to give and take pleasure. He pressed her body close to his, and his fingers moved lovingly against the back of her neck, stroking and caressing, robbing her of the will to resist . . .

His lips moved to her throat, and he whispered her name. "Oh, Madeleine, my dearest, sweetest Madeleine . . ."

Shivers of desire passed through her. This was ecstasy. From the moment she'd met him, he'd never been out of her thoughts. She'd looked into his eyes and had awoken from a long slumber. Now she was alive, her heart beating to the rhythm of his, her body quivering with a need for his.

They were locked in each other's arms, so oblivious to everything around them that they didn't hear the crunch of carriage wheels at the door. They knew nothing until the sound of two laughing, chattering female voices alerted them. With a guilty gasp Madeleine pulled sharply away from his embrace. His sister had arrived! Gathering her skirts, she hastened to the fireplace where Margaret still slept on in the chair, and she just had time to compose herself when the doors burst open and two fashionably dressed ladies entered.

The first one was so like Philip that she had to be his sister Elizabeth. She was tall and graceful, and looked very *à la mode* in a pink muslin gown and a gray woolen spencer that came down to the new natural waistline. The gown had a wide hem, stiffened with rouleaux and embroidery, and an elaborate Elizabethan ruff that stood outside the spencer. The spencer's upper sleeves were puffed and slashed with pink, adding to the Elizabethan effect, as did her wide-brimmed gray velvet hat with its lavish pink plumes. She had her brother's dark hair and blue eyes, and her curls had been parted in the center of her forehead and gathered on either side of her pretty face, a coiffure as bang up to the mark as her clothes.

The other lady was tawny-haired, with lustrous gray eyes, and a heart-shaped face that was so beautiful she almost resembled a porcelain doll. Her figure was enviably petite and curved, and she was perhaps even more stylishly and fashionably turned out than her companion. She wore a close-fitting black pelisse with the very latest capes, and it was elegantly piped with white. Her black velvet bonnet was tied on with wide white satin ribbons and was adorned with eye-catching scarlet aigrettes. The same scarlet was repeated again on her gloves and ankle boots, and she was so perfect in every way that she might just have stepped out from the pages of *La Belle Assemblée*. She paused just inside the door and smiled at Philip. It was an enigmatic smile, conveying both a becoming hesitance, and a silent promise that she meant to make up for something.

He seemed rooted to the spot on seeing the second lady, and hardly noticed as his sister went to hug him and kiss his cheek. "Philip, it's wonderful to see you again," Elizabeth declared warmly, hugging him again and then kissing his other cheek.

He tore his eyes away from the figure by the doorway, and returned his sister's smile. "It's good to see you again too, Sis."

She turned. "Look who I've brought with me. Now I'm sure all will be well after all."

He looked at her companion. "Delia?" he said at last.

"Can you ever forgive me?" she breathed, going slowly toward him, her lovely eyes beseeching his kindness.

Elizabeth stepped smilingly aside. "Of course he forgives you, don't you, Philip? After all, it was only a silly misunderstanding. Poor Delia wasn't guilty of anything, and you were a sulky bear to believe ill of her. Come now, tell her you love her." She prodded his arm playfully.

"Forgive . . . ? Yes, of course." He ran his hand uneasily through his hair, his glance moving fleetingly toward Madeleine and then back to Delia.

With a relieved cry Delia hurried to him, linking her arms adoringly around his neck and kissing him passionately on the lips. "Oh, my darling, my darling!" she cried then, her voice shaking with emotion. "I was so afraid that I had lost you forever, and now I will never let you go again. I accept your proposal, my dearest Philip, and will gladly be your wife."

By the fireplace, as yet unnoticed by either of the two new arrivals, Madeleine could only stare. She was numb with pain. Proposal? His wife?

At last the voices disturbed Margaret's sleep, and with a slight sigh she awoke, stretching her arms above her head. "Goodness, have I been asleep for long?" she asked, looking up a little sheepishly at her sister.

Elizabeth turned swiftly, and at the same time a rather surprised Delia drew back from Philip's arms. "I . . . I had no idea anyone else was here," she murmured, her sharp glance raking the sisters from head to toe.

Elizabeth's sister looked inquiringly at him. "I trust you mean to introduce us," she prompted. Her glance wasn't sharp, just a little quizzical as she began to detect a swirl of undercurrent in the air.

"Er, yes, of course." His eyes were almost haunted as he turned to the fireplace and spoke to Madeleine and Margaret. "May I present Lady Delia Fitzroy, and my sister, Miss Elizabeth Levington?" His glance returned to Elizabeth and Delia. "Allow me to introduce Miss Madeleine and Miss Margaret Charlton."

Delia gave a very cool nod of the head, for she had already correctly interpreted Madeleine's disconcerted reaction.

Elizabeth's smile was warm and open and she approached the fireplace. "Charlton? Isn't that the name of the family who resided here before?"

Margaret returned the smile. "Yes, it is, Miss Levington."

"Oh, how agreeable it is that you and my brother have become acquainted." Elizabeth's thoughtful gaze encompassed Madeleine for a moment, and then swept back toward Philip.

He shifted uncomfortably. "They, er, have very kindly consented to decorate the house for me."

Elizabeth glanced around approvingly. "It's charming, quite charming. How clever you are," she said, smiling at the sisters. There was still no hint of rancor about her; indeed she seemed genuinely pleased to speak to them, but Delia was the very opposite, exuding suspicion and ill-will as she watched from beneath the kissing bough.

Guile and artifice were second nature to the tawny-haired widow who'd been the cause of his hasty departure from the capital, and now that she was suddenly faced with a possible rival, she was more than equal to the moment. She glanced up at the kissing bough as if noticing it for the first time. "Oh, how very fortuitous! Philip, do let us seal our match with a kiss."

Without giving him the chance to refuse, she slipped her arms around his neck again and pressed her lips lovingly over his. It was a rather shameless kiss, especially in company, and she employed every sensuous wile in her considerable repertoire.

Madeleine's heart felt as if it were breaking in two, and she was immeasurably relieved when they heard another carriage arriving at the door, for this time there were no voices to indicate further guests, which meant that it was the carriage to take Margaret and her back to Ferncombe Cottage.

Margaret realized it as well and got up from the chair, but then she swayed a little and gave a low moan before sinking to the floor in a faint. Shocked, Madeleine knelt anxiously beside her. "Margaret? Margaret, can you hear me?"

Elizabeth was too startled to do anything, but Philip hurried over. Delia remained where she was beneath the kissing bough, her gray eyes cold and angry she witnessed how fleetingly but deliberately Philip put his hand over Madeleine's, and how equally deliberately that lady flinched away.

Crouching over Margaret's unconscious figure, Philip tried to rouse her. "Miss Charlton?"

But although she gave another soft moan, her eyes didn't open.

Madeleine was distraught. "She's been so ill recently

with influenza, and she isn't very strong! Can someone please go for the doctor in Lyme?"

"Yes, of course." Philip nodded at his sister. "Ring that bell over there; the servants are all in the kitchens, celebrating the finishing of the decorations, and no one will hear unless you ring loudly."

"I'll go to the kitchens, so as not to waste any time." Elizabeth replied promptly. "Which way are they?"

"That door." He pointed.

Without further ado Elizabeth hurried away, and then Philip carefully gathered Margaret into his arms and placed her carefully in the chair once more. He pushed her tangled russet hair back from her pale face, and said her name again, but she didn't respond at all.

Madeleine was beside herself with worry, clasping her sister's hand and rubbing it as she tried to arouse her. "Margaret, please answer me," she begged.

Philip put his hand firmly over hers, not allowing her to snatch away this time. "Madeleine, I'm sure she has only fainted and will soon be herself again. I am also sure that there is no question of either of you returning to Ferncombe Cottage tonight. I will take her up to one of the bedrooms, and I absolutely insist that you stay here with her."

"But, my parents—"

"I will send word to them the moment the doctor has been here and we know what is wrong. I am still sure it is no more than a faint, but if it is more, I will despatch my carriage to bring them here immediately."

Tears shone in Madeleine's eyes. "Thank you," she whispered.

"You surely did not expect me to let you leave after this?"

She met his gaze accusingly. "I no longer know what to expect of you, sir," she replied.

"Madeleine, you must allow me to explain."

"There is nothing to explain, sir, for it is all amply clear."

He straightened guiltily and said nothing more because at that moment Elizabeth returned with some of the servants, including Mrs. Crayforth.

Madeleine stood back as he gently lifted Margaret again and carried her across the hall toward the staircase. But as she followed him, Madeleine was aware of the silent, thoughtful figure beneath the kissing bough. When she paused at the foot of the staircase to meet Delia's gaze, she knew that in Sir Philip Levington's beautiful future wife she had made a very bitter enemy indeed. But such jealousy was unnecessary, for it was only too plain that she, Madeleine Charlton, had been a means of passing the time.

Elizabeth glanced at Delia as well, and then went to Madeleine, kindly linking her arm. "I'm quite certain that all will soon be well again, Miss Charlton," she said. "I too had influenza earlier this year, and I fainted once or twice when I was recovering. There wasn't anything wrong; it was just that I was still weak, and I'm sure that's what has happened to your sister now. Come, I'll accompany you to see that all is well."

They began to climb the staircase, and Delia's spiteful gaze followed, lingering on Madeleine's all the while.

Margaret recovered consciousness shortly after being taken to the bedroom and declared that there was no need at all for the doctor to examine her, but both Madeleine and Philip were adamant, and so she reluctantly submitted when Doctor Hemmings arrived half an hour later. She was swiftly diagnosed as having simply overexerted herself, and he prescribed a good night's sleep and a cup of Mrs. Crayforth's rosemary infusion, a tonic that was renowned throughout Lyme Regis. He said that if she felt well enough, she was quite at liberty to go home the next morning, but that on no account was she to consider such a thing tonight, and then he left again. A footman was immediately dispatched to Ferncombe Cottage to inform Mr. and Mrs. Charlton of events, and to reassure them that Margaret was not in any danger and that both daughters would be safely home in the morning.

The rosemary infusion took swift effect, and not long after taking it Margaret sank into a comfortable sleep. Elizabeth kindly sat with Madeleine for a while, but such consideration inevitably meant that Philip was alone with Delia, a fact not lost upon Madeleine, whose emotions were in wretched confusion after all that had happened. From the peak of ecstasy during the kiss beneath the bough, she had been plunged into the deepest trough of misery, and she would never forgive herself for having been so duped by a man she now knew to be little more than a callous womanizer. He had amused himself with her, and if his bride-to-be hadn't come when she had, who knows how much further into temptation she, Madeleine Charlton, might have been drawn?

She was glad when Elizabeth at last decided to leave her alone with Margaret. It wasn't that she didn't like Philip's sister; on the contrary she found her very warm and agreeable, it was simply that she needed time to think and to collect her scattered senses. She intended to be mistress of herself when next she had to face Sir

Philip Levington, a meeting she did not believe would take place before the following morning. Having been found out in his baseness, she was certain he would avoid her all he could, but she was wrong, for he came to the room only minutes after his sister had left.

He entered quietly, after knocking so softly upon the door that she didn't hear him. She was seated by the fire and leaped hastily to her feet. He closed the door and then took several steps toward her. "I came to see if there was anything you require, Madeleine."

She was as cold and stiff as she could manage. "A servant could have been delegated that task, sir, and I would be obliged if in future you would address me more appropriately as Miss Charlton."

A shadow passed through his eyes. "Madeleine, there is no need for this to—"

"There is every need, sir," she interrupted, trying to despise him as much as she despised herself for her gullibility. But she couldn't despise him. She loved him . . .

"You misunderstood what Lady Delia said."

"Did I? I think not, sir, for it was clear enough, and I suppose I should be grateful that she arrived here when she did. At least I was spared the humiliation of making an even greater fool of myself."

"Madeleine, I can understand that things appear as they do to you, but if you will allow me to explain—"

"No doubt your explanation will be as smooth and almost faultless as your skill at seduction."

His manner became cooler then. "It would seem you are determined to believe ill of me, Miss Charlton."

"What else am I to believe? I was a means of passing the idle hours until your true love arrived."

"That isn't so."

"Sir Philip, while I am grateful for your kindness

toward my sister, I assure you that our stay here will be limited to one night. We will return to Ferncombe Cottage first thing in the morning."

"As you wish," he replied stiffly. "The adjacent room is at your disposal, Miss Charlton."

"I will stay here with Margaret."

"Very well. Good night, madam." Turning on his heel, he strode out.

She gazed wretchedly after him, wanting with all her heart to call him back, but knowing that that was the last thing she should do. Tears stung her eyes, and she hid her face in her hands.

Late that evening, when he believed Elizabeth and Delia had retired, Philip went to the billiard room. He was far too wide-awake and restless to sleep and thought he might divert himself for a while with a little idle play, but almost from the outset he simply leaned upon his cue, gazing absently at the scoreboard. The fire had burned low, and the room was shadowy and dimly lit, except for the green baize table with its colorful scattering of ivory balls.

He didn't hear Delia's soft step behind him and knew nothing of her presence until suddenly her slender arms slid around his waist, and her seductive voice whispered in the silence.

"Have you missed me, my darling?"

"Delia!" He turned sharply.

She wore a flimsy muslin wrap over a diaphanous nightgown, and her smooth tawny hair tumbled loose about her shoulders. Her lily-of-the-valley perfume pervaded the room, as fragrant and alluring as ever. She smiled, slipping her arms around him again and moving close so that her body pressed to his. "You should not have left London like that, my dearest, for I have seen the folly of my ways," she breathed.

"Perhaps I was the one guilty of said folly," he replied.

"I know you don't mean that. You love me, Philip, and I now know that I love you." For a fleeting moment she remembered Madeleine's face. It did not take a genius to guess what had been going on. Well, the little redhead in the outmoded crimson velvet dress was about to be taught a very salutary lesson in not reaching up above oneself. The likes of Sir Philip Levington weren't for her.

The clock on the wall began to chime midnight. Delia glanced at it and then smiled up into Philip's eyes. "It's Christmas Eve now, my darling, and I have the most perfect of gifts for you." She stretched up to kiss him on the lips.

Christmas Eve dawned very frosty and white, and Lyme Bay was wreathed in mist as the servants arose at Fairhill Park to go about their tasks. Mrs. Crayforth supervised them in the beginning, but then adjourned to her parlor to take a dish of tea. She sat comfortably by the fire, enjoying a few moments to herself before the business of preparing breakfast for Sir Philip and his guests. After that the day promised to be very hectic indeed, with all the remaining guests set to arrive. By tonight the house would be full to overflowing, and she and the other servants would be rushed off their feet. Maybe it would be like old times again, when the Charltons had been here . . .

Firelight flickered over the room and upon the housekeeper's prized collection of little china figurines, acquired over many years of service to the Charlton family. Each figurine recorded a special event, whether it was Miss Madeleine's eighteenth birthday, Mr. and Mrs. Howard's wedding anniversary, or Miss Margaret's first ball. Mrs. Crayforth gazed fondly at them, but then her expression saddened as she looked at one figurine in particular. It was a Wedgwood shepherdess and had been given to her as a parting gift when the Charltons had left Fairhill Park. Oh, what a dreadful day that had been, with all the servants in tears, and poor Mr. Charlton looking as if the world itself had come to an end.

The housekeeper sipped her tea, her thoughts moving on to her new master. Sir Philip Levington was a gentleman, and no mistake, and the servants all held him in high regard. At least they did so far. All that might change now that it seemed there was a fancy London lady on the scene. There wasn't much that took place beneath this roof that Mrs. Crayforth did not know, so that his obvious interest in Miss Madeleine had been a source of great joy. But that had been before the arrival of Lady Delia Fitzroy, who wasn't at all to the housekeeper's liking. That one was trouble, with a capital *T*, and everything would have been much better if she'd stayed in London where she belonged. The Lord alone knew what would happen now.

The door opened suddenly, with no polite knock beforehand, and Mrs. Crayforth gave such a start that she almost spilled her tea. A frown darkened her brow as she prepared to chastise whichever maid it was, but then she got up hurriedly as she saw that her visitor was none other than the London lady herself.

"My lady?" she said, endeavoring to bob a neat curtsy at the same time that she set her cup and saucer down.

"Mrs. Crayforth, is it not?"

"It is, my lady. May I be of assistance?"

"I trust so," Delia murmured, going to the window and looking out over the frost-whitened kitchen garden. She wore a very stylish morning gown made of blue-and-white-striped silk, and her hair was twisted up beneath a dainty little lace cap from which fluttered blue satin ribbons.

"Did you sleep well, my lady?" the housekeeper asked, feeling the need to say something.

"Adequately." Delia turned from the window. "I trust you aren't busy, Mrs. Crayforth?" Her glance deliberately took in the cup of tea.

"I was just taking a moment or so before resuming my duties in the kitchens, my lady," the housekeeper replied a little defensively. She was insulted, for she took her position very seriously indeed and did not like the implication she might be less than constantly diligent.

"Please do not misunderstand, Mrs. Crayforth," Delia murmured, a faint smile still playing upon her lips as she went to take the chair opposite the housekeeper's. "Actually, I was hoping that you might be able to tell me something about this beautiful house. I can tell that you love it very much, for you take such pride in looking after it."

The flattering words were chosen carefully, and they had an immediate effect, for Mrs. Crayforth softened with pleasure. "Why, thank you, my lady."

"Do sit down and tell me all about Fairhill Park and its history, Mrs. Crayforth. I understand you were here when the Charltons owned it?" She smiled agreeably as she set about enticing the unknowing servant into divulging all manner of interesting tidbits about the former owners—and about Miss Madeleine Charlton in particular.

Delia emerged half an hour later with everything she needed to know, and with the very weapon to wound Madeleine most.

Madeleine had slept in the chair in Margaret's room and was awakened by the sound of sawing from the park outside. For a moment she didn't quite know where she was, but then memory returned and she got up swiftly to hurry to her sister's bedside.

Margaret stirred at her touch. "Madeleine?"

"How are you?"

"I feel much better, thank you."

"Are you quite sure?"

"Yes." Margaret struggled to sit up, and then her curious gaze went toward the curtained windows. "What are they doing out there?"

"I don't know." Madeleine went to pull the curtains back, and then her breath caught as she saw the scene outside. Her beloved spruce tree lay upon the grass, and some of the men were preparing to carry it into the house.

"What is it?" Margaret asked, watching her.

"My tree has been cut down," Madeleine whispered.

Margaret stared at her. "But whatever for?"

"I don't know." Madeleine fought the tears back. Why would Philip issue such an order? Trees were felled only when they were old and dangerous, or when their timber was required. Her tree was neither old nor dangerous, and it was too small to provide timber. Was this simply petty revenge—the angry response of a man who had failed in his shabby seduction?

The men picked up the tree and began to carry it toward the house. Without saying anything more to

Margaret, Madeleine gathered her skirts and hurried from the room. As she neared the top of the staircase, she heard Delia's imperious tones in the great hall. "No, no, dolt, don't put it there, put it over that side!"

Madeleine's steps faltered, and instead of going down the stairs, she went on to the minstrels' gallery, from where she could see what was happening. Placing her hands on the green-garlanded balustrade, she looked down into the hall below and saw a scene of considerable confusion. Her tree had been carried to a place by the foot of the staircase, and two men were holding it steady in a large tub of earth while two more were endeavoring to prop it up firmly with stones. A fifth man had secured it with a rope, tying it to one of the banisters so that it couldn't fall over. Elsewhere in the hall some more servants were engaged upon rifling the decorations, taking all the brightest things, stars, rosettes, everlasting flowers, ribbons, and candles, and bringing them to place on the floor by the tree.

Delia had taken charge and looked very much the lady of the house as she stood there in her blue-and-white-striped gown. It was as if she was already Philip's wife, and therefore at liberty to do as she pleased beneath his roof.

At that moment Elizabeth descended the staircase in a flurry of jonquil muslin. She didn't notice Madeleine standing in the shadows of the gallery, and her steps faltered as she saw what was happening in the hall. "What on earth—?"

"It's a Christmas tree, Elizabeth," Delia explained. "The royal family has them at Windsor, you know, and it is becoming quite the thing to have them in fashionable residences. It has always been the tradition in Hanover and other German places."

"This is Fairhill Park in Dorset," Elizabeth responded

dryly, glancing around a little unhappily at the way the other decorations had been looted for ornaments to put on the tree.

"It may be a rustic corner of England now, Elizabeth, but I intend it to be a *fashionable* corner. Fairhill Park is going to be one of *the* places this Christmas."

"I hardly think my brother's house will ever rank alongside the likes of Windsor," Elizabeth murmured, still looking around. "Oh, whatever have you done—?"

"Done?"

"To the rest of the decorations. It all looked so lovely."

"It was adequate, I suppose, but hardly stylish. Miss Charlton may know what is what out here in the sticks, but she has no idea at all about London ways."

"That is surely for Philip to decide."

Delia's eyes flickered. "He has given me *carte blanche*."

"He has?" Elizabeth was obviously surprised.

"Oh, do stop looking so disapproving, Elizabeth. You brought me here to be reunited with him, and that is what has happened. The past is the past, and from now on I intend to be everything he wishes of me."

"Then I trust for your sake that this is indeed what he wishes," Elizabeth observed, looking at the tree again.

"It is, you have my word upon that. I told him I would like to put up a German Christmas tree, and he told me to take this particular one."

Up on the gallery Madeleine's eyes stung anew with tears. So it *was* angry spite, nothing more and nothing less. Oh, how very wrong she had been about him.

Elizabeth wasn't impressed by this newfangled form of decoration, no matter how traditional it might be in Germany. "It seems a waste of a good tree to me," she observed with crushing practicality.

"Trees like this will soon be all the rage, Elizabeth,

and Fairhill Park will have been one of the first houses to boast one."

"I'm sure you will receive all the necessary credit," Elizabeth replied, not without a touch of acidity. Then she gathered her skirts and walked away across the hall in the direction of the dining room, where breakfast was being served. She was puzzled by the encounter with Delia, for she had been so sure the previous night that it was Miss Madeleine Charlton who now occupied Philip's heart. What was going on? He had yet to come down from his room, but when he did, his baffled and slightly cross sister intended to have a word with him.

Delia seemed sublimely unconcerned by her friend's strained reaction, and resumed supervising the tree. Her eyes slid knowingly up to the minstrels' gallery, where she had known all along that Madeleine was watching. If she had planned it precisely, things could not have gone better than this. The presumptuous little redhead was learning her lesson very neatly and very painfully indeed!

Not realizing that her presence was known, Madeleine remained unhappily where she was for a moment or so, and then she turned to leave the gallery to return to Margaret, but as she did so she saw Philip walking along the passage toward her. He wore a pine green coat, gray marcella waistcoat, and cream trousers, and there was a gold pin in his neckcloth. He looked a little tired, as if he hadn't slept a great deal.

He was the last person she wished to see, and so she cast around desperately for somewhere to draw out of sight, but there was nowhere, and anyway, he had already seen her. He halted, his blue eyes guarded because he was uncertain of the reception he would receive. "Good morning, Miss Charlton. I trust your sister has recovered?"

"We will be leaving as soon as possible, sir."

"It would seem that you have not personally improved since last night," he murmured.

"Did you honestly imagine that I would?

"Madeleine, this is all so unnecessary—"

"No, sir, it is very necessary indeed. I marvel at your ability to ape the innocent, for to be sure you are very convincing, but I happen to know that you are far from innocent."

"Meaning what, precisely?"

"That your wife-to-be has carried out your instructions to the very letter."

He looked blankly at her. "I'm afraid I don't understand."

"No? Forgive me if I choose to doubt that claim."

His eyes darkened then. "This is becoming a little wearisome, madam. If I tell you that I don't understand, then you may be sure that that is precisely what I mean. You may also take my word for it that Lady Delia Fitzroy is not my wife-to-be."

"That is not what she says, and at this precise moment I am more inclined to believe her than you."

With two strides he had closed the physical distance between them, if not the emotional. Seizing her arms, he shook her slightly, his blue eyes bright with anger. "Damn you, Madeleine! I haven't done anything to warrant your doubts, and I certainly do not deserve to be shut out of your heart. Yesterday in the great hall I thought—"

"Yesterday in the great hall I was a fool, sirrah. Unhand me, if you please!"

"No, madam, for it is *now* that you are being a fool," he breathed.

"Let me go!"

"I will release you when I'm ready," he said softly, pulling her slowly toward him.

She began to struggle, but before she could cry out his lips were over hers, and his arms had moved inexorably around her, crushing her close as if he would never let her go. It was a harsh kiss, angry and strong, and when his fingers twined in her hair, they did so with a force that hurt.

But if the embrace was cruel, it was also impassioned and burning with a rich desire that threatened to overwhelm her. Her senses betrayed her, and luxurious sensations began to stir irresistibly through her body, making her ache with a need to submit.

But then she remembered his lies, and with a cry forced herself away. Tears were wet on her cheeks, and she trembled with feeling. "I despise you," she whispered. Then she fled past him toward Margaret's room.

He was also in the grip of emotion, but as he tried to regain his composure, he became aware of Delia's voice in the hall. Puzzled, he went to the edge of the gallery and looked over. What he saw made his eyes harden with fury, and with a smothered curse he strode toward the staircase.

Delia paused as she saw him descending toward her, and for a moment her confidence fluttered, but then she smiled at him. "Good morning, Philip."

"What is the meaning of this?" He gestured toward the tree and the spoiled decorations.

"Why, I thought you would appreciate a German Christmas tree," she replied.

"You had no business touching anything."

"Oh, Philip, don't be such a sulky bear. I know you were a little upset last night, but I'm sure you didn't mean it. Let us forget all about it and begin again." She was at her most winning and beguiling.

"I meant everything I said last night, and any new beginning I make this morning will be made without you; indeed I expected you to be long gone from here by now."

Specks of high color touched her cheeks, for the servants had all stopped their tasks to listen to such an interesting exchange. "Please, Philip, we should be more private . . ." she began.

"No, Delia, for it seems to me that speaking to you in private does not have the desired effect. I spurned your advances last night, and I am still spurning them now. You no longer mean anything to me, madam, and I wish with all my heart that you hadn't tricked my sister into bringing you here. Your continual lies, stratagems, flirtations, and shameless capacity for infidelity have finally opened my eyes and earned my contempt, madam, and I wish you to quit this house as soon as it is humanly possible."

There was a shocked hush in the hall.

She was bitter then. "I suppose I have your little Miss Charlton to thank for this!"

"No, Delia, you have only yourself to thank. If you hadn't behaved so badly, you would never have forfeited my love."

"And *she* is my replacement?"

"That is no concern of yours."

"Well, I suspected it might be a vain hope that you would have changed your mind this morning, and so I took a certain elementary precaution to make certain that you won't find it easy to convince her you are all that is noble and gallant. An amusing gesture on my part, do you not agree?" she breathed, her eyes bright and taunting as they moved deliberately past him toward the tree.

He followed her gaze and suddenly recognized it. He whirled bitterly back to face her as he realized what had been done in his name. "Damn you, Delia," he breathed.

"No, sir, damn *you*! How dare you set me aside in favor of that nonentity of a creature! I promise you that it was very satisfying to order her pathetic little tree to be cut down, very satisfying indeed!"

"If I were not a gentleman—"

She goaded him bitterly. "You'd what, sir? Strike me in front of the servants?"

Elizabeth's angry steps suddenly broke into the silence as she came toward them, having heard the whole conversation. Her face was flushed with resentment as she halted in front of Delia. "My brother might be too much of a gentleman to stoop to the necessary action, madam, but I am most certainly not too much of a lady!" With that she struck Delia's cheek and would have done it again if Philip hadn't swiftly caught her wrist.

"That's enough, Elizabeth."

But his sister's rage was still burning bright as she continued to hold her former friend's gaze. "You viper! You swore to me that you had never done anything to warrant my brother's mistrust, but it's now clear that you were guilty of all those whispers! And since you arrived here you've caused as much spiteful mischief as you can! You even lied this morning when you claimed you were to be my sister-in-law! You are no longer any friend of mine!"

Philip looked at Delia. "I think you had better leave forthwith, madam. You have relatives in Weymouth, as I recall. The mist has lifted, the roads are clear, and

I see no reason at all why you should not be with them well before darkness."

"Philip—"

"Please go, for there is nothing for you here."

Her eyes flickered with loathing, and she gathered her skirts to go to the staircase, and as she went up it she did not deign to glance back.

Elizabeth was close to tears. "Forgive me, Philip, both for making such a public display and for bringing that creature here."

"You acted for the best," he replied, giving her a quick hug, but then his gaze went back to the tree.

Elizabeth looked as well. "I . . . I know that this particular tree is of some significance, Philip, but I don't understand what."

"It's Madeleine's tree, planted for her by her grandfather, and now she thinks I sanctioned its felling."

"You must tell her the truth," his sister urged.

"She is set upon believing ill of me."

"That's nonsense. You must go to her now and explain," Elizabeth advised quickly. "You do love her, don't you?"

"Yes." He gave a short laugh. "Dear God, yes, I love her! I hardly know her, but already she means everything to me."

"Then don't let this misunderstanding persist for a moment longer."

"It isn't as simple as that, Elizabeth. You see, although I may love her, she despises me."

"I don't believe that."

"It is the truth."

"Yes, but surely it's only because she misunderstands about you and—"

Elizabeth couldn't say anything more, for Mrs. Crayforth suddenly hurried up to them. "Sir Philip? I must speak with you!"

"Yes, what is it?"

"There's some trouble in the stables, a fight, and I think you should go there immediately!"

"A fight?"

"Yes, sir. Please go before someone is badly hurt."

"Oh, very well."

Elizabeth caught his arm. "What about Miss Charlton?"

"There is nothing further to discuss. It is at an end," he replied, and then he hurried away.

Elizabeth looked helplessly after him. "Oh, Philip, Philip, why choose this of *all* times to show how proud and obstinate you can be?" she murmured and then turned swiftly to detain the housekeeper, who had begun to walk back toward the kitchens. "Mrs. Crayforth, a word if you please," she said.

"Madam?"

Elizabeth searched her face. "How adept are you at the art of conspiracy?" she asked.

The housekeeper blinked. "Conspiracy, madam?"

"Yes. Am I right in thinking you would welcome the prospect of Miss Madeleine becoming my brother's bride, and therefore mistress of this house?"

Mrs. Crayforth hesitated and then nodded. "Yes, madam, you are quite right."

"Then you and I have some plotting to do. I want you to return to the kitchens and then send for Miss Madeleine to come and help you with some problem. I want you to keep her there for a few minutes, long enough for me to have a private word with her sister."

"But what problem can I invent, madam?"

"I'm sure you can think of something, Mrs. Crayforth. Ask her about some point of etiquette over serving the Christmas meals, *anything*, just detain her for a little while."

"Very well, madam."

Elizabeth smiled. "Send someone to ask her now, and be quick, for we must accomplish this before my brother comes back."

"Yes, madam." The housekeeper turned swiftly away. A minute later a maid hurried up the staircase, and Mrs. Crayforth went back to the kitchens.

Madeleine had returned to Margaret after her brief confrontation with Philip by the gallery, but before going into the room she paused to collect herself. She didn't want her sister to know how upset she was about everything and strove to overcome her emotions. Thus Margaret had no idea what Delia had been overheard saying or about the last, painful encounter with Philip.

Margaret had been sitting up in bed, but now felt unwell again and was lying down, saying she needed to rest for a little longer. Madeleine was dismayed, both because her sister had apparently not recovered completely after all, and because they would now have to delay their departure for Ferncombe Cottage.

She stood by the window, gazing out over the park toward the sea, and deliberately not glancing toward the stump that told of where her tree had been. There was a tap at the door, and she steeled herself in case it was Philip.

"Yes?"

The door opened and one of the maids came in. "Begging your pardon, Miss Madeleine, but Mrs. Crayforth wonders if you would be so kind as to go to the kitchens. She has some difficulty she thinks you will be able to sort out."

"But what of Lady Delia? Or Miss Levington? Shouldn't they be consulted first?"

"Mrs. Crayforth sent me to you, Miss Madeleine."

Madeleine didn't want to go, for it was hardly her place, and the last thing she wished was to be caught in circumstances that might be construed as intruding upon the domain of others. But then she remembered the back staircase, which could be used without anyone in the main house being any the wiser, and so she nodded at the maid. "Very well, I'll come now." She went to the bed. "Will you be all right, Margaret?"

"Yes, of course," Margaret replied sleepily.

Madeleine hurried out with the maid, and as the door closed, Margaret sat up in the bed with a heartfelt sigh. "Oh, Madeleine, what am I going to do with you?" she murmured.

There was another tap at the door. "Miss Charlton? May I come in?"

Margaret recognized Elizabeth's voice. "Yes, of course," she answered, wondering what on earth Philip's sister would wish to see her about.

Elizabeth came stealthily in and closed the door softly before hurrying to the bedside. "Miss Charlton, I know that this may sound strange coming from me, and that you probably think I am intent upon some mischief, but the truth is that I am on your sister's side in all this, and you and I must work together if we are to help my brother and her settle their foolish differences."

Margaret stared at her.

Elizabeth gave a little smile. "Philip loves Madeleine, you know, and I have the strongest feeling that she loves him."

Margaret looked a little uncertainly at her. "Forgive me for saying this, but yes, I do think it a little strange that you should come to me on such a mission. You brought Lady Delia here and are apparently her close friend. Why then do you support my sister?"

"Because I now know Delia Fitzroy for the scheming, dishonest, exceedingly disagreeable cat she is, and because it took me all of a minute or so on arriving to realize how it was between my brother and your sister. Mule that he is, Philip is all-important to me, Miss Charlton, and his happiness comes first as far as I'm concerned." Elizabeth smiled again. "Was that frank enough for you?"

"Yes, I believe it was."

"And you are prepared to admit that your sister loves my brother?"

"Yes, she does." Margaret grinned. "And as to helping them sort themselves out, why on earth do you imagine I'm pretending to be ill?"

Elizabeth's eyes widened. "Are you saying that all this is a sham?"

"From the very first swoon. I'd fallen asleep by the fire in the great hall, but I woke up without them knowing. They were beneath the kissing bough in a very warm embrace, and so I feigned to be still asleep. Then you arrived with Lady Delia. I realized how it was going, and so I saw to it that Madeleine didn't scuttle home and leave the field free to her rival."

Elizabeth's eyes shone. "Oh, you are indeed a creature after my own heart! I'm filled with admiration at your quick-wittedness."

"I felt very guilty for deceiving poor Doctor Hemmings, for he is an old friend of the family, but I made myself think of how Madeleine had kissed your brother. She wouldn't have done that unless she loved him, and that was spur enough for me to press on with my play-acting."

"We have to bring them together again, but it will be difficult after what has happened this morning."

"This morning?"

"Oh, I suppose there's no way you could know. Let me explain." Elizabeth sat on the edge of the bed and proceeded to relate the story of the tree, and of Philip's furious reaction. "So you see," she finished, "Delia was given her *congé*, and in front of the servants! It is a measure of my brother's rage and dismay that he spoke publicly to her like that, for under normal circumstances he would never have done so. But the thought of what had been done to Madeleine's tree was too much for him, especially as Delia had been pretending that she'd carried out his instructions."

"What a horridly spiteful and mean-hearted vixen she must be," Margaret breathed.

"She is. Listen, I think that must be the men taking her luggage out now."

They both heard footsteps passing the door and the murmur of male voices as some of the servants carried Delia's two heavy trunks. A moment later there were light female footsteps and the rustle of fashionable clothes as Delia herself followed.

Elizabeth turned urgently back to Margaret. "We must think of what to do now. Philip has no intention of speaking to Madeleine because he believes she despises him. You've already heard me call him a mule, and he is, believe me. Once his heels are dug in, it takes heaven and earth to make him budge."

"I fear that Madeleine can be much the same. She's anxious to get away from here as quickly as possible, and I'm finding it more and more difficult to keep pretending I'm ill. I won't be able to fool her for much longer."

"I thought that might be the case, not about your

pretend illness, you understand, but about Madeleine's reaction to all this. That's why I decided you and I must join forces. If they can't be persuaded to see wisdom, then they must be duped into it. But how, that's the problem. We haven't much time to dream up a stratagem, for Mrs. Crayforth won't be able to keep Madeleine in the kitchens for long."

"Mrs. Crayforth is in on this?" Margaret was taken aback at the thought of the housekeeper stooping to such chicanery.

"Yes, and while she keeps Madeleine busy, Philip is in the stables sorting out some quarrel between the men. We must think quickly."

They were both silent for a moment, and then Margaret suddenly straightened excitedly. "You're right about them both refusing to see wisdom, so we must try a little trickery."

"Yes, but how?"

"I've thought of that. When Madeleine and I leave, we will go through the great hall, for I will refuse to countenance scurrying down the back stairs like parlormaids in trouble with Mrs. Crayforth. Do you think you can get him into the dining room when he returns from the stables?"

"The dining room? Yes, I suppose so, but how will that achieve anything?"

"See that he's there with you at eleven; that's in exactly half an hour. Leave the door ajar so that you can see into the great hall."

"What then?"

"When Madeleine returns here, I will say that I feel sufficiently recovered to go home, and we'll come down to the great hall to leave. Then I'll pretend to have left my gloves behind, and I'll come back here on my own, leaving her in the hall. You must then make absolutely certain that he has no option but to go out and speak to her. Browbeat him. Call his honor into question if he refuses. If that doesn't work, I'll come back down and start on her. I'll tell her that Delia was lying, and I'll challenge her to hear his side of it. We have to make it virtually impossible for them to be defiant, and between us we *have* to succeed!"

Elizabeth smiled. "If we don't, it won't be for lack of trying. I'll go now, and I'll do all I can to have my brother in the dining room at eleven o'clock precisely."

"With the door ajar," Margaret reminded her.

"With the door ajar," Elizabeth confirmed, and then she got up and hurried from the room. She'd only been gone a minute or so when Madeleine returned.

Margaret glanced at the clock on the mantelpiece. If she got up now and took her time about combing and pinning her hair, washing, dressing, and so on, she could make certain that it was eleven o'clock when they went downstairs to the great hall. She smiled at Madeleine. "I feel better again now, so we can go home if you wish."

"It's definitely what I wish," Madeleine replied with feeling.

"Very well." Margaret drew the bedclothes aside and got up. "What did Mrs. Crayforth want?"

"Oh, it was something about how to arrange all the guests at the table. I don't know why she needed my advice, for she's done such things time and time again in the past, and anyway, she should have asked Lady Delia or Miss Levington." Madeleine lowered her eyes. "You were right about one thing, anyway."

"And what is that?"

"This Christmas *is* the worst one ever."

"Oh." Margaret sat by the dressing table and picked

up a hairbrush. Was the elaborate plan with Elizabeth really necessary? Could Madeleine be brought around by being told the truth about Delia? Surely it was worth a try. She glanced at her sister in the mirror. "Did you know that Lady Delia has left?" she asked lightly.

"Left?" Madeleine looked swiftly at her. "How do you know that?"

"Miss Levington came to see how I was, and she told me. It seems that Sir Philip isn't going to marry her; indeed there has been a very definite parting of the ways. She had no permission to cut down your tree and certainly had no business saying she was to be his bride."

Madeleine was silent for a long moment.

Margaret turned to look at her. "Have you nothing to say?"

"Not really. Why should I?"

Margaret was a little exasperated. "Madeleine Charlton, you surely don't imagine that your *tendresse* for him has passed me by? You are in love with him, and if Lady Delia has now been removed from the scene then—"

"He didn't spurn her when she rushed into his arms, did he? Nor did he tell her there and then that he no longer wished to marry her."

"I know, but—"

"It is therefore clear to me that no matter what has happened since to bring about a parting of the ways, at the time of her arrival she had every right to think of herself as his prospective wife. I just want to forget all about him. I wish I'd never decided to come here for those horrid cones, and I certainly do not ever mean to come here again."

"What if you're wrong about him?"

"And what if I was a mere fleeting fancy, a means

of forgetting the ennui for a while?" Madeleine's voice was small, for this was what she truly thought.

"I don't believe that of him," Margaret declared stoutly.

"How well do you know him?" Madeleine asked bluntly.

"I . . ." Margaret shrugged. "Not well, I suppose, but I still don't believe he would behave like that."

"I do. I think he is a practiced seducer, and that I made a fool of myself by being taken in. Now, can we please leave the subject alone?"

"As you wish." Margaret resignedly returned her attention to the mirror and her hair. Well, now it was up to the plan she and Elizabeth had concocted. May it have more success than a straightforward appeal to her sister's suddenly nonexistent common sense!

It was five to eleven, and Elizabeth waited anxiously in the dining room, for Philip had yet to return. She had had no option but to send him a message, requesting his immediate presence in the dining room. The virtually untouched breakfast had been cleared away, and on Elizabeth's swift instructions Mrs. Crayforth had brought some hastily prepared mulled wine flavored with oranges and cloves. It was a drink of which Philip was particularly fond, especially at Christmas.

The hall was quiet now, for she had told Mrs. Crayforth to order the servants back to the kitchens, leaving the decorations in the confusion Delia had caused. It was best to have no one else around if the all-important confrontation was to be brought about successfully. Oh, where was he? Why didn't he come?

To her relief she suddenly heard his steps, and then he was there. "I came as soon as I received your message. What is it? Has something happened?" he asked.

"Er, no, I just thought you'd like to join me for a glass of this." She indicated the wine.

He looked irritably at her. "Damn it, Elizabeth, I thought there was something wrong!"

"Well, I didn't think you'd want your wine to go cold." She met his eyes with as much innocence as she could, only too aware that she sounded far from convincing.

With a sigh he turned to close the door.

"Please leave it open, it's very hot in here," she said quickly.

"Hot Elizabeth, it's barely warm."

"*I* feel hot."

"Oh, very well." He took a glass from the tray and then went to stand by the window, gazing out at the sunken garden, and the sparkling water of Lyme Bay beyond the park. There was no sign of the frost now, but the beautiful clear day it had heralded had now come to its full glory. He swirled the wine in his hand. "I saw Delia's carriage leaving."

"Good riddance, say I."

He nodded. "She really took me in; indeed, I can't believe I was so blind to her faults for so long."

"Blindness of that sort appears to be your specialty, Philip," Elizabeth observed cordially.

"And what is that supposed to mean?"

"That you are closing your eyes now, rather than go to Miss Charlton and tell her you love her."

"It's none of your concern, Elizabeth."

"No?"

"No! And if you mean to roast me about it, I'll leave you to it."

She sighed and then glanced toward the door as she detected the faint sound of two sets of steps descending the staircase to the hall. From where he stood, Philip couldn't hear anything at all. She smiled as she heard Margaret's voice. The stratagem had commenced!

Margaret paused at the foot of the staircase, surveying the tree, which had been left in its half-finished state. "How horrid it was to do this," she said sadly.

Madeleine couldn't bear to look at it and wanted only to escape. She glanced toward the main door. "Let's go, for I want to leave here as quickly as possible," she pleaded.

"We must take one last look around," Margaret replied.

"Please, Margaret. It's bad enough that you wouldn't go by the back way, but to insist now upon lingering here like this . . ."

"Just a moment more. After all, we may never come here again." Margaret deliberately strolled into the center of the hall, standing directly beneath the kissing bough as she took her time about gazing around.

Reluctantly Madeleine joined her, glancing uneasily toward the various doors for fear of seeing Philip emerge through one of them.

Margaret smiled at her. "You surpassed yourself with the decorations this year. I don't think I've ever seen it look better."

"Lady Delia's activities haven't exactly helped," Madeleine responded, surveying the pile of bright ornaments still waiting to be put on the tree.

Margaret looked across at the dining room, where Elizabeth was waiting to catch her eye. But where was Philip? Seeing her inquiring expression, Elizabeth nodded and indicated that he was by the window.

Madeleine's attention was diverted by the kissing bough above their heads. Seeing her looking up at its gently floating ribbons, rich greenery, and suspended ball of mistletoe, Margaret seized the opportunity. "Oh, no! I've left my gloves in the bedroom!"

"I'm sure they'll be sent down to the cottage," Madeleine began quickly, fearing another delay to their departure.

"There's no need for that. All I have to do is go back and get them."

"Margaret—"

"I won't be a moment." Gathering her skirts, Margaret hastened away.

Seeing Madeleine standing on her own beneath the kissing bough, Elizabeth turned to Philip. "There is something I wish you to do for me, something very important indeed, and that is why I've lured you here now."

"What is it?" He looked at her from the window.

"I wish you to speak to Miss Charlton."

"Elizabeth—"

"She is out there in the hall now, and she is entirely on her own."

He moved slightly and looked out into the hall, where Madeleine still hadn't noticed anyone in the dining room.

Elizabeth reached out to take his hand. "She loves you, you fool, and if you don't speak to her now, then all my plotting, and that of her sister, will have been for nothing. Please, Philip, don't let her go. I can tell that she is the one for you; it's written in your eyes."

He hesitated.

Elizabeth was merciless. "If you don't, I'll never forgive you, and I certainly won't let you forget what an idiot you are."

He smiled a little. "You drive a cruel bargain, madam."

"One has to be cruel to be kind," she replied.

Putting his glass down, he left the room to go out into the hall.

Hearing his step, Madeleine turned with a quick gasp. Their eyes met, and then she looked away again, wishing Margaret had agreed to use the other staircase. If she had, they'd have reached Fern Combe by now.

"Madeleine?"

"I'm only waiting for my sister and then will be gone, sir," she replied.

"I must talk to you."

"I would rather not."

"Don't I deserve at least deserve the chance to explain?"

She looked unwillingly at him. "If you mean to tell me that Lady Delia has left, you may spare yourself the effort, because I already know."

He crossed toward her. "Maybe you know that, but do you also know that she is not going to be my bride?"

"Yes."

He halted a few feet from her. "And that makes no difference to you?"

"No."

"I cannot believe that you are as steely-hearted as you pretend, not when I recall the last time we stood here together." He glanced up at the kissing bough.

She colored. "Please do not remind me of how gullible I was."

"Perhaps I was the gull, Madeleine, for I believed you loved me."

She didn't reply.

"Do you make a habit of indulging in such passionate kisses?"

The question stung her. "No!"

"Then it *did* mean something to you?"

"You know that it did."

"Yes, I know because it meant the same to me. Do

you imagine that *I* am disposed to making such ardent advances to anyone who catches my eye?"

She looked at him. "I don't know. Are you?"

"I vow you would make an excellent card player, Madeleine, for your face gives nothing away."

"If I mean so much to you, why didn't you come to tell me Lady Delia had gone?"

"And if I mean so much to you, why would you have left without speaking to me?" he countered.

"This avails us of nothing, sir."

He smiled a little. "That is very true, so I will tell you why we have both been behaving so ridiculously. It's called pride, Madeleine, and pride is one of the seven deadly sins. Did you mean it earlier, when you said you despised me?"

She couldn't answer.

"Are you still too prideful to be honest?"

"What do you want me to say? That I love you? Very well, I will say it. I love you, Sir Philip Levington."

"Oh, Madeleine . . ." He reached out to her, but she drew back.

"No!"

"Why? What obstacle is there now that wasn't there last night when you kissed me?"

"Lady Delia Fitzroy stands between us."

He stared at her. "That's nonsense."

"Is it?" Her eyes were bright. "All I know is that when she ran into your arms, you embraced her and kissed her on the lips. And you did not protest when she mentioned marriage. I don't know what occurred between you after that, but I know what I saw at that precise moment."

"You saw a man who was caught unawares, a man who was so surprised to see her that his responses were automatic and certainly not thought out. I do not deny that I loved her once, or that I was misguided enough to ask her to marry me, but that was before I saw the real Delia Fitzroy. I'd fallen out of love with her before I left London, and she was certainly not on my list of guests for Christmas here. My sister was duped into bringing her. I don't profess to know why Delia decided she wanted me after all, for I thought I'd made my disillusionment very clear indeed before leaving town. No doubt it was just another example of the perversity of her nature, wanting that which she thought she'd lost. Believe me, Madeleine, I was dismayed to see Delia come through that door, and if you intend to turn your back on me simply because of a few foolish seconds of surprise, indecision, witlessness—call it what you will—then perhaps you *should* go."

Madeleine stared at him, a million emotions swirling confusingly through her.

His voice was soft then. "You've already admitted that you love me, Madeleine, and now you know that I love you, too, so what is there left to keep us apart. It cannot be Delia, so what new defense do you have?" He put his hand out, and touched her pale cheek with his fingertips.

Her breath caught, and she closed her eyes.

"Oh, Madeleine," he breathed. "My sweet, sweet Madeleine . . ."

Suddenly she was in his arms, her lips raised gladly to meet his. His heartbeats were close to hers as he held her, and his kiss was long, passionate, and tender. He held her as if he feared to ever let her go again, and she met his desire with equal ardor.

At last he drew back slightly, cupping her face in his

hands and gazing down into her loving eyes. "I so nearly lost you, my darling," he whispered.

"I've been so idiotic . . ."

"We both have." He kissed her forehead and then brushed his lips over hers again. "We've put foolishness behind us now and must look to the future. It's Christmas Eve, and two things are very clear to me. The first is that you belong with me. The second is that you belong in this house. Those two things could so easily become one. All you have to do is say you'll be my wife. Become Lady Levington, my darling, and make this the most memorable and magical Christmas possible."

She stared at him. "Philip, I—"

"Just say yes," he interrupted softly.

"Yes," she whispered. "Oh, yes . . ."

Smiling, he kissed her again, and the ribbons on the kissing bough trembled gently, just as she did in his arms.

Mrs. Crayforth peeped out from the entrance to the kitchens, and her heart quickened gladly at what she saw. This was perfect, quite perfect.

Others watched with satisfaction as well, Elizabeth from the door of the dining room, and Margaret from the minstrels' gallery. The two main conspirators then looked at each other and smiled, before returning their triumphant attention to the two lovers beneath the kissing bough.

Season of Joy
by
Gayle Buck

1

THE HOUSE PARTY had been in full swing for days. Upwards of twenty relatives and neighbors had descended at some point to celebrate the Christmas season with the Huntingtons.

Some had expressed surprise and disapproval that the family should enter into the frivolities of the season while still in mourning, but Sir Henry had decreed that the happy traditions were to be observed despite the loss of the scion of the house.

"Tony would have been the last to have wanted the living to be buried with the dead during Christmas," he had declared.

And so the decorative fir garlands and red ribbons had gone up; tantalizing scents of roasted goose and Christmas puddings had wafted through the house;

laughter rang out as children dashed to and fro under their elders' feet; the ladies chattered as though they had not seen one another for years, while the gentlemen's deeper tones provided a fine counterpoint.

Miss Huntington paused at the bottom of the stairs, her hand resting lightly on the balustrade, as she gazed thoughtfully around.

The manor house had never appeared more handsome bedecked in its fragrant greenery, red bows, and tinsel. Everywhere one looked, there was the scent and sight of Christmas. Fir decorated the mantels in every room and was wound through the balustrade and up to the upper balcony. For days the sideboards had groaned with the scrumptious offerings from the kitchen— roasted fowl, hams, puddings, pastries, sweetmeats, sweetbreads, and pies. The heady scents of the traditional eggnog and rum punch hung on the air.

Miss Huntington crossed the hall to join the rest of the household in the parlor. Here, too, the signs of the holiday were lavishly displayed. A kissing bough hung from the chandelier in the parlor, heavily laden with bright red apples and candies and tiny gifts and candles. Mistletoe, lavishly ribboned, garnished the center of the bough. It was unfortunate that she would not herself be the object of sweet gallantries under that same bough, came the traitorous thought. She suppressed it at once.

Miss Huntington quietly greeted everyone with a smile and a gracious word as she made her way across the room. She took her place at the periphery of the company, preferring the semi-solitude near the draped windows to the excited conversation closer to the blazing hearth. This evening, as had every previous evening, was to be solemnly marked by the lighting of another of the kissing bough candles that symbolized the twelve days of Christmas. The candlelighting was always followed by the traditional joyous carols.

Miss Huntington turned to the window behind her and lifted the heavy velvet drape aside. She did not know whether she could bear another moment of frolic and good spirits. This day had been particularly trying, simply because it was the eve before Christmas, and as the hours had drawn on toward evening, the time she most dreaded had also drawn nearer.

She stared out on the quiet winter night, reflecting, quite without bitterness, that much of the heartache of the past months could have been avoided if she had not gone up to London for a Season.

It had been her first Season, and toward the end of it, Miss Theresa Huntington had done her duty and accepted Lord Robert Houser's suit.

It had not been expected that Miss Huntington would make a spectacular match, for she was not an heiress nor a diamond of the first water. Oh, her portion was known to be well enough. And certainly there was nothing to complain of in the thick dark tresses that accented her deep blue eyes, which could spark alike with laughter or temper, nor in her slender graceful figure.

However, it could not be denied that the Huntingtons, though a very old family, were rather obscure, having had a preference for some generations for their country holdings over the position that they might have otherwise enjoyed for themselves in London society.

There had been other suitors, of course. Miss Huntington was one of those who did not cause ripples, but neither had she sunk out of sight. She had enjoyed a certain measure of popularity and had even been honored with two other offers. But Lord Robert had seemed to her fond family to be the best of the lot, and so it had not come as any great surprise when she had chosen his lordship.

Lord Robert was the youngest son of the Earl of Hampton, and with two elder brothers, it could be safely said that he could not expect ever to aspire to the title. Yet since he had his own inheritance from the maternal side of his family, his was a position of comfort and prestige in society. It had therefore not been necessary for him to marry an heiress.

In point of fact, Lord Robert had not thought of marriage at all, having toyed with the notion of leaping into the war being waged on the Peninsula, until he had met Miss Huntington. His restless boredom had vanished and become supplanted with a feeling of contentment that his life was at last taking direction. Thus, Lord Robert was suitably pleased that his suit had prospered.

By and large, the match was thought to be a respectable one by both families. The betrothal contract had been duly signed, and the date of the nuptials set.

Then the brother closest in age to Lord Robert was killed in a driving accident, leaving a widow and infant daughter. Lord Robert stepped into his brother's shoes, as joint guardian to his niece, and the wedding was postponed until the family had come out of deep mourning.

Before the six months was completed, the earl, who had suffered for some years from an incurable illness, also succumbed, and the family was plunged once more into deep mourning. The countess took to her bed, too overwrought by these successive blows to contemplate the planning of the forthcoming happy event.

Lord Robert, who had sustained the loss of his favorite brother and his father with admirable fortitude, became the mainstay of his mother's tottering strength and the patient recipient of the new earl's alternating flashes of ill temper and uncertainty. There was no question of setting aside the needs of his family in the pursuit of his own selfish wishes. The date for the wedding was once again postponed, this time being consigned to an indefinite future.

His betrothal had obviously been entered into at the worst of times.

Indeed, the whole affair had been plagued from the beginning with bad timing, and what with one thing and another, had become a source of great frustration to a gentleman who had thought his future in a fair way to being securely settled.

Perhaps, then, it was not surprising that Lord Robert reacted in the manner that he did when he discovered his betrothed in the arms of another man.

Lord Robert had accepted an invitation from his prospective in-laws to a long weekend in the country, and he had looked upon the opportunity to be away from London with weary relief. For weeks he had accepted the condolences of acquaintances, managed the slow business of probate, and soothed his mother's distraught humors. He had also endured his eldest brother's sudden pomposity upon inheriting the responsibilities of the earldom.

The new earl was jealous of his own newfound authority. He came to resent that Lord Robert should be so capable and cool, when he was himself terrified of the position that had been thrust upon his shoulders. At the same time, the earl felt that as head of the family, he should be consulted in all matters. He also demanded that their mother look to him for the advice and support that she had asked of Lord Robert. Matters came to a head between the brothers, ending with the earl hurling shouted insults, which Lord Robert had received with icy disdain.

Lord Robert had begun to give more serious thought than he had ever done before to the notion of buying a commission in the army, but no longer simply out of patriotic conviction; rather, as a way of shoving aside everything that had become so onerous to him. The deaths of his father and brother had profoundly shocked him, and shown him how insignificant his role was in society. It would be far better to be a soldier fighting for a worthwhile cause. However, he was uncertain how his betrothed would feel if he were to ask her to follow the drum.

When the invitation from the Huntingtons came to him, Lord Robert thought a few days rusticating in the country would be just the respite that he needed. It would, as well, give him an opportunity to become better acquainted with his prospective bride, whom he had not had the opportunity to speak to more than a few dozen times in all these months.

On that fateful evening the Huntingtons had invited their close friends, the Stanhopes, to stay the weekend and to provide a social atmosphere to his lordship's visit. Though the company was nothing like the sophisticated set that Lord Robert was used to mixing with, he discovered it to be a convivial gathering with Squire Stanhope and his lady, their son and two daughters.

After dinner, the gentlemen joined the ladies for coffee in the parlor. Lord Robert noticed when Miss Huntington slipped away into the gardens, and he waited a suitable interval before he followed her out onto the veranda.

The early summer sky had just come into dusk, the smell of roses was still heavy on the warm air, and the leisurely drone of insects could be heard. It was an exceptionally beautiful evening, except for the sight that greeted Lord Robert's disbelieving and affronted eyes.

Miss Huntington was wrapped in a fierce embrace. She was not struggling with Mr. Stanhope. On the contrary, she seemed to be returning the liberty with equal passion. Even worse were the sound of her choked words on Lord Robert's ears.

"Oh, John! I shall miss you so!"

Mr. Stanhope released her to put up a hand and brush away a tear from her cheek. "None of that, my girl. You knew it was going to happen sooner or later. Now put away the sad face and go back in to your betrothed. He seems a good enough fellow."

A swift tide of emotion almost choked Lord Robert with its intensity. He said bitingly, "Thank you for that at least, Stanhope."

The two sprang apart, staring at him with equal expressions of shock and consternation. Lord Robert regarded them with a cold smile.

Stanhope recovered himself first and, with a quick glance at Miss Huntington, said, "It is not what it must appear to you, my lord."

"Indeed. You must take me for a flat, Stanhope, if you think that I shall doubt the evidence of my own eyes. It is patently clear that I have interrupted a lovers' tête-à-tête," said Lord Robert with cold fury. The thought arrowed through his mind that it was all of a piece with the way fortune had been dealing with him lately, and the maelstrom of emotion he had endured for the past several weeks coalesced into sheer rage.

"How dare you!" Miss Huntington exclaimed, her eyes flashing in the setting light. "Why, I have known John forever. We have always been—"

Lord Robert threw up his hand, distaste for the inevitable denial strong in him. "Spare me, I beg. Stanhope, you shall name your seconds."

He had the bleak satisfaction of watching Miss Huntington's lips part in speechless shock, her lovely eyes widen with incredulity. She would know that his had not been a casual promise made for a marriage of convenience and small honor, he reflected savagely.

Mr. Stanhope squared his shoulders. There was a rigid line about his mouth. "Very well, my lord."

"No!" Miss Huntington threw herself in front of Mr. Stanhope, as though she braved a brace of pistols. "I would rather shoot you myself, my lord, rather than allow a duel to take place between you."

Mr. Stanhope grasped her shoulder. "Theresa—"

Lord Robert stared across the short distance at her defiant face. Her eyes had regained the spark of spirit that had so entranced him upon their first meeting. He hardened his heart, ignoring the ache of loss for something that had never been his to possess, after all. A muscle jumped in his jaw, quite discernible in the candlelight from the windows. "Do you love him so much?"

"Of course I love John!" she exclaimed indignantly. "He is like my—"

"No more need be said. I withdrew my challenge, Stanhope."

Lord Robert made a jerky bow before turning on his heel and striding back inside.

The two stood where he left them, quite stunned by what had happened.

"How perfectly awful," said Miss Huntington.

Mr. Stanhope laughed shortly at the absurd understatement. "Quite. You realize, of course, what his lordship thought."

"But it is ludicrous. We have been best friends from the cradle, you, Tony, and I. I feel the same for you as I do for Tony, the only difference being that he is my twin. For Lord Robert to imply that—that—" Miss Huntington felt at a loss for adequate words. She sighed. "I must go explain the matter to his lordship at once. I don't mind telling you that I don't relish the necessity."

"No, by Jove," said Mr. Stanhope feelingly.

As she started away, he reached out to stop her. "Wait. His lordship appeared to be in an icy rage. He won't want to give you an audience. He'll freeze you with a bow and a stare. Let me draw off the worst of his anger, try to smooth things down first, man to man, as it were. He can't very well avoid me if *I* choose to beard him."

Miss Huntington bit her lip in uncertainty. "I do see your point, John. If I were to approach him now, when he is still so very angry, he could simply excuse himself to his rooms, and that would be the end of it; whereas you could follow him to his chambers."

Mr. Stanhope thought privately that his chances of gaining admittance to Lord Robert's dressing room were outside at the least, and definitely not what he would wish to do in any event, but he did not say so. He placed a brotherly kiss on Miss Huntington's brow. "Right, then. I'll see the matter straightened out before I leave."

Miss Huntington caught his arm as her previous concerns came rushing back on her. "Oh, John, I do wish that you would change your mind! Tony has already gone, and now you mean to follow him. I don't see why either of you feel it incumbent upon you to join in this awful war."

Mr. Stanhope laughed. "No, I don't suppose you do, my girl. Nor do my mother or sisters. But the squire does and, what's more, he has given me his blessing, even though I am his only heir."

"The squire knows that he can't stop you," said Miss Huntington bitterly.

Mr. Stanhope instantly sobered, saying gravely, "You know that is not true, Theresa. If the squire had forbidden it, I would have accepted his wishes. You know I would have."

"Oh, go away," she said crossly, because she knew that he spoke the truth. He had always held his parents in greatest respect, and the squire's word was Mr. Stanhope's own final judgment in nearly every instance. It was not that Mr. Stanhope lacked initiative or boldness; far from it. The squire had molded his heir into a strong personality who was at once his own man, and yet, honored the wisdom of his elders.

"I'll leave you to your crochets while I forge off on your behalf." Mr. Stanhope dropped another careless kiss upon her. "I will doubtless see you in the morning. Lord, I hate leave-takings. My mother and sisters will cry, of course. I will be drenched before I manage to tear myself away."

That made her laugh at last, as he had intended. She tucked her hand into his arm. "I shan't promise you it, but I shall try not to add to your baptism."

As they entered the drawing room, he said, "Oh aye, just as you didn't when Tony rode off."

"Fiend," she said, hiding her very real sorrow beneath the teasing scowl she turned on him.

Lady Amelia came up to them. "We will have coffee in a moment, dears. John, the squire has just announced that you are joining the army. I must say that the news was not entirely unexpected, though we had hoped— but there, I can see from your expression that the matter is quite settled. I must not nag at you. It did not do the least good to do so with Tony, so I shall save myself the trouble."

Mr. Stanhope grinned, pressing the hand that she had given to him. "Indeed, ma'am. My mind is quite made up and has been for some time."

"Futile, just as I suspected," Lady Amelia nodded, sighing. She smiled in understanding at her daughter's somber expression. "Theresa, I should like your assistance with the coffee. If you will excuse us, John."

2

Miss Huntington followed her mother across to the coffee urn and was soon dispensing cakes with the refreshment. Lord Robert refused both coffee and other refreshment. She watched John Stanhope approach his lordship and speak quietly to the gentleman. Lord Robert returned a short reply, one which caused Mr. Stanhope to flush, then bow and walk away.

Miss Huntington was incensed by Lord Robert's show of arrogance. What right had his lordship to judge either her or John, for he knew nothing at all about them. He had quite mistaken the entire matter, but was proving himself too distastefully proud to admit to his error.

Her indignation so consumed her that she scarcely realized that she had actually risen from her place and had acted upon her feelings, until she found herself standing before her betrothed.

He stared down at her with cold gray eyes. One dark brow arched as though in well-bred, bored surprise. "Yes, Miss Huntington?"

She quailed in inward amazement at her own unthinking action. As she gathered her wits, she faltered, "You do not wish refreshment, my lord?"

His lip curled. Disdain entered his eyes. "I think not from your lovely traitorous hands, ma'am."

All of her indignation came to the fore, giving her the courage of anger. She said in a furious undertone, "You have no right to judge us thus, my lord, I assure you."

"Forgive me, but I think that I do stand in some position to do just that. You are, after all, my betrothed," he retorted.

"But you know nothing of me or my family or my friends. You cannot possibly place the proper construction on what passed between John and myself without some insight into our history," said Miss Huntington.

"I have discovered as much as I wish to, Miss Huntington, believe me," said Lord Robert in an indifferent voice.

Miss Huntington strove for a reasonable tone. "You quite mistake the matter, my lord. John Stanhope and I are friends only, and have been these many years."

"The only mistake I have made is in our betrothal,

Miss Huntington. No, do not be anxious, ma'am. You may rest easy. I have no intention of repudiating you before your good and kind family."

She gasped in shock.

Lord Robert gave a mirthless laugh. "I had expected to bestow my name on a lady of unquestionable character and virtue, one whom I would be proud to call my wife. Now it seems that all that I hoped for is but a mockery." He smiled again, as though he spoke more to himself than to her.

Miss Huntington whitened at the insult. Her eyes flashed with anger and the hint of tears. "You are an arrogant fool, my lord, as any person in this room would tell you if you had the intelligence to inquire the truth."

She whisked herself about, and for the remainder of the evening she did not speak another word to him. Nor did she acknowledge his lordship's presence unless the flow of conversation demanded that she do so, for she did not wish to create an unpleasant scene before her parents and the Stanhopes.

Fortunately for the preservation of her equilibrium, a game of cards was proposed. As the numbers were uneven, Miss Huntington chose to settle into conversation with one of the Misses Stanhope, who did not play, and thus escaped her own place at one of the tables. Mrs. Stanhope was also content to be left out of the entertainment, urging her eldest daughter to take her place.

Presently, with the end of his own game, Mr. Stanhope came over with the sister who had partnered him to join the other ladies. While his sister was engaged in describing the plays to her mother and sibling, he drew

Miss Huntington a little aside and asked quietly, "Did you not have any luck, Theresa?"

"His lordship is totally unreasonable and persists in holding to his ridiculous assumption," said Miss Huntington briefly.

Mr. Stanhope frowned. "I did not find him at all amenable, either. However, I do not accept defeat so tamely. I shall try again to reason with him at the next earliest opportunity."

"Thank you, John. I do not know that it greatly matters, however, for I have come to have the gravest doubts over the wisdom of the connection between myself and Lord Robert," said Miss Huntington.

"The devil! Here's a fine thing, I must say. You can't be thinking of jilting the fellow," exclaimed Mr. Stanhope, appalled.

"Can I not?" asked Miss Huntington, looking thoughtfully in her betrothed's direction. The other table had also finished their play, and Lord Robert was saying something to her parents, the faintest of smiles on his handsome face.

"Now there you're out. How would it affect your parents, the scandal and all? Think long and hard about it first, that's my advice," said Mr. Stanhope earnestly.

Miss Huntington frowned, unwilling to agree yet knowing that his assertion had validity. She sighed. "You are in the right of it, of course. I mustn't let my temper blind me, as surely as his lordship's abominable pride has blinded him. I must count the cost to others."

Lady Amelia came up then, barring any further conversation of the topic. "Dearest, Lord Robert has requested that I extend his apologies to the company. He confessed to feeling somewhat out of sorts, having contracted the headache during cards, and he is retiring.

There is not the least need to look so anxious, for he assured me it was due to nothing more than fatigue. I imagine our cheerful little gathering proved unexpectedly trying to one who has sustained such recent grievous losses. Your father said all that was proper, of course, and invited his lordship to accompany him out on the estate on the morrow. As Sir Henry says, there is nothing like a good tramp or long ride to blow away the cobwebs from a man's head."

"I am positive that Lord Robert will profit from just such exercise," Miss Huntington said tartly. She ignored Mr. Stanhope's warning glance. "Perhaps Papa should mount his lordship on Sultan. That would certainly take Lord Robert's mind off his brooding reflections."

Mr. Stanhope gave a strangled cough and muttered an excuse as he moved away to address his father.

"Sultan! Why, what are you thinking, my dear? You know that Tony is very nearly the only one who can control that brute. I am astonished by your suggestion," said Lady Amelia, her expression reflecting her words.

Miss Huntington felt herself flush. She was instantly ashamed for her uncharitable words, borne as they had been out of pique. Before she could offer her mother a stammering excuse for her rash suggestion, Sir Henry, who had joined them, spoke up.

"It might suit very well, actually," he said. "I do not know Lord Robert well, of course, but I have heard of his reputation. He is accounted a very knowledgeable whip and a bruising rider."

"Well, if you think so, Henry, then of course there can be no question. However, I wish you to know that I shan't be a bit pleased if a guest of ours is brought home on a door with every limb broken," said Lady Amelia.

Sir Henry sent a considering glance toward his daughter. He had noted that Lord Robert's attention to the cards had been haphazard at best, and that his lordship's eyes had more than once strayed in his daughter's direction. That, coupled with Lord Robert's graceful excuse to retire, made him wonder whether there had not been some sort of falling out. "In that unlikely event, our daughter must be persuaded to sit beside his lordship's bed and entertain him until he mended."

Miss Huntington's cheeks deepened in color. She was at once shocked by her father's outrageous suggestion and relieved that Lord Robert was not present. She did not think that, harboring as he was under his misbelief, Lord Robert would have welcomed such a witticism. "I do not think that a proper suggestion, even in funning, Papa."

Lady Amelia smiled even as she shook her head in gentle rebuke of her lord. "No, it certainly is not. Really, Henry. At times you allow your teasing to cross the line of what is tolerable."

"Do I, my dear? I apologize for causing your blushes, Theresa. However, there is no denying that the attention of a pretty woman can jolly a man out of the doldrums," said Sir Henry.

Miss Huntington's eyes flew to her father's face. He raised a questioning brow as his intelligent gaze met his daughter's. She knew that he had somehow guessed that there was something amiss between her and her betrothed.

Miss Huntington quite suddenly decided that she had endured enough for one evening. Her father's perception had never more unnerved her. She was certainly not prepared to withstand his gentle probing. "I do hope that everyone will excuse me. I fear that I myself have become very poor company."

"The megrims seem to be running rampant this evening," remarked Sir Henry.

Miss Huntington ignored her father, instead drawing upon a smile to extricate herself from the company as she said good night all around.

The squire patted her arm in affection. "Don't be too anxious over that young buck of yours. You've had a bit of a tiff this evening, and no doubt you are thinking it is the very end of the world. Pooh! No point in denying it, my girl, for it was written all over your face and his lordship's. You'll find, however, that the morning light shows men what fools they are."

"Thank you, dear sir," said Miss Huntington, deeply embarrassed by the squire's bluff comfort. She avoided her father's eyes and fled.

As she exited the drawing room, Mr. Stanhope gave her a smile of reassurance that to a small degree comforted her exacerbated feelings. She knew that her best of friends would not willingly fail her in setting right the misunderstanding that had arisen with her proud and arrogant betrothed.

The following morning Miss Huntington saw Lord Robert only briefly: once as they passed one another in front of the breakfast room, and again when Lord Robert and her father returned from a brisk walk about the estate. She thought it just as well, since his lordship was freezingly polite on both occasions. She wished very much that the misunderstanding that lay between them could be rectified, but she did not know how to go about it, since his lordship had refused to listen to either herself or to Mr. Stanhope.

She felt unduly restless because of the troubling

problem with Lord Robert, so much so that she was
unable to fully enjoy the bright weather. There had
been a time not so long past that she would have hared
off to the stables, dressed in her twin brother's cast-off
breeches, and gone for a long, tiring ride in order to
rid herself of such bothersome thoughts. But that was
not possible for her now, she thought with a sigh. She
was not a miss still in the schoolroom, trying the pa-
tience of her governess with hoydenish tricks. She was
betrothed, and must behave with all the circumspection
that was required of a well-bred young lady.

Miss Huntington went out into the rose gardens, her
hands encased in light gloves, armed with basket and
scissors. If she could not ride, then she would vent her
frustrations in a useful fashion. She was absorbed in
the task of ridding the bushes of half-blown blooms
when a heavy step sounded on the gravel. She glanced
up, expecting to see one of the gardeners, but instead
met Lord Robert's cold eyes.

Miss Huntington straightened to give him a cool
greeting. "My lord."

"Miss Huntington." He bowed slightly.

There was a moment's silence while she snipped yet
another bloom and put it in her basket. She was aware
of his lordship's scrutiny, but she did not look again in
his direction.

"My father is doubtless in his study at this hour if it
is he that you are looking for," said Miss Huntington.

"Thank you, but it is not Sir Henry that I wished
to speak to," said Lord Robert.

She did glance at him then, her brows rising slightly.
"Oh, was it not? Then you must wish directions to the
stables, for I am very nearly certain that my father gave
orders that you could have your pick of mounts. Allow

me to suggest Sultan as a challenging mount. He belongs to my brother and has sadly gone without proper exercise since Tony was last home."

"Nor am I interested in the stables at this particular time," said Lord Robert from beneath his teeth, obviously annoyed by her less than subtle hint that she had no desire for his company.

"Forgive me, my lord. It seems that I am unnaturally slow-witted," said Miss Huntington with false brightness. "Do enlighten me as to your wishes, I pray."

"What I wish is to speak to you about Stanhope, Miss Huntington. I wish to make it quite clear that you are not to associate with the gentleman in future, for as my intended bride I shall not countenance rumor nor scandal," said Lord Robert in clipped accents.

Miss Huntington gasped, color flying into her face. "Of all the effrontry!" She regarded him for a short moment, all of her contempt plain in her eyes. "You are far out of water, my lord, and so you shall swiftly discover. I do not turn shoulder on any friend." She made to brush past him.

His hand shot out, his fingers wrapping around her wrist. "Not so quickly, my lovely betrothed. We have not yet come to an understanding," he said grimly.

"Oh, but I think that we have," she countered, her angry flush belying her coolness of tone.

"You will not give up Stanhope?" It was a harshly voiced demand.

Miss Huntington gave him a cutting look. "You will do me the favor of unhanding me, my lord!"

Instead of releasing her, Lord Robert yanked her close to him. One arm imprisoned her, his fingers locking her own arm behind her. His other hand caught up her chin. "I am a jealous man. I do not share that which is mine," he breathed into her shocked face. Then he bent his head and brutally took possession of her half-parted lips.

The kiss was thorough and unquestionably shattering. Miss Huntington had accepted her fair share of flirtatious salutations in the past, but nothing had ever prepared her for this deliberate onslaught to her senses.

Through the drowning mists that fogged her paralyzed mind emerged one solid thought. Rage consumed Lord Robert. He had kissed her for only one purpose, and that was to brand her as his own.

As swiftly as she had been gathered to him, she was set free. Miss Huntington rocked back on her heels. If it had not been for his hand under her elbow, she was dazedly certain that she would have fallen.

Meeting his cold, satisfied smile, she lifted her hand and slapped him full across the face. The imprint of her hand was clearly visible against his tan.

His hands curled into fists at his sides. His eyes were alight and hard. Softly, menacingly, he said, "Jade."

She fled, giving not a thought for the roses strewn wildly on the garden path.

3

For the remainder of the afternoon, Miss Huntington kept close to her rooms. She was not a coward, but she shivered each time she recalled that quite diabolical look in Lord Robert's eyes. He had appeared ready to strangle her.

Miss Huntington wondered what she could ever have

seen in his lordship during the Season that had led her to accept his suit. He was dictatorial, arrogant, cold. She must have been daft. However, she could not forget the instant attraction she had felt toward Lord Robert. It had been that spark between them that had led her into her present situation.

She knew that something had to be done. Lord Robert had made it so jarringly clear what he thought of her. Her cheeks warmed even now at the insult. He had called her a jade.

It was really too awful to contemplate marriage to a gentleman who had such a mistaken idea of her character. She was too much of a realist to believe that somehow it would all simply fade away like a bad dream. The misery and injustice that she would be forced to bear each day of her life would be intolerable.

She desperately wanted to confide in someone, for she was at a total loss to explain her confused feelings or her fear that her contracted marriage would be a dreadful mistake.

When the misunderstanding with Lord Robert had arisen, she had wanted to confide her perturbation to her parents. However, the embarrassment such a course would have brought to everyone concerned was not to be contemplated. Now Miss Huntington wondered whether that was the only option left open to her.

Miss Huntington hoped even more fervently that John Stanhope would not fail her.

Mr. Stanhope took leave of his family and friends soon after tea. The good-byes were just as tearful as he had predicted. Miss Huntington tried valiantly to keep her promise, but it was too much in the end and she threw herself into his arms.

Mr. Stanhope hugged her, not completely dry-eyed himself, before gently putting her away from him. "I left a letter for his lordship. It was the best I could do," he whispered.

Miss Huntington nodded. Under the greatcoat he had donned, he wore his regimentals. The sight of him in such brave colors had been her true undoing, because it had brought back in painful clarity her brother's leave-taking. "Thank you, my best of friends. Pray take care."

"Oh, I will; never fear," said Mr. Stanhope with a show of heartiness.

She pressed his hand one last time, and turned away to allow the squire and her father to say their own farewells. She met Lord Robert's stare and read condemnation in it. Miss Huntington deliberately turned her shoulder, unwilling to have the poignancy of the moment spoiled by the gentleman's unpleasant suspicion. She waved along with the rest when Mr. Stanhope climbed into the carriage and then trust his head out the window to shout a final farewell.

The carriage rolled down the drive, and Miss Huntington turned to mount the front steps.

Lord Robert stepped over to her side, politely offering his arm. She glanced up at him warily. But there was nothing in his inscrutable face to give her a clue to his thoughts. Dropping her eyes, she accepted his escort into the house.

"I wonder, Miss Huntington, shall you take my own leave-taking equally to heart?" he asked quietly.

She turned her face to him, startlement in her eyes. "What do you mean, my lord?"

He smiled, but there was no actual amusement in his expression. His gray eyes were too cold. Without replying to her question, he lifted her hand to his lips. "I shall see you again at dinner, Miss Huntington." Then he turned and walked away, leaving her to stare after him.

That same evening, soon after dinner, Lord Robert left.

Miss Huntington heard nothing from Lord Robert for several weeks. In fact, she was rather relieved. Despite John Stanhope's best efforts and her own, matters between herself and Lord Robert had not been restored before his lordship's departure. Since she and Lord Robert had never been on such terms as to correspond, she thought little more about it.

At the breakfast table one morning, she received a short note from his lordship that, as she read it, caused her to turn white.

> "I write to inform you, Miss Huntington, that due to the circumstances which bar our nuptials from taking place for the foreseeable future, and in view of my own restless desire to be a part of the fight on the Continent, I have taken a commission. I will already have sailed for Portugal by the time this communication reaches you. I am confident that the war will soon be over. However, I understand fully that you might not wish to remain affianced under such peculiar circumstances, and for an indeterminate time. I assure you, therefore, that I shall harbor no ill thoughts toward you if you should choose to dissolve our connection. My apologies, etc. R."

"Why, whatever is amiss, dearest?" asked Lady Amelia.

Without a word, Miss Huntington passed the short note over to her mother. She stared at the sideboard opposite, numbed by his lordship's terse words. She was completely certain that Lord Robert had chosen his course based on his misinterpretation of what had transpired during that fateful weekend. She understood, too, that he was making available to her an honorable release from their betrothal. It was quite apparent that was what he desired of her, and he had gone to what she thought of as quite desperate lengths to obtain it. He had gone off to war rather than stay in England and wed her.

"How extraordinary! Henry, do read this. Lord Robert has sailed for Portugal!"

Sir Henry perused the note in his turn. His brows formed a frowning line over his eyes. "Extraordinary, indeed. Though, as I now recall, Lord Robert had seemed most interested in the war, discussing its course with feeling and concern. But I had suspected nothing like this to be in his mind."

"It is like a fever. No doubt the notion took hold of his lordship's imagination when John Stanhope left us," said Lady Amelia. She glanced at her daughter's perfectly still figure. "I cannot imagine how his lordship could think that our daughter was so shallow as to turn aside from her pledge to him. Theresa, had Lord Robert hinted at any of this on the occasion of his visit?"

"No, I had no inkling that he was contemplating such a step," said Miss Huntington. She was vaguely astonished at the composure of her voice. She shook her head, trying to clear her thoughts. "First my brother, then John, and now Lord Robert. Is this war fever so catching, then, that everyone I know must rush off?"

"Men have heeded the call to arms from time immemorial," said Sir Henry somberly. "War is an ugly mistress, and one that we would all do altogether better without." He refolded the sheet and gave it back into his daughter's hand.

"You must write Lord Robert at once and release him from that anxiety that so patently preys on his mind. He is obviously laboring under great emotion concerning the status of the betrothal, and no wonder when the wedding has been put off these several months. I think it would be wise to reassure his lordship that you have not had a change of heart," said Lady Amelia.

"A wise suggestion, dear lady. A man about to go into battle should not be thinking about anything but the task ahead of him," said Sir Henry, his frown deepening.

"Yes, of course. I shall do so at once," Miss Huntington agreed. She excused herself from the breakfast room and withdrew into the library. Not very happily, she sat down at the writing desk, only to stare at the opposite wall.

Her position was peculiarly confusing. It was obvious to her, if not to her parents, that Lord Robert wanted assurance, not of the continuance of their betrothal, but of his release from a connection grown repugnant to him.

In addition, his lordship apparently believed that she would be relieved by his suggestion that she jilt him. She thought, in view of what had passed between them and of the glimpse she had had of Lord Robert's intractable character, that she would be doing herself a favor in obliging him. However, to do so while he was away fighting for his country smacked of such heartlessness that she could not bring herself to do the thing just yet. Others would not condemn her half as harshly as she would judge herself if she abandoned a gentleman in such a callous manner.

Undoubtedly, it would be best to wait until Lord Robert returned to England. It would surely not be thought strange that after such a protracted separation, they should each experience a reversal of feeling.

Her decision made, Miss Huntington produced after much struggle her reply to Lord Robert. The letter was so stilted that she grimaced upon reading it over, but nevertheless it was the result of her best efforts, and so she franked it and sent it on its way.

Nearly two months later, she was astonished to receive in the post a letter from Lord Robert. His letter was as stilted and guarded in tone as had been her own, yet he had answered her. Miss Huntington felt obliged to extend to him the same courtesy, and so was born a correspondence between them. It was, moreover, one which gradually evolved to the point that Miss Huntington began to receive each successive missive with increasing interest and even a certain measure of pleasure.

Ever since her brother Tony had gone overseas nearly two years before, she had been in the habit of writing to him. It came as a surprise to her when Tony mentioned in his less-frequent communication that he had met up with Lord Robert. ". . . Though he is something of a sobersides for my taste, I like him well enough and wish you well of him, sister."

She put away Tony's letter, her cheeks still warm from the inexplicable pleasure that her brother's careless approval had given her.

That was the last letter that Miss Huntington received from her brother.

In late summer 1812, the year that the tide of the war

turned at last, the name of Anthony Huntington appeared on the casualty lists published in the London *Gazette*.

The devestating blow of her twin's death was swiftly followed by the horrible dawning realization that letters from Lord Robert, and from John Stanhope as well, had become increasingly overdue.

The slow months passed, and the Christmas season inevitably arrived.

The clock on the mantel struck the hour, startling Miss Huntington from her somber reverie. She stirred restlessly at the window. Her image stared starkly back at her through the soft flakes swirling gently out of the night against the frosted panes of glass.

Behind her, she heard the murmur of conversation, the occasional rise of laughter. The warmth of hearth and family were all around her, but she felt herself to be separated from the joyous spirit of Christmas.

Miss Huntington dropped the velvet drapery and turned away from the cold window. She could not avoid what was to take place. It would be the height of bad manners to excuse herself before the most cherished tradition of all had been honored.

She rubbed her hands up and down her arms. She felt chilled, but she knew that seating herself in a chair close to the fire or taking a cup of the fragrant hot rum punch would do little to warm her spirits.

Miss Huntington looked around at those gathered in the parlor. Much of the company had dwindled in the last two days, some of their relations who lived farther away having preferred to take advantage of the unexpected stability of the weather and return home in relative comfort.

Most of their neighbors had also chosen to observe

Christmas Eve in their own homes, but the Hunting-tons' closest friends had remained, so that there were still a good number in attendance. The Squire and Mrs. Stanhope and their two daughters; the reverend and his good wife and their daughters, the Misses Clarence; and old Mrs. Princeton, a distant cousin. The elderly lady nodded in her chair now, her ever-flashing knitting nee-dles for once stilled in her lap. Miss Huntington's brother-in-law and sister, Mr. and Mrs. Hopstead, with their numerous progeny had elected to remain the entire holiday. Most of the children were already abed in anticipation of bringing the dawn on more swiftly, but the older twin boys had been permitted to remain up despite the lateness of the hour.

As she listened to the cheerful conversation, Miss Huntington felt herself to be the only one not infused with the Christmas spirit. Everything was the same as in past years, yet so very different. She wore half-mourning now, as did her parents and her sister and brother-in-law and their children. The somber colors were in mute contrast to the gay decorations and, for Miss Huntington, so eloquently pointed out the incon-gruity of this Christmas season.

It was the first Christmas without her twin brother, Anthony. Dear Tony, killed by a spent ball on a hot Span-ish plain. John Stanhope was also gone, it seemed. As for Lord Robert—but she cut off that train of thought.

Miss Huntington had exercised the tightest rein on her emotions. For weeks after learning of her brother's demise, she had gone about dry-eyed, completely in control of her expression and her manner, agreeing with calm to whatever suggestion was put to her. The con-trol she had maintained had become even more rigid when it became more and more likely that she would never receive letters from John Stanhope nor Lord Robert again. She knew of the worried glances that her parents had bent in her direction, but she had not acknowledged their concern.

She had believed she had successfully walled herself off, so that even her innermost thoughts were ruthlessly monitored. But when it became obvious that her father meant to hold to every Christmas tradition, her careful control cracked just for a moment. An instant later, she nodded and smiled. "Of course, Papa." Even then, she did not speak of her brother.

She would not think of Tony. She would not think of John.

Most of all, she would not think about Lord Robert. Especially on Christmas Eve, she could not allow herself that.

Unbidden, a phrase or two of Lord Robert's last letter came to mind. He had said that he might request leave for the holiday and had hinted that he would call on her then.

Tears threatened her, and she blinked them away. She raised her chin in a proud tilt. No, it would not do to think about Lord Robert.

With a word or two, Sir Henry rose from his chair. Miss Huntington stiffened, aware that the moment she had most dreaded had arrived.

4

Sir Henry smiled, his glance touching each of those present before he spoke. "My family and friends, as you know, we are gathered together to celebrate a very special season. It has been a difficult year for many of us."

There was a stirring, a murmur of agreement. Lady Amelia slipped her hand into her husband's. He glanced down at her, the flicker of a smile touching his face. "Nevertheless, it is right and proper that we observe those traditions that illustrate the joy and wonder of the birth of our Lord. On this, the eve of His birth, we celebrate our good fortune in possessing the love of family and friends. Good Reverend, if I may prevail upon you at this time?"

"Of course, Sir Henry. It will give me the greatest pleasure to do so," said Reverend Clarence, rising, to take the large tooled leather Bible that Sir Henry offered to him. He opened it, turning a few pages to find his place, and cleared his throat.

Miss Huntington clenched her hands, digging her nails into her palms. For as long as she could recall, each eve before Christmas, her father, or another designated to stand in his place, had read the story of the birth of Christ.

Last Christmas, Sir Henry had relinquished that honor to his son, when Tony had been on leave from the army.

Her brother had flushed with pleasure. "Thank you, sir." Standing tall and proud in his regimentals, firelight glinting off his brass buttons, his strong young voice had uttered the same words that now rolled so beautifully off Reverend Clarence's tongue.

" 'And lo, the angel of the Lord came upon them, and the glory of the Lord shone round about them; and they were sore afraid.

" 'And the angel said unto them, Fear not: for behold, I bring you good tidings of great joy, which shall be to all people. For unto you is born this day in the city of David a Savior, which is Christ the Lord . . .

" 'And suddenly there was with the angel a multitude of the heavenly host praising God, and saying,

" 'Glory to God in the highest, and on earth peace, goodwill toward men.' "

There was silence, only the muffled tumble of kindling falling into the heart of the fire breaking it, as the reverend slowly closed the Bible. He looked up. "War is the curse of mankind. But God in His mercy always brings such strife to a close."

"Aye, and so must we hope to see a swift end to this ghastly war," said Mr. Hopstead somberly. "We've lost too many of our brave fellows."

"It cannot end too soon for my taste," said the squire gruffly.

Lady Amelia put on a determined smile. "Henry, I should like very much to taste the rum punch, as I am certain as do the others. Will you do the honors?"

"Of course, my dear," said Sir Henry.

Miss Huntington did not join the rest of the company in crowding about the punch bowl. She wandered instead over to the pianoforte and trailed her fingers over the keys.

She was recalling other times, when the world had seemed one of quiet conversation and simple pleasures. She would sit, there, in a wingback chair where the candlelight could best strike the pages of her book. Her mother and Mrs. Stanhope would embroider in the straight chairs opposite with the box of tumbled silks at their feet, their soft voices in direct counterpoint to their husbands' genial arguments on politics and agriculture as they stood at the mantel. Her sister had already married Mr. Hopstead by then and gone to her own home. The two boys, Tony and John Stanhope, would likely as not be hunched over the chessboard, the hearth fire casting a ruddy glow over their intent faces. John's sisters had always been poring over the latest lady's magazine, exclaiming with much animation over the latest fashion plates and occasionally calling upon her to leave off reading her book long enough to give her opinion on some furbelow or other.

In the last few years, the chess game and the talk of agriculture had given way to disturbing talk of revolution and war. The women had listened, wondering and anxious about what it could possibly mean to them all. Then had come the time when Tony said good-bye, his face solemn above the brave red regimentals that appeared too big for his thin wiry body.

Miss Huntington looked around the parlor. Though it was cheery with company and the warmth of the fire in the grate, she thought she would never see it again as it had been. Tony was dead, and there was little hope held out for John Stanhope. As children, she and Tony and John had been inseparable; but she had had to let them go without her, and now she had lost them both.

Miss Huntington had held to the thought that the casualty lists in the *Gazette* had never included John Stanhope's name, but even that comfort was gone from her now.

The squire, ill at ease and fidgeting with his stock, had brought a creased letter from his son's senior officer only days ago. Long delayed, it told painfully of how John had fallen during a bloody retreat and of his body's subsequent disappearance. The officer could only speculate that John's body, stripped of uniform and identity, had been buried anonymously in a mass grave.

The squire had turned his sad face to Miss Huntington and said gruffly, "I am more sorry than I can ever say, my dear girl, for I know how close you and Tony and John have always been."

Miss Huntington had listened to the letter's contents without moving and with a perfectly expressionless face.

"Perhaps—perhaps dear John was taken prisoner by the French instead," said Lady Amelia faintly.

The squire dismissed the suggestion out of hand. "That would have meant no chance at all for the boy. If John was taken prisoner, he in all probability died hideously of festering wounds."

The squire's words left silence in their wake. Rumors of French cruelty and neglect of prisoners had filtered back to England and even to their own quiet countryside.

"A quick death on the battlefield would have indeed been more merciful," said Sir Henry quietly. The squire had nodded sad, heavy agreement.

Her fingers trailed the keys again, picking out a melody familiar to her. Miss Huntington realized of a sudden it was a waltz, the first waltz she had ever danced with Lord Robert.

With a quick, sharp movement she turned from the pianoforte, uttering, "Damn this war!"

All heads turned, expressions of shock on their faces.

Miss Huntington realized that she had spoken her thoughts aloud. She flushed hotly. "Forgive me. I—I fear that I am overwrought. Pray excuse me." Tears burned her eyes, filled her throat, as she rushed to the door.

"Theresa!"

As she ran out into the hall, she heard her father's voice. "No, Amelia. Let the poor girl go. She'll do better for a good cry."

Miss Huntington fled to her bedroom, but she felt trapped there. She did not throw herself across the bed.

She was too wound up. She paced, dashing the tears angrily from her cheeks. She could think of nothing except of her longing to escape.

Miss Huntington turned abruptly to her wardrobe and searched out her oldest riding clothes. It was not her riding habit with its full skirt and close-fitting jacket that she sought, but the worn shirt and vest and breeches that she had appropriated from Tony before he had left. He had not minded, since he had outstripped her in height and girth; instead, he had treated it as a very good joke that his sister should be able to wear his hand-me-downs.

She ripped off her gown, heedless that a button or two popped and rolled across the floor. Letting the gown fall to a puddle on the carpet, she pulled on the riding clothes. The outfit still fit her slender frame comfortably. Stomping into her boots, she paused only long enough to snatch up a muffler and coat, her whip and gloves, before she returned swiftly downstairs. Avoiding the more-traveled passages, she let herself out the small door at the back of the manor.

The cold struck her at once, freezing the traces of tears on her cheeks and lashes. Snowflakes eddied about her, then swept away in a gust. Bundled in the long coat and gloves, the muffler wound over her head and neck and tucked securely inside the top of the coat, she was unrecognizable in the dark as the daughter of the house as she half stumbled, half ran to the stables.

Miss Huntington entered stealthily, even though she knew that as likely as not that the grooms were up at the kitchens at that hour with the other servants enjoying their own Christmas celebration. A swirl of snow and cold entered with her before she had pushed the door closed again.

There was a stamp of hooves, the soft whicker of curiosity. Yellow lantern light shone in the dark intelligent eyes as heads were put over the stall doors. She spoke softly to the horses, reassuring them as she walked down the line of stalls. When she reached the stall that was her goal, she did not hesitate.

What she contemplated doing was sheer madness, and she knew it.

Quickly she set about the business of saddling Sultan, her brother's stallion. The sly eyes and red flaring nostrils of the bay had at times made her uneasy, but she gave no thought to that now. She quieted the animal with low words as it snorted and shied away from her.

When she had finished saddling the stallion, she led him out of the stables. The bay threw up his head at the cold, but not in objection. The stallion snorted, his neck arching. She could see that he was eager to run.

That was what she wanted of him.

She got up onto the mounting block and agilely leapt into the saddle. Instantly the stallion stepped out, his hide quivering in anticipation.

Sultan was a fiend only the strongest hands could control. Miss Huntington, though an excellent rider in her own right, could not hope to equal her twin brother's mastery over the animal. If the stallion spooked and took the bit—but she dismissed the thought.

A short laugh escaped her. "Come on, boy. Let's fly."

The stallion needed no other encouragement. He bounded forward in powerful strides, and the manor house was swiftly swallowed up in the night.

Miss Huntington put the stallion to a cross-country steeplechase. Together she and the stallion soared over fences and ditches, while the moon played skulk with the clouds.

The eery light brushed the landscape in shades of grays and dark shadows. The snow was spread like white iron in the fields. An unnatural stillness pervaded the night, except for the occasional sharp crack of a tree branch exploding from the ice and the muffled thunder of hooves. A few flurries of snow here and there cloaked rider and mount, but as swiftly were swept behind by their headlong passage.

The swiftness of the ride was exhilarating. It was frightening, and she gloried in it. The stallion was a handful, seemingly tireless. Her fingers were clenched on the reins, numbed and without feeling. The cold air seared her lungs with each breath, while the whip of the wind scorched her cheeks.

For the first time in many weeks she felt alive again, and she laughed breathlessly.

She took several gates, then a high rail fence, landing on the bank beyond it. A short distance farther, she was plunging down a slope into the road. She had the impression of an oncoming carriage, of the startled and shying team. Then the stallion lifted for the fence, and she was gone into the field beyond.

5

The gentleman inside the rocking carriage had a fleeting glimpse of a lithe dark figure on an immense stallion before horse and rider cleared the fence on the side of the road and thundered across the field.

"Damned bloody fool!" he exclaimed, even as he admired the rider's form and style.

As the carriage resumed its steady progress, he settled back against the squabs. A frown carved his lean face. There had been something strikingly familiar about the horse, even in the dim moonlight. Something about the extravagant way it jumped, its obvious strength.

A few minutes later, he had forgotten the incident when the carriage stopped at its destination. The carriage door was opened, the iron step was let down, and the gentleman descended.

He looked up at the manor house. Though heavy draperies had been drawn against the night, here and there slits of warm light escaped from the windows to throw uneven zigzag patches on the snow.

The gentleman reached his right hand up to arrange his coat closer over his useless left shoulder. His appearance would cause some surprise, but he knew it was the news that he had come to impart that would generate the greater pleasure.

Ascending the front steps, he let fall the knocker. The front door was opened to him. The butler's eyes opened wide in recognition. "Lord Robert!"

Lord Robert stepped inside, brushing flakes of snow from his coat. He smiled. "Dare I hope for a warm welcome, Simpkins?"

"Indeed yes, my lord!" The butler motioned for a footman to divest the visitor of his greatcoat, himself taking his lordship's beaver and gloves. Surreptitiously he eyed the broad bandage adorning his lordship's brow and the sling that supported his lordship's left arm. Lord Robert's left coat sleeve hung empty, and the sling that supported his arm was clearly visible beneath the drape of the coat itself.

"You will find the family in the parlor, my lord."

Lord Robert nodded and stepped through the familiar doorway as the butler announced him. He paused on the threshold, becoming suddenly the focus of all eyes. Lord Robert smiled crookedly. "A merry Christmas to all."

His greeting appeared to release the company from their stupefaction and several surged toward him, their voices raised in mingled welcome and amazement.

"My lord! It is damn good to see you, sir," said Sir Henry, seizing Lord Robert's hand. He nodded at the sling. "Nothing of a serious nature, I trust?"

"A trifle only," said Lord Robert.

"Why, what have we been thinking to keep you standing about? You must come sit down," said Lady Amelia, urging him over to a settee before the fire.

Lord Robert allowed himself to be coaxed to the comfortable site, his glance encompassing the company. He experienced a sharp knife of disappointment when he did not see Miss Huntington at once, but he assumed that she had left the gathering on some errand and would soon return.

A glass was pressed into his hand. The heady aroma arising from the glass was instantly recognizable, and he nodded his thanks to the squire. "Rum punch is just the thing one needs on such a cold night, sir," he said.

"Aye, it will warm you and loosen your tongue, as well, I hope," said the squire.

"Indeed, we are all agog. How came you to us, my lord?" asked Lady Amelia.

"I am certain it is a vastly romantic tale," said Mrs. Hopstead.

"It is a tale scarcely worth sharing, actually," said Lord Robert.

There was an immediate protest.

"Come, my lord. We all know better than that. There was no word of you for too many weeks," said Lady Amelia.

"My part will keep for the moment, my lady. As it happens, I have come under dispatch to the squire and his lady, to inform them that Mr. Stanhope is even now laying in his own bed and that he is most anxious to see them," said Lord Robert.

Mrs. Stanhope gasped, turning perfectly white. She uttered faintly, "My John is home? He's alive?"

Lord Robert nodded, his voice unexpectedly gentle. "I left him barely an hour ago, ma'am. He suffers a little still from his wound, which causes him to become easily fatigued, or otherwise he would have accompanied me to greet you for himself."

"Praise God for His gracious mercies," exclaimed Reverend Clarence. "This is, indeed, wonderful news, my lord!"

Mrs. Stanhope took urgent hold of her husband's sleeve. "We must go to him at once, dear sir."

The squire shook himself free of his paralysis. He nodded, his own normally ruddy face showing his shock. "Aye, at once. Thank you, my lord. You could not have brought better tidings." He had seized Lord Robert's hand in a painful grasp, expressing mutely what mere words could not.

Lord Robert nodded his understanding, flexing his hand unobtrusively when the squire released it. "It was my pleasure, sir, I assure you."

The squire and Mrs. Stanhope took hurried leave of their host and hostess and the remainder of the company. "I know that you will not be offended that we do not stand on ceremony, Sir Henry," said the squire.

"Of course not. Give our best regards to John. We

are only too happy that he is returned safely to his family and friends," said Sir Henry.

"Oh yes, indeed! We shall come over tomorrow to welcome him home," said Lady Amelia.

When the Stanhopes had left, the Reverend and Mrs. Clarence and their daughters also stood ready to take their leave. They offered to take up Mrs. Princeton in their carriage and deliver her home, which invitation the elderly lady was glad to accept.

Lady Amelia protested that it was still early. "For you must know that we do not quench the candles until after midnight on the eve before Christmas."

Smiling, the reverend shook his head. "Your kind hospitality is truly appreciated, ma'am. However, this is such a wondrous time for both families and should properly be enjoyed by those most concerned without thought for entertaining guests. We shall leave you to treasure it in privacy," said Reverend Clarence, with a glance in Lord Robert's direction.

Lady Amelia was left with nothing more to say, and truly, she was rather grateful for the Clarences' consideration, so she did not urge them further but instead pressed the reverend's hand in a telling manner. "Thank you, good sir." She wished the Clarences and Mrs. Princeton good-bye, promising faithfully to call on them all very soon and to bring all the news.

Sir Henry added his own assurances, but as soon as the door closed, he turned at once to the unexpected caller. "Now you must tell us how this happy event has come about," he said, renewing Lord Robert's empty glass with more rum punch.

"There is not much to tell, as I said," said Lord Robert, accepting the punch with a flicker of a smile. "I was wounded in a spot of action and then knocked senseless. I wakened to find myself to have been taken prisoner by the French. There were others such as myself, most wounded. Stanhope was among them. He and I managed to escape together and make our way back to our own lines. From there, we were sent to a hospital and then packed off back to England."

Sir Henry's penetrating gaze rested on Lord Robert's expressionless face. He felt that there was more to the tale than his lordship had related so laconically, but he thought he knew better than to push for details that Lord Robert was reluctant to divulge. He contented himself with an observation. "I am happy that you and John made your way at once to us."

"Stanhope was naturally anxious to return to his home and, at his insistence, I accompanied him. I had thought, too, to relieve your minds about my own safe return," said Lord Robert. He glanced again toward the door.

Sir Henry noted but did not comment on the glaring omission that Lord Robert had dealt to his own family in coming first to Huntington Hall. Again, Sir Henry had the strongest impression that Lord Robert had stated less than was actually the case. He had not missed the glances that Lord Robert had cast toward the door. Obviously, his lordship's overriding intent was to be reunited with his betrothed.

"We are glad to have you with us," said Sir Henry. His quiet tone caught Lord Robert's attention, and his eyes swung around to meet Sir Henry's in a long silent communication. Sir Henry nodded, as though to himself. "My daughter will be happy to hear that you have returned safely, my lord."

"I had hoped to greet Miss Huntington this evening,"

said Lord Robert with a tentativeness at odds with his characteristic self-assured manner.

"Theresa!" Lady Amelia rose from her chair and crossed to the bellpull. "I had quite forgotten in all the excitement that she was not here with us. Of course you must wish to see her! I shall send up to her on the instant."

A faint flush colored Lord Robert's lean cheekbones. "Pray do not disturb Miss Huntington on my account if she has already retired," he said politely, dropping a mask over the sharp knife of disappointment he felt that the lady was not apparently going to appear.

"Oh, as to that, I doubt that my sister has precisely retired," demurred Mrs. Hopstead, exchanging a swift glance with her husband. Mr. Hopstead frowned and gave a slight shake of his head, as though in reproval.

Lord Robert caught the wordless exchange. His brows came together. "Is there something amiss with Miss Huntington? Is she ill?"

"My daughter excused herself from the company earlier, my lord, when she became overcome by recollections of a happier Christmas season," said Sir Henry quietly.

"It is the first Christmas without her beloved brother," said Mr. Hopstead, his frown deepening. "Theresa and Tony were quite close, more so than either of them were to my wife."

Mrs. Hopstead gave a trembling smile of acknowledgment. "It was very wonderful to see. Theresa and Tony, and of course John Stanhope, were always together as children. I was a bit older and therefore had my own set of friends."

Lady Amelia turned from giving a quiet order to the footman who had come in answer to her summons. She seated herself in a wing chair. "Tony was her twin," said Lady Amelia softly. "I think more than any of us, Theresa was affected by his death."

Sir Henry's hand descended comfortingly upon his wife's shoulder. "Indeed, that is true. It has been a difficult time for us all, but for Theresa it was a sort of lonely nightmare. I do not think that I ever saw her shed a single tear when we read of Tony's death. I had hoped that observing our Christmas traditions as closely as possible would serve to break through that shield she erected against us all. It was perhaps a rough-and-ready method, but I am persuaded that she will be the better for it."

"I see." Lord Robert turned the empty wineglass over and over between his fingers. He had forgotten that Miss Huntington's brother was her twin. Now, recalling the face of the lively young gentleman whom he had known but briefly, he thought there could have been little doubt that in looks Mr. Anthony Huntington and his sister had borne an extraordinary likeness to one another. They had apparently shared that special bond of affection that was said to exist between twin siblings.

He wondered whether they had also been similar in temperament. He had had far too little time with Miss Huntington to accurately judge her character, but only a little exposure to Tony Huntington's animated company had been enough to impress upon him that gentleman's high spirits and great courage.

On the thought, he said, "I became acquainted with Mr. Huntington while in Spain. I thought him a fine young fellow, extraordinarily brave and gallant."

Sir Henry raised his brows. After the initial surprise at Lord Robert's words, there came a decided twinkle into his eyes. "I should think reckless would be a fitter description of my son."

"Reckless on occasion, perhaps, but still impossibly brave," said Lord Robert. He hesitated, then said, "When he found himself in desperate straits, instead of abandoning his wounded fellows, he stood his ground and almost single-handedly beat off the enemy until others could come to his aid. Those men owed him their lives."

"You saw him die?"

He did not know who had asked the startled question. "Yes. He turned toward me, laughing and making a joke. The next instant he was crumpling to the ground. I do not believe that he ever knew that he had been shot." Lord Robert looked up at the sound of a muffled gasp. "Forgive me. I should not have opened so painful a subject."

There was a moment's silence, broken by his host.

"On the contrary, we are indebted to you, my lord. You have given us an invaluable gift," said Sir Henry, very softly.

The door opened and the footman entered. He crossed to Lady Amelia's chair and bent to her ear. The effect of his few quiet words was electrifying. Lady Amelia's eyes widened, and she started up from her chair. "Gone! Whatever can you mean? She couldn't possibly have left!"

"What is the matter?" asked Sir Henry sharply.

Lady Amelia turned to him, forgetting her usual restraint before company in her alarm. "Theresa has disappeared! Her maid found her gown tossed onto the floor, and Tony's old riding clothes are missing."

"What time was this?" demanded Sir Henry of the footman.

"The maid was sent up to inform miss of his lord-ship's arrival and returned just this instant, sir," said the unhappy footman.

"Riding clothes? Surely Theresa could not have gone out on such a freezing night," said Mr. Hopstead disbe-lievingly. His wife murmured horrified agreement.

"But that's just what she 'as done, sir, and what's more, she 'as taken the young master's horse."

All turned their faces to the short stocky man who had entered, unnoticed until that moment. Lord Rob-ert's sharp glance raked him, at once placing the man as a groom by his garb. The groom's grim pronounce-ment had been met with stunned silence, but then amazed exclamations rang out.

"Sultan!" Lady Amelia's face turned white. "She'll be killed!"

At her mother's horrified words, Mrs. Hopstead gave a cry and hid her face in her hands. Mr. Hopstead patted his wife's shoulder, murmuring abstractedly through a worried frown.

"Theresa is a fine horsewoman. We must trust in that," said Sir Henry firmly. But his expression and his tense stance gave the lie to his calm assurance.

"Has Miss Huntington ridden the stallion before?" asked Lord Robert sharply.

He was recalling his own ride on the horse not many months before. After the disastrous meeting with Miss Huntington in the rose garden, he had felt savage satis-faction in riding roughshod over the countryside. The stallion had had a hard mouth and had been headstrong. Lord Robert had enjoyed mastering Sultan, appreciat-ing the stallion's stubborn spirit and strength. But now, envisioning Miss Huntington on the horse's back, he felt a cold shaft of fear.

Sir Henry shook his head. The lines creasing his face deepened. "Sultan was my son's mount. Tony was the only one who could control him well."

The groom cleared his throat. "Begging your pardon, sir, but miss 'as been on the beast. The young master thought it a rare joke to put 'er up on Sultan."

"Is Miss Huntington capable of controlling the stallion?" demanded Lord Robert, returning his hard gray gaze to the man.

The groom hesitated a shade too long. "Miss is a rare 'un on 'orseback."

"But if Sultan were to bolt—"

Lord Robert did not finish his sentence; it was unnecessary. He could see the same apprehension that he felt in the expression of those around him. He swung around on the groom. "I will go after her. Bring 'round a horse immediately." The groom nodded understanding and hurried out of the parlor. The footman also retreated, carrying the news to the rest of the house.

Sir Henry's brows rose. His daughter was more his responsibility than Lord Robert's, as certainly the younger man knew, but he was given pause by the grimness of his lordship's expression. He decided to await events.

"You, my lord! Why, you haven't the use of your arm," said Lady Amelia. "We could not possibly ask it of you."

"Nevertheless, I shall go," said Lord Robert brusquely. He smiled suddenly, lightening the severity of his expression. "You need not fear on my account, ma'am. I have ridden before with such a handicap, having broken my arm in a fall and finished a twenty-mile course over some of the roughest hunting country known. I shall do very well, I promise you."

Lady Amelia appealed to her husband. "Henry, surely you will go after Theresa."

"I think that we may leave our daughter safely in his lordship's capable hands," said Sir Henry. His eyes were fixed on Lord Robert, an odd smile in their depths.

Upon meeting Sir Henry's gaze, Lord Robert gave a short ironic bow. He well understood that his prospective father-in-law was acknowledging an extraordinary trust in him.

Mr. Hopstead stepped forward. "I shall accompany you, my lord." His wife gave a small gasp of protest, but he said firmly, "No, my dear. It is my duty to our sister."

Lord Robert glanced from Mrs. Hopstead's distressed countenance to the face of the stocky gentleman whose steady regard did not waver under his frowning scrutiny. He said quietly, "Thank you, Mr. Hopstead. I am obliged to you."

"Good, Herbert. You know the country roundabout wilst his lordship does not," said Sir Henry, clapping his son-in-law on the shoulder.

The butler entered, Lord Robert's greatcoat laid over his arm, while the footman came hovering behind bearing his lordship's beaver and gloves. Sir Henry's eyes fell on the footman. "You, there! Run up for Mr. Hopstead's coat and riding gloves, and be quick about it. And send word for another mount to be brought up." The footman handed over the beaver and gloves to the butler, and virtually ran to accomplish his errand.

"That was my own thought, sir," said Mr. Hopstead gravely. "My only concern is that we have not a clue as to what direction she might have taken."

"But I do know," said Lord Robert calmly. He had

put on his beaver and accepted the butler's help with the greatcoat, and was engaged in pulling on his gloves. He glanced up at the murmur of astonishment, a grim smile playing about his mouth. "As it chances, on my way here tonight, what I took to be a madman plunged his horse across the road directly in front of my coach. I'd lay odds now that it was Miss Huntington."

"The horse, my lord?" asked Sir Henry urgently.

"I thought at the time it was one I knew," said Lord Robert. "There was something strangely loose-limbed about its jumping style that caught my eye."

Sir Henry nodded, satisfied. "That was Sultan. Thank God. You'll find her and bring her safely home, my lord."

Lord Robert gave a grim smile. "You have my word on it, sir."

The footman had returned with Mr. Hopstead's outer garments, and Lord Robert had waited impatiently for the gentleman to bundle himself into them. When he saw that his companion was ready, he said, "Let us go, Mr. Hopstead."

6

Lord Robert and Mr. Hopstead went down the front steps of the manor house, ice crunching audibly under their boots. There were three horses saddled and waiting, their reins held in the groom's firm grip. Sir Henry, who had stepped outside to see them off, said, "What's this?"

The groom touched his forelock. "Begging your pardon, sir, but I'll be needed to deal with that contrary beast."

"Aye, I should have thought of it myself," said Sir Henry, nodding. He looked up at Lord Robert, who had managed awkwardly to swing up into the saddle. "You will bring her safely home, I do not doubt," he repeated.

"There is no question of that, sir," agreed Lord Robert. He swung the horse around. Accompanied by the other two riders, he cantered down the drive.

His breath frosting on the air, Lord Robert described to his companions where the rider had so precipitously startled his coach horses. Mr. Hopstead nodded thoughtfully. "I know the place you speak of, my lord. It's fast beside the ford at the stream. We'll reach the field soon enough."

"Aye, it be a likely place to run that brute. As heavy as 'e is, there'll be sign of his passing," said the groom.

Lord Robert cast a calculating glance up at the leaden sky. "Yes, as long as the weather continues to hold. I suspect there will be snow again before morning."

Silence greeted this pronouncement, and greater urgency was felt by each man. If the snow should begin to fall before they found Miss Huntington, even if they had already struck her path, it would conceal any track. In that event, there would be the grave chance of not finding her at all that night.

The possibility was unthinkable, as was proven by Mr. Hopstead's observation. "The best thing for all of us is to discover that we have engaged on a wild-goose chase, and that my sister-in-law will have made her own way safely back to the Hall."

"In that case, I should very likely wring her lovely neck," gritted Lord Robert.

His sentiment, though startling at first to his companions, was upon reflection heartily understood. Certainly it was to be hoped that Miss Huntington had not come to grief on the hard-to-manage stallion. However, if she was unhurt and their own misery was to be the only underscoring of this cold night's ride, then his lordship had their unqualified approval in his determination to bring the young lady to a proper understanding of her thoughtless actions.

Very soon the horsemen reached the field that Lord Robert had described. They rode close to the rail fence and stood in their stirrups to examine the snowy ground on the opposite side.

"There, my lord. I'd wager a fortnight's pay that those marks were made by that great scrambling brute," said the groom, pointing.

"Aye, the hoof marks are plain as day. It must be my sister-in-law," said Mr. Hopstead.

Lord Robert acknowledged the assertions with a nod. He backed his horse and leaped it over the fence, followed by the groom on his own mount. Mr. Hopstead elected a more sedate crossing, trotting a few yards to the gate and slipping into the field through it.

The drifting snow had been swept away by the wind, leaving only the hard white frozen surface across the face of the field. The hoofprints they followed were frozen solid and easily discernible.

"Aye, I'd recognize the print of those shoes anywhere. See there, the mark cut into the shoe 'as printed pretty as could ever be 'oped. That's the mark of John Rider the blacksmith. 'E signs 'is work, as it were," said the groom.

"Thank God. We've found her," said Mr. Hopstead.

"We haven't yet, but we undoubtedly will," said

Lord Robert. He touched spurs to his mount, quickening the pace of the party. There was no danger of overlooking the trail at this juncture, for the hoofprints continued as starkly visible as before.

"Judging by the length of the stallion's stride, it was going at a good clip cross-country," said Lord Robert. "I hope Miss Huntington had the sense to pull him up before she went into those trees up ahead."

"If miss was able," muttered the groom.

As the small copse was neared, it was discovered that the trail gradually veered, finally to be seen to be paralleling the trees rather than going under them. "Good girl," murmured Lord Robert approvingly. He was fast coming to an appreciation of his betrothed's riding skill. Her seat must be magnificent to stick this long to the stallion's back, and as for her ability to force the stallion to change direction when it was still so fresh, he thought that she must be a rare rider, indeed.

Mr. Hopstead had lapsed into silence some minutes before. He blew alternately on his gloved hands. "It's becoming colder."

"Yes," agreed Lord Robert. Though aware that the cold had penetrated his coat and set up a dull throbbing ache in his weak shoulder, he gave no real notice to it. His whole determination was upon overtaking Miss Huntington as quickly as possibly. Nothing else seemed to matter beyond the anxiety that he felt for her safety.

Mr. Hopstead's horse staggered, then recovered as the gentleman dragged it up. "Hold up, my lord!"

Lord Robert turned his mount. "What is it?" he asked impatiently.

Mr. Hopstead had dismounted to examine his mount's front foreleg, which it touched hesitantly to the ground. He straightened. "My horse broke through the crust over a hole. The gelding is lame. Jem, you'll have to lead him back while I take your nag."

The groom objected, though respectfully, "Begging your pardon, sir, but who'll take that brute in hand when we come up to it? Him not knowing you and all."

"The man is right. Neither of us can hope to manage Sultan well enough to lead him back to the stables," said Lord Robert, indicating his wounded shoulder with a flick of his rein.

"Then it is I who must leave you, my lord. I wish it were otherwise," said Mr. Hopstead. He held up his hand.

Lord Robert leaned down to grip the gentleman's hand. He understood and appreciated Mr. Hopstead's genuine regret. "At least you may lay some fears to rest, Mr. Hopstead. Sir Henry and Lady Amelia will be glad to know that we have indeed discovered Miss Huntington's direction," he said.

Mr. Hopstead's glum face lightened a fraction. "Aye, there's that, of course." He turned the limping gelding, and began trudging back over the way they had come so shortly before.

A swirl of snow almost obliterated his stolid figure before Lord Robert once more turned his mount to the track and, in company with the faithful groom, continued on his quest.

An hour later, after crossing a tall rail fence and scrambling their mounts through the ditch beyond it, Lord Robert's sharp eyes caught sight of a small dark shape half-covered with drifting snow. He and the groom walked their horses closer.

Lord Robert bit off an exclamation. He sprang out of the saddle, at the same time tossing his reins to the groom. Taking the tips of his leather glove between his teeth, he ripped off the glove and let it drop as he knelt down beside the still figure. Roughly he pulled aside the muffler about Miss Huntington's neck to feel for a pulse. It fluttered beneath the press of his fingers. He let go his breath on a soft sigh, not knowing until that moment that he had been holding it.

"What be the verdict, my lord?" asked the groom anxiously.

"She's alive," said Lord Robert tersely, exploring for injury with his one good hand. "Other than a knot the size of an egg on the side of her head, she appears to be all right. Damn it, she's practically frozen! We've got to get her out of this cold."

The groom twisted in his saddle, thoughtfully inspecting the rail fence and ditch, half-hidden by lazily blowing snow. "Aye; I'm thinking miss put Sultan to that break and lost her seat on landing. 'Tis likely 'e didn't quite clear the ditch, and she went over 'is 'ead, 'ard like. 'E'll be 'alfway 'ome by now, as there's no sign of the brute that I can see."

"I don't give a tinker's damn about that cursed horse!" exclaimed Lord Robert, clumsily replacing the muffler as best he could about his betrothed's neck. "We must get Miss Huntington to shelter before she freezes to death." He abruptly rose to his feet. "Curse this shoulder of mine. You'll have to hand her up to me, Jem."

"Aye," agreed the groom laconically.

Lord Robert mounted and then took both sets of reins so that the groom's hands could be free. The groom carefully lifted up the young woman onto the horse in front of the viscount.

Lord Robert helped clumsily to settle her against

him. She stirred weakly, a low moan escaping her pallid lips. "Softly, sweetheart, softly," murmured Lord Robert, gathering the reins. "I'll have you home shortly."

Miss Huntington stretched languorously. She had had the most extraordinary dream. Yet half-asleep, a smile touched her lips.

The bedroom door opened, and she opened her eyes. Her maid quietly entered to pull open the window drapes. Thin sunlight streamed into the room. Miss Huntington voiced a cheerful greeting. "Good morning, Maggie."

The maid gave a violent start and shrieked as she spun around. "Oh, miss! Such a start you gave me." The woman's eyes widened. "Miss, you're awake!" She ran out of the room.

Miss Huntington was left openmouthed by the maid's strange behavior. She pushed herself up, grimacing at how her body protested the small movement. Her head pounded ominously. She could not remember having had the rum punch, but she must have done so. Otherwise, she would not have this abominable head.

Seconds later the bedroom door flew open, and Lady Amelia rushed in. "Darling! You are awake at last."

"Is it so very late?" asked Miss Huntington, throwing a startled glance at the wan daylight visible at her windows.

Lady Amelia gave a catch of laughter. "Oh, my dear. No, it is just before nine of the clock. The family was just rising from breakfast when Maggie brought me word of you. Everyone is naturally anxious to hear how you are feeling."

"Mama, why such a fuss?" asked Miss Huntington,

a frown forming between her delicate brows. "Did I make such a fool of myself, then?"

"Indeed you did," said Lady Amelia with unusual emphasis. She seated herself on the edge of the bed. "But we shall not speak of that just now. Your father shall have something to say about it, I don't doubt. But at the moment, I think it best if you remain in bed to rest a bit longer. I've sent Maggie to bring up some tea and toast, and then she will see that you are made presentable."

Lady Amelia laid a cool hand on her daughter's forehead and smiled, saying softly, "I am so thankful that you were not the worse for that idiotic ride of yours."

The beginning of suspicion took definite shape from out of the midst of Miss Huntington's bewilderment. "Mama, I do not precisely recall, but I seem to remember—yes, I went down to the stables and took out Sultan! Oh, my word! How could I have been so stupid?"

"I really do not know," said Lady Amelia, laughing, but with a shade of concern in her eyes. "Do you truly not recall what happened? Why, my dear child, you were thrown by Sultan! You have been unconscious for nearly two days. The doctor warned us that the knock you took on the head had rendered you quite senseless, and that you would most likely awaken feeling dazed and disoriented. But you mustn't be anxious, for you will be right as rain with a bit of rest."

Miss Huntington was exploring with tentative fingers the source of her headache. She winced at the tenderness of the swelling in her hairline. "It is no wonder that I have the headache this morning. Sultan must have tossed me straight onto my head."

"The wonder is that you did not suffer a broken neck," said Lady Amelia with asperity. "When I think of you up on that brute, and learning that Tony had actually encouraged you to ride Sultan—" She stopped, apparently overwhelmed with her emotions.

Miss Huntington was beginning to recognize that she had indeed behaved foolishly. If her mother, normally so placid in character, was expressing herself so forthrightly, then she could well imagine how Sir Henry had reacted at her foolhardiness. "Is Papa very angry with me?"

"Your father wished to come up at once and speak to you most firmly about your folly. But I have persuaded him to wait until you are more yourself, for nothing is worse than a thundering scold when one feels unwell," said Lady Amelia.

"Oh, dear," said Miss Huntington.

"I should think so, indeed."

The maid returned to the bedroom, bearing a tray. Lady Amelia rose from the bed. "Here is Maggie with your tea. When you have finished, Maggie will see you tidied, for I do not intend to allow you to receive everyone's well wishes in your crumpled gown and with your hair all tumbled. Nothing could be more calculated than that to convince the high-strung that you are in severe straits. And I do think we have had enough high drama, do you not, my dear?"

"Yes, Mama," said Miss Huntington meekly.

An hour later Miss Huntington had finished most of her breakfast, though only at the scoldings of her maid, and had submitted to changing into a fresh gown covered with an elegant wrapper. Her hair was brushed, but it had been left loose to curl silkily about her shoulders, as Miss Huntington had complained that she could not bear to have it up because it pulled and made her head ache that much more.

She had not needed the maid's urging to return back to bed, but had gratefully slipped back under the coverlets, more tired than she could ever recall. The maid slipped pillows behind her back and left her alone at last, taking away the breakfast tray.

Not long afterward, just as Miss Huntington was drifting back to sleep, Lady Amelia reentered the bedroom. She regarded her daughter critically and nodded. "Much better, dearest. You are still too pale, but there is nothing that can be done about that. There is someone outside in the hall who has urgently requested word with you. I have given my permission for a few minutes." She opened the bedroom door and gestured permission for the visitor to enter.

A gentleman walked into the bedroom, pausing beside Lady Amelia.

Miss Huntington stopped breathing. She stared at him, quite certain that she must be hallucinating. Lady Amelia apparently had no such difficulty, for she smiled up at him. "You will not tax her too strongly, my lord?"

"I promise that I shall not," said Lord Robert gravely.

Miss Huntington's heart tripped, then began to beat at an amazing rate. The feeling of unreality closed tighter around her. Horrified, she realized that her mother was actually preparing to leave her alone with his lordship. "Mama!"

Lady Amelia paid not the slightest heed to her daughter's agonized plea, nor to the expression of shock on her face. She simply smiled, walked toward the door, and gently shut it after her.

Miss Huntington's eyes flew swiftly to Lord Robert's inscrutable face. A bandage decorated his brow. She saw, too, that one arm was laid in a sling. The evidence of wounds should have taken away from his formidable presence. However, he appeared to her no less than dangerous.

She had never felt so vulnerable. It was unthinkable that a gentleman should have been allowed to enter her bedroom, but it struck her as particularly so when she was half reclining in the bed. Miss Huntington sat up straighter, only belatedly realizing that the covers would slip lower, revealing the front of her wrapper. She did not want to betray her nervousness by yanking up the blankets, yet it did not occur to her that crossing her arms over her breast accomplished the same thing.

After all that had happened, she was alone with Lord Robert. And in quite unnerving circumstances.

7

They gazed at one another for a long moment, neither moving and seeming to scarcely breathe. Miss Huntington felt her pulse pound wildly in her veins. She was sitting in what she thought of as intimate disarray, and though fully covered, she felt peculiarly naked to the somber gaze of the tall gentleman who stood silently at the end of her bed.

As for Lord Robert, he beheld a frightened beauty. Her eyes were huge blue pools in her pale face, and the pulse beat quite plainly at the base of her slim throat. The wrapper she wore was closed modestly to the throat, but nevertheless it clung faithfully to her soft curves. He felt the stirrings of desire, and he dared not visualize what lay beneath the hinting of the soft mounds of the bedclothes.

He stepped around the end of the bed.

Miss Huntington's eyes dilated, and she shrank back against her pillows. Lord Robert merely seated himself in the chair beside the bed. She plucked nervously at the coverlet. If only she could sink up to her chin in the concealing folds. She cast a desperate glance toward the door with the devout wish that her maid would return to interrupt this tête-à-tête.

Apparently drawn by the restless movement of her hand, Lord Robert caught it in his own. He raised her fingers to his lips in a warm salutation that sent shock waves to the very ends of her nerves.

She went utterly still, only the tremor of her fingers betraying her agitation.

"You still wear my ring," he said quietly.

"I—I have never removed it, my Lord," she whispered through the dryness of her throat.

"I am glad of it," he said, still in that quiet tone. He frowned at her slim hand, which he still had not released. He said slowly, "Your letters to me were enlightening, Miss Huntington. I gained a familiarity with your character that I would not have come to appreciate in the general way."

"As yours were to me, my lord," she said. The circumstances were odd, but the conversation was carried on in the tones of the drawing room, decorous and polite. "I learned much about—about the war and your opinions of it."

That was not the whole truth, she thought. His letters had revealed a man of deep compassion, one who had cared for his fellow soldiers and who had pitied the peasants whose lives had been reduced to harsh hunger and brutal conditions. He had revealed a sensitivity and caring that put to the lie all that she had concluded about him during that one disastrous weekend.

She had long since stopped thinking of him as the cold, arrogant lord who had attempted to order her life and who had written that stiff letter giving permission for her to jilt him. His harsh manner toward her had been only a shield that had hidden and protected his true nature. It was a great pity that she had not known it at the time.

Her regretful reflections were routed in an astonishing fashion.

Lord Robert was suddenly seated on the bed. His good arm slipped behind her shoulders, drawing her close, while his weight on the mattress persuaded her to roll into even closer proximity.

Miss Huntington's face was pressed against the warmth of his shirt. Instinctively her fingers reached up to clutch his coat lapel. She felt his lips moving on her hair.

"My love; my darling love."

Shockingly, she realized how familiar was her position, how familiar the murmur of his soft words. She stiffened, endeavoring to straighten.

He allowed her only a little latitude. "What is it?"

She stared up into his face, utterly appalled. "It was not a dream!"

"What was not, my lady?" he asked, somewhat amused by her agitated exclamation. Bright color had come up in her pale cheeks, and her eyes held an emotion that he could not quite read.

"This! Your holding me like—like this," she stammered.

"No," agreed Lord Robert, smiling openly now. "I

had you up before me on the horse on our return to the Hall. I did not realize you were conscious, however." His brow slanted in wicked speculation.

"I wasn't! At least—I couldn't have been, or I wouldn't have allowed you to—"

Miss Huntington's face flushed brighter as she recalled another important aspect of the dream that she had remembered upon wakening.

"To do what, my dear Miss Huntington?" he drawled politely, his breath feathering her skin.

Unconscious of the action, her lips parted, and his mouth closed the remaining distance between them. It was a searching kiss, hungered and promising all at once. It was nothing like his kiss had been in the rose garden, when he had humiliated and enraged her.

Lord Robert raised his head at last, and Miss Huntington opened her eyes dazedly. She became aware that she was lying pressed back against her pillows, Lord Robert's arm beneath her and the considerable weight of his upper body imprisoning her own. Oddly enough, she did not feel the least bit entrapped.

She slipped her hands up over his shoulders and slid her fingers into his hair. "I fear you have compromised me most wantonly, my lord," she murmured. "It is really quite shocking."

Lord Robert's breath was coming somewhat harshly. His eyes glittered with a smoldering intensity that she found immensely satisfying. "Conventions be hanged. I have played the utter fool. I should have wed you out of hand these several months past. Then I could be making love to you properly now without worrying about your mother standing outside the door."

Miss Huntington blushed charmingly, completely unvexed by this hasty speech. However, there was one point that needed still to be aired. "But what then of John Stanhope, my lord? Have you still a jealous heart?"

Lord Robert bent to press a fleeting kiss on the corner of her mouth. "My heart is exceedingly jealous where you are concerned," he assured her. She was not altogether displeased by his declaration when he became engaged in exploring her throat with shivery butterfly kisses.

At length, Lord Robert murmured, "Have I told you that Mr. Stanhope and I escaped from the French in one another's company? I regretted it, believe me, for he was quite persistent throughout all our long trek that I be made to understand the true relationship between you."

Miss Huntington sat up abruptly, her head coming into sharp contact with Lord Robert's. "John is alive? He's home?"

Lord Robert complained at her rude treatment. "I shall know better than to bring the fellow along with me out of French hands the next time if this is to be my reward."

Miss Huntington had difficulty grasping the enormity of it all. "But I—we had not received any word of John until the squire got that horrible letter from his commanding officer. He was supposed to be dead. How did you come up with him?"

"Toward the end of the last action I was in, I took a ball in the shoulder and then I was grazed by another." He briefly touched the intriguing bandage on his brow. "I must have been knocked out for a time, for when I came to my senses, the fighting had stopped. It was eerily quiet, except that I heard French being spoken quite near me. Too near, as it turned out. I was taken prisoner. Stanhope was among others who had also been so unlucky. The rest is obvious."

"You could not have given me more wonderful news," exclaimed Miss Huntington. "How deliriously happy the Stanhopes must be. They do know?"

"He is well and safely at home, yes." Lord Robert sighed and drew back, perceiving that her attention had quite strayed from more important matters. "We shall have the curst fellow at the wedding, I suppose."

Miss Huntington threw her arms about his neck and bussed him so wholeheartedly that he quite lost his resigned air.

Much later, after many words had been exchanged intermingled with wonderfully warm kisses, Lord Robert said idly, "You have not yet told me what madness possessed you to take out Sultan."

"My mad folly, indeed," said Miss Huntington with a small embarrassed laugh. "I was attempting to escape the Christmas season. It—it was proving so painful since Tony was gone forever, and it seemed so certain that John was, also."

"And what of me?" he asked quietly.

She played with his lapel. "That was the worst." She raised her face, tears glistening in her eyes. "I had thought my heart had died, you see, and I had never had a proper chance to give it into your keeping."

His arm tightened about her. "You have held mine all unknowingly since the first moment that I saw you," he said softly. He hesitated, then said, "I hated Stanhope for standing, as I thought, so much closer in your affections."

A blaze of happiness went through her. "I think this is the most glorious Christmas that I have ever known," said Miss Huntington.

The bedroom door opened, and Lady Amelia stepped in. What she thought of finding her daughter wrapped in a fierce embrace, she did not voice. However, she did say, "I do think weddings at Christmas are so very appropriate, for the joy of the season lends itself so well to the occasion."

The Viscount
and the Hoyden
by
Laura Matthews

"BET YOU half a crown!" Ralph exclaimed, his nose pressed against the schoolroom window. "Look! He's definitely riding this way. It's the viscount, I tell you."

"Oh, it isn't either," his sister Brigid scoffed. "He would be riding in a carriage with his crest on the door. Viscounts don't just ride about in the snow when they're on their way to visit someone of Papa's importance."

"A viscount can do whatever he wishes," Ralph informed her, shifting his gaze from the gathering gloom on the landscape outside to his younger sister's face. "Maybe he's not so toplofty as an earl or a marquess would be, and certainly not so much as a duke, but enough. More than a baronet!"

"Well, Papa is grand enough for me," Brigid sniffed.

She sighed and rubbed clear the spot her warm breath had misted. "He rides well. Hally will like that. If it's the viscount," she remembered to add. "And I did not accept your bet, Ralph, for I haven't a half crown to my name."

Ralph narrowed his eyes against the dusk, squinting to keep the moving form in his view. "I don't really understand why he's coming to spend the Christmas holidays here when his seat is in Somerset. We don't know him, and he'll just be in the way," he grumbled. "You just can't be as comfortable with strangers in the house."

"Well, Papa invited him because his mama and our mama were friends," Brigid explained. "That's why he's come."

"That's no reason!" Ralph glared out into the gloom. "I'll bet he wants to marry Hally."

"Marry Hally? He doesn't even know her!" Brigid's eight-year-old face had gotten red at the very thought. "Don't be absurd! Besides, Hally doesn't wish ever to marry."

"Girls marry," Ralph pronounced with all the wisdom of his own eleven years.

"Not Hally," Brigid insisted. She jumped down from the chair she'd drawn over to the bank of windows. "She wants to stay here with us as she always has."

"Lot of good that will do her," Ralph said knowingly. It was too dark now for him to see the rider, and he was satisfied as to the viscount's identity in any case. "Hally's getting old."

"Old! She's only twenty. And she could have married Tom Parsons last year if she'd wished."

Ralph snorted. "Tom Parsons. As if he were anybody. A nodcock of the first order. No one would want to marry Tom Parsons."

"He's very handsome," Brigid protested.

"And without a lick of sense. Hally sent him on his way with a flea in his ear."

Brigid's brow creased. "Why wouldn't the viscount marry someone he knows?"

Ralph, who hadn't considered this possibility, dismissed her reasoning with a wave of his fingers. "Oh, you don't know anything, Brigid."

There was a quick knock on the door of the schoolroom, and the children turned to see their older sister, Hally, thrust her head into the room with the air of an innocent intruder. "I'm not interrupting, am I?" she asked. "Not disturbing your lessons, or preventing you from studying?"

Her short, curly hair, only allowed by her Papa after numerous arguments in which she'd pointed out that Lady Caro Lamb was all the rage for having it, seemed well suited to the vivacious cast of her face. With deep blue eyes, gleaming black hair, and a mischievous dimple in her right cheek when she grinned, she looked more like an Irish milkmaid than the daughter of a Hampshire family that traced its lineage to William the Conqueror.

"Miss Viggan has gone off for her tea," Brigid said. "Oh, Hally, he's here!"

"Who's here?" her sister queried, coming into the room with her usual energy, her cheeks still pink from outdoors and her hair disheveled.

"Viscount Marchwood, silly," Ralph said. "We saw him riding toward the house."

Hally cocked her head at him. "Riding? I should think he'll arrive in a carriage, or perhaps in a stylish curricle." Her voice held a trace of sarcasm, which she made little attempt to hide. "John would have it that the viscount is a noted whip."

Since their brother John's one aberrant passion was horseflesh, this was something of a compliment. John, a sturdy, unimaginative fellow of nineteen, saw no need for light diversions from his self-imposed estate work schedule of dawn to dusk, but his siblings knew that he could often be distracted by some variation on the theme of riding, driving, or hunting. Which, as Hally was wont to say, "is a very good thing, for otherwise he would certainly be no more than the paltriest clodhopper."

Brigid was squirming on the chair she'd taken. "But, Hally, aren't you going to change? He will be here any minute."

"Pshaw! What does it matter? Williams will show him to a room. And if he's ridden, he'll need to remove his dust. John or Papa will see him then. No one asked me to be there."

"But, Hally, you're the mistress here!" Brigid nearly wrung her small white hands. "We wouldn't want him to think that he wasn't welcome. I should hate it if I arrived at a country house and there was no one to welcome me."

Hally tapped her kindly under the chin. "Don't fret, sweetheart. Papa has been sitting in the winter parlor for the last three hours with a toasty fire going and a blanket over his legs waiting to greet his lordship. I was only teasing."

"But you should be there! What will he think?"

"That I have other important things to do—like visit my brother and sister in the schoolroom."

"I think he's come to marry you," Ralph interjected.

Hally stared at him. "My dear boy, he doesn't even know me! His mother particularly wanted him to spend Christmas with us so he could tell her how we go on after all these years. She has to spend the holidays with her ailing sister and didn't want him to be without family."

Ralph looked unconvinced, but linked his arm with hers—he was almost as tall as Hally—and led her to the abandoned tea tray. "Have a biscuit with us, Hally, before you go down, and tell us about the ice skating. Miss Viggan wouldn't let us out today. She said tomorrow the ice would be safer. Papa really should not make me mind her. I'm far too old to be shut up in the schoolroom."

"Oh, indeed," his sister agreed as she took the chair he gallantly offered. Her eyes sparkled with excitement. "I raced Francis Carson on the ice today, and I won!"

Before she had finished describing this latest adventure, Miss Viggan entered the room and announced with truly remarkable gravity, "Your Papa wishes you to join him in the winter parlor, Hally."

Hally sighed. "Thank you, Miss Viggan. I shall present myself immediately."

Miss Viggan, who had been at Porchester Hall since Hally was a child, added diffidently, "I believe Lord Marchwood is with the baronet."

Hally winked at her sister. "As I suspected. Behave yourselves, urchins," she instructed with her usual lack of sincerity. "I'm off to do my duty."

The Hall was not yet decorated for the holiday season. Hally had hoped to take the younger children out to gather holly and evergreen boughs that afternoon, but Miss Viggan had been adamant that the two of them had not deserved the special treat. It was her one method of maintaining order in her small ranks, disallowing treats with Hally, but it was an effective one. Even Hally had to admit that Ralph and Brigid were more likely to listen to the governess if they knew a promised treat lay in the balance.

Hally wore an everyday dress of lavender wool, chosen by her Aunt Louisa in absentia, which was no more suited to Hally's tearing spirits than it would have been for a small terrier. Still, Hally wore it religiously as a sort of lesson to her father and John, who seemed to believe that were she to somehow manage a bit of decorum their lives would be immeasurably better.

Not that she doubted for a moment their devotion to her! Hally knew they both loved her—and appreciated her role as well. With the baronet never remarrying and John still too young to marry and bring a wife there, Hally had served as mistress of Porchester Hall since she was old enough to order a proper tea.

Mama had died when Brigid was born, more than eight years previously. Hally had practically raised Brigid, with some help from Miss Viggan, and felt proud of the results. And Ralph. Of course Papa and John had had a lot to do with raising Ralph, but there too she'd had her influence, keeping them from making him stodgy and bland as they seemed intent upon doing. Poor Ralph. He should go away to school, certainly, but until recently he'd been adamant about staying in Hampshire. Hally had encouraged him, pointing out the good things—as John was all too capable of inadvertently alluding to the worst—in going off to school. They were trying to convince him to try the spring term at Greenwald, a smallish school no more than fifty miles distant. Hally would miss him if he went, but she thought he'd benefit from the experience.

When she reached the hallway outside the winter parlor, Williams sprang to open the door for her, giving her a slightly questioning look as he did so. Hally supposed he wondered if she knew that she was about to encounter an important visitor, and if she did why she hadn't dressed more stylishly. Her dimple appeared briefly, but she said nothing as she composed her face into a semblance of innocent properness and walked swiftly into the room.

A cozy tableau greeted her: Papa wrapped up in his blanket before a roaring fire; her brother John in buckskins and top boots, pouring tea; and a stranger in town clothes seated as far as possible from the source of the heat. The two able men rose to their feet, John with startled alacrity and the viscount with a more languorous grace.

Though John stood almost six feet, the stranger outdistanced him by an inch or two and Hally was forced to look up quite a ways when her father exclaimed, "Good, my dear! We should have waited tea for you, but no one seemed to know where you'd gotten to. Come in, come in. Let me introduce you to Viscount Marchwood. Marchwood, my daughter Alice Halliston Porchester."

"Miss Porchester," the viscount murmured, his brows slightly elevated over his dark, quizzical eyes. "Your servant."

"Lord Marchwood." Hally dropped an energetic curtsy before moving to her father's chair to bend down and drop a kiss on his raised cheek. "Papa. John. There was no need to wait for me. I've been in the schoolroom with Brigid and Ralph. Miss Viggan said you were looking for me."

She seated herself in the chair her brother John had been occupying and proceeded to finish pouring tea. Her own particular manner of pouring tea bore little resemblance to her mother's. Lady Jane had been a delicate, feminine woman who did everything with exquisite taste and simple elegance. Hally's style was a good deal more spirited. Tea invariably splashed over the rim and onto the plate when she poured it. Lumps of sugar splashed determinedly into the brew, and biscuits were offered with an enthusiasm few could resist.

Lord Marchwood accepted a biscuit, a slice of seed cake, and buttered bread sprinkled with nuts, a concoction of Hally's invention. He eyed the last with uncertainty, but Hally was insistent. "We invented them quite by chance, Ralph and Brigid and I," she explained. "It was on a picnic in the walnut grove where Ralph had climbed a tree and sat above us cracking nuts. Then he used the buttered bread for target practice. It's delicious, isn't it? You'll be fascinated by some of the dishes they prepare in the Porchester kitchens."

"Oh, no, Hally!" John protested. "You haven't ordered curried fowl for tonight's menu, have you? You'll kill the poor man!"

Hally's chin went up. In a haughty voice she informed her brother that he did not need to eat the curried fowl if he did not wish to, but that the rest of the family were looking forward to it. "Aren't you, Papa?"

Sir Thomas valiantly agreed that he was, but with a commiserating look at John that did not escape Hally's attention. "Not everyone has the taste for spicy cookery," she informed Lord Marchwood.

"Or the courage," her brother said in his own pungent fashion.

"Exotic cookery is one of my few domestic interests," Hally admitted to the viscount, her dimple appearing. "I don't play the pianoforte, I don't sing at all well, I don't sketch or draw and my needlework is abominable."

"She's a very fine horsewoman," John hastened to interject, as though to offset this list of negatives. Then fearing that this sounded like a boast, his face grew flushed. "Not that it matters," he mumbled. "I'll have another of the Christmas biscuits, Hally. Today's the first time this year Mrs. Goodin has served them. They're one of the signs we look for that the festive season is here," he explained to the viscount with a forced heartiness. "Perhaps you have something of that nature at Millway Park to welcome in the season."

The viscount nodded. "From the week before Christmas until a week after, each night a candle is placed in the window of every room. It's a charming sight from outside, especially coming home from church on Christmas Eve. I believe my mother brought the tradition from her home in Yorkshire when she married my father."

Sir Thomas, who had been toasting a piece of bread at the fire, remarked that he liked that tradition very well. "What do you say, Hally? Shall we make his lordship feel right at home by having the servants put candles in all the windows this evening?"

Hally was always inclined to please her father. "If you should like it, Papa. Though I'm not at all sure we have such a generous supply of wax candles. It would not offend you, Lord Marchwood, if we used something a little more economical, would it?"

"You must do as you see fit," the viscount assured her at the same time her brother protested, "Well, of course we'll use wax candles, Hally. I'm sure we must have enough and I will go into the village myself tomorrow to get more if we need them."

The two fell to bickering about who was responsible for such a chore and the baronet raised his eyebrows in exasperation to his visitor. "We're not accustomed to company," he explained. "They haven't the habit of it."

John, embarrassed, immediately broke off what he was saying and sat back, ruffled, in his chair. Hally, unconcerned, smiled cheerfully at the viscount. "Well, really the only company we're accustomed to is family, and we're to have Mary Rose Nichols with us. Her father is my father's cousin, and she's the most charming girl. She's very down to earth but joins in all our flights of fancy, too. We couldn't ask for a more perfect companion at this time of year."

"She sounds delightful," the viscount said.

"And she's beautiful," Hally added. "Truly the most attractive girl in the county, isn't she, John?"

John's hand stopped on its way to his mouth with a biscuit. "Well, yes, I suppose so. In a quiet way. There's nothing dashing about Mary Rose. She doesn't call attention to herself."

"Certainly not. A very proper, well-behaved girl," Hally agreed. "She arrives tomorrow for a fortnight. We haven't seen her since last summer and she is long overdue for a visit."

Lord Marchwood regarded her with interest. "My mother remembers visiting here when there were just the three of you children but several of your cousins as well. She said the house absolutely rang with laughter and adventures."

Hally considered. "That would have been a long time ago, when I was ten or eleven perhaps. I think I remember your mama but I'm not sure. Does she smell of violets?"

The oddness of the question did not seem to perturb his lordship. "It's a scent I remember very clearly from my childhood, though she has taken more recently to wearing attar of roses or some such thing."

Sir Thomas was nodding reminiscently as he listened to the young people. "I remember the scent of violets, too. Your mother told us all about you when she visited then, and she regretted not bringing you. But you'd gone to stay with your grandparents for the spring holidays, as they were nearer your school. It seems a long time ago."

"Almost ten years." Hally patted her father's hand. "But now we have Lord Marchwood in his mother's stead. I fear he'll find us very dull after London. Perhaps we should have an evening party."

"There is no need to go to any extra lengths for my entertainment," Lord Marchwood hastened to assure her, a decidedly amused light in his eyes. "I wish no more than to be a part of your family for my stay."

Hally wondered why he continued to regard her with such intensity. The whole problem with sophisticated people, she mused, was that they regarded such situations with a tolerant amusement, which did nothing to elevate one's spirits. Well, Hally was not going to let the viscount's attention, whether it was teasing or not, discompose her. He was, after all, just a man like all the men she'd met previously in her life, and she had had no trouble conversing with them.

Not that she found the Viscount in any way objectionable in his person. He was tall, and broad-shouldered, having rather the type of build a farmer might have, though of course Lord Marchwood had never in his life done such a thing as drive a plow horse or pitch a bale of hay onto a wagon. If he had indeed ridden to the Hall, he had changed quickly, and not to buckskins as her brother wore, but pantaloons over his shining black Hessians. His brass-buttoned blue coat was worn with a buff waistcoat and fit him like a glove. Hally suspected that he was a dandy, though in truth she had not a complete knowledge of what that term meant.

But Lord Marchwood had a head of curly brown hair that seemed barely tamed by his barber's scissors. In fact, Hally suspected that Lord Marchwood had not been to his barber in a period of time a little longer than her father would have approved of. Both the baronet and his son wore their hair quite short, and certainly not curling down over their ears or onto their necks. Hally rather liked it.

The viscount sat at his ease in the chair farthest from the fire and explained to John and Sir Thomas that he had only taken to his horse the last few miles because he had felt cramped from the long carriage ride. "And it's beautiful country here," he added, a description bound to please his hosts. "The light covering of snow was just what we needed to make it feel like winter. I noticed that your pond was solidly frozen."

Hally's eyes sparkled. "Yes, and you shall come to skate with us tomorrow. My younger brother and sister and I have made plans already."

Lord Marchwood held up a defensive hand, laughing. "Oh, no. I haven't been on skates since I was a boy, Miss Porchester. You must excuse me."

"Pshaw," she declared, "one never forgets how to skate, sir. Don't be so stuffy."

"Hally," her father said warningly, "his lordship isn't here to break his neck on the ice."

Hally's nose went up fractionally. "Well, I for one shall think he is a poor sort of fellow if he doesn't come skating with us."

John hastened to change the subject. "I had hoped Lord Marchwood would join us in gathering the greens for the Hall tomorrow. Tame sport, perhaps, but it is one of our traditions here. We take a jug of hot spiced cider with us, and hot chocolate for the younger ones."

Hally could not detect any condescension in the viscount's ready acceptance. It wouldn't be as much fun having him along, though; usually they sang Christmas carols and danced some circle dances in the woods as though they were sprites. She could not picture Lord Marchwood, even after a few glasses of cider, wishing to participate in their youthful fun. But Mary Rose would be there and perhaps he would want to please Mary Rose.

Her father was saying, "My daughter will give you a tour of the house before the light entirely fades, Lord Marchwood. The Hall is not so large that you could get lost, but I always found that I appreciated knowing the lay of the land when I visited far afield."

Hally hadn't the faintest idea when last her father had visited any spot farther than twenty miles from the Hall, but naturally she made no remark to that effect. "I would be honored to show his lordship around the Hall," she said grandly, which made her brother regard her suspiciously.

Showing people around the Hall was actually one of Hally's favorite duties as de facto mistress. The modest but beautiful Palladian mansion had been designed almost a hundred years previously by Colin Campbell after the previous structure had burned to the ground. Hally led Viscount Marchwood through a succession of rooms on the ground floor, filling in a little family history as she went. With a wave in the direction of the west wing, she said, "My grandfather had the kitchen wing attached to the house because he was tired of his food arriving cold."

"An eminently sensible move," the viscount agreed. "I'm afraid we haven't made that kind of progress at Millway Park."

She blinked at him. "You haven't? But how do you keep the food warm?"

"We invested in a monumental stock of silver covers, I believe. Kept the industry alive years after it should have failed."

A chuckle escaped her. "Well, I'm surprised you haven't done something to rectify the situation. Our neighbors the Carsons still have a separate building for the kitchens, and I can tell you it is a dreary business dining there. Even when they have company, they cannot manage to bring a warm roast of beef to the table. It's very discouraging."

"Yes, indeed. Too much of this sort of thing is carried on in the name of tradition. My mama will have it that it has always been done that way and that it should continue. One does not wish to discompose one's mama, even for a warm meal."

Hally could not tell if he was teasing her, despite the wicked gleam in his eyes, so she merely sniffed and pushed through the door into the hall. "I believe your mother and mine were close as young women."

"Bosom friends from what I hear."

He had continued to regard her with an absorbed interest that surprised her. Not that there was anything so crass about his brown-eyed gaze as to be impolite. It was merely that he never took his eyes off her, and he seemed to approve of what he saw. Hally felt slightly self-conscious. "And your mama probably thought I would be something like my mother."

"I imagine she did."

"Well, I should tell you that I am not at all like my mama. Your mother would be greatly disappointed. My mother was a very sweet and gentle woman, by far too accommodating to everyone around her. I have an entirely different disposition."

"So I see."

"I believe, in fact, that I was named Alice after your mama, though as you have heard, my family calls me Hally. Another disappointment for your mama, no doubt."

"Oh, I think she would be able to handle such a setback," he said, reaching past her to adjust a candle that she had inadvertently knocked to a precarious angle. "My mama is by nature an imperturbable woman. I think you would like her."

"Well, as to that, I don't remember." Hally was beginning to wonder, though, if the particularity of his interest had anything to do with Ralph's suggestion. Surely that was absurd! If the viscount's attention had wandered, or his gaze wavered, she might have dismissed it entirely. But the dark eyes, under the darker brows, remained locked on her face.

"The main hall serves as our gallery," she said. "There are family portraits from as far back as the fifteenth century. They were the first thing the baronet at

the time thought to save when the house was burning.
Imagine!"

Marchwood bent his head slightly toward hers and
asked, "And what would you save in the event of a fire,
Miss Porchester?"

"As to that, only the portrait of my mama. Other
than that I would save the people and the animals and
maybe a few personal treasures that I could get my
hands on."

"Did people die in the fire then?"

"No, but they might have," Hally insisted. "I'm sure
the baronet didn't manage all these heavy old portraits
by himself. He must have kept the servants carrying
them out well past a time when it was dangerous."

He grinned. "I see. You're speculating."

"A very reasonable speculation it is, too. Just for the
sake of some family history." Hally tugged at the
sleeves of the lavender gown. "Surely you can picture
the scene yourself."

"My imagination is not so fertile as yours," he admitted, turning to study a dark, stern-faced man in the
portrait at his elbow. "I would be tempted myself to
save paintings as old and fine as these. The ones at
Millway Park are from a more recent period. But show
me the portrait of your mother, Miss Porchester."

Suddenly Hally wasn't sure she wanted him to see
it. He seemed so sure of himself, so ready to claim a
relationship with her mother through his own. The portrait, though done locally, was remarkably good in its
resemblance to its subject and in the artist's skill. She
hesitated, but eventually moved to the foot of the staircase, indicating that the painting was on the first
landing.

"It was done two years before she died. About the

time your mother must have been here, actually. Papa says he likes to pass it every day as he comes down or goes up the stairs. And it's good for Brigid to see it, since she never knew Mama. At first, though, it was . . . well, never mind." What had she been about to tell this stranger, anyhow? What did he care for her feelings about the portrait?

Marchwood had climbed the stairs and stood easily before the full-size painting. "Is it a good likeness?"

"Yes, very like."

"Then I can see some of her in you. She was a beautiful woman, with such an angelic smile."

"You certainly don't see *that* in me!"

Marchwood turned to gaze down at her, wearing a rueful look. "Not the angelic smile, perhaps."

Hally felt a flush rise to her cheeks. Had he just called her beautiful? Surely not. She didn't really look at all like her mother, aside from some similarities of coloring and facial shape. He was, perhaps, teasing her again. Hally was finding it very difficult to understand what was happening.

"Lord Marchwood, why have you come here?" she asked, blunt to the point of rudeness, perhaps, but unable to restrain her need to know.

"My mother asked me to come. She was especially curious about you. She remembered you very well from when you were a child, and she wanted to know what had become of that spirited little girl. You see, I was the only child she ever had, though she would have liked a daughter, too." He cocked his head to one side, regarding her seriously. "She wondered how your mother's death had changed you and whether you had become more like her as you grew up. I'm expected to drink in every detail and report back to her."

Hally was only partially convinced by this explanation. She suspected that there was more to the story than he had related, but that he was unlikely to be more forthcoming at this point. "I'll just show you the library and the common parlor on the first floor," she said.

There were six bedchambers on the first floor as well as the common rooms. Hally made certain to point out the corner where her father was installed in the master suite, next door to the chamber given over to Lord Marchwood.

"And on the other side is my brother John's room and then mine, which shall be Mary Rose's for the fortnight. I'll stay on the second floor next to Miss Viggan. She's our governess. Perhaps you met her."

"No, I don't believe so." Lord Marchwood had paused outside his own chamber. "Perhaps Miss Nichols could have this room, and I could take the room on the second floor."

"Surely you jest," Hally mocked him. "And put you beside Miss Viggan? Why, her reputation would not be worth a fig after a night of that."

Marchwood laughed. "Very well. I can see that you've taken everything into consideration, Miss Porchester. But I hate to think of you being dispossessed of your room on my account."

"It's really on Mary Rose's account, and I could not be doing it in a more worthy cause."

He gave her a slight bow, that same gleam in his eyes. "You are all kindness."

"I think you know better than that." Hally turned away quickly and led him down the hallway to the library. The room was a treasure of leather-bound volumes, with comfortable chairs and tables, a grate set with logs for a fire, and a generous supply of candles. At his murmur of pleasure, she said, "Please make yourself at home here. My father and John seldom use the room."

"If they don't use it, then you must," the viscount surmised. "Because I've seldom seen a room with the look of comfort and convenience this one has. My own library isn't half so welcoming."

Hally, under his renewed scrutiny, flushed again. "I come here sometimes," she admitted, backing out of the room. "It's a pleasant place to sit and read."

"What is it you read here?"

She shrugged. "A bit of everything. Mrs. Radcliffe's novels. Books on brewing beer. Biographies of famous people. I don't have a disciplined mind, Lord Marchwood. If something interests me, I take it down from the shelf and read it."

"My mother would be enchanted," he murmured, just loud enough for Hally to hear.

She closed the door of the library behind them, rather sharply, vowing to avoid the room while he was at Porchester Hall. Let him enjoy the full use of it; it was only a fortnight out of her life, after all. She would spirit a few books up to the second floor when she knew he was occupied elsewhere.

"We dine at seven. I suppose that seems early to you, but it is our way in this part of the country."

"My dear Miss Porchester, we dine at six at Millway Park. And I shall be delighted to try some of your culinary experiments if they are half as tasty as the walnuts on buttered bread."

"Did you really like that?" she asked, surprised.

"Very much. One day I'll treat you to my own speciality."

"What is it?"

"No, no." He wagged a playful finger. "You'll have to wait and see. But I should let you go. I've taken up more than enough of your time. Thank you for the fascinating tour."

Hally readily left him standing there in the hallway, watching her retreat. Really, a most unaccountable man. He was not at all what she'd expected, and he seemed to have some deeper motives than those he claimed. Surely not marriage. And yet, those eyes. That incredible attentiveness to her. Really, it was very distressing. But also intriguing, she admitted to herself as she wandered off to her room to change for dinner.

Hally had arranged for Miss Viggan and her younger brother and sister to join them for the evening meal. Marchwood was seated to Hally's left. She had placed Brigid on his left and Ralph across from him, with Miss Viggan beside Ralph. The two youngest members of the party regarded the viscount with wide, curious eyes. Miss Viggan had obviously instructed them in their manners, for they remained unnaturally quiet until Marchwood spoke to them.

When Ralph was asked if he was at school, he shook his head emphatically. "I don't wish to go to school. The masters are mean and the other boys are rough, and I can't have my pony with me," he said.

The viscount nodded. "That's what I thought before I went, too."

"Well, it's true enough," Ralph insisted. "John was beaten several times when he was at Harrow, and all for the stupidest things. I shouldn't like that at all!"

"No, it's certainly not pleasant to be beaten," the viscount agreed in all seriousness.

Hally expected that at any moment he would lay out the beneficial aspects of school life, but he remained mute, awaiting Ralph's next remarks.

"And the boys were mean to him when he first came. They made fun of his clothes and kept him from playing on teams with them," Ralph pursued.

John felt it necessary to protest this description. "Only until I showed them how well I played," he pointed out to Ralph. "It's all part of hardening you up."

"I don't wish to be hardened up," Ralph muttered mulishly. "What's the point of that?"

The viscount took a bite of the fowl and a startled expression registered on his face. Hally, who had been watching him with interest, laughed. "I believe John warned you about the curried fowl, my lord. Sometimes it's best to eat it with a goodly quantity of small beer." She pushed her untouched glass to him, and he gratefully took a long sip. "That's how they make the curried fowl in India, I'm told. Very spicy."

"Indeed," he murmured.

"I told you you shouldn't have served it," John insisted, glaring at his sister.

"No, no, I was just taken by surprise." Marchwood helped himself manfully to another bite, which sent him for another long draft of the small beer. "Actually it's quite tasty. One need only accustom oneself."

"One is better off skipping that dish," John suggested, though he had himself taken a small portion. Both Ralph and Brigid were so used to the curried fowl that they downed it without even the aid of small beer.

"Well," the viscount said, turning back to Ralph, "you would have no difficulty with the food at school."

Hally took exception to this. "Are you suggesting

that if he is so lacking in taste as to enjoy the curried fowl, nothing they could prepare at school would bother him?"

"Something like that," the viscount admitted, "though you have put it in rather a different light than I should have. I meant that if Ralph is accustomed to eating a variety of unusual dishes, he would probably tolerate the school food better than most."

"I'm not going to school, so it doesn't matter," Ralph said.

Abandoning this lost cause for the moment, Marchwood turned to Brigid. "And, Miss Brigid, what are you learning from Miss Viggan?"

"She has made me a set of piquet cards with names of English towns and rivers on them. I can find them all on the map now," Brigid said proudly. She shifted uncomfortably in her chair and added, "But I think Hampshire must be much nicer than Somerset for it has the downs."

"Well, Somerset is lovely, too, with its moors. Do you go for long walks on the downs?"

"Almost every day," Brigid said. "Miss Viggan says the exercise is good for me. She doesn't approve of running, of course, but Hally and I do it sometimes just for fun when she's not there."

Marchwood shared a rueful look with the governess, who made no comment, though she appeared pleased by the viscount's notice. It was Ralph who added, "Hally is quite the fastest of all of us. And she skates like the wind. She beat Francis Carson in a race today."

"Did you, by Jove?" Marchwood murmured, intrigued. "Then perhaps I shall have to try on a pair of skates after all. Tell me, Miss Porchester, how do you keep your skirts from tangling with your legs."

"I wear an old gown of my grandmother's which has stiffened skirts that don't cling. They sway back and forth like a bell, but they don't get in my way."

"Ingenious."

"Don't you skate in Somerset?" Brigid asked.

"There's a pond that freezes solid almost every year, but I have to admit it hasn't occurred to me in years to skate." He glanced at Hally. "My mother used to skate."

"Mine did as well. Papa and Mama and John and I skated together years ago." She smiled fondly at her father. "Remember the year the tree fell at the edge of the pond, and we had a log to sit on in the perfect spot?"

Her father nodded, a reminiscent smile tugging at his lips. "Jane could almost dance on the ice. She would spin around without falling down, and glide in loops like a country dance. You could hear her laugh like a bell tinkling across the pond." He sighed, cleared his throat, and took a sip of his wine.

Brigid tugged at Marchwood's sleeve. "Why doesn't your mama still skate?"

He bent his head to her. "I'm not sure. I suppose she feels too old to skate, though she will still stand up with me at the local assemblies. I shall have to ask her."

"They have assemblies in Somerset?" Brigid asked.

Marchwood laughed. "Yes, we are not so much in the wilderness that we lack a local assembly. They even," he whispered, as though it were a secret, "dance the waltz there."

"Hally says they don't do the waltz at the Winchester assemblies. I suppose it is that no one knows how."

The viscount looked questioningly at his hostess, who said, "Well, perhaps some of them know how to waltz, but it isn't done here. If it were, we should have to learn it."

"I'll teach you," he suggested, smiling lazily at her. "Perhaps Miss Viggan would play the pianoforte for us."

The governess gave her ready assent. Hally regarded him with keen interest. "Would you teach Mary Rose as well?"

"Of course. And John. With Sir Thomas's approval . . ."

Sir Thomas smiled benevolently. "I see no harm in it. You're very kind, Lord Marchwood."

"It will be my pleasure," Marchwood said, his eyes once again on Hally and sparkling with good humor.

"Humph," she said.

Hally was not surprised to see the Nichols's carriage come rolling up the drive at shortly before eleven o'clock the next morning. Mary Rose was a conscientious young woman, and she would have been up early and ready to start her journey of twenty-two miles before most households were wide awake.

As the footman let down the carriage steps and handed Mary Rose down to the snow-covered ground, Hally watched with satisfaction from the window of the breakfast parlor. Yes, indeed, Mary Rose would be the perfect addition to their house party. In her emerald green cloak and wide-brimmed bonnet she looked as fetching as any woman of eighteen years that Lord Marchwood was likely to have set eyes on in his perambulations about London or Somerset. If the viscount was wife-hunting, Hally was about to present him with the perfect woman.

Mary Rose took dainty little steps in her matching emerald green half boots toward the stairs leading up to the entrance hall. Her blond curls peeked out from her bonnet, framing her heart-shaped face quite perfectly. Hally grinned with mischief, quickly wrapped a shawl about her shoulders, and hastened out to greet her guest.

"You must be chilled to the bone!" she cried as she hugged her cousin to her. "I'm so glad your family could spare you to come, Mary Rose."

Since Mary Rose's family spared her quite regularly to every relation known to them, this was almost a piece of impertinence, but Mary Rose knew Hally well enough to realize it was not meant unkindly. "Papa gave me a locket before I left, since I would miss the holiday there. Mama sent several jars of marmalade. And my sister Martha insisted I wear the traveling outfit her godmamma gave her. Isn't it splendid?"

"Absolutely delightful. Shall I see you up to your room for a bit of a rest before luncheon? You may be fatigued from your journey."

"Me?" Mary Rose laughed gently. "I think traveling well is my most special talent. No one I know travels so easily as I do."

Hally took the parcel of marmalade from her cousin's hand. "You're a great gun as Ralph would say, Mary Rose. Come, let me introduce you to our guest."

The delicate features drew into something of a frown. "I didn't know you were to have other guests. Dear me, I scarce brought anything out of the ordinary to wear. It's not someone of fashion, is it, Hally?"

Hally laughed, "Today he seems to have dressed like the rest of us, but yesterday he appeared something of a Tulip, I believe. Perhaps he's being on his best behavior, though it is hard to know what his best behavior is. Come, I'll introduce you."

Mary Rose had given up her cloak and bonnet to the waiting footman and now pushed ineffectually at the blond curls. "Do I look presentable?"

"You never look anything less than lovely," Hally assured her, guiding her by the elbow toward the winter parlor, where she flung the door open dramatically and announced, "Mary Rose is here."

Sir Thomas struggled to his feet and made the girl a deep bow. "We're honored, my dear Mary Rose. Let me present Viscount Marchwood, who is the son of a very dear friend of my late wife's. Lord Marchwood, Mary Rose Nichols, our cousin."

Mary Rose, surprised by the title of the viscount perhaps, dropped her eyes modestly to her half boots and curtsied. "My lord."

"Miss Nichols. A pleasure to meet you." The viscount's gaze swept over the newcomer and then back to Hally with an appreciative grin.

"John asked your pardon for his not being here when you arrived," the baronet explained. "He promised to join us for luncheon."

"Oh, please do sit down, Sir Thomas!" Mary Rose begged, and then added, a little diffidently, "John always works so hard."

"Well, he's going greenery hunting with us this afternoon." Hally patted the chair beside her. "Here, sit by Lord Marchwood and let me ring for some tea to warm you."

She watched with satisfaction as the viscount settled down to bring the shy young woman out. Mary Rose, owing to her own family's size and lack of funds, had not been properly presented to society and thus had never been made aware that her beauty was remarkable and her gentility captivating. Surely, aside from her lack of dowry, an excellent match for any young man of breeding. And what could a lack of dowry mean to a man of Marchwood's situation? Absolutely nothing, Hally felt sure.

"Eight brothers and sisters!" Even Marchwood looked startled. "And where do you fall in the family?"

"I'm the second oldest," Mary Rose said. She blinked somewhat sheepishly at her questioner. "My sister Elizabeth has married and left home, but the rest of us are at Chalford. It's a little crowded."

"Well, we're delighted to have you here," Sir Thomas insisted as Hally tucked the blanket back around his legs. "We have plenty of room."

"You're to have my bedchamber," Hally explained. "I'm going to take the room next to Miss Viggan."

"Oh, no, you mustn't!" Mary Rose turned to her hostess with an alarmed look. "I wouldn't for the world dispossess you of your room. Let me sleep on the second floor."

"And be something less than the perfect hostess?" Hally scoffed. "Certainly not. What would his lordship think of me?"

Mary Rose flushed with embarrassment, and the viscount considered his hostess with a doleful expression. "I tried, too, Miss Nichols. She told me that Miss Viggan's reputation would be destroyed were I to occupy the room on the second floor."

"And so it would. No arguments, please. I shall be quite content there, I promise you."

A servant came in with the tea, and Hally moved closer to her companions to pour. "Lord Marchwood has brought us a new holiday tradition, Mary Rose. We are putting candles in the windows each night, and one evening I thought we might take a sleigh ride to get the full effect of them from outside at night. Does that not sound like fun?"

The girl's large eyes lighted with pleasure. Yes, Hally thought, she is a very taking thing and the viscount seems to appreciate her loveliness. Hally was rather pleased with her endeavors thus far and sat back to allow their guests to get to know one another better.

Hally had organized their expedition to the home wood with her usual skill. Refreshments were ordered, tools for cutting the boughs and holly branches sought out, the sleigh for carrying them to the woods and two servants to bring the trap were arranged for.

A light snow was falling as they set out in the sleigh. Brigid and Ralph were seated with Hally on the driver's seat, while Mary Rose, Marchwood, and John squeezed together on the seat behind. When John had arrived for luncheon, he had been a little stiff with their newest guest. Hally hardly understood this, since they had all known one another all their lives. Mary Rose had seemed slightly awkward with him as well, saying nonsensically that she thought he was taller than he used to be, which was certainly not the case.

Well, it was probably the excitement of the day. The younger children were certainly in tearing spirits, unable to stop chattering for even a moment as the sleigh glided toward the woods. Mary Rose regarded them with delight, just as though her own younger brothers and sisters did not give her quite enough of that sort of entertainment every day of the year.

"Miss Viggan says we may make bells to go on the green boughs in the hallway," Brigid chirped. "Paper bells out of special silver paper she brought back from her trip to Winchester last week."

"How lovely," Mary Rose said. "I have brought some ribbons that I thought we might use as well for decorating."

Perfect, Hally decided, smiling. The viscount would see how good Mary Rose was with children. She glanced behind to see if he had noted this. The viscount winked solemnly at her. Really, he was too exasperating. Hally looked sharply away.

Not quite sharply enough, however, for the sleigh hit a hidden rock and its occupants bounced hazardously off their seats. Hally braced Ralph and Brigid on either side of her as the horses came to a halt. Turning to assess any difficulties behind her, she noted that John and Marchwood had likewise thrown their arms around Mary Rose. Color instantly flushed the young woman's cheeks, almost as if an impropriety had been taken. John's arm instantly withdrew, but the viscount's remained long enough for him to assure himself that his companion was safely settled.

"Oh, thank you," Mary Rose murmured. "I was caught off guard. That's what happens with sleigh rides, isn't it? You can't see everything under the snow and you have these unexpected bounces. I'm fine now, thank you. Not at all shaken, actually."

Inane chatter was so unlike her cousin that Hally regarded her with suspicion. Had the viscount perhaps allowed his arm to dwell a little too long and frightened the girl? Mary Rose was notoriously skittish with men, but Hally had every confidence that a man of Marchwood's address would have no difficulty in allaying her fears. It might, in fact, provide just the sort of challenge his lordship needed.

Certainly it was Marchwood who handed Mary Rose down from the sleigh when they reached their destination. He handed Hally down as well, and Brigid very nearly jumped into his arms when he attempted to gallantly see her to the ground. Amused, he laughed and swung the child around in a wide circle, making Brigid squeak with delight. Mary Rose smiled approvingly at him. Hally felt almost smug.

Lord Marchwood had not, after all, had the opportunity earlier in the day to see Mary Rose in her delightful emerald cloak and bonnet, with her blond curls peeking out. Now he walked with her to the spot where John was already spreading out the hot cider and chocolate. He helped Brigid, Ralph, and Mary Rose to chocolate, while John poured cider for Hally and Marchwood.

John lifted his own cup in a toast. "To the greenery, which will make the Hall smell rich with pine and glow from the holly berries."

"Very poetic," Hally proclaimed, before downing the better part of her cider in a single gulp. This was something of a tradition, too, but she neglected to inform the startled viscount.

John, however, frowned at her. "That's for the men to do, Hally. Not the women."

"I've done it every other year," she protested.

"Yes, well, we're far too indulgent of you."

Hally snorted and picked up a saw. "I can drink you under the table, John."

Which was true enough. For some reason spirits never seemed to have the least effect on her, whereas her brother became slightly foxed with even small amounts. She was not, it was true, in the habit of imbibing, but that was another thing the viscount needn't concern himself with. Let him assume the worst if he chose.

But the viscount apparently assumed nothing. He

walked between her and Mary Rose to the holly bushes where he insisted that the two ladies would not wish to tear their gloves on such sharp leaves. "Let me do the cutting. My gauntlets are old and scarred from driving. One more scratch won't do them a bit of harm."

Hally wouldn't yield the saw. "It's part of the fun," she insisted, reaching into the thick of the prickly leaves and aiming for the base of a branch. "I do it every year. Ouch! See, even Brigid takes a turn."

Not far from them John was indeed allowing Brigid, who had put on his enormous gloves, to hack away at a holly branch. Marchwood took the opportunity to insist that Hally put on his own gauntlets, which were infinitely more protective than her gloves. Not really relishing the pain of continued pricks and scratches, Hally submitted to his request. Marchwood pocketed her gloves with a faintly triumphant air.

Hally drew on his gauntlets, feeling the warmth of his hands still in them. It was a strange sensation. She felt protected and somehow cherished. Looking up into his alert eyes, Hally grudgingly thanked his lordship and returned to her task. But the gesture had made her, surprisingly, feel feminine and fragile. How ridiculous! As though she were a ninnyhammer of a girl. Nothing could be further from the truth.

For the next hour the small troop of gatherers chose the most heavily laden holly branches, and the bushiest greenery to take back to the Hall. Hally watched as Marchwood even climbed a tree to reach a branch Brigid insisted was quite the loveliest they had seen all afternoon. She stood with her heart in her throat as he leaned out to slice at it, and thought that Mary Rose must be quite terrified for him.

Her cousin, she found on turning around, was not

even looking at the viscount, but helping John decide on whether to discard a slightly crushed pine cone. Probably Mary Rose, tender hearted as she was, could not bear to witness such a callous act. Brigid and Ralph and Hally applauded the viscount as he bowed from the tree, then leaped to the ground in front of them, did a somersault and landed on his snow-covered boots.

"By Jupiter, I think he could perform at Astley's," Ralph said, all admiration.

"He was much better than Will Dudly at the fair," Brigid agreed.

Hally walked over to scold the viscount. "You are shamelessly intent on winning them over, aren't you, my lord? An easy victory. They're just children, after all."

He grinned. "But they are your brother and sister. How could I not want to encourage them to like me, any more than I would encourage you, my dear Miss Porchester? Though I do admit that they are a trifle easier to please than you are."

"I'm sure I like you well enough, Lord Marchwood."

"You relieve me. My mother would be disappointed indeed were I to return to Millway Park with the sad news that her namesake held me in the greatest aversion."

Before Hally could respond to this patent attempt to bribe her, her hand was clasped by her brother Ralph, who was the last of the line that Mary Rose led, singing a round as they began to wind themselves in and out through the trees. Well done, Mary Rose, Hally thought, as she allowed the viscount to grasp her hand in turn and bring up the rear of their line. Usually it was she who began the chain, because John, though he would join in, found it somehow too childish to do.

Their voices echoed through the woods as they marched and danced to Mary Rose's leadership, following her every move and tone with an exact mimicry that made Hally laugh with sheer exuberance. When Mary Rose gestured to Lord Marchwood to reverse their direction and become the leader in turn, Hally was surprised at the ease with which he joined in the activity. He had them hopping in the snow and jumping over logs and doing bird calls. She laughed until her sides ached at his attempts at whistling.

"I never could do it," he grumbled, wrinkling his nose at her amusement. "Watch your head now," he instructed as he took her under a low-hanging branch. Her bonnet caught the side of it, and a pile of soft, wet snow landed directly on her neck, causing her to squeal with the shock. "Serves you right," he declared as he made an attempt to brush the icy slush away.

Hally found the closeness of his face disconcerting, and the warmth of his hand on her neck startling. His lips seemed almost close enough to touch hers, but he made no attempt to move away when she protested that she was quite all right. "No, you must let me clear all this snow away. I don't wish you to take a chill."

She could bear his ministrations only for a few moments. Not that he repulsed her. Quite the opposite. She found that his touch sent a decided thrill through her, that the closeness of his lips made her wonder what it would be like to kiss him. Where did such a thought come from? Hally could not remember any such serious consideration in her life, especially when some local lad had attempted to steal a kiss. Ugh! Such clumsy oafs they'd been. Well, it was no wonder she wanted nothing from them.

But Marchwood. Somehow she knew he would not

be the least bit clumsy. That he would, from un-
doubted great experience, know quite how to kiss a lady
so that she knew she was being kissed properly. Hally
shrank back from the viscount, scarcely able to meet
his eyes. "Thank you, sir. I feel not a trace of snow
left upon me."

"Wonderful. Then we shall proceed."

Only then did Hally become aware that the others
had been waiting for them, that John and Mary Rose
and Brigid and Ralph had watched this strange little
interlude. And probably thought not a thing of it, she
assured herself, lifting her head high. "Lead on, Lord
Marchwood," she insisted.

For the better part of the next twenty-four hours she
managed to avoid him. Oh, there was plenty to do,
what with decorating the Hall and going into the village, alone, to see if she could not find the perfect gift
for her father. She had already found something special
for each of her brothers and her sister, but her father,
and Mary Rose, were more difficult to truly please.
Hally had no intention of getting a gift for the viscount.
He was not, after all, one of the family.

The viscount himself had reminded her that they
were to go skating. This happening within Ralph and
Brigid's hearing, there was nothing for it but to accept
his challenge and prepare for an expedition to the pond.
But Hally was in uncertain spirits. She was beginning
to find the viscount intriguing, and she realized that
she rather liked his smile, and the way he seemed to
understand her, and his good-natured acceptance of her
attempts to palm him off on her cousin.

And yet it was Mary Rose who really deserved to
have him. It was her cousin who needed to be married

and away from her large family. It was Mary Rose who had no dowry to speak of. And it was Mary Rose who was the most beautiful girl ever to come out of Hampshire, by almost everyone's accounting. Surely the viscount must have been impressed by Mary Rose's beauty and her truly gentle spirit. Who would not?

So Hally felt a little uncomfortable about the growing interest she was taking in Lord Marchwood. She did not wish to mislead him, for she had no intention of leaving her home to marry him or anyone else. Not that he had asked her! She wanted him in no doubt that Mary Rose was the one whose attentions he should vie for. Mary Rose herself seemed more shy than ever, keeping more to the family than to his lordship's vicinity.

Hally donned her grandmother's old polonaise dress, the one with stiff, billowing skirts, in which she was wont to skate. It was actually quite an attractive dress, blue like her eyes, and the wrap she wore over it matched quite to admiration. Her fur-lined cap and muff were a little too stylish for such an occasion as a skating match, but she wore them nonetheless because they were the warmest things she had for such cold and snowy weather.

Ralph and Brigid were already in the hall waiting for her when she descended. "Did you bring a pair of skates for Lord Marchwood?" she asked, smartly pulling on her gloves.

"John said we could use his," Ralph said, pointing to where John's skates lay on the floor by the winter parlor door. "You know, Hally, John's feet may be a trifle larger than his lordship's. Perhaps we should bring Papa's old skates, too."

"Oh, they'll be quite covered with dust," Brigid protested. "Lord Marchwood shan't mind John's being a little large."

"Shan't I?" The viscount had appeared on the landing of the stairs, looking quite the handsomest man Hally had ever seen in his buckskin breeches and a wine-colored coat. His curly hair crept down over his ears, giving him a youthful look. He regarded his booted feet and frowned. "You don't think your sister is trying to take advantage of me?"

"Never!" Ralph cried. "Hally would not do such a poor-spirited thing. It's all fair and square with her. She doesn't have to play off tricks to win her races."

"I see." The viscount descended the rest of the way and reached down to pick up John's skates. "Perhaps they *will* be a little large, but I shall tie them tightly. Are we all ready? Will Miss Nichols not join us?"

"Mary Rose preferred to stay and finish decorating the saloon with John and Miss Viggan," Hally explained. Her voice made it clear that she considered this something of a betrayal of her plans. "And she doesn't skate herself."

"Well, we will just have to manage without her." Marchwood took one of Brigid's hands. "To the pond, then."

Brigid giggled and led the way, with Ralph and Hally following. Hally reflected that the viscount seemed to have had no difficulty endearing himself to her sister. Even Ralph was coming around after the greenery gathering. Marchwood had proved himself a "right one" in the boy's eyes then, someone who could enter into their conversations and interests with ease. Hally felt almost envious of the children's uncomplicated relationship with him. Her own encounters seemed fraught with danger. And though the path to the pond had become icy and somewhat hazardous, Hally refused Marchwood's offer of support. "I'll be all right," she assured him, with a careless swing of her skates.

One side of the pond was open to the lawns while the other followed the wooded verges of the property. Hally and her siblings had skated there since they were tiny and knew every inch of the water and its banks. Hally sat on a log to one side and tied her skates securely over her half boots. She'd worn the same skates for three years now and had not a qualm about their giving her trouble. Lord Marchwood, on the other hand, found John's skates even larger than he'd expected and had to tie them quite tightly to keep them on.

"You'd best have a run to get the feel of them," Hally suggested. "I don't want you saying you weren't prepared when I beat you."

"Ho!" Marchwood laughed and did indeed glide over the ice, carefully taking stock of the feel of the blades and how he balanced on them. "I think I'll just run once along the course, if you'll show me, Ralph."

Hally swung around in loops and circles while he sped off on his dry run, with Ralph skating beside him. Watching him she acknowledged that he would provide a skating challenge, certainly, but she rather fancied she had a surprise in store for him. He was so overconfident, too sure of his own prowess. Though Hally was very much aware that men did not like to be outmatched by women, she had never lost a race on purpose. She was a female, after all, and could be handily beaten by most of them if taken seriously. Too often her opponents assumed they could win and failed to put forth the necessary effort. Her eyes danced as she watched Marchwood skate back to join her.

He tipped his hat and smiled. "A very fine course you've laid out, Miss Porchester. I especially appreciate the brandy barrels. Aren't they a trifle difficult to negotiate with those skirts of yours?"

"I manage."

"Yes, I imagine you do. Shall we have Ralph count us down?"

Brigid stood by the bank at the end of the course, which wound down along the pond, round not one but three barrels, and back up to a spot close to the beginning. Ralph was declaring what good sport it would be, "For he may not have skated in years, Hally, but he's no bad hand at it either."

"Three, two, one. Go!" he cried, bringing his hand up with a flourish.

Hally knew her best bet was to get ahead of Marchwood from the start and try to maintain her lead. She was accustomed to racing and had set herself to be off like the wind at Ralph's signal. Her skirts swayed dramatically as she raced along, swinging from side to side. She could tell that Marchwood was startled, but he quickly settled down to skate fast and hard after her. The most important part of the race was rounding the barrels, when her skirts did, indeed, give her trouble. If he had caught up to her by then, she would have very little chance.

Coming to the barrels she scarcely slowed at all, still ahead of him by several yards. Her skirts knocked against the first barrel, but swung wide of the second as she wove past it. Marchwood wouldn't be able to pass her at this point unless he planned to knock her down, because her skirts took up so much room that he wouldn't fit between her and the barrel. Hally took advantage of this situation and swept through the last narrow bit to hit the open pond again with a slight advantage over his lordship.

She could hear the hissing of his skates right on her heels and she increased her effort. This was going to be even more challenging than she had thought! But she would not let him win. Not a man who hadn't been on skates for years. And it was more than that, she knew. Somehow if he won this race, it would be like his triumphing over her, without any effort at all. She simply refused to let it happen.

Her heart beat so fast it almost frightened her as she put on a final burst of speed. Brigid was jumping up and down and clapping her hands. Ralph was frankly staring at her. Never had she skated this fast before. She simply *had* to win. But she could feel Marchwood almost at her elbow, coming on strong. And then she was flying past the marker.

"Hally won! Hally won!" Brigid called. "Just barely, but she most certainly won, didn't she, Lord Marchwood?"

With a grimace Marchwood admitted that it was so. Hally could see in his eyes that he had tried to win, but that he too had underestimated her until too late. "Your skates were a little large," she conceded, when she could get a breath to speak. "And I've never skated so well."

He looked down at her, a skeptical light in his eyes. "Haven't you? I wonder why it was so important to beat me."

"I always play to win."

He restored a black wing of her hair to its place under her cap, his finger lingering on her cheek. "So do I, Hally. So do I."

*　　*　　*

After they had dined that evening, Hally suggested a sleigh ride in the moonlight. This was a treat she had promised Mary Rose and it seemed to her that with a little management she could see her cousin bundled under a warm wrap beside Lord Marchwood. In the event, no one was willing to fall in with her schemes.

John objected to her sharing the driving with him. "For you nearly overthrew us in the daylight, Hally, and it's dark now!"

"Nonsense. There's plenty of moonlight," Hally insisted.

But when the sleigh was before them, the viscount brooked no argument. He handed Hally into the back and tucked a rug snugly about her before positioning himself directly beside her, touching from shoulder to hips. Hally remarked that he need not sit so close to her as there was plenty of room on the squabs.

"Yes," he agreed, "but the cold wind will whip between us if we don't present a united front."

The night air was indeed icy, with stars dotting the black sky above and a wind whirling past on the snow and through the spidery branches of the trees overhead. Marchwood shifted his arm to a position along the back of the seat, just lightly resting along her shoulders. Hally gave him a look of suspicion, but made no comment. The viscount remarked that the moon was nearly full, and didn't she find that a delightful circumstance. Hally agreed to it.

John drove sedately down the drive and took a turn across the lawn and around the east woods. The jingling of the bells on the horses' harness and the swishing of the sleigh blades over the snow were the only sounds for some time. No one seemed in a mood to talk, until John guided his team back toward the house and they could see the pinpoints of light in each window. The Hall looked quite enchanted.

"That's how it is at Millway Park," Marchwood said, gesturing toward the tiny lights with his free hand. "My mother's family has done it for eons. But the Park is a Gothic fantasy in itself, and the candles in the windows make it look quite fey. Sometimes, lights seem to appear at spots where there are no windows, and others seem to move where there is no possibility of someone carrying them."

"Really?" Hally bent toward him, her eyes wide. "How do you account for that?"

"The magic of the season," he suggested, his eyes alight. "Miracles happening. Being overcome with wonder."

She could tell that once again he was teasing her. "They don't move at all," she scoffed, leaning back, but only to find that his arm had dropped closer about her shoulders.

"Oh, they do," he assured her. "I imagine your brother Ralph could figure out a way to make lights move where they shouldn't."

"Ralph? Well, I daresay I could do so myself." Hally considered the possibilities. "First I would go up to the attics and lower a lantern on a rope. Then I would swing it back and forth. From a distance it would appear to be moving."

From the other seat Mary Rose's muffled voice asked, "Is that how it was done, my lord?"

"Perhaps. No, no, I am not going to tell you all my secrets, Hally. I want you to consider other possibilities."

Hally grumbled that she would certainly do so, that no Somerset mystery could stump her for long, and that she thought the Hall looked very beautiful. John seconded her opinion, saying, "It's a wonderful idea,

Marchwood. Somehow it makes one remember the true spirit of the holiday."

"It does, doesn't it?" Mary Rose said through the scarf wrapped tightly about her neck and chin. "Like the night sky and the star of Bethlehem over the stable. Like a Christmas spectacle."

Under the cover of Mary Rose chatting away to John about Christmases celebrated at Chalford, Marchwood tightened his arm around Hally's shoulder and murmured, "Are you cold? This icy air is going to get on your neck. I could hold you a little closer, if it wouldn't discompose you."

Here was a challenge if ever she'd been offered one, Hally thought. And as with her skating challenge to him, she must try not to underestimate the viscount. The problem was that she liked his arms around her. She felt very comfortable that way, and rather daring. When she said nothing, he drew her closer to him, so that her head rested against his shoulder and she could feel the warmth of his breath when he spoke.

"Sometimes it's hard to think of making a major change in your life," he said. "More often than not you've got things set up just the way you like them. And yet, life moves on and things never stay the same, Hally. Your brothers will get married and your sister will grow up. Even, sadly, your father one day will be gone. You need to think about the future and what you really want to have for the next twenty years."

"My brothers and sister are still young," Hally murmured against a flapping cape of his greatcoat. "Brigid is only eight. I've been like a mother to her."

"Brigid has Miss Viggan."

"It's not the same!"

"I know. Truly I do. But even she will one day be

a young woman. You wouldn't want to keep her here any more than she would want to keep you."

"I'm the only one who lets her have the freedom she needs. Everyone else is so intent on making her into a proper young lady. Brigid has spirit. I couldn't bear to see it broken."

"It was never broken in you. I see no reason why it should be in Brigid."

Hally sighed. "I was only twelve when my mother died."

"A terribly difficult time for you."

"Oh, what do you know?" Hally twisted restlessly against his shoulder. "I don't know why I'm telling you any of this. It's no concern of yours."

"But it is. I want to know everything there is to know about you, Hally. Because I think you're a very special person." He ran a finger along her cheek, tracing its shape down to her chin.

Hally swallowed nervously. Even in the dim light she could see a question in his eyes. He was going to kiss her, right there in the sleigh, with John and Mary Rose laughing merrily on the seat in front of them. Unless she stopped him. Unless she turned her head aside or held up a restraining hand. She did neither of those things.

His lips were cold from the night air, and yet they seemed warm, too. A shiver ran through her and he held her more tightly against him. And then, all too soon, he drew back slightly, studying her. "Perhaps next time you'll kiss me back," he whispered, smiling languidly.

Unable to speak, she turned her head once again into his shoulder. What was happening here? Either he was courting her or treating her quite cavalierly, and she could not believe the latter. But why would he wish to marry her? He hardly knew her. She was not beautiful and pretty-behaved like Mary Rose. She was not a brilliant match in any respect. And she had let him put his arm around her and pull her to him and . . . kiss her. What would he think of her now? Probably he had gotten quite the wrong impression.

The sleigh was closer to the house now, and the light of the candles danced as they glided over the snow. Hally watched silently until they drew near the stables. Then she straightened against the squabs and said to Marchwood, "There has been one good thing come from your visit, then—a new Christmas tradition. I shall see that it is carried out every year," she added, somewhat defiantly.

"Wherever you are," the viscount suggested, giving her shoulders a slight squeeze.

"I shall be right here," she retorted.

The next morning Hally lay in bed longer than usual. Though she had slept perfectly well, she had awakened with a thousand thoughts in her mind, and all of them seemed to do with Marchwood. Quite vividly she remembered his lips on hers, gentle and undemanding. What did he mean by her kissing him back? It seemed a very bold thing to do, and surely one that would indicate that she had some affection for him.

Well, she did have some affection for him. In spite of her very strong will to be indifferent, she found herself decidedly attracted to him. She liked the way he talked, the way he smiled, even the way he treated her—with that odd little sparkle in his eyes that was not the amusement she had at first suspected but something else—as if he was conspiring with her. Almost as if he knew her and cherished her. Which was a great deal of nonsense, after all, since he had only arrived a few days previously.

But Hally could feel her heart beat a little faster at

the thought of seeing him at breakfast. She was suspicious of this symptom, however. Maybe that's what he wanted, for her to fall in love with him. It could very well be that he had responded to the challenge she'd laid down by indicating she had no intention of falling in love or marrying. His pride might have insisted that he wrap her round his finger before he left Porchester Hall. Some men were like that, she knew.

How was she to know what kind of man Marchwood was? Everything he had done and said so far could be playacting, or unfeelingly falling in line with his mother's desire for him to attach himself to her. Why, after all, would a man of Marchwood's address show up in Hampshire to court a woman he had never met? There was something decidedly suspicious about that. According to John he could have his pick of the ladies of *ton* in London. So why hadn't he?

Confused, Hally climbed out of bed and allowed her abigail to assist her into her most attractive day dress. And what if Mary Rose was already particularly taken with the viscount?—Mary Rose with her exquisite face and blond locks and sweet manner. She deserved someone like Marchwood. Hally could not conceive of someone preferring her own Irish milkmaid looks and hoydenish manner. When her abigail suggested a slightly more modish hairstyle for the day, with her black hair swept back to a loose knot and tendrils framing her face, Hally sighed and agreed.

Mary Rose was the first to comment on this change. She had just lifted a piece of toast, but put it back down, exclaiming, "Why, how charming you look, Hally! Such a becoming way of doing your hair."

Naturally the rest of the family, and Marchwood, turned to regard her. John and Marchwood rose to bow.

Hally felt a blush rise to her cheeks. "Millie suggested it," she mumbled, helping herself from the platters on the sideboard.

Sir Thomas, whose legs had been particularly painful the last day, remained seated and excused himself for the discourtesy. "I think Millie has been studying *La Belle Assemblée*," he teased. "Mary Rose is quite right, my dear. You look charming."

Hally thanked him and allowed Marchwood to hold her chair for her. She was not able to look him in the eye, but muttered her thanks and immediately began to eat her breakfast. The talk that she had interrupted gradually revived around her, and she heard Marchwood tell of his plans to drive his curricle into the village. "And I had hoped you'd come with me, Hally," he said. "Perhaps you have some shopping left to do."

It was the first time he'd called her Hally in front of her family, and she could see John's brows rise. Brigid giggled but Ralph frowned slightly. The baronet's smile was kindly but a bit absent. "Won't the snow be a problem?" she asked, stalling.

"My pair are accustomed to it. I could use your help with some purchases I have in mind."

There was a determined light in his eyes that Hally could not ignore. "Very well. Right after breakfast would be best for me." She did, certainly, have household duties but nothing that could not be delayed for a few hours. And she wanted to see some of this famed driving ability of his.

Which was immediately apparent when he brought round his curricle from the stables. If Hally had known there was a pair of matched bays of that distinction in the Porchester stables, she would have paid them a visit before this. Their spirits were high enough to require a firm and experienced hand. But they were glorious! Watching from the stairs as Marchwood brought them under control was spectacle indeed. His lips twisted quizzically as a footman handed her into the curricle.

"They're a bit fresh! My own fault, of course, for not taking them out yesterday. I had intended to, but other matters claimed my attention. You won't be too alarmed, will you?"

Hally, allowing him to tuck the rug around her, assured him that she wouldn't. And neither was she, though all things considered it might have been wise. The lane was icy from an overnight freeze, and the horses occasionally slid. But Marchwood kept a steady hand on them, and by the time they reached the main road the traveling was easier. Marchwood gave the bays a little more room and their gait stretched out to a remarkable smoothness.

"I'd like to shake them out a little. Show me a more circuitous route than this, would you?" he asked.

She would have been willing to drive with him for hours. There was something about his competence as a whip that thrilled her. His spirited horses gave him no trouble, even once when they passed another carriage that was taking up far more than its share of the road. She could only guess the strength in his hands and arms that held the bays steady even as they attempted to shy from the approaching vehicle. A lesser whip would have had them in a ditch, no doubt about it. Hally wished her brother John could have seen Marchwood's feat.

But the viscount seemed hardly to notice as he kept up a stream of questions about the neighborhood. Within the span of half an hour she had pointed out all their neighbors' homes and her favorite summer rides and the spot where foxes invariably went to ground.

Eventually they ended up in the village, where there were not really more than half a dozen shops, and only two of those a place where they might find the gifts Marchwood was intent on buying for her siblings.

She led the way into a general mercantile business where bolts of cloth were heaped high on shelves from front to back of the room. There were also bonnets and muffs and gloves and ribbons and a variety of trims. Marchwood paused in front of the bonnets, reaching one down from its stand and turning it from side to side. "For Brigid," he explained.

"It's a little grown-up for her," Hally protested.

"That's why she'll like it," he rejoined. "Show me what it looks like on."

He placed the bonnet of white watered *gros de Naples* on her head. Hally knew Brigid would love the turned-up brim and the ornamental band of blue tufted gauze. Mrs. Windom, the shopkeeper, came over to point out unnecessarily that the *gros de Naples* at top and bottom was cut in the form of leaves, with a bunch of the leaves and a bouquet of marguerites placed on one side of the crown. Marchwood tied the white satin ribbons in a full bow on the left, as Mrs. Windom instructed him.

"Very fetching." He turned to Mrs. Windom to say, "It's not actually for Miss Porchester, but for her sister Brigid. Just the sort of thing she shouldn't wear for another few years, don't you agree?"

"Oh, decidedly." Mrs. Windom smiled. "And if you purchase it for her, you will win her heart forever."

"Just so. I shall take it."

Hally shook her head in mock disapproval as she removed the confection, but she was charmed. He did seem to have an understanding of people that impressed her. And when he took her next to the almost hidden section of books Mrs. Windom kept at the back of her store and ran his finger along the titles, she knew he was looking for something in particular. At length he shook his head. "Well, I don't suppose I should have expected to find it in a village," he said as he straightened up. "How far is it to Winchester?"

"Much too far to go in a morning."

Mrs. Windom asked if she might know what book it was his lordship was seeking. When he had given her the name and author, she excused herself to look through a ledger she kept with her accounting materials. Smiling rather delightedly, she came back and pointed to the entry. "I got it for James Bilbury just a month ago. If you wouldn't mind its having been read already, I daresay I could cozen him into parting with it on the promise of another copy. I could have it sent up to the Hall."

Marchwood agreed to it, explaining to Hally that he most particularly wished to give the book to Ralph. "Because it's all about going away to school and the mischief they get up to there. The author describes cricket matches and hockey games and football matches. Ralph would find it very enlightening, I think."

Hally felt that peculiar palpitation in her heart that was becoming more familiar to her. She hadn't expected someone like Marchwood. She wasn't aware that people like Marchwood existed, handsome and funny and thoughtful and interesting. Surely he was too good to be true. He would either disappear in a puff of smoke or turn out to be a highwayman.

"Did you wish to look for something for John or Papa?" she asked through a constricted throat.

"No. I brought their gifts with me." *And yours,* his eyes seemed to say.

Hally's eyes dropped before his. There was still time to get him a gift, of course, but she wouldn't be rushed into it. It made no sense to get him something meaningless, and she could not for the life of her consider getting him something important. "Then let me stop at the butcher for the veal cutlets for cook, and we'll head back to the Hall."

He tucked her hand through his arm. "It's all right, Hally. I don't expect a gift from you."

"I should think not!"

The saloon was a fairyland of twinkling candles, silver paper bells and bright red holly berries nestled on prickly green leaves. Swags of evergreen boughs hung everywhere and the room was redolent with their scent. Marchwood had insisted that this was the perfect time for them to learn the waltz. Miss Viggan, who had settled Sir Thomas comfortably in a chair by the fire, agreed to play the pianoforte, and John reluctantly assented to make the fourth in their group.

"Mary Rose is a superb dancer," Hally pointed out to the viscount when he approached her. "She will learn the waltz a great deal easier than I. John and I will watch and attempt to copy what you do."

Marchwood regarded her with his usual good humor and presented himself to her cousin, who shyly allowed him to take her in his arms. They glided effortlessly about the room; Mary Rose seemed to follow with no difficulty. Hally could hear Marchwood talking with his partner with his usual ease.

John was a stiff dancer, and when he realized that he was being asked to take his sister in the next best thing to an embrace, he was properly shocked. "No wonder they don't do it at the Winchester assembly," he grumbled.

Hally laughed. "Don't be so stodgy, John. It's quite like skating, actually."

"Indeed it is," Marchwood agreed as he and Mary Rose passed by.

John was watching the other couple and his foot tangled with the base of a plant stand. "I'm no good at this," he declared, moving toward the side of the room. "You and Marchwood have a go at it, Hally. He's the expert, and you'll not learn how to do it properly with me as your partner."

Mary Rose instantly offered to watch with John. Marchwood opened his arms to Hally, who reluctantly came to him, placing her hand in his. Marchwood said, "Look at my eyes, Hally. Let me guide you just by my touch and the music."

Hally, who had been trying to puzzle out just where they were to move next, as one might in a country dance, regarded him with skepticism. "I'll fall flat on my face."

"No. I wouldn't let that happen, my dear. Trust me." He hummed the tune in her ear and swung her around the floor in flowing circles. Hally moved like a skater now, grasping the essence of the dance, and bringing her own special zest to it.

"I want you to call me Frederick," he said.

"Why?"

"Because I've asked you to, of course. And because you haven't objected to my calling you Hally. Hally suits you."

John and Mary Rose had begun to dance on the opposite side of the room and Hally gave a *tsk* of annoyance. "Now why will he listen to her and loosen up when he was stiff as a poker dancing with me? You know, John didn't seem at all keen on my inviting Mary Rose for the holidays, but he gets along swimmingly with her."

Marchwood regarded her curiously. "Yes, I've noticed that myself."

"I suppose you've also noticed that Mary Rose is the most beautiful girl. And so very ladylike, don't you think? Her family, though astonishingly large, is quite respectable. My father could tell you anything you wanted to know about her family."

"I know everything I need to know about Miss Nichols's family."

"Are you going to call her Mary Rose?"

"No."

Hally was actually relieved to hear him say it. The time had long since passed when she really wanted Marchwood to be interested in her cousin. She said, rather diffidently, "Did it bother you that I won the race, Lor . . . Frederick?"

He smiled. "Very good. No, but I think I deserve a rematch."

"Oh, I never give rematches," she said airily.

"I'm not surprised. You wouldn't win another time, would you?"

"Not against you," she admitted. "I probably wouldn't have won the first time if John's skates hadn't been so large for you."

"Well, you're hampered by your skirts, so it was an even handicap. Only next time I wouldn't underestimate you."

Hally kept her eyes locked on the neat folds of his neckcloth. "Did it shock you, being raced against by a woman?"

He considered this seriously for a moment. "Not particularly. I like you just the way you are, Hally. Dancing, skating, sleighing, singing. Your vitality is infectious. I don't know any other young woman who could bring such exuberance to her pursuits."

Hally frowned. "From what I hear, London ladies are very stiff and proper. Which sounds very boring, but I imagine you would require that kind of behavior from someone of interest to you. Such as a sister," she hastened to add. "Otherwise she would be looked at askance and considered a hoyden, wouldn't she?"

"Probably."

"Well, that is how it would be with me. I would be considered a hoyden in town."

"I imagine you're considered a hoyden in the country," he retorted.

"Well, and if I am, so what? My family accepts me. This is the person I am. I don't want to change."

"No, but you will as you get older, Hally. It's inevitable."

"I'll never be suitably refined for a London drawing room, Frederick."

"Perhaps I should be the judge of that."

He had continued to guide her effortlessly over the floor. When Miss Viggan appeared about to pause at the end of the waltz, Hally caught Marchwood's entreating glance at the governess, and Miss Viggan, being a very perceptive woman, had straightened her narrow back and started in again at the beginning. Marchwood returned his attention to Hally, a slight frown pulling his brows together.

"I understand what you're saying, Hally. You think London society would be too restrictive for you. But London is an exciting place: the sights and the theater and the opera and all manner of other activities to catch your attention."

"It simply wouldn't do," Hally said, with regret in her voice. "I would get restless and shock everyone by riding through Hyde Park at a gallop."

"You underestimate my resourcefulness in keeping you distracted, Hally." She flushed, but Marchwood continued, "I do not envision spending the rest of my life with a woman whose every thought is of balls and gowns and receiving morning callers. I want someone out of the ordinary, a wife with a mind of her own, even if she does sometimes offend the finer sensibilities of the *ton*. Someone bright and vivacious and dashing. Someone like you, Hally."

"Oh," she cried, "but you hardly know me, Frederick! You cannot realize what you are saying."

"But I do." He drew her closer. "I've known you for a very long time. Let me show you something."

With very little commotion he guided her to the pianoforte, thanked Miss Viggan for her playing, explained to Sir Thomas that he wished to show Hally something in the library, and drew her away from the saloon. Hally followed him, curious but with great trepidation. He really was talking about marrying her and taking her away with him. She could scarcely bring herself to consider the implications of this. When he left her alone in the library after starting the fire and lighting a branch of candles, her heart was beating so quickly she had to calm herself with words of sternest good sense.

When he returned, he was carrying a very small case that he set on the oak table. "My mother had this done when she visited here years ago. You were ten at the time."

From the box he drew a miniature Hally had never seen before. It was a picture of herself astride her favorite pony, McDougall, flying over a small hedge. Her black hair streamed behind her and her cheeks glowed with excitement.

"My mother kept it in her dressing room, and she would tell me tales about you. She used to say, 'Oh, Frederick, you would have had such adventures with her had you been there.' Apparently all in the space of a month you managed to get lost in a cave, find three stray kittens, scare your brother John by pretending to be the ghost of a former resident of the Hall, build a secret fort in the woods that you took her to see, race every boy who would accept your challenge, and insist on going pigeon shooting with your Papa."

Hally smiled reminiscently. "They were wonderful times."

"They sounded wonderful to me, too, growing up alone in that huge house at Millway Park. I envied you your brothers and your cousins and all the companionship that I missed so much. Your family sounded so warm and happy and special. And you, you sounded like the most delightful free spirit, so unconventional and so full of boundless energy. I've wanted to meet you for years."

"You could have come any time."

He brushed a lock of the raven hair back from her face. "But I'd built up a boy's fantasy. Coming here was likely to be such a rude shock."

She swallowed against the lump in her throat. "And wasn't it?"

"You know it wasn't."

His voice, soft as a caress, reached her through her growing panic. Hally was trying to keep her mind clear but his nearness was undermining her resolve. She believed him, how could she help but believe him? "But,

Frederick, we aren't children anymore. You can't have the kind of childhood I had."

"No, but together we could give it to our children."

When his lips came to meet hers, Hally felt excitement race through her body. This time she had no hesitation in kissing him back. In fact, she would have been quite incapable of restraining her natural urge to indulge fully in the experience. The thrill she felt was so overwhelming that it almost frightened her. Every sense seemed alive to his influence, his lips against hers, his arms around her body. Nothing had prepared her for the total involvement she felt. And it alarmed her into drawing back from his hold.

Marchwood studied her face in the candlelight. "I think perhaps your papa would wonder at our staying here any longer, my dear. Would you like to join the others in the saloon for tea?"

"Yes, please," she said, shaken. "I need time to think."

The next morning Marchwood had allowed Hally to take the reins of his spirited bays once he had seen them past their freshness. He had not pressed her about other matters, and she had been grateful. Because it all seemed so new to her, so impossible that this could be happening. And yet it was. Alice Halliston Porchester, who had never given a serious thought to marriage or the possibilities of finding a man to her liking, had fallen head over ears in love with this curly haired, provocative, laughing stranger.

It was possible that he was deluding himself about her, she reminded herself. That he had built up an image which she didn't really fit and that she should warn him away from. But she had tried, hadn't she? She had offered him Mary Rose, the dearest, prettiest woman in Hampshire—and Marchwood would have none of her. Was it possible that he wanted Hally herself in all her imperfection, in all her boisterous exuberance?

She remembered the previous evening and the way he'd looked at her, the way his voice had caressed her and the way his lips had roused her. Nothing had prepared her for someone like Marchwood. Nothing had prepared her for falling in love.

Marchwood had invited Hally to drive with him to church on Christmas eve in his curricle. All day she tried to sort things out in her head, but all she could do was look forward to sitting beside him, to the time they would spend alone together. Surely she would know what to say to him then, to let him know how full her heart was. Even if she couldn't marry him.

The snow had melted down to a last few patches here and there, and the rest of the family drove in the family barouche. But now, as Marchwood and Hally drove home, he made a point of allowing the barouche to pass them, and urged his bays to their least energetic efforts. As though even a walk were too much, after a while, when they had come far enough up the drive to see all the candles in the windows, Marchwood drew his team to a stop.

"I think it would be best for me to offer you my present now, Hally, so that you will feel the greatest freedom in answering me as you wish." He drew a jeweler's box from the pocket of his greatcoat and opened it to show her the diamond-and-sapphire ring inside. "It's a family heirloom. My mother wished you to have it, as a keepsake, no matter how you felt about me. But I wish to accompany it with an offer of marriage. I have fallen desperately in love with you, my heart, and nothing will do but to have you as my bride. If you could see your way clear to have me, that is."

All Hally's intentions otherwise seemed suddenly to have melted away with the vanishing snow. She could think of nothing but the bursting love for him which filled her heart. Hally allowed him to slip the sparkling ring on her finger. Her eyes rose to his and her hand came up to touch his cheek. "Oh, I do love you, Frederick. And I would be honored to be your wife."

The viscount, grinning outrageously, crushed her against his chest. Then he tilted her face up to his and brought his lips down to meet hers. Again the most luscious of sensations raced through her body, tingling all the way from her head to her toes. He tasted of fresh cold air and the warmth of love and the excitement of sensuality. Hally's response was rich with her newfound appreciation of this delightful form of expression. She had never realized what piquancy, what vitality, what desire there could be in a simple meeting of lips. She discovered that a kiss could make one wish for a great deal more . . .

At length, disheveled and deliriously happy, she was brought to her senses by the jolting of the carriage. Marchwood had lost control of the horses in his distraction and he now laughed and drew them to a halt again. Hally, trying once more to bring some reason to her life, said, "But think, Frederick! There is still Brigid to be taken into account. And my father, and John, and Ralph. I know they can manage without me, but I do make their lives more comfortable."

"So you do." He pressed her fingers to his lips. "Well, let us dispose of these matters in an orderly fashion. Brigid, I think, must come to us part of the year, with Miss Viggan. You will keep her from becoming stuffy and proper, I trust. And your father could come as well, though I think we would do better to visit him here, as he is most comfortable in his own home. Seeing you settled would please him more than anything. Now, John. There I believe you have been missing the drama that has been going on beneath your nose."

"I don't understand."

"Well, there may be no proper understanding yet, but if my eyes do not deceive me, John and Mary Rose are intent on making a match of it. John may be a little young as yet, but . . ."

"John and Mary Rose!" Hally looked back over the past week and realized that she had indeed been blind to their courtship, being far too busy with her own. "Well, my word. The Nichols probably will put no rub in the way, though Mary Rose could do a great deal better, I dare say."

"How unflattering of you to say so!" Marchwood laughed and drew her into the circle of his arms. "And I think I have Ralph convinced that school would be just the place for him." He cocked his head at her. "Have I covered everything?"

Hally sighed and snuggled closer. "If you please, tell me again that you love me."

"I will be happy to tell you every day for the rest of your life," he promised.

Hally sighed. "Before you came, I thought things would go on the way they were forever. That nothing would change, and that I would be quite content. How is it possible that everything has changed, and yet I'm happier than I have ever been?"

"As I am," he agreed. Then he motioned toward the Hall with its dancing candlelight and said, "Perhaps it's the season, my love. The season of miracles."

The
Christmas Mouse
by
Emily Hendrickson

AMANDA peeped out of her window, drawing the sheer curtains back just enough so she might see without being observed. A sense of peace crept over her while she watched the traveling coach disappear down the avenue to the main road. Outriders surrounded the elegant equipage. The coachman, resplendent in his many-caped driving coat with a bunch of Christmas greens tucked into his buttonhole, grandly tooled along in high gig. The children had waved for a few moments until hauled inside the coach by an indignant Margaret.

Amanda touched her throat in a gesture of guilt.

"Oh, but I am a wicked woman—lying to my brother and dear, dear Margaret," Amanda murmured, genuinely distressed. But truly, had she been compelled to travel with them and spend her holiday once again cooped up with the children at the top of some great house while all the other adults enjoyed the festivities below, she would have gone mad. Even the nannies and the other governesses celebrated belowstairs. But shy, diminutive Amanda, belonging to neither group, was left out. She simply could not bear it once more.

"I do not know where I found the courage to tell them such a tarradiddle. Fancy!" Amanda thought as she shook her head in bemusement. "Margaret grew most alarmed at the mere thought of my having an infectious cold. It would never do for her to be required to nurse her four darlings." She recognized this without malice, for Amanda quite understood her sister-in-law and her sensitive nerves.

That the eldest of those darlings was as tall as his aunt and terrorized her daily was beside the point. No nanny or governess occupied the nursery suite, for with Amanda in residence, why go to such expense? So Margaret had taken a nursemaid along to handle the four Barkley offspring, resolved to make the best of things rather than cancel what promised to be a delightful holiday. She never allowed consideration for her young sister-in-law to intrude on her plans in the least.

Amanda let the curtain drop from her chilled hands. She rubbed them together, wishing she might have a bit of a fire in her room. There was precious little heat allowed on the top floor, and it made winters exceedingly nasty to endure.

Then realization hit her. With those insufferable children gone, she, dear George's young and willing-to-serve sister—the mousy girl who had never "taken" during her appalling Season in London—would be able to enjoy a roaring fire in the library with none to say her nay! The very thought of it made her heady with anticipation.

She slipped quietly from the small and sparsely furnished bedroom at the top of the house, where Margaret had felt it best for her to reside these past years since the death of her parents—so that Amanda might be close to the children—and tiptoed down the three flights of stairs until she reached the ground floor. Here she espied George's stuffy butler.

"I should like my nuncheon brought to me in the library, Leeson. I shall spend the day in there." Her brave words faltered at the narrow look from Leeson, who knew perfectly well that Amanda had informed the Viscount and Lady Rosling that with a dreadful cold it was impossible for Amanda to join the traveling party. It might be expected that Amanda would take to her bed, but certainly not to occupy the library. Leeson barely nodded in reply.

With a defiance Amanda hadn't known she possessed, she tilted her pretty little nose and marched to the library, all the while quaking in her sensible half boots of dull brown morocco. Perhaps if she assumed her instructions would be followed, someone might actually bring her food.

A proper, spinsterish cap—one created for her by Margaret—sat correctly atop soft ash brown hair that was swept into a tidy bun at the nape of her neck. The muslin cap—with no frills or lace to soften it—was neatly tied beneath her chin in a no-nonsense bow. Her dull gray dress primly covered her ankles—which were delightfully trim if one managed to catch a glimpse of them.

After adding some more wood and nudging a log or two, Amanda settled into a leather chair by the deliciously roaring fire, her dark brown eyes lit in anticipation of her splendid treat. George had occupied the room earlier, writing orders for his steward to follow during the family's absence. He always enjoyed a good fire, as did Margaret. Amanda would have as well, had she the opportunity to sit with them of an evening.

Instead, piles of mending found their way to her little bedroom. Amanda often huddled beneath her coverlet while straining to see her stitches. She prided herself on her excellent needlework, even if it was tablecloths and linens for the most part rather than pretty gowns or perhaps infant dresses for a babe of her own.

She sighed with regret that she could not be more forceful, make her wishes known to her brother. But then, he would think her silly to be dreaming of a tiny house all her own, where she might be a spinster with cats by her side and flowers in the summer.

Oh, what wicked sinfulness, to be actually *sitting* in the morning with nothing more contemplated than enjoying the latest novel Margaret had ordered from London. A rather feline smile crept over Amanda's sweet face.

Some hours later, when her stomach protested the scantiness of the toast and tea she had consumed early that morning before her courageous declaration, the library door creaked open. The youngest of the housemaids, little Fanny, entered bearing a tray.

"If you please, Miss Barkley, your nuncheon as you asked." Fanny set the tray on a small table near the chair where Amanda had curled up, utterly lost in the tale spun by a Miss Austen.

"Oh, my! Fanny! How you startled me." Amanda placed her novel aside, then inspected the tray. How dismaying to see a bowl of gruel, a wafer of bread with butter, and weak tea. "This is not quite what I anticipated," she murmured.

Fanny heard her clearly, for the girl had remained close by as though waiting for some reaction. Unruly brown curls escaped from beneath her mobcap to frame a too-thin face, the dominant feature of which was a pair of enormous pale brown eyes. She pleated the apron covering her neat print dress with nervous fingers.

"Cook said seein' as how you were not fit enough to go with Lady Rosling, you could scarcely expect a decent meal. I fear 'tis what you are likely to get, Miss Barkley," the girl announced in a soft, hesitant voice.

"This will never do," Amanda said firmly. She found it was not at all difficult to talk to Fanny. The girl seemed as timid as Amanda, sort of a kindred soul as it were.

Most of the servants in this household looked down on Amanda, she knew, making their opinion of the young woman who so quietly slaved for her brother and his wife quite clear. Fanny was the only one who seemed to view Amanda with something like compassion, and for that Amanda softened her normal reserve.

"Tell me, do you think you might manage to bring me something else? And you may toss this to the pigs, if you please." Taking an audacious breath, Amanda gestured to the tray of despised food.

"Oh, miss, I dunno. I kin try," Fanny replied with equal daring.

Two pairs of eyes met, recalling how Cook ruled her kitchen with an iron hand. Poor little Fanny would be risking her job to attempt such a request.

Amanda could not ask her to do such a thing. With a resigned sigh, she said quietly, "Never mind. I find this will do after all." She picked up a spoon to sample the detested gruel, finding it worse than expected. She barely repressed a shudder of revulsion.

"I'm that sorry, miss," Fanny apologized in her little voice, looking quite as though she was about to burst into tears.

"It is not your fault, my girl," Amanda said with equal quiet. "Perhaps you might sneak a few lemon biscuits with a pot of tea shortly. Tell Cook I am all admiration for her thoughtfulness, but I crave a taste of lemon."

Fanny nodded, her eyes wide with unaccustomed spirit as she contemplated the cook's reaction. "That I will, miss," she declared before marching timidly from the room.

Pushing aside the wretched gruel, Amanda concentrated on the bread and butter while hoping that more tea and those lemon biscuits could be hers before too long. Actually, the bread and butter was not too far from her customary fare, although they were her usual supper instead of a noon meal.

The three boys and little Emma were given bread and butter with their porridge and tea in the morning. They had roast meat, potatoes, followed by some sort of pudding about one o'clock. Late afternoon saw the bread and butter with tea again. Amanda sighed at the thought of wickedly rich puddings and sauces, veal fricassee and turbot, with a nice roast duck occasionally. Vegetables and fruit would be most welcome with her meals. These things were deemed unnecessary for the children—and so, of course, for Amanda.

Her mouth watered at the mere thought of such a repast. Somehow she suspected that the servants would dine better than she did in the ensuing days. If only she had the courage to demand better food.

A timid scratching on the door was followed by an equally timid Fanny. She clutched a tray in her hands, looking fearful. Did she expect Cook to barge into the library demanding the return of a few biscuits?

"Your tea and lemon biscuits, miss. And a nice juicy apple as well," Fanny declared with triumph.

"How utterly wonderful," Amanda replied with heartfelt gratitude. Here she had been wishing for fruit, and it magically appeared . . . via Fanny, of course. Why, perhaps she might wish for something else and have it materialize as well! Then Amanda smiled at her foolishness.

The ever-lurking desire for a tiny cottage of her own—where she might be mistress and not the helper—surfaced only to be tucked away for later dreaming.

"Tell me, Fanny, are you happy here?"

"Happy, miss? Lawks, I dunno. I suppose so. I've a bed to sleep in and food to eat and work aplenty. Figure that I best content myself with that." The maid shot a curious look at Amanda, as though wondering what had prompted such a peculiar question.

"I see what you mean," Amanda said reflectively, reluctant to let Fanny return to her duties. "I imagine I had better satisfy my longings the same way."

"Longings, miss?" Fanny queried before she recalled she ought not embark on a conversation with her employer's sister, even if she was treated like help.

"Oh yes. I should dearly love a little house of my own . . . one with a thatched roof and a cat by the hearth, flowers in the summer, and a roaring fire come winter." She stared at the present fire for a moment before recalling the impropriety of her chat with the maid.

"Begging your pardon, miss, but I think there should be a fine gentleman in that picture you paint so pretty."

"Not for me, Fanny," Amanda replied with a shy smile. "I would expire at the very thought of talking to an ordinary man, much less a fine gentleman. You see," she confided, "when I went to London for my Season, I didn't take. I could have been invisible, for all I was noticed."

"Dressed in white, no doubt," Fanny added, wise to the ways of the gentry.

"True. I must have looked dreadfully insipid. Margaret insisted I wear my hair as it is now, only without this sort of cap. I did not like what I saw in my mirror, but I lack the spirit to demand my own way, you see."

"You ought to have soft-like curls about your face," Fanny said suddenly, tilting her head to study Amanda with disconcerting intensity. "And you ought to wear blues and greens to look nice with that pretty skin you have. Looks just like the cream that comes from the dairy, it does." Then Fanny blushed when she realized how forward she'd been.

"That is very kind of you to say, my dear girl," Amanda said amiably. It might be improper for Fanny to be so daring, but thoughtful compliments rarely came Amanda's way. They were to be cherished, not scolded about.

Fanny was about to depart when the door opened without warning and Leeson stood there, staring at the tableau by the fireplace. When the maid backed away as though to take her leave, Amanda lifted a hand to stop her. She'd not have Fanny punished for being kind.

"What is it, Leeson?"

"There is a person to see you, Miss Barkley," he intoned in that dreadfully starched-up manner he had.

"To see me! But, whoever might that be?" she wondered aloud to Fanny.

"The fine gentleman," whispered the maid with spirit.

"Rubbish," Amanda replied with a chuckle. Nonetheless, she left the security of the library to venture into the hall with some trepidation. The hall was drafty, making Amanda wish she had dared to tell Leeson to bring the person to her. But years of bustling to do the bidding of others had conditioned her. She went, rather than summoned.

The person proved to be a well-garbed servant dressed in gray livery trimmed in wine with pewter buttons down the front. He bowed, then presented a large letter to Amanda, saying, "I shall await your orders, miss."

Absently instructing an inquisitive Leeson to see to the comfort of the servant, Amanda wandered back to the library, her curiosity aflame. What could someone have sent her? Someone, moreover, who had a liveried servant?

Settling on the leather chair once again, she took a deep breath while examining the outside of the letter. No clue, other than her name and direction. The spidery handwriting looked to be that of a clerk.

With her heart pounding wildly, Amanda broke open the seal, then unfolded the missive. What could it be?

Her dark eyes grew wide with amazement as she skimmed over the contents once, then reread with greater care each word of the incredible letter.

"Dear Miss Barkley," the letter went. "It is my great pleasure to inform you that you are sole heir to the estate of Mr. Andrew Prewbody." Amanda suspected the estate was modest. How could it be otherwise? What man would leave a vast estate to a woman? She continued to study the letter, concentrating on the sentences she found intriguing.

"Mr. Prewbody—in the event you are unaware of the connection—was a dear friend of your father, meeting with him every year until your father's death. Mr. Prewbody, having no immediate heirs, decided to leave his property to the girl of whom he had heard so much over the years." She wondered precisely what her dear papa had said.

"I respectfully urge you to assume control of your inheritance at your earliest convenience. I shall meet with you before long, should you accept this estate, to discuss the details. Should you wish to return with Jervis, the bearer of this missive, you are at liberty to do so. He has a sum of money for you sufficient to cover expenses you might incur on your trip." The momentous letter concluded, "Respectfully, Osbert Rushbury."

After the third reading, she held the letter to her bosom, hope rushing madly to her heart. A house! She had been given a house to have for her very own. Her long-held wish had been granted!

The letter did not specify when she must go, but urged speed. She really ought to consult George and Margaret. They stood in lieu of parents to her. After all, she was only one and twenty. They were older, wiser.

Yet, why should she? she argued. She held the letter away, to study it again. There was the sum of money available for her to use as necessary. If she waited to discuss the inheritance with George and Margaret, she sensed they would declare the entire scheme improper. They'd likely convince Amanda to sell the house, never to know what it might be like to enjoy a life of her own.

Could she? Dare she? She could have a cat!

She hurriedly rose and crossed to the hall, going to look out of one of the front windows. There stood an elegant carriage that put George's to shame. It appeared to be the latest in style and comfort from what she could tell at this distance. Well sprung, polished to a fare-thee-well, it waited for her to flee. Horses stamped impatiently, eager to be on their way.

Flee? Where had that word come from, pray tell?

Amanda returned to the library where Fanny still stood, her curiosity getting the better of the knowledge that she might well be punished for being absent from her duties so long.

"I have inherited a house, Fanny," Amanda said quietly, but with an inner elation that no one could fail to see. Her dark eyes gleamed with excitement.

"Oh, miss. What will you do?"

"I am going to pack my things and depart at once," Amanda declared with great daring. Oh, she was wicked, but the lure of a place of her own overcame all thoughts of propriety.

"Will ye?" the girl asked, seeming to sense that Amanda needed someone to talk to about this momentous decision.

"Well, I have little enough to pack. That would be simple to do. The thing of the matter is . . . *can* I do such a thing?" still wavering a bit, her dark brown gaze sought the pale amber stare of the thin little maid.

"I dunno. Seems like you might, seeing as how you

were a-wanting such a house for a long time and all," Fanny asserted with spirit.

"What would George and Margaret, that is, Lord and Lady Rosling, say? It would be wrong of me to take off like this without a proper consultation with them." Amanda held the stiff parchment to her, reluctant to so much as put it down lest it evaporate like a dream upon wakening.

With great daring Fanny said, "Her what puts you in a poky little room at the top of the house to work for her like a servant when you are his lordship's sister? She'd most likely find some way to stop you from going, miss. After all, she'd have to hire a governess to take your place, she would." Then Fanny compressed her lips as the realization of what she'd uttered appeared to hit her.

Fanny was right, Amanda acknowledged. The little housemaid knew whereof she spoke. It might be difficult to face, but the admission that Amanda was nothing more than an unpaid governess to children who utterly terrified her could not be denied. William threatened to outgrow Amanda soon, with James and Giles not far behind. Little Emma followed her brothers example and teased Amanda unmercifully. They were spiteful, mean children try as she might to love them.

In a voice that could barely be heard, Amanda looked at Fanny and said, "I shall do it. Now!"

"Oh, miss," Fanny responded, her happiness for Amanda shining forth from her eyes.

Clearing a sudden obstruction from her throat, Amanda looked at the letter she held as though it might explode in her hands, then began to walk to the door. At the sill, she paused, turning to face the maid again.

"Would you come with me, Fanny? Or is there a

young man or family you must stay here for?" Amanda waited, frozen while she wondered if the first request she'd made upon hearing of her good fortune would be granted.

"Lawks, miss, there's nothing to hold me here. I'll come with ye, and gladly." Fanny hurried after Amanda as the two crept silently up the stairs to the top of the house.

Amanda giggled, something she hadn't done since a little girl. "I do not know why we pussyfoot around like this. Leeson and the others shall know all about it before long—that is, if the groom, or whatever he is, hasn't already informed them of his mission."

"Most likely he'll preen himself a bit, miss. Most fellows like to have a spot of glory when they can."

Amazed at this bit of wisdom from the girl, Amanda merely nodded, then set to work. All the while she placed her skillfully mended and carefully tended garments into her little trunk, she wondered if she did the right thing.

"I never seed you wear this, miss," Fanny said with an awed voice as she took a simple silk gown from the wardrobe.

It was a pretty Clarence blue round gown with delicate embroidery around the modest neckline and hem. Wispy lace trimmed the neck and edged the puffed sleeves. It had never been worn, hanging in the wardrobe for the day when Amanda would be called to fill in at the table, a day that never seemed to arise.

"I made that," Amanda confessed. "I had hoped to use it at a dinner or some sort of party."

"But madam would never want you around to take away from her," Fanny concluded sagely.

"Fanny, you ought not say such a thing," Amanda

rebuked, all the while suspecting the maid spoke the truth.

Once Amanda's cherished bits and pieces were tucked in along the sides of the trunk, the lid was dropped down and the two women stared at each other.

"Well, we had best find you a portmanteau, then inform the young man that we wish to depart today."

Fanny giggled, a nervous little sound.

Within a short space of time, baggage for the maid was found in the form of an old portmanteau that had belonged to Amanda's mother, and was most likely to be forever ignored by Margaret.

About an hour had passed when Amanda and Fanny presented themselves in the central hall, warmly cloaked in worn gray wool and feet encased in snug boots.

"You may tell the young man that we wish to depart now, Leeson." Amanda enjoyed seeing the look of shock that flashed over the normally impassive face of the haughty butler.

"But, Miss Barkley . . . Lord Rosling . . . her lady-ship . . ." He sputtered a few moments, then observing that Amanda stood quietly waiting without replying, he marched off to the rear of the house.

"I had best leave a message for George, I expect. I would not wish him to be upset." Amanda hurried to the library desk to dip the quill pen into the ink, penning her brief missive with care, yet speed. She would not lose courage now. She thanked her brother for his care these past years and informed him of her legacy. She declared she'd not wanted to trouble him with her decision to claim her house, for she knew he would wish her to accept. She promised to write before long, she concluded vaguely.

"The coach is ready to leave, miss," Leeson announced from the doorway with a distinct note of disapproval.

Amanda sanded her letter, then sealed it, tucking it beneath the paperweight on the center of the desk.

"Tell Lord Rosling I have left a message for him." Amanda deliberately had not left her direction. She knew her brother and Margaret, particularly. They might try to force her to return to Rosling Hall. She had no intention of coming back here, ever.

When Amanda went to enter the grand traveling coach, Jervis presented her with a leather pouch he said was from Mr. Rushbury. She assumed it contained the money.

The greatest sense of adventure settled inside the coach as the two young women, both diminutive in size and looking more like excited children, embarked on their journey. If the groom had been surprised that they had chosen to leave immediately, he gave no indication.

Amanda investigated the contents of the bag, gasping when she realized all that was within.

"The groom said we shall stop when we please. I was given a sum for expenses!" Amanda declared, holding up the soft leather pouch that contained more gold coins and bank notes than Amanda had seen in her lifetime.

"I think ye done a fine thing, miss. I feel sure ye won't be sorry ye left this place."

Amanda did cast a brief glance back at the house where she had spent so many hours in tedious labor. Then, as the beautiful coach turned the corner, she resolutely faced the road ahead, feeling as though the cares of many years slid from her shoulders.

"We are free, Fanny. From now on we shall live snug

as a bug in a rug in my little house. We shall have a pretty cat, an orange tabby, I believe. And we shall dine on turbot and veal with sauces galore whenever we please. Oh," Amanda suddenly cried, "do you cook, Fanny?"

"Not much, I don't," the maid confessed. "I do buttered eggs a real treat, and my mam taught me to fix a tasty rabbit stew."

"Well, then, we shan't starve until I can find us a cook." Amanda sighed in happy speculation.

The two settled back against the softly cushioned squabs to contemplate the things they would need and wonder about the little house they would occupy. They ignored the many pauses for a change of horses until the hour grew late and the coach drew up before a fine-looking inn.

Amanda began to appreciate what a nice thing it was to travel in style, when the innkeeper—after a glance at the remarkable equipage—bowed low, offering her the best the inn had to offer.

The following morning after a lovely repast of buttered eggs, toast and berry jam, with lashings of hot tea, the two young women again set off, this time wondering how long they would be required to travel.

"The directions are very obscure, you know," Amanda explained to Fanny. "I wonder if Mr. Prewbody did not wish me to tell George where I am to live?" This thought so intrigued her that she remained silent for several miles.

Her musings ceased when the coach drew to a halt in a pleasant little market town. The door opened, and Jervis bobbed his head in deference.

"If you please, miss, we wondered if you wished to do a bit of shopping. The house is not too far from here, but not convenient to the shops what with the snow and all."

Dismayed that she would not be able to walk to the shops when she needed something, Amanda nodded gratefully, beckoning Fanny to follow her from the coach.

"Come, we had best select what we need for a few days." The two set off along the street to have a glorious time of it. At a fruiterers shop, they bought fancy apples for a pudding and a nice sack of oranges. Amanda paused at another shop to buy spices and honey and all manner of staples—including some very fancy tea—for she was unsure as to what she would find at her new abode. At the bakery, Amanda purchased bread and scones and a number of other delicacies that soon filled several parcels.

The butchers shop was a final stop. A fine green duck soon found its way into the market basket, followed by a sizable rabbit, a perfect veal roast, a ham, and other luxuries that Amanda had not tasted since her parents died.

The flitch of bacon stuck out of the top of the basket in a comical way, but Amanda paid it no heed. Her cheeks flushed a charming rose-pink, she marched along the walk with Fanny at her side, the burdened groom following closely behind.

"You ought to have a proper kerseymere pelisse," Fanny urged as they passed a mantua-maker's shop.

Amanda stopped to peer in the window of the elegant little establishment.

"I could, could I not?" Amanda said wonderingly. Her cloak might be serviceable, but it lacked a certain something. Before she could change her mind, she instructed the groom regarding all the parcels and baskets, then hurried inside the little shop in search of a pelisse that would be warm *and* pretty.

When they left, Fanny carried more parcels and wore a smug expression that might have annoyed Amanda had she not been so delighted. It seemed that the mantua-maker had made a number of festive garments for a young woman just about Amanda's size who had failed to pick them up.

Her happy reflection faded when she bumped into a gentleman right in the middle of the walk. "I do beg your pardon," she said while she gazed up into a pair of the bluest eyes she'd ever had the pleasure to see.

Amanda's lashes dropped over her cheeks in mild confusion at the sight of the handsome gentleman who barred her way back to the coach.

"It is all my fault, miss. Please accept my humblest apologies," the man said in a voice that met Amanda's ears with pleasing mildness. George had a loud voice, most likely acquired from giving commands all the time. How lovely to hear a man speak with something less than a shout and in such cultured accents.

Fanny cleared her throat, reminding Amanda that it was unseemly to be chatting with a total stranger on the walks of the market town, even if she wasn't a resident and most likely able to ignore censuring looks.

"I must be going, sir. Please excuse me." Amanda glanced helplessly at the parcel that had dropped to the ground, or more accurately, on the gentleman's boots.

Following her look, the gentleman bent down to pick up the parcel—which contained a perfectly lovely Norwich shawl in shades of blue and green—and clasped it to his chest.

"Allow me to escort you to your carriage. Dare I hope it is the one over there?" He nodded in the direction of the coach in which Amanda had traveled.

Not knowing quite how to handle the somewhat audacious man, Amanda nodded, wondering why the information should have any influence on him in the least.

"Indeed, it is," she said in her gentle way, then walked toward the coach.

It was the first time she could recall that she had a gentleman escort her anywhere, let alone a man this handsome. He was just enough taller than she so that she didn't have to crane her neck to see him. He didn't frighten her in the least, as most gentlemen did. And she rather liked the deferential touch of his gloved hand at her elbow when they crossed the cobbled street. Her foot slipped on one of the stones. How lovely to have someone skillfully steady her, bringing her safely to the far side with no further mishap.

"Thank you, very much," Amanda said fervently when he handed her into the carriage. "You are too kind, sir." She caught an exchange of glances between the groom and the gentleman, but expected that it was a male sort of thing.

He waited until Fanny plumped herself on the opposite cushions, arranging the assorted parcels on one side away from the baskets bought earlier. He handed the parcel he'd carried directly to Amanda, his gaze meeting hers.

"Perhaps we may meet again," he said. It seemed to her his nice blue eyes lit up with pleasure at the thought.

"Perhaps," she replied, demurely concealing her wishes behind rapidly lowered lashes.

She heard the door shut, then she watched as the coach pulled away from where the man stood. How she would like to know who he was. It would not have been proper for them to introduce themselves, although she would have liked him to know her name as well. Odd, it seemed that with every mile she traveled, she shed some of the timidity she possessed while in her brother's house. Still she was not so daring as to forget all propriety.

He did seem to recognize her coach, she recalled.

"Fanny, I wonder if the gentleman knew Mr. Prewbody?" She had discussed her benefactor, the unknown Andrew Prewbody, with Fanny at some length, having no one else with whom to air her conjectures during the journey. All the letter had said was that Mr. Prewbody was a good friend of her father's. Having no children of his own, he wished to bestow his home on a worthy young woman. Amanda had blushed at that sentiment. While it was sad that he'd had no children, Amanda confessed that she was most grateful for his gift of the little cottage.

The horses clopped along, the sound almost like music to Amanda. She wished she might sing a song of freedom, but Fanny would think her a silly goosecap.

When the coach slowed, she ventured to let down her window to catch a first glimpse of her new home. The coach swept between an elegant stone gate with room to spare.

Amanda wondered at this. Surely they had taken a wrong turn. They ought not be trotting along this impressive avenue lined with holly and yew trees. However, she was far too timid to say a word, so watched, eyes wide, as they drove through the lovely parkland.

"Fanny, look at the rolling lawn falling away from the avenue. There is the nicest blanket of snow on the ground. Is it not the prettiest thing?" Amanda said, trying to keep her worries from creeping into her voice. She just knew they were to be shooed away. She dreaded scenes.

"Yes, miss. Appears to me that you best think about something other than a thatched cottage. Just look."

Amanda looked, too awed to say a word in reply.

Coming into view was not a humble cottage but a large manor house of hewn stone topped with an impressive pediment in the Doric style! There must be a mistake. Why there were at least three floors counting the attics.

The carriage halted. The groom opened the door, let down the steps, then offered the faintest of smiles to Amanda. "Miss Barkley, may I welcome you home."

She couldn't prevent a shocked gasp. Home? Not likely. But he ought to know. Then she recalled the looks exchanged between the groom and that gentleman in town, and she wondered if he had known about her. The thought was disquieting.

As graciously as possible Amanda descended from the traveling coach, walked up the broad steps to the front of the house, then paused before the door. Did one knock at one's own front door? She couldn't have waited another moment. Trembling, she opened the door and entered with Fanny close behind her.

"Good gracious!" Amanda exclaimed. "This is most elegant." Before them was a pleasant oak-paneled entrance hall with a neat black and white tiled floor. A curving staircase rose gracefully upward on one side of the room. Fine paintings and statues were placed about, perhaps offering a taste of what was to come.

There was not a soul to be seen.

"Let's have a look-see," Fanny whispered, awed to near silence by the size of Amanda's "cottage."

With a careful swallow, and almost wishing the groom had tagged along with them, Amanda hesitantly walked toward the first of the doors on her left.

Upon opening it, she saw attractive sofas and comfortable chairs arranged about the spacious room. "The drawing room, I expect." Then she espied a pianoforte close to a lovely marble fireplace. "I could play," she exclaimed in delight. She had barely touched an instrument since coming to live with George and Margaret.

They backed out, then went on to open the next of the hallway doors.

"Lawks, miss, such a heap of books!" Fanny declared before Amanda could announce that they had found the library, a truly masculine place.

"So it is," Amanda murmured, almost overcome with the extent of her new abode. Deciding she had best continue before she collapsed with the sheer enormity of it all, she crossed the hall, a part of her wondering at the lack of servants around. The house bore the touch of well-loved care; not a trace of dust nor a dull window to be seen.

Inside the next door she discovered a small sitting room, just the place to do accounts and work on her embroidery. She sighed with pleasure at the thought.

Tugging Fanny along, she continued the exploration to see a room that held a collection of tapestries and other art objects. Beyond this was a small breakfast room with cheerful green and white decor. The last of the ground-floor rooms remained.

Here they reached a comfortable dining room done in pretty yellow and white. The cherry table gleamed with polish, yellow draperies added charm. No fire burned in the grate of the lovely marble fireplace. Amanda shivered, drawing her worn cloak more closely about her.

"Let us inspect one of these doors. There must be some servants about somewhere." She peeped around the first, but found a butler's pantry. Behind another was a flight of steps. Fanny hurried along with her until they reached the high-ceilinged kitchen.

Polished copper and tin vessels hung neatly on the walls. Hams, tongues, and flitches of bacon were suspended from the ceiling. Amanda thought of the small slab of bacon that reposed in one of her baskets, and exchanged a rueful look with Fanny.

"La, miss, this be a grand kitchen." The maid frowned at the smokejack sitting empty beside the fireplace, also empty. The clock in the corner of the room reminded them it was time for a meal. But where was the cook to prepare it? No sign of a fire upon which to cook could be seen.

The door opened, and the groom entered bearing several of the baskets and parcels containing the things purchased in town. He stopped when he caught sight of them. A frown of enormous proportions spread across his face as he surveyed the otherwise vacant room.

Amanda wondered if he would tell her it was all a hum, that she was to go elsewhere.

"I don't understand it. Believe me, miss, you have a full staff. Usually," he muttered in an aside.

"Were we expected today?" Amanda inquired, having a slightly better knowledge of how households were run.

Such a peculiar expression crossed over his face that Amanda longed to laugh.

"As to that, miss, it may be that they have taken themselves off on a holiday, most likely thinkin' that you would not be here until after Christmas."

"Well," Amanda said briskly, taking charge as though she had done it before in her life, "we shall just make the best of things until they return."

"I kin fix ye a plate of buttered eggs with a slice of that lovely bread we bought in town," Fanny offered.

"And some ham, I believe," Amanda added, eyeing the nearest one with hunger. It had been ages since she had tasted a well-cured ham, and her mouth fairly watered at the thought of it.

Before long Fanny and Amanda sat down to a lovely

supper of eggs, ham, and bread spread with the finest marmalade Amanda had ever tasted. Fanny had been reluctant to join Amanda until persuaded it was practical. Once replete, Fanny said she would wash up if Miss Amanda would take herself off to find a place to sleep.

Amanda set off to explore with a lit candle in hand. With the passing of daylight the house seemed somewhat ghostly to her, the lofty ceilings possessing an elegance she found hard to accept as hers. The stairway led up to the bedrooms, precisely as she had expected.

"This will do nicely," Amanda announced to no one when she stopped in the doorway of a pretty room decorated in shades of blue and gold with a painting of cupids floating in a painted sky overhead. "Just the thing for a maiden lady." She giggled, then lit several more candles, preparing for her first night in her new home.

When Fanny joined Amanda, she found her humming to herself while she emptied the trunk, which the groom brought up as soon as she informed him of her wishes. He had started a fire, although that was not his normal job, and it now burned brightly in the hearth.

"Lawks, miss, I think this house be right nice," Fanny said in what had to be an understatement of the day.

Amanda agreed, then put the last of her things in a splendid wardrobe twice the size of the one at her brother's house. She shut the door to it, turning to face Fanny.

"Your room is through here, for I do not fancy having you upstairs when there is but the two of us here," Amanda joked.

After inspecting the pleasant little room with a window overlooking a grand spread of lawn that swept to a dimly perceived lake some distance away, Fanny could only nod her agreement.

Once settled in a most-comfortable feather bed with a charming view of the cupids over her head before she blew out her candle, Amanda reflected on the great change in her life. Had Mr. Prewbody known her family so well that he would have realized that George and Margaret would go away at Christmas? But what if Amanda had gone as usual? She would have missed the news of her inheritance and the chance to escape. It was all beyond her. She could only be thankful that she had deviously remained behind.

The last thought before she drifted to sleep was of the gentleman she had encountered in town. Would she ever see him again?

Come morning, Amanda and Fanny again made shift for themselves at breakfast. Amanda left Fanny exploring the pantry while she decided to look about outside.

She left off her spinsterish cap at Fanny's insistence and felt wickedly exposed with nothing more than the hood of her cape to cover her head. Once outside, she began to explore her new domain.

With Christmas only days away, Amanda wished to cut greens to decorate. The day was fresh but not too brisk. She reveled in the neatly kept lawns and sweeping views. Could this really be hers? Contentment surged through her.

Once she had her first armful of holly and ivy, she returned to the drawing room prepared to garnish the mantelpiece. When she reached the doorway, she halted in her steps. There atop the lovely mantel sat a mouse. It stared at her with large sharp eyes, head tilted to one side, a long tail curved about it while it prepared to bolt.

Amanda did what any young woman of sensibilities would do. She screamed. It was a tiny sound as screams go, for Amanda was a timid person, not given to unseemly displays.

To Charlie Dane, crossing the entrance hall after finding the door left wide open, the noise sounded more like a squeak. He hurried forward, ready to do battle for the young woman his good friend Prewbody had settled his estate upon.

Just inside the door, he found the shy young woman he had encountered the day before while in town. Her dainty yet pleasing figure was complemented by a wealth of brown hair curled about her heart-shaped face. When she turned to face him, her pretty dark eyes were filled with distress. Such elfin beauty went straight to Charlie's heart. He approved her wary curiosity, for he ought to have informed her yesterday that he lived nearby.

"Charles Dane, at your service, miss." He bowed his most elegant, then stepped forward to help if he could.

"There is a mouse on the mantel," she declared in wavering tones.

"No dragon?" he said, disappointed when he saw his levity was not appreciated. Glancing at the mantel, he caught sight of a tiny yellow-necked mouse, the sort that enter unoccupied homes comes winter in search of a dry, sheltered place for the season. "Aha!" he confirmed. "A little fellow, and not too alarming if he is alone."

Seeming to forget the mouse for the moment, the young woman advanced a step. "I bumped into you yesterday."

"And we still do not have anyone to introduce us. Unless"—he cast a glance at the mantel—"we ask friend mouse to perform the task."

A charming, most musical laugh followed his silly remark. "I am Amanda Barkley, and I seem to have inherited this lovely house. Did you know Mr. Prewbody, sir?"

"Indeed, I did," Charlie said proudly. "I also benefited from his benevolence with a generous gift. He was a fine man. I understand he and your father were the best of friends. He did not wish to see his home occupied by complete strangers, so when he learned that you resided with your brother and sister-in-law, he decided to give you his house. He was quite ill toward the end of his life, but his mind was as sharp as ever."

Charlie decided that giving the house to Miss Barkley was perhaps the nicest thing Andrew Prewbody could have done under the circumstances. Charlie continued to share information with his lovely new neighbor.

"You will soon meet with Hodgkin, the solicitor, who will explain the terms of the will. In the meantime, know that you have inherited a sizable estate." He went on to tell about the place in glowing detail.

"You seem to know a great deal about it, sir," Miss Barkley said at last with a small smile peeping out that made Charlie wish to keep her amused forever. Her eyes sparkled and her creamy skin acquired a delicate pink hue that was most becoming.

"I should," he replied. "I have served as the manager here for the past few years when Andrew became too ill to handle matters for himself." At her bewildered expression, he gathered she wondered why a gentleman should be working at such a job, and he hastened to explain.

"My brother holds the family title and has four potential heirs to the viscountcy. I do not feel cut out for the law, the church, or the army. So Andrew encouraged me in something I enjoy, managing land."

"How fine of him. I wish I had met the gentleman."

"He knew a great deal about you, if I may reveal his secret. He and your father corresponded all the years after they left school, meeting when they could. They both enjoyed hunting, so that was their time together, usually. He liked the miniature of you that your father showed him." Charlie gave her a considering look, then went on, "Although you were younger, you have not changed all that much, I believe. You were a very pretty girl."

She blushed and looked away in modest confusion. "This is all quite unsettling."

He noticed that she still clutched the greens to her, so offered to help.

"If that mouse will go away, I would like to begin decorating the house for Christmas. I have never attempted to do so before, but I should like to try."

"A goodly amount of greenery, of which you have plenty, and a cluster of mistletoe, perhaps?" He chuckled at the blush that again suffused her cheeks.

It was a devilish thing to do, to tease her, but he felt daring. Usually he was more retiring around women, knowing they were not likely to be interested in a second son with no chance of acquiring the title. Now that he had the inheritance from his grandmother and Andrew Prewbody, a circumstance he had kept to himself, he was more eligible, but felt no different. There was in Miss Barkley a shy reticence that he found disarming and comfortable.

She cleared her throat. "I believe I should like a Yule

log here in the drawing room. My father always had one, but Margaret thinks them a deal of nonsense and bother. I wish one again. He sat beside it to tell us tales of the ghosts of Christmas past."

"While you kept an ear alert for the singers from the village with their caroling?" He smiled down at her, knowing full well that he ought to leave here, for it was the height of impropriety for a bachelor to remain closeted with a young lady.

"Oh yes. Did you do that as well? Am I likely to hear the harmonizing of familiar songs on a frosty winter's night? I do hope so." She crossed the room to place the greenery on a table by the fireplace. A small fire burned to take the chill off the room. The mouse had disappeared.

"I would not be surprised." To fulfill her simple wish, he'd be willing to hire singers if necessary.

Amanda tucked the first of the holly branches behind the clock on the mantel. This was followed by several others, handed to her by her new friend.

"I gather you live not far from here?"

He gave her a startled look. "Did I not tell you? I am your neighbor to the west. Or, my brother is. They are off for the holidays, leaving me to manage the place."

"Goodness, so many go away. My brother and his family did as well." She considered her subterfuge employed to avoid that trip and blushed again. "I shall be happy to stay by my hearth."

She knew the urge to invite her new neighbor, but was far too shy to be so bold. Yet, he would be alone. Perhaps. She would think about it, although it would take every bit of her nerve.

They walked out of the front door and down the

steps to the area where holly and ivy could be found in abundance.

Amanda looked about her, commenting to Mr. Dane, "One would almost think that Mr. Prewbody had these all planted expressly for Christmas decorating." Then she laughed at her silly notion.

"I would not be surprised. He liked people and often entertained."

"Oh, my. I do not know anyone at all. The house will feel neglected, I fear."

"You know me, Miss Barkley. No reason to fear being alone."

Amanda felt her heart perform the most peculiar little flips and flops when she gazed up into the clear, trustworthy blue of Mr. Dane's beautiful eyes.

How long they might have stayed there staring into each other's eyes was never known. A tan and black terrier came gamboling up to where they stood, eager to be included in the outing. He at once altered the mood.

"Hello there," Amanda said, suddenly grateful to have something else to look at, for Mr. Dane's eyes were far too intriguing. She knelt to gingerly pat the little fellow.

"He's a sturdy boy. Won't do you a bit of harm, but is dandy at hunting rodents and the like."

"I suppose I ought to borrow him to catch that mouse." She exchanged an amused look with her neighbor, relieved to find that odd expression had gone from Mr. Dane's face. "I had hoped to find a kitten that might prove to be a mouser as well as a companion." She omitted the knowledge that her sister-in-law detested dogs and cats, so none were allowed at Rosling.

"If you are troubled by our little friend again, just

let me know. I'll stop by to check on you in any event. There may be other problems that pop up."

"Like all the servants taking off on a holiday, not expecting me to arrive until after Christmas?" Amanda tossed him an expectant glance, not disappointed in the least at his reaction.

"No!" he exclaimed, darting a horrified look back at the house. It sat in peace, absorbing the gentle winter sun in utter silence.

"Fanny and I are rubbing along quite well together, all things considered. My needs are simple."

"Ah, but your wants!" he declared with that twinkle back in his eyes. "I'll wager that you would like a plum pudding, perhaps some other treats for the season?"

"We have the ingredients if we can manage to put things together. I was never permitted in my brother's kitchen, but I have fond memories of my childhood, licking spoons while observing preparations for the holidays."

"And did you watch to see where the little charms were put in the cake?"

"Of course," she retorted, "for all the good it did me." She subsided at that, recalling the numerous times she had wished to be elsewhere. And now she was.

She also recognized that were her house to be filled with people, she would be far too shy to speak to so dashing a gentleman as Mr. Dane. Perhaps it was as well that she remain alone, with Fanny and later the other servants to care for the house. She tried not to think of the day when the dear house would have to go to another. She ought to find a worthy spinster.

"What has brought that sad expression to your eyes, I wonder?" he said. "Come, forget the past and let us gather more greenery to bedeck your new home."

With deliberate care, Amanda shook off her memories to join in the fun. For Charles Dane made it fun for her, spouting jokes, brandishing holly branches, and finally locating an elusive bunch of mistletoe for her to hang.

Amanda well knew the tradition surrounding the mistletoe. It hung in a doorway, and every lad who could steal a kiss from an unwary young miss while beneath it, claimed a white berry as a trophy. When all the berries were gone, the kisses ended. She noted that this particular example contained an abundance of little white berries. She said nothing about it, for who would there be in her empty house to claim kisses?

They returned to the drawing room, shedding cloak and coat to work in harmony while arranging the profusion of greenery about the room. There was so much that they went to the dining room to continue their task there, all the while talking about memories of other Christmases.

Charlie noted that while Miss Barkley mentioned her childhood, she never spoke of recent years. It was most curious, since he was certain that with children in the house, her brother must celebrate in generous style. Finally he inquired.

"Your family . . . I suppose they observe the holiday, with puddings and green ducks, great fires in the drawing room and the like?"

"The past few years they have gone to visit friends or Margaret's family," she replied in a pinched little voice.

"They?" He hadn't missed that word nor the bleak expression that had crossed her face.

"Well, I traveled along, but the children require tending, you see."

"Surely their nanny took care of that."

"They do not have a nanny or governess."

Her simple words painted a picture of the little sister conveniently at home to take over the unpaid—and likely unthanked—job of caring for the children. He was utterly appalled that this young woman, barely out of the schoolroom as far as he could see, would be saddled with the task.

"How many children do they have?"

"Three boys and a girl." Amanda shivered at the memory of the eldest boy, William. The very thought of him had fired her determination to flee Rosling when she could.

The door opened, and Fanny poked her head around to survey the two who decorated the house.

"What is it?" Amanda said.

"I found the makings for a Christmas plum pudding but for the brandy. I wondered if perhaps the gentleman might know where it be kept, since he knew the late master, as it were." Fanny slipped around the door, hiding her hands beneath her apron.

Glad to have a diversion, for the scene had become too intimate for Amanda's liking, she turned to her neighbor with a questioning look. "Well, sir?"

He nodded, then left the room.

"It looks real pretty in here," Fanny said shyly, her too-thin face lighting up with a smile. "I found a cookery book in the kitchen, and since I kin read, we'll do right fine until those others come back."

It was clear to Amanda that Fanny was not only proud of her ability to decipher the cookery book, but pleased that she might test her skills.

"I hope you find a recipe for apple tart in that book," Amanda said, thinking of green duck for a dinner.

"Never you worry about a thing, miss," Fanny assured.

At that moment Mr. Dane returned bearing a bottle of brandy. He offered it to Fanny. "I suspect it is quite a fine old brandy. Best use with caution."

"Thank ye, sir, I shall," she said timidly, then whirled around the door and was gone.

Shortly after that Mr. Dane took his leave.

Amanda watched from behind a dining room drapery as he strode down the avenue, then with his dog at his heels cut across the snowy fields toward the west. He had promised to check on her, to come again, she recalled. She hugged her arms around her with quiet pleasure at the mere thought of seeing the gentleman once more. Then she ordered herself to stop being a ninny and cleaned up after the decorating for her Christmas. Would she dare hang up the mistletoe that Mr. Dane had picked? She gathered it in her hands, wondering if she would be foolish to even hope for a kiss. After contemplating the white berries amid the greenery for a few moments, she tucked them up on the fireplace mantel in the drawing room.

Not wishing to be alone with her thoughts, she joined Fanny in the warmth of the kitchen where Jervis helped the maid stone the raisins for the grand Christmas pudding.

Who was to consume this magnificent pudding was not clear, but Amanda nurtured a tiny hope within her that Mr. Dane might be persuaded to join her for a Christmas dinner. He had told her that his family was away. How sensible to share the meal, she thought with a small glow in her heart.

"I shall mince the suet, then prepare the currents,"

Amanda offered, accustomed to a subservient role in life.

Fanny gave her a startled look. "Whatever you wish, miss."

Amanda reflected that she must become familiar with giving orders rather than receiving them. She merely smiled, then found the suet to begin mincing it for the pudding.

The room was fragrant with the scents of Christmas. Brandy mingled with the ingredients in the pudding when it was set to boil. The aroma of ripe apples being peeled for a tart added to the pre-Christmas impression.

How pleasant, Amanda thought. Her own kitchen filled with the promise of her first Christmas. For it seemed as though she had been reborn, experiencing life for the first time.

Her dreams that night included the shadowy form of a handsome young gentleman, which didn't escape her when she woke the next morn. " 'Tis not you who will be picking a white berry from the mistletoe," she scolded the woman in the looking glass while she brushed her curls.

"You ain't a-going to put on a cap again, are you?" Fanny asked in dismay when Amanda picked up one of the muslin caps her sister-in-law had given her.

Amanda looked at the hated cap. Not even so much as a frill or a scrap of lace, but plain, as plain as her life was supposed to be if Margaret had her way. She turned to face Fanny, cap in hand. "Do you think you could find a use for these?"

"Not on me," the little maid denied stoutly in a soft voice. "I prefer me mob." She patted the ruffled cap on her head, a most becoming article. "I kin use 'em for dusting," she finally declared with a cautious glance at Amanda.

Rather than scolding, Amanda grinned, then gave Fanny a reproving look. "At least they shan't be wasted."

"No, miss," Fanny replied, a hint of laughter lurking in her voice.

"Ham and buttered eggs again, with biscuits, perhaps?"

Obviously enjoying her foray into the culinary arts, Fanny proudly proclaimed that to be the menu for breaking the morning fast.

Giving her ash brown curls a final pat, Amanda followed Fanny down the back stairs to the kitchen, welcoming the warmth of the fire.

Her own small blaze had scarce had a chance to warm up her bedroom, yet she had been comfortable beneath the down comforter on her huge bed. She was becoming accustomed to the sight of those silly cupids on her ceiling. The modest array of clothing inside her wardrobe did not disturb her in the least. She reveled in her freedom.

Following her breakfast, she decided to investigate the drawing room again. Cautiously opening the door, she peered around, staring intently at the mantel. Would the mouse still be there?

Two beady little eyes above a fine set of whiskers stared back at her. Its enormous ears were alert to the entrance of the outsider. A crumb filched from the dining room floor was held in two paws, awaiting consumption.

"Good morning," Amanda said politely, for she was less frightened today and considered the mouse in a more kindly manner when she recalled how it had more or less brought Mr. Dane into her life.

The elegant whiskers twitched.

"You ought not be here, for I intend to have a rousing fire, which I suspect you will most heartily dislike."

"What's this? Given to talking to yourself?" Mr. Dane inquired in a jovial manner from behind her.

"I'll have you know that I was passing the time of day with our mouse." She beamed a shy smile at him, forgetting to be timid in her complete delight at his appearance. Although he really ought not enter other people's houses without at least knocking. Not but what she'd have hurried to open the door for him.

Charlie noted the use of "our" and smiled. "I have a surprise for the mistress of the house." He reached inside of his coat where he had sheltered the animal since he'd left the barn.

"A kitten!" she exclaimed with evident happiness. "Oh, look, Fanny," she said to the maid, who had entered with a bucket of coal for the fire. "A marmalade kitten. I fancy it will be some time before it will be a challenge to our Mr. Mouse on the mantel, however."

"Mr. Mouse, is it?" Fanny said with a gleam of laughter in her pale brown eyes. "I best find a box for the kitten, miss."

"I shall wish to keep it upstairs with me at night, I believe. The poor little thing will be lonely at first." She inspected the kitten, then added, "I shall call him Punch, for he reminds me of the color of the punch my sister-in-law makes in the summertime."

Pleased to see the tenderhearted reception to his gift, Charles divested himself of his greatcoat and muffler, placing his hat on top of the pile. Not having a servant about had drawbacks, but advantages as well. There was not a soul around to overhear his conversation with Miss Barkley.

"I fear we are to have another spell of bad weather, Miss Barkley. Since we cannot go hunting for a Yule log, perhaps I could instruct you on the running of your new estate?"

Amanda would have done almost anything to acquire his company, even study accounts. She nodded demurely. "That would be extremely thoughtful of you, if you would not mind, that is."

"Splendid," he declared. "Let us repair to the library, for that is where the estate books are kept."

In the following hours, Amanda gained a far better understanding of precisely what she had inherited. Hundreds of acres, a home farm, a sizable establishment fit for a man to run. How could she hope to manage such a place?

She looked at Mr. Dane, wondering, speculating. Would he consider helping her? Now was not the moment to ask, she supposed. But someday she would have to inquire of him if he would continue to handle the affairs of the estate.

Fanny peeked around the corner, hesitantly announcing a nuncheon.

"Good, simple country fare," Mr. Dane pronounced when he saw the beef soup, sliced bread, cold meats, and the apple tart.

"Good food for a winter's day," Amanda agreed. She glanced out of the window at the wisps of snow that drifted down from time to time. It swirled about the holly trees, dusting them with a delicate tracery of white powder.

A fire crackled in the hearth, warming the room. Amanda felt as though the two of them were on an island in time, secluded and remote from the dictates of society. A society that made harsh pronouncements, declaring a spinster must not enjoy the company of a gentleman without a gathering about her.

"I thank you for your taking pity on a poor gentleman left on his own," he inserted into her thoughts.

"You are most welcome, sir. I believe we help one another, for I am sadly in need of your advice." She wondered if now was the time to ask for his help with the estate, then decided to wait.

"Good food and company are truly agreeable to one who must remain with the house while my family is gone."

"The kitten seems to be settling in well," she said sprightly, wishing to change the subject. The little fellow had followed Fanny into the dining room and now curled up not too far from the fire. No doubt he recalled the cozy warmth of the barn where he could snuggle up to his mama cat.

They discussed the fate of the mouse for a brief time, then shifted to other, more interesting topics. Amanda reflected that never could she recall having her opinion sought on any matter. Early on, she had been in the schoolroom. Later, when she moved to live with George and his family, she did not frequent the drawing or dining rooms when they had company. In that house, not even the maid sought her opinion.

"I fear you were correct about the weather, sir. The snow looks to worsen very shortly," Amanda reported after a glance out of the window.

"I had best leave soon, then. But not until I sample this apple tart."

Since Amanda had helped peel the apples for the tart and suggested the amount of seasoning required, she glowed with pride when he took a taste, pronouncing it fine indeed.

He left shortly later, obviously reluctant to go and promising to keep an eye on her at least until the servants returned to their proper places.

Once again alone, Amanda returned to the drawing room with the kitten at her heels. Mr. Mouse looked down from the safety of the mantel, surveying the new addition to the household with what certainly seemed like scorn.

For his part, the kitten paid the mouse not the least bit of attention. Amanda collapsed on one of the sofas close to where a small fire burned to keep the room pleasant. "I do believe I shall have a severe case of the giggles if you two keep this up."

The kitten merely purred as it settled down on Amanda's lap. She considered this an excellent excuse to curl up with one of the books she had placed near by for such a purpose and before she knew it, time for the evening supper had arrived.

"It does my heart a treat to see you taking your ease for a bit," Fanny said as she served up a tasty rabbit stew for their meal. Her cheeks were rosy with her triumph.

"Well, I cannot continue in this manner or I shall become a sloth," Amanda said with a hint of a smile.

Another night in her elegant bed, with a peep at those silly cupids before blowing out her candle, and Amanda began to feel that her life at Rosling Hall was quite remote, another lifetime, perhaps.

Morning brought a delightful view to her eyes when she chanced to go to the window. A fresh snow blanketed the ground, revealing nothing more than a few bird tracks below her window. Just outside of her window, a robin perched atop a mountain ash preparing for its Christmas feast, found in clusters of red berries hanging from a branch. At the bottom of the lawn, across the winding stream, a herd of deer meandered. Pale winter sun gave a delicate sparkle to everything in sight. Amanda was enchanted.

While eating her porridge and bread, she reflected that she would not see Mr. Dane this day, what with the new snow and all. Although the snow had been slight, one did not traipse about the country with the roads possibly blocked with drifts. She resigned herself to a day of work.

Dusting, sorting linens, all those dreary tasks had taken on a luster of sorts when it was *her* furniture to be dusted and *her* linens to be sorted. If all were like the fine linen sheets on her bed, she doubted if she would be faced with a stack of mending.

Since all her despised muslin caps had disappeared into the rag bag, Amanda did her best to neatly confine her hair. However, wisps insisted upon curling about her face while she worked at her task, delicately framing her face with an ash brown halo.

"Halloo!"

The shout came from the ground floor. Amanda hurried to the top of the stairs, amazed to find Mr. Dane below. He was garbed in his many-caped greatcoat, his hat displaying a small bunch of greens in honor of the season.

"There you are. I feared that the house was deserted once again, for I could find no one about."

"La, sir," she rebuked gently, "some of us must do a bit of work now and again."

"Not today. 'Tis two days before Christmas. I have come to take you sleighing!"

With a cry of delight, Amanda forgot her earnest intent to put the linen closet in order and flew down the stairs. A peep out of the front door revealed a lovely sleigh pulled by two stalwart steeds.

"Oh, my," she softly exclaimed. "I have never gone sleighing in my life. Dare I?" she whispered.

Fanny, like the excellent maid that she was, scurried down the stairs with Amanda's warm kerseymere pelisse over one arm, stout half boots in one hand, and a velvet bonnet dangling from the fingers of her other.

"Well, I see that I shall have to go, for I'd not disappoint Fanny," Amanda said with a shy smile lurking about her pretty mouth.

"I promise to take good care of you," Mr. Dane said. "I have a warm rug, with hot bricks for your feet. And here," he produced a beautiful fur muff from behind his back, "is something to keep those dainty fingers warm."

Amanda knew she must be blushing with his attentions and words. "How kind, sir."

He ushered her into the red sleigh with great courtesy, making Amanda feel like a countess at the very least. With a flick of the reins, they set off along the avenue. The faint sun had yet to melt the bit of snow, and they made fine progress.

"This is beyond anything lovely, sir," Amanda said. Ahead of her the horses tossed their heads, tiny clouds rising from their mouths in the frigid air. She tucked her hands more deeply inside the fur muff, relishing the day and the company. How kind of Mr. Dane to offer her this treat.

"I am glad you are not a hothouse flower, but like a hellebore that blooms in midwinter."

"Blooms, sir? Well . . ." Amanda laughed with joy,

but couldn't think of a reply to his gallant words. No doubt her blush was bloom enough.

Having the roads to themselves, they continued until they reached the edge of the village, where Mr. Dane drew up before the local inn with an elegant flourish. They entered, Amanda with not a little trepidation. She had never been in a country inn like this before.

"Charlie, my boy," said a plump gentleman who wore the most violently red waistcoat that Amanda had ever seen.

"Evan," Mr. Dane replied. "We are trying out the sleigh, for you must know that this is the first winter in some time that there has been sufficient snow for it.

"Bless you, Mr. Dane," the mistress of the inn said, bustling forth from her kitchen with great ceremony. "What a day it is, to be sure. You'll have a taste of my mince pie, I'll wager. And a cup of hot coffee would not come amiss either, if I don't miss my guess." She wiped her hands on a spotless apron that nearly covered her from neck to hem, and curtsied both to Mr. Dane and Amanda.

She suited her words to actions, and before Amanda could consider that she would be sitting in the common room of the local inn enjoying a piece of mince pie and hot coffee, it was placed before her.

"Oh, it is good." Amanda savored the delight of warm mince pie and hot coffee after being out in the frosty air.

"Can anything be better?" Mr. Dane added with a look at Amanda that set her heart to fluttering.

The man named Evan joined them, sitting close to Mr. Dane while studying Amanda. "Nice weather we're having," he observed.

Amanda concentrated on her pie.

"Miss Barkley, may I present Evan Heppell. Evan, Miss Barkley is my new neighbor, and I'm showing her about the area today. Becoming acquainted, you might say."

"Jolly good of you, especially when Miss Barkley is a treat for the old eyes." Mr. Heppell's eyes were pensive.

Mr. Dane glanced at his friend, then said, "I wonder that you are here. Thought you were on your way south."

"To m'brother's house," agreed Evan. "Slowtop that I am, I delayed too long. Now I shall stay home instead." This last was said with so much satisfaction that Amanda had to smile. Apparently he did not care overmuch for his brother or his family. "Intend to visit old George instead."

At the mention of someone named George, Amanda's head went up, startled. Deciding it wasn't *her* George, she returned her gaze to her plate and the last crumbs of her pie.

"We had best depart before the sun warms the roads too much and we become stuck in the mire." Mr. Dane gently guided Amanda to the door and out to the sleigh.

His friend peeped out at the sight, then disappeared.

"Your gentleman friend seems pleased enough to remain at home this season," Amanda said while the sleigh set off in the direction of home once again. She thrust her hands deeply into the muff, and enjoyed the comfort of hot bricks against the soles of her half boots.

"Well, George Pilkington has a bang-up party this time of year. No doubt but what Evan is headed that direction." Her escort gave Amanda a speculative look she chose to ignore.

Amanda wondered if that was where Mr. Dane intended to go for his celebration, then chided herself for being nosy. What was it to her if he enjoyed the company of his friends at holiday time?

Mr. Dane skillfully guided the sleigh around a small drift of snow, then smartly along the roadway. The long whip beside him had not needed to be used, for the horses responded beautifully to the merest touch of the ribbons.

The sleigh flew over the frozen road, going so fast that Amanda felt her breath snatched from her, grabbed by the wind to be given to another. The deer had strayed farther afield from the meadow. Their heads came up in startled awareness as Mr. Dane and Amanda sailed past them on the near-silent runners. Only the sound of the horses could be heard. Otherwise they were like the wind.

Amanda knew a deep sense of peace and utter happiness. This wonderful man was giving her a Christmas gift beyond price. Thankfulness welled up inside her, and she wondered how she would ever have survived living had she remained with her brother. Thank the good Lord for Mr. Prewbody.

"Andrew liked to go sleighing," Mr. Dane said, as though he knew Amanda's thoughts had turned to that gentleman.

"How nice," she replied. They had turned into the avenue leading up to her house. She bravely faced up to the end of the delightful ride. After all, good things had to come to an end.

Jervis materialized around the side of the house, taking the reins when they halted. Tossing him a word of appreciation, Mr. Dane drew Amanda along with him to survey the countryside from the terrace.

"The snow is so perfect. I imagine by tomorrow it

will warm up and become a memory," Amanda said, trying not to be sad at the thought.

"You look rather angelic with the frost decorating your bonnet."

"Have you ever made angels?" she said by way of her reply. When he declared he had never heard of making angels, Amanda took him by the hand, having left the fur muff in the sleigh as was only proper.

He followed her out on the snowy ground, watching with a puzzled look as she carefully stepped to a fresh patch of snow, then proceeded to spread herself on the ground, sweeping her arms in an arc.

"Help me up, please. I do not wish to spoil what I am sure is a very nice angel." She held out one little hand to him with evident trust he would obey her nice command.

He did as asked. Then a smile of comprehension came over his face as he viewed the pretty silhouette of an angel in the snow.

Amanda turned to him, her face glowing with happiness and her eyes sending messages to Charlie. He wondered if she realized what they contained.

"I think we had better return you to the house before you become as cold as your lovely angel," Charlie said, tucking her close to his side while they walked swiftly to the house.

"Oh, fiddlesticks. I never take ill. Fortunately. Even when the children had the flu, I was spared."

"I would rather not take any chances. I want you to remember this day as something very special, not as a day when you contracted a dreadful cold."

He led her into the house, quietly shutting the door behind them as though not to break the spell that had fallen over them when they first entered the sleigh.

She paused in the entrance hall to stare thoughtfully at him. Charlie wondered what went on inside that pretty head of hers. Tendrils of her soft brown hair curled charmingly about her heart-shaped face. Those melting brown eyes studied him with such tender regard. Had she begun to care just a little for him? He hoped so, for he was coming to care a great deal for his new neighbor.

He stepped forward to assist her with her bonnet, thinking it was rather nice not to be overrun with servants at this moment. His hands brushed her cheeks as he undid the ribands. The bonnet fell disregarded to the floor while the two were totally lost in each other's eyes.

He moved to gather her to him.

She fitted in his arms just exactly right, and she met his lips with none of the timidity he expected. Had the perfect day bewitched her as it had him?

"Oh!" she whispered, blushing a bright pink when she stepped away from him, her confusion appearing at war with another emotion yet undefined. She stared at the floor, obviously embarrassed. But he detected a faint smile curving her lips, and felt he had not blundered in his gentle kiss.

At that romantic moment, Fanny came sailing down the stairs with a shawl in her arms. "Ye'll be a-wanting this, Miss Amanda." She accepted the pelisse in exchange, her amber gaze darting between the pair just in from the cold.

Charlie impulsively reached out to adjust the pretty shawl about Amanda's slim shoulders.

"You must come in to see our friend Mr. Mouse," she said in her quiet way, moving toward the drawing room door.

A feeling of triumph swept over Charlie at her words. She accepted his kiss and invited him to join her. How much better could things be? He loosened his greatcoat, dropping it on a chair inside the drawing room before striding to survey the mantel.

"Where is it? Hiding?" He glanced over the pretty arrangement of greenery, but missed any sight of the little mouse. Punch curled up on the carpet near the fire.

"Oh, I hope so. I should hate to think of the poor little thing in the cold."

"This is the young lady who screamed when she first saw a mouse, is it not?" He grinned at her discomfiture, feeling very much in charity with that particular mouse at the moment.

She did not meet his gaze, but searched the room for her visitor. Charlie suspected that she was still somewhat reserved, the memory of their kiss—as gentle as it was—lingering in her mind. He wondered what it might be like to introduce Amanda to the wonders of true romantic loving, and felt a warmth seep through him that had nothing whatsoever to do with the fire blazing in the hearth.

"Will you join me for supper, Mr. Dane? I cannot promise you a roast, but Fanny and I have contrived a very nice pheasant pie. Jervis obliged us with a brace of birds this morning."

"I should like nothing better." Charlie hoped he didn't seem too eager when he agreed to the invitation.

She finally looked at him then. A hesitant smile curved her lips, then she softly squealed, "There it is."

Glancing behind him he discovered the little fellow peeping from beneath a clump of red berries. Those whiskers appeared to have a crumb or two still clinging to them.

"So I see. Pity he could not enjoy the sleigh ride."

"I fancy he was enjoying something much more to his liking. I do hope he has not invited a friend to join his party." A little frown worried her brow. Charlie found to his surprise that he longed to take her into his arms to assure her that she need not worry about a thing as long as he could be around to protect her.

I am being a silly goose, to talk so about one little mouse." Amanda gave Mr. Dane a tentative smile, then crossed to the door. "Allow me to tell Fanny that we shall have a guest this evening for our modest supper. You see I did not grace it with the title of dinner. Perhaps . . ." She permitted that sentence, so filled with hope for the future, to trail off into silence.

"It didn't take much to see that the gentleman from next door will be sampling our pheasant pie this evening," Fanny said when Amanda told her about the guest.

"See if there is anything in the pantry you might add to the menu, please?" Amanda gave her maid a bemused look, then drifted from the kitchen to the dining room to check the table setting she had arranged this morning just in the event of this very occasion. The sight of pretty Wedgwood china, fine crystal, old silver, with a small epergne holding bright red apples with holly leaves tucked in for contrast brought a sigh of pleasure. Amanda adjusted a linen napkin, then whisked herself across the hall to the drawing room where her important guest awaited.

"Tomorrow I intend to put together a few baskets to give those tenants on my land . . . the ones you told me about. What is customary in this area on Christmas

Eve? I think a sack of coal, perhaps a blanket or two, some useful clothing?"

"Just the thing," he declared with obvious approval.

Amanda was not in the least accustomed to such admiration in the eyes of anyone, let alone a presentable gentleman—even if he was a younger son of a peer and not the most eligible man in some eyes. That meant nothing to her. Her Season in London had not brought any masculine attention from anyone remotely considered eligible. She was quite thrilled to have company. Of any kind. And if the gentleman revealed admiration for her charitable instincts, she was in high alt.

"Would you like to have me take you about to the tenants? Jervis could, I realize, but I know these people well. It could serve to introduce you, break the ice as it were." He seemed almost eager to be of help.

"That would be most kind of you, sir." She could not believe she had been so forward as to broadly hint for his company. At least, she suspected that was the result of her inquiry. The tongue-tied Miss Barkley of Rosling Hall would not have dared to open her mouth. But then, the Miss Barkley of Rosling wouldn't have had the chance, would she?

"I wish you would call me Charlie. Everyone does, you know."

"Everyone?" she said with a smile.

"Near enough so," he replied acknowledging her little joke. "At any rate, I intend to call you Amanda from now on . . . unless you object?"

She could scarcely credit that he could give her such an uncertain look. Surely he must know that she had little resistance to him. "No, I have no objection. I must admit that having someone call me Miss Barkley seemed strange. I found myself looking about to see who else was here."

He gestured to the sofa by the fire, and they both sank down to discuss the visits to be paid on the morrow, and just what to bring along to the tenants.

When Fanny popped her head around the corner to inform them that the pheasant pie would spoil if they didn't come at once, they promptly rose. Continuing to chat about the coming day, they walked to the dining room.

Here Charlie came to a halt when he surveyed the prettily set table.

"I say, Amanda. That table looks as elegant as any I have ever seen."

Amanda doubted that very much, but thought him tactful and kind to shower her with praise.

After the simple but tasty meal they decided to play cards, Charlie apparently having no inclination to take himself home. Amanda was quite certain she had never been so happy in her entire life as this very moment. To have someone who expressed interest in her and who seemed to enjoy her company was a far cry from being relegated to the nursery or a quiet corner with a pile of mending.

When at last he left, Amanda searched the mantel for a sign of her mouse. He was not to be seen. She hoped he was safely asleep and had not become a meal for Punch. Although the kitten was most well behaved, Amanda suspected he had been taught by the barn cat to chase a mouse when one was seen.

Before going to her room, she paused by the front windows, the ones that faced the west and Charlie's home. He was out of sight by now, riding his horse across the fields to reach the warmth of his bed. She hadn't dared to dash to the windows to watch him depart lest she look a silly green girl. But she had followed his path in her mind. The thought of having him introduce her to the tenants on the morrow gave her deep satisfaction.

She reminded herself that she really would have to discuss the future with him. She knew she could not manage this fine estate all by herself. Oh, she might be able to locate a steward for it, she supposed. But Charlie knew it intimately. And, she admitted, she wanted him. To oversee it, naturally, she scolded herself.

The cupids hovering over her lovely bed seemed to be dancing when she studied them before she went to sleep. Tomorrow, her heart sang after she blew out her candle and closed her eyelids. Tomorrow and tomorrow and tomorrow. She quite forgot that when Macbeth had uttered those words, he had been on the brink of disaster.

Come first light, Amanda popped from her bed as though on a spring and dashed to the window, wrapping her shawl about her to ward off the morning chill.

The sun shone, although gently. And the roads were somewhat more clear, enough so they could use the carriage rather than the sleigh. She had enjoyed the sleigh, with the sound of the runners hissing over the snow so quietly. Even the horses usual clip-clop had been muted. And she had been alone in the world, or near enough, with Charlie.

The presence of Evan Heppell at the inn yesterday had not dimmed her pleasure. Nonetheless the memory of that party, the splendid one presented by their friend Pilkington gave her pause. She wondered if Mr. Dane, that is, Charlie would attend. Well, she decided, it was beyond her control, one way or the other.

She dressed herself hurriedly, sending a brush through her soft curls while she wondered what in the world Charlie thought of a spinster who didn't wear caps.

Following a light breakfast, she persuaded Fanny to help her decide what might be given to the tenants. She located several warm coats as good as new that had belonged to Mr. Prewbody, and set them aside so to obtain the advice of Mr. Dane. Charlie.

"Be a right shame to let these good clothes go to dust with no one to wear them," Fanny declared, stroking her hand over the fine broadcloth of the top of the pile.

"Blankets, next. Are there some that are in excellent repair that we may spare? next year I shall purchase new things, I vow." She exchanged a look with Fanny, both recalling the hand-me-downs given to Amanda at Rosling Hall.

Amanda led the way to the large linen closet where linen sheets, creamy wool blankets, and soft towels— both huckaback and a different sort that had a looped pile—were stacked. Amanda believed these last ones were referred to as Turkish towels, and were considered fine for drying after a bath. She had not been allowed to use them at Rosling.

"Your thoughtfulness will be honored for what it is, miss," Fanny assured her. "Never worry about them being used. There's been hard times in the country." She accepted a modest pile of blankets that Amanda deemed fit to bestow on the tenants, then led the way downstairs.

Jervis had consented to put up neat sacks of coal to present as seasonal gifts, so after their morning's labors

Amanda felt ready to depart. Whenever Charlie would come, that is.

She waited by the front windows for a time, wondering when he might arrive. When she realized that she was behaving like a green girl again, she scolded herself.

Whisking off to the drawing room, she inspected the mantel to see if the mouse might still lurk there. Slowly she advanced upon the spray of holly, wondering if that bunch of berries didn't move a trifle when she grew closer.

Two ears popped up, followed by a pair of bright eyes and the elegant whiskers.

"Ah, Mr. Mouse. You still visit us, I see."

"I have brought a friend for him." The voice at the doorway caused Amanda to spin about, quite unable to conceal her delight.

"I do hope it is not a lady mouse, sir. I have no desire for our little friend to set up housekeeping." She blushed a deep pink when she realized how forward her words might be considered.

In reply, and totally ignoring her lapse, Charlie advanced with his hand held out to her.

Amanda crossed to meet him, her curiosity driving away the chagrin at her indiscretion. "It is a mouse," she cried as he placed a beautiful carving of a mouse into her hand.

Mr. Mouse's ears and eyes, right down to the splendid tail were duplicated in this tiny sculpture. "How dear!" she exclaimed in delight.

"I thought that when this little fellow decides to depart for the out of doors, you might still have a memory of our happy days together this winter," Charlie confessed.

Amanda blushed again, for she had been thinking

along the same lines, only she hoped that it would be shared memories. Together. Apparently Charlie had different plans. Without a doubt she would have to adapt hers a trifle.

"Well, I do thank you, sir." At his admonishing look, she dropped her lashes, blushing modestly.

"I see I must work on persuading you to think of me as a friend," Charlie said.

Her lashes flew up, and she gave him an earnest look. "Oh, I assuredly do that . . . Charlie." Then to cover her feeling of confusion, she slipped on her pelisse, gesturing to the pile of blankets near the doorway. "I wonder if these will be acceptable? They have been used, you see. Next year I shall be careful to have new things. I would not wish to insult the tenants. Will these, do you think?" She searched his face for his reaction.

Knowing these soft woolen coverings were finer than anything the tenants could afford, Charlie said, "These will do well enough."

In short order all the practical gifts commonly given to tenants on the estate were loaded into the carriage, and the two set off, watched by a smug Fanny and a curious Jervis.

Amanda felt as though she had joined the silly cupids on her ceiling—heavenly. Her cheeks were pink from the cold, and her eyes sparkled with happiness.

Charlie thought she looked beautiful. Gracious in all she said when presenting the practical gifts—for she well knew what it was to do without, he surmised—and charming in a most unassuming way, she won the hearts of all she met.

Mrs. Midgly clasped her hands to her ample bosom in pleased amazement when Amanda praised her youngest as being a bright lad. Young Tom Bingely gratefully accepted one of Andrew Prewbody's old-but-good coats to cover up his missing arm, lost in the Peninsula. Old Mr. Sneyd was overwhelmed at the presentation of one of Mr. Prewbody's best pipes and a tin of tobacco.

Amanda threw a grateful look at Charlie at this latter sign of approval. She'd not have known to do this had not Charlie suggested it.

By the end of the afternoon, Amanda thought she had reached the peak of happiness. She had not missed the speculative looks in the faces of the women as they glanced from Amanda to Charlie. It gave Amanda more hope than she had known in her young life. Perhaps were she to persuade Charlie to assist her with the estate someday, they might reach a more satisfying accord?

"I trust you will join us for supper again, sir. It will be a simple affair but ample for a gentleman, I fancy. It is little enough that I may do to repay you for all your help this afternoon." Amanda held her hands together before her, beseeching him with her eyes if she but knew it.

Charlie wondered if she realized how she sounded, like the lady of the manor speaking to a steward. He dismissed the thought as unworthy, but it lodged in the back of his mind, not to be brushed away.

"I should be pleased to join you, Amanda," he said with deliberation. He would bring their relationship to that of a closer connection.

They had spent more time together than many an engaged couple, giving them a chance to know each other better than most. His brother had proposed to his wife after three dances, a ride in the park, and a consultation with her father. Charlie liked his time with Amanda better.

It was difficult for him to believe they had met only a few days past. She was all he had ever hoped to find in a wife: thrifty and practical, yet delightful and full of imagination. And she possessed a rare sort of beauty a man would never tire of if he lived to be a hundred.

They decided to play a game of cards after Amanda put away her things and saw to the table setting. While she busied herself at her brief tasks, Charlie sought out Jervis to see how things went in the stables.

The estate went well, like the well-tended farm he intended to have. He wouldn't deny that he had hoped to buy it from Amanda when first he knew of her inheriting the place. He had even dreamed that Andrew might bequeath it to himself. And now he hadn't the heart to ask Amanda to sell. Perhaps he might later on when she tired of being lady of the manor. Now she was far too delighted to have her own home and be her own mistress to consider another change.

And while Andrew had bestowed an extravagant sum of money on him, Charlie wasn't sure it would be sufficient to buy the estate outright. He would have to arrange some form of payment schedule. Then again, perhaps that would not be necessary. If he married Amanda he would have it all, plus the most lovely woman he had met in a long time, if not ever.

Consequently Charlie was a bit subdued when Amanda had put her bits and pieces away to join him at the card table.

Amanda wondered at his pensive state. Had something happened? He had spoken with Jervis.

"Please, is something wrong? Did Jervis tell you of a problem—other than the absent servants, who truly are not all that missed for the nonce." She placed one slim hand over his in her anxiety.

He studied that little hand, then glanced over to the wooden mouse. "No, nothing at all. Jervis tells me that all goes well. Apparently you are an easy mistress to please. A bit of coal, a fire now and again. He is free to tend the stables as he must and still accommodate your wishes."

Amanda gave Charlie a puzzled look. He was in an odd humor. She didn't tease him about it, for she really did not know him so well, did she?

The game of cards proceeded quietly, with both parties somewhat distracted and not playing their best. Following the simple supper Charlie excused himself, but not before Amanda extended her invitation for the following day.

"You will join us for Christmas dinner, will you not? The holiday would not be the same without company," she explained, although she had always been relegated to entertain the deaf uncle, or the difficult aunt when asked to join the relatives. He would be alone with his family gone, and she had no one to invite. "Fanny and I have put together a respectable menu, and even made a mince pie. Perhaps you might help with the Yule log?" she added as an enticement. He had seemed interested in that before.

"I should like to join you, but I must insist on bringing something for the festivities. I have sampled your fine bounty every day. Since I cannot in all propriety ask you to dinner at my brother's home, I would have his cook prepare something special for our holiday meal. A roast goose, a trifle, or something perhaps a bit difficult to concoct. Would that be acceptable?"

"Of course," Amanda said graciously. "Although it is not necessary in the least, it would be lovely to have a real cook's additions. Fanny and I are learning, but our failures are almost as numerous as our successes."

She compressed her lips before she burst out with an unseemly giggle. Burned porridge and scorched potatoes were part of their instruction, she supposed. But they had not been edible.

His murmured agreement said all it should, but a shiver of unease came over her. Then she decided she was being fanciful. She waved him farewell from the doorway before he disappeared into the gloom of the early nightfall.

Amanda found the little carving of the mouse where Charlie had placed it on the drawing room mantel and clutched it to her. Meeting the beady eyes of the live mouse, Amanda said softly, "But something is not quite as it should be. I can feel it in my bones."

With a twitch of its whiskers, the real mouse vanished behind the red berries with no solution for her.

She had wanted to go to church this evening. If possible, and the roads permitted, she would attend divine services tomorrow to proffer her thanksgiving for all her many blessings. The welcome sound of a choir and the peal of the organ would make Christmas all it should be. It brought peace and love to mind. Did petitions go with thanksgiving? She could place her appeal for her future at that time as well.

Amanda strolled slowly up the stairs to her room, totally forgetting to bring a book along as she often did. Instead, she undressed, donned her voluminous night rail of worn cream flannel, and climbed beneath her bedcovers to stare at the silly cupids for a long time before she finally blew out her lamp and went to sleep.

Charlie rode along the road, ignoring the shorter route across the fields. He had much on his mind. The problem had come to him this evening while they had dined so simply and yet so acceptably. Lingering snow offered a trace of added illumination to the starlit night while his horse carefully picked its way along the dimly lit road.

The problem was that Amanda Barkley was an heiress. A considerable heiress. He ought to know. He had managed this estate for the past few years, learning from Andrew as he went along how to handle each situation as it arose. The effort was to prepare Charlie for the life of an estate manager. He knew to a pence what the income of her estate was, how productive the land had become with all the innovative methods Andrew had encouraged him to try.

Yet nothing Andrew had taught him had prepared Charlie for his present dilemma. The rather mercenary thought that had occurred to him earlier returned. Marry Amanda and he would have this all. But how could he? She would consider him the veriest fortune hunter. And she would be right in the eyes of the world. It certainly would be a fortune for him.

How could he convince that sprite of a girl that he had tumbled into love with her the moment he had laid eyes on her, screeching in her minuscule way at a foolish little mouse. A grin lit his face for just a few moments as he recalled that time. She had appeared such a timid little thing, a merest wisp of a woman with those large dark eyes looking so terrified of such a very small mouse.

Yet he well knew from the kiss they had shared that she was all woman. And that was the trouble. For not only had she fit in his arms like she had belonged, but she had proved to be a very fine person to boot. Scarcely into her new home, not truly settled in the least, she had worried about gifts for tenants she didn't even know.

Only someone of the highest principles would evidence such concern. And what did that make him? Unprincipled?

It would never do. He could not continue to see her, for he suspected there already was much speculation. He had not missed the looks from the tenants, nor the conjecture lurking in Evan Heppell's gaze. Only the absence of his own family and the lack of hers sheltered their meetings and the amount of time he'd spent at Prewbody House. Time? Charlie had all but taken up residence there.

However, he did not think he had compromised her reputation, for there was no one to know of all the hours he spent at the house. His servants knew only that he had gone to instruct the new owner of the estate. He doubted that Jervis and Fanny would say a word, for they appeared devoted to their new mistress.

But Charlie knew, and therein was the problem. His solution was a painful one. Perhaps he could find a way around the dilemma. He couldn't think of one at the moment.

No, he'd just have to bite the bullet, do what he knew he must. She'd never forgive him for what he intended to do. But most likely, she'd not forgive him were he to follow his desires and marry her. Someday someone would say something, or perhaps the thought would come to her unbidden. He could not take the chance of having those charming glances turn to cold stares.

It was for the best.

Charlie turned his horse over to the groom with scarcely a murmur for the beast or man, an occurrence most unlike him. He paced the distance to the family home with reluctant steps, then entered.

First, he left instructions for the cook to follow in

the morning. If the lavish order for a new neighbor surprised the cook, not a word was uttered.

Then Charlie took himself up to bed, but not to sleep until he finally succumbed at a late hour, frustrated and angry at his lot.

Amanda rose early, determined to be happy this holy day of all holy days. She sang as though to cheer the house and hurried through her breakfast, although she savored the slice of ham that she and Fanny enjoyed every day since arriving.

Dressed in her best, she bade Jervis bring the coach around to the front. Miss Barkley was going to church.

Seated in splendor with Fanny at her side, Amanda drove to the village then entered the lovely old church to the accompaniment of the organ's peal of joy.

Although she tried to keep her eyes fixed to the front where a perfectly splendid arrangement of holly and ivy decorated the altar, she could not prevent little side glances. Was he here?

Oh, she knew he could not come to share the pew with her. That would be unseemly. It would give rise to all manner of speculation. But she wished she could glimpse his handsome face among the throng of worshipers. Mrs. Midgly nodded with a smile. On the far side of the church she espied Mr. Sneyd. The other tenants were also in attendance.

But she did not see Charlie.

That peculiar sensation that all was not well assailed her again, then she decided she was being exceptionally foolish. Charlie was most likely sound asleep, having quite forgotten the hour.

When the lovely service was concluded, she began to make her way out of the building. It was then that she

saw him. He was flirting with a young miss, a highly
suitable girl if her elegant clothes and indulgent-looking
parents were any sign. He did not cast a glance in
Amanda's direction.

She hoped he might at least bid her Happy Christmas. He did not even turn her way.

"Come on, Fanny. We must hurry or that green duck
might burn to a cinder," Amanda declared in a tight
little voice.

Fanny, having eyes in her head, hurriedly agreed and
marched her mistress to the carriage where she gave
Jervis a speaking look. They were off with a flurry,
leaving curious folk to speculate on the shy young
woman who had inherited Andrew Prewbody's fortune.
Tales of her goodness had preceded her, so none
thought her haughty, merely timid.

Once she entered her new home, Amanda set about
preparing for their guest. The table was arranged with
the best china and silver, the arrangement of holly and ivy
enhanced with the addition of the little wooden mouse.

In the kitchen, Fanny surveyed her efforts with
pride. Come the addition of the offerings from the
neighboring estate, the dinner would be as fine as anything presented at Rosling Hall.

Dressed in her pretty blue silk gown with the lovely
blue and green Norwich shawl purchased in town that
day that she had first set eyes on Charlie draped about
her shoulders, Amanda waited.

And waited.

"The duck is a-drying out, Miss Amanda," Fanny
said, reluctant to intrude, but knowing something had
to be done sooner or later.

"Hush. I believe I hear a carriage." Amanda froze in
place, scarcely daring to move.

Fanny heard it as well. She bustled to the front door, then paused with puzzlement when the carriage continued around the house to the rear.

Scurrying through to the kitchen door, Fanny met the footman from the Dane household with an anxious gaze. The elegant roast goose, potato *rissoles*, and the fresh pineapple from the Dane succession house was impressive. Strawberry ice cream, stuffed quails, and a hot-raised pie of mixed game completed the assortment. When it all sat on the well-scrubbed center table, Fanny studied the footman.

"Will Mr. Dane be along directly?"

The footman handed Fanny a folded piece of fine paper with a blob of wax sealing it.

"What's this?"

"A message for Miss Barkley. Don't know what's in it. He just said to hand it to you when I delivered the food." The fellow shuffled his feet, then fled the house.

Fanny, not in the least slow, watched the man leave and muttered to herself, "Fine thing to send all this food if he ain't gonna come."

"What was it, Fanny?" Amanda said from the shadowed doorway. She had wrapped the shawl around her as though to ward off a chill, although the kitchen was actually quite warm. The elegant Rumford stove housed the efforts of the morning, emitting delicious smells that mingled with those sent from Dane house.

"A message for you . . . along with enough food for a small army." Fanny picked up the ice cream to take it outside to keep it frozen.

"I see." Amanda extended her hand to take the missive, then walked in measured steps to the drawing room. Here she crossed to the sofa nearest the fireplace. Once seated, she broke the seal.

A dismayed flush crept over her cheeks. He wasn't coming. Most likely he was off to that dratted Pilkington party. Why had he told her he would join her for dinner, then fail to come with nothing more than an exceedingly brief letter saying that "something" prevented him from sharing the dinner with her?

That pretty miss at the village church? No. He might be attracted to that girl, but he seemed a most honorable gentleman. If he accepted an invitation, he would come. So . . . why didn't he?

Amanda rose from the sofa and began to pace back and forth before the fireplace, glancing from time to time at the curious little mouse. It peeped from behind the red berries again, its bright eyes watching her intently.

"So, you miss him as well, do you? Well, he does not wish to join us," Amanda declared with unaccustomed spirit.

"He ain't coming, is he? What am I to do with all this food?" Fanny said from the doorway.

"If I knew anyone, I should invite them, but it is far too late for that, even if I did have an acquaintance who might oblige me."

"Well, then?" Fanny persisted.

"Give me a moment," Amanda said with a wave of her hand. She continued her pacing, fighting the waves of despair that assaulted her when she considered that if she found no solution to this, Charlie might well avoid her forever. Something had occurred, but she could not think as to what it might be. But, whatever it was, it was serious.

"I would swear that he cares for me," Amanda said to the mouse, Fanny having retreated to the kitchen. "Surely he is not the sort of man to kiss a lady, then shab off. No, there must be something. Why, he spent

so much time explaining the workings of the estate."
Amanda paused, staring at the mouse. "I never did ask
him to assume the stewardship of the estate," she said
in a considering way. "Not that *that* particular title is
what I would wish for him."

But was that how he saw things? Did he foolishly
believe that now she had acquired an estate that she
would think herself above him? Surely not.

"Fanny!" she called to the rear of the house.

The maid ran to the entrance where her mistress now
stood staring out of the front window.

"Fanny," Amanda repeated quietly, "do you imagine
that Mr. Dane thinks me an heiress?"

"Well, and you are, miss. A pretty fine heiress, if
you were to ask me, or anybody."

Amanda stamped her tiny foot. "That is precisely
what I feared you might say. Oh, that nodcock, that
buffleheaded, cork-brained, utter fool!"

"Miss?" Fanny said, looking as though her mistress
was a bit of a peagoose herself.

"My pen! Paper!" Amanda whirled into action, scrib-
bling a note that brought a flush to her pale cheeks. "There!
Fanny, request Jervis to take this to Dane House, and
Fanny . . . tell Jervis that it is most urgent."

Mystified, Fanny rushed to the stables to hand the
message to the groom, who, when told it was serious,
dashed off to the west on the fastest horse in the stables.

Back in the drawing room, Amanda affixed the cluster of mistletoe to the doorway with a length of red
riband and a small nail.

At Dane House, Charlie read the note that the butler
had hurried to deliver upon being told the matter was
a pressing one.

In short order there was a pounding on Amanda's

front door, which was immediately thrown open. Charlie dashed into the drawing room, freezing in horror upon finding her stretched out on the sofa.

"Oh, my dearest," he exclaimed as he dashed to her side to begin chafing her dainty hands.

Amanda's lashes fluttered, and she gave Charlie a demure look before glancing off to the mantel.

"What is it, dear girl?"

"Oh, Charlie, I am besieged." She sighed in dismay. Not far from her side was a broom, which upon rising she brought into play.

"Who dares beset you? Mice? I shall bring in all the cats." He eyed the broom, then searched about the room with a puzzled expression.

"Oh, I daresay I have chased them into their holes for the moment. No, 'tis not just the mice."

"A man has threatened you? I'll have him clamped in irons. How dare anyone frighten a little thing like you?"

Amanda placed the broom against the sofa, then crossed her arms in front of her. She tapped a diminutive foot, and gave him a most daring and un-Amanda-like glare.

"But, Charlie, you are my dilemma. You and the mice, for I just know I am about to be overrun."

His look of confusion was nearly her undoing. Still Amanda continued. "I have reached the conclusion that I must sell my inheritance, for I cannot manage it myself. If I cannot cope with a few mice, how could I dream of supervising a great estate?" She ignored his mutters of an agent. "Besides, when the neighbors are so unkind, I could not bear to remain here."

"Who was unkind to . . . Oh. The dinner."

"When you merely sent those lovely foods and did not come, I feared I had somehow insulted you, possibly angered you beyond all redemption. And then I remembered what day this is. It is Christmas, Charlie."

He drew back until he again stood in the doorway, uncertain of what might come next.

She crossed the small space that separated them to confront the man she had come to love in such a short time. Standing directly beneath the mistletoe she had tacked to the doorway, she said. "It is a day when love and peace are to reign, at least for a time. Forgiveness, too, Charlie."

Amanda reached up to touch his cheek in a tentative gesture. Still unsure, she continued, more daring than ever in her entire life, "I love you, Charlie Dane. I want nothing more in life than to be yours and have you as mine. Of course, it would mean you must take over the estate for me, but that is something you would do well. I fancy a few might say you were a lucky fellow to marry the heiress. But we would know the truth of the matter."

Charlie looked at his precious darling girl. Hope rose wildly within him, and he asked, "And what is that?"

"That we are the ones who are truly blessed to find each other. Happy Christmas, Charlie." She extended one hand to pull several white berries from the dangling cluster, offering them to her Charlie.

And Charlie, to his credit, needed no other invitation.

On the mantel, the mouse was whisker to whisker with its wooden counterpart, and one might almost say it smiled.

No Room
at the Inn

by
Mary Balogh

THE White Hart Inn, somewhere in Wiltshire—it had never been important enough for anyone to map its exact location on any fashionable map or in any guidebook fashionable or otherwise—was neither large nor picturesque nor thriving. It was not a posting inn and had no compensating claim to fame—not its location, nor the quality of its ale or cuisine, nor the geniality of its host, nor anything in short. It was certainly not the type of place in which one would wish to be stranded unexpectedly for any length of time.

Especially at Christmastime.

And more especially when the cause was not a heavy snowfall, which might have added beauty to the surroundings and romance to the adventure, but rain. Torrential, incessant rain, which poured down from a leaden sky and made a quagmire of even the best-kept roads. The road past the White Hart was not one of the best-kept.

The inn presented a picture of squatness and ugliness and gloom to those who were forced to put up there rather than slither on along the road and risk bogging down completely and having to spend Christmas inside a damp and chill carriage—or risk overturning and celebrating the festive season amidst mud and injuries and even possibly death.

None of the travelers who arrived at the inn during the course of the late afternoon of the day preceding Christmas Eve did so by design. None of them did so with any pleasure. Most of them were in low spirits, and that was an optimistic description of the mood of a few of them. Even the landlord and his good lady were not as ecstatic as one might have expected them to be under the circumstances that they had rarely had more than one of their rooms filled during any one night for the past two years and more. Before nightfall all six of their rooms were occupied, and it was altogether possible that someone else might arrive after dark.

"What are we going to give 'em to eat?" Letty Palmer asked her husband, frowning at the thought of the modest-size goose and the even more modest ham on which the two of them had planned to feast on Christmas Day. "And what are we going to give 'em to drink, Joe? There is only ale and all of 'em are quality. Not to mention the coachmen what brought 'em 'ere."

"It'll 'ave to be ale or the rainwater outside," Joseph Palmer said, a note of belligerence in his voice, as if his guests had already begun to complain about the plain fare at the White Hart. "And as far as vittles is concerned, they'll 'ave to eat what we 'as and be thankful for it, too."

But the guests had not yet begun to complain about the food and drink, perhaps because they had not yet had an opportunity to sample the fare on which it seemed likely they would have to celebrate Christmas.

Edward Riddings, Marquess of Lytton, cursed his luck. He had been fully intending to spend the holiday season in London as he usually did, entertaining himself by moving from party to party. The ladies were always at their most amorous at Christmastime, he had found from experience. Yes, even the ladies. There was always pleasure to be derived from a sampling of their charms.

But this year he had been persuaded to accept one of the invitations that he always received in abundance to a private party in the country. Lady Frazer, the delectable widow, was to be at the Whittakers' and had given him an unmistakable signal that at last she would be his there. He had been laying determined siege to her heart, or rather to her body, since she had emerged from her year of mourning during the previous spring. She had the sort of body for which a man would be willing to traverse England.

Yet now it was evident that he was neither to reach that body in time for Christmas nor to return to London in time to console himself with the more numerous but perhaps less enticing pleasures of town. Even if the rain were to stop at this very instant, he thought, looking out of the low window of the small and shabby room to which he had been assigned at the White Hart, it was doubtful that the road would be passable before Christmas Day at the earliest. And there were still twenty miles to go.

The rain showed no sign of abating. If anything it was pounding down with greater enthusiasm than ever.

If he were fortunate—but events were not shaping up to bring any good fortune with them—there would be a beautiful and unattached lady of not quite impeccable virtue also stranded at this infernal inn. But he would not allow himself to hope. There could not be more than five or six guest rooms, and he had already seen five or six of his fellow strandees, none of whom appeared even remotely bedworthy.

It was going to be some Christmas, he thought, gritting his teeth and pounding one fist against the windowsill.

Miss Pamela Wilder gazed from the window of her room and felt all the misery of utter despair. She could not even cry. She could not even feel all the awkwardness of her situation, stranded as she was at a public inn without either maid or chaperone. It did not matter. Nothing mattered except that her first holiday in more than a year was to be spent here at this inn, alone. She thought of her parents and of her brothers and sisters, and she thought of Christmas as she had always known it—except last year—at the rectory and in the small church next to it. There was warmth and light and wonder in the thought until nostalgia stabbed at her so painfully that the memories could no longer bring any comfort.

They did not know she was coming. It was to be a surprise. Lawrence, one of Sir Howard Raven's coachmen, had been given a few days off for Christmas and had even been granted permission to take the old and shabby carriage that was scheduled for destruction as soon as the new one was delivered. And his home was not ten miles from the rectory where Mama and Papa lived. Pamela had broached the subject very tentatively and quite without hope, first with Lawrence and then with Lady Raven, and wonder of wonders, no one had raised any objection. It seemed that a governess was not particularly needed at Christmastime, when young Hortense would have cousins with whom to play and greater freedom to mingle with the adults.

Pamela was free until two days after Christmas. Free to go home. Free to be with her family and spend that most wonderful time of the year with them. Free to see Wesley and hope that finally he felt himself well enough established on his farm to offer for her. Free to hope that perhaps he would at least ask her to betroth herself to him even if the wedding must be postponed for a long time. Having an unspoken understanding with him had not soothed her loneliness since she had been forced to take her present post more than a year before. She craved some more definite hope for the future.

Yet now she was to spend Christmas at the White Hart, eight miles—eight impossible miles—from home. Even if the rain were to stop now, there seemed little chance that she would make it home for Christmas Day. But the rain was not going to stop now or before the night was over at the very earliest. There was no point in even hoping otherwise.

She was hungry, Pamela realized suddenly, even though she was not at all sure she would be able to eat. How could she do so, anyway? How could she go downstairs alone to the dining room? And yet she must. She was not of any importance at all. There seemed little hope of persuading anyone to bring up her dinner on a tray.

What a Christmas it was going to be, she thought. Even last year had been better—that dreadful Christmas, her first away from home, her first in the status of a servant and yet not quite a servant. She had been able to celebrate the coming of Christ with neither the family nor the servants. Perhaps after all she would be no more alone this year than last, she thought in a final effort to console herself.

Lord Birkin stood at the window of his room, his lips compressed, his hands clasped behind him and beating a rhythmic tattoo against his back. What a confounded turn of events.

"We should have come a week ago, like everyone else," Lady Birkin said, "instead of staying in London until the last possible minute."

She was seated on the edge of the bed behind him. He knew that if he turned and looked at her, he would see her the picture of dejection, all her beauty and animation marred by the rain and the poverty of her surroundings. She would hate having to spend Christmas here when they had been on their way to spend it with the Middletons and more than twenty of their relatives and friends.

"You would have missed the opera and the Stebbins' ball," he said without turning.

"And you would have missed a few days at your club," she said, a note of bitterness in her voice.

"We could not have predicted the rain," he said. "Not in this quantity anyway. I am sorry that you will miss all the Christmas entertainments, Sally."

"And you will miss the shooting," she said, that edge still in her voice. "And the billiards."

He turned to look at her at last, broodingly. Marriage had turned out to be nothing like what he had expected. They were two people living their separate lives, he and Sally, with the encumbrance of the fact that they were legally bound together for life.

Were things quite as bad as that? They had been

fond of each other when they had married, even though their parents on both sides had urged the match on them. He still was fond of her, wasn't he? Yes, he was still fond of her. But somehow marriage had not drawn them closer together. The occasional couplings, now no more frequent than once or twice a month, though they had not been married much longer than three years, brought with them no emotional bond. They both behaved on the mornings after the couplings as if they had never happened.

"I am sorry about the sparsity of rooms," he said. "I am sorry we must share."

His wife flushed and looked about the room rather than at him. It was going to be dreadful, she thought. Dreadful to be alone with him for what would probably be several days. Dreadful to have to share a room with him and a bed for that time. They had never shared a bed for longer than ten minutes at a time, and even those occasions had become rarer during the past year.

She had married him because she loved him and because she had thought he loved her, though he had never said so. Foolish girl. She must have appeared quite mousy to such a blond and beautiful man. He had married her because it was expected of him, because the connection was an eligible one. She knew now that she had never attracted him and never could. He rarely spent time with her. Their marital encounters were a bitter disappointment and so rare that she did not even have the consolation of having conceived his child.

She knew about his mistresses, though he did not know that she knew. She had even seen his latest one, a creature of exquisite beauty and voluptuous charms. She herself had come to feel quite without beauty or charm or allure.

Except that she had not allowed herself to give in to self-pity. She had had a choice early in her marriage. Either she could retreat into herself and become the mousy uninteresting thing he saw her as, or she could put her unhappiness and disappointment behind her and live a life of busy gaiety, as so many married ladies of her acquaintance did. She had chosen the latter course. He would never know for what foolish reason she had married him or what foolish hopes had been dashed early in their marriage.

"There is no point in apologizing for what cannot be helped, Henry," she said. "Under the circumstances I suppose we are fortunate to have a roof over our heads. Though I could wish that it had happened at some other time of the year. It is going to be an unimaginably dull Christmas."

She wondered what it would be like to lie all night in the large and rather lumpy bed with him beside her. Her breathing quickened at the thought, and she looked up at him with an unreasonable resentment.

"Yes," he said. "Whoever heard of Christmas spent at an inn?"

"It would not have happened," she said, hearing the irritability in her voice and knowing that she was being unfair, "if we had come a week ago like everyone else."

"As you keep reminding me," he said. "Next year we will do things differently, Sally. Next year we will see to it that you are surrounded by friends and admirers well before Christmas itself comes along."

"And that you have plenty of other gentlemen and gentlemen's sports with which to amuse yourself," she said. "Perhaps there will be some gentlemen here, Henry. Perhaps you will find some congenial companions with whom to talk the night away and forget the inconvenience of such congested quarters."

"I can sleep in the taproom if you so wish," he said, his voice cold.

They did not often quarrel. One or other of them usually left the room when a disagreement was imminent, as it was now.

"That would be foolish," she said.

He was leaving the room now. He paused, with his hand on the doorknob. "I doubt there is such a luxury as a private parlor in this apology for an inn," he said. "We will have to eat in the public dining room, Sally. I shall go and see when dinner will be ready."

An excuse to get away from her, Lady Birkin thought as the door closed behind him. She concentrated on not crying and succeeded. She had perfected the skill over the years.

It was an excuse to get away from her, Lord Birkin thought as he descended the stairs. Away from her accusing voice and the knowledge that the worst aspect of the situation for her was being forced to spend a few days in his dull company. She did not sleep with any of her numerous admirers. He did not know quite how he could be sure of that since he had never spied on her, but he did know it. She was faithful to him, or to their marriage at least, as he was not. But he knew equally that she would prefer the company of any one of her admirers to his.

But she was stuck with it for several days. And at Christmas of all times.

The Misses Amelia and Eugenia Horn, unmarried ladies of indeterminate years, had left their room in order to seek out the innkeeper. The sheets on their beds were damp, Miss Amelia Horn declared in a strident voice.

"Perhaps they are only cold, dear," Miss Eugenia Horn suggested in a near whisper, embarrassed by the indelicate mention of bedsheets in the hearing of two gentlemen, not counting the innkeeper himself.

But her elder sister was made of sterner stuff and argued on. They were bitterly disappointed, Miss Eugenia Horn reflected, leaving the argument to her sister. They would not make it to dear Dickie's house fifteen miles away and would not have the pleasure of their annual visit with their brother and sister-in-law and the dear children, though the youngest of Dickie's offspring was now seventeen years old. How time did fly. They would all be made quite despondent by her absence and dear Amelia's. Dickie was always too busy, the poor dear, to have them visit at any other time of the year.

Miss Eugenia Horn sighed.

Colonel Forbes, a large, florid-faced, white-haired gentleman of advanced years, was complaining to Lord Birkin, the innkeeper's attention being otherwise occupied at the time. He deplored the absence of a private parlor for the convenience of his wife and himself.

"General Hardinge himself has invited us for Christmas," the colonel explained. "A singular honor and a distinguished company. And now this blasted rain. A fine Christmas this is going to be."

"We all seem to be agreed on that point at least," Lord Birkin said politely and waited his turn to ask about dinner.

Sometimes the most dreaded moments turned out not to be so dreadful after all, Pamela realized when the emptiness of her stomach drove her downstairs in search of dinner. Although the dining room appeared alarmingly full with fellow guests and she felt doubly alone, she did not long remain so. Two middle-aged ladies looked up at her from their table, as did all the other occupants of the room, saw her lone state, and took her beneath their wing. Soon she was tucked safely into a chair at their table.

"Doubtless you expected to be at your destination all within one day, my dear," Miss Eugenia Horn said in explanation of Pamela's lack of a companion.

"Yes, ma'am," she said. "I did not expect the rain."

"But it is always wiser to expect the unexpected and go nowhere without a chaperone," Miss Amelia Horn added. "You would not wish to give anyone the impression that you were fast."

"No, ma'am." Pamela was too grateful for their company to feel offended.

The Misses Horn proceeded to complain about the dampness of their bedsheets and their threadbare state.

"I suppose," Miss Amelia Horn said, "that we should have expected the unexpected, Eugenia, and brought our own. It is never wise to travel without."

The rain and all being stranded at the very worst time of the year had appeared to draw the other occupants of the room together, Pamela noticed. Conversation was becoming general. She looked about her with some curiosity, careful not to stare at anyone. A quiet gentleman of somewhat less than middle years sat at the table next to hers. He said very little, but listened to everyone, a smile in his eyes and lurking about his mouth. He was perhaps the only member of the party to look as if he did not particularly resent being where he was.

An elderly couple sat at another table, the man loudly

and firmly condemning England as a place to live and declaring darkly that if the government did not do something about it soon, all sensible Englishmen would take themselves off to live on the Continent or in America. He did not make it clear whether he expected the government to do something about the excessive amount of rainfall to which England was susceptible or whether he was referring to something else. Whatever the cause, he was very flushed and very angry. His wife sat across the table from him, quietly nodding. Pamela realized after a while that the nodding was involuntary. They were Colonel and Mrs. Forbes, she learned in the course of dinner.

A young and handsome couple sat at another table, perhaps the most handsome pair Pamela had ever seen. The lady was brown-haired and brown-eyed and had a proud and beautiful face and the sort of shapely figure that always made Pamela sigh with envy. Her husband, Lord Birkin, was like a blond Greek god, the kind of man she had always found rather intimidating. They were clearly unhappy both with each other and with a ruined Christmas. Apparently they were on their way to a large country party. They were the sort of people who had everything and nothing, though that was a flash judgment, Pamela admitted to herself, and perhaps unfair.

There was another gentleman in the room. Pamela's eyes skirted about him whenever she looked up. On the few occasions when she looked directly at him, her uncomfortable impression that he was staring at her was confirmed. He was not handsome. Oh, yes, he was, of course, but not in the way of the blond god. He was more attractive than handsome, with his dark hair and hooded eyes—they might be blue, she thought—and cynical curl to his lip. She had met his like a few times since becoming a governess. He was undressing her with his eyes and probably doing other things to her with his mind. She had to concentrate on keeping her hands steady on her knife and fork.

"Oh. On my way home, ma'am," she said in answer to a question Mrs. Forbes had asked her. "To my parents' home for Christmas. Eight miles from here."

Everyone was listening to her. They were sharing stories, commiserating with one another for the unhappy turn of events that had brought them all to the White Hart. Only the quiet gentleman seemed to have had no Christmas destination to lament.

"I am a governess, ma'am," she said when Miss Eugenia Horn asked her the question. "My father is a clergyman." The gentleman of the lazy eyelids—the innkeeper had addressed him as "my lord"—was still staring at her, one hand turning his glass of ale.

The conversation turned to the food and a spirited discussion of whether it was beef or veal or pork they were eating. There was no unanimous agreement.

A governess, the Marquess of Lytton was thinking, daughter of a clergyman. A shame. A decided shame. Governesses were of two kinds, of course. There were the virtuous governesses, the unassailable ones, and there were the governesses starved for pleasures of the sexual variety and quite delightfully voracious in their appetites when one had finally maneuvered them between bedsheets or into some other satisfactory location. He judged that Miss Pamela Wilder was of the former variety, though one never knew for sure until one had made careful overtures. Perhaps she would live up to her name.

She was certainly the only possibility at the inn.

There had not appeared to be even any chambermaids or barmaids with whom to warm his bed. He had the uncomfortable feeling that he might be facing an alarmingly celibate Christmas if Miss Wilder was saving herself for a future and probably illusory husband. There was the delectable Lady Birkin, of course, but then he had never made a practice of bedding other men's wives or even flirting with them, whether the husband was in tow or not.

Miss Pamela Wilder was the only possibility then. And a distinct possibility she was, provided she was assailable. She was slim, perhaps a little slimmer than he liked his women when there was a choice, but there was a grace about her figure and movements that he found intriguingly feminine and that stirred his loins, though he had drunk only two tankards of the land-lord's indescribably bad ale. Her face was lovely—wide-eyed, long-lashed, with straight nose and soft, thoroughly kissable mouth. Her hair was smooth and tied in a sim-ple knot at her neck, as one would expect of a govern-ess, but no simplicity of style could dim its blond sheen.

Two nights, probably three, at this inn, he thought, if they were fortunate. She could help Christmas pass with relative comfort, perhaps with enormous comfort. She might console him for the fact that the consumma-tion of his lust with Lady Frazer must be postponed beyond the festive season.

The innkeeper and his wife did not seem to feel it would be diplomatic to discuss private business in pri-vate. Mr. Joe Palmer was refilling the gentlemen's glasses with ale when the inevitable new arrivals came to the inn, looking for a room. Mrs. Letty Palmer came and stood in the doorway to discuss the matter with him just as if the room was not full of guests who had their own conversations to conduct.

"We don't 'ave no room for 'em," Mr. Palmer said with firm decision. "They'll 'ave to go somewhere else, Letty."

"There's nowhere else for 'em to go," Mrs. Palmer said. "We're full with quality and their servants. They aren't quality, Joe. I thought p'raps the taproom?"

"And 'ave 'em rob us blind as soon as we goes to bed?" Mr. Palmer said contemptuously, earning a roar of fury from Mr. Forbes when he slopped ale onto the cloth beside that gentleman's glass. "We don't 'ave no room, Letty."

"The woman's in the fambly way," Mrs. Palmer said. "Looks as if she's about to drop 'er load any day, Joe."

"Oh, dear," Miss Eugenia Horn said, a hand to her mouth. Such matters were not to be spoken aloud in genteel and mixed company.

Mr. Palmer put his jug of ale down on the cloth and set his hands on his hips. "I didn't arsk 'er to get in the fambly way, now did I, Letty?" he said. "Am I 'er keeper? What are they doin' out in this weather anyway if she's close to 'er time?"

" 'Er man's in search of work," Mrs. Palmer said. "What shall we do with 'em, Joe? We can't turn 'em away. They'll drownd."

Joe puffed out his cheeks, practicality warring with compassion.

"I won't 'ave 'em in 'ere, Letty," he said. "There's no room for 'em, and I won't risk 'aving 'em steal all our valuables. And all these qualities's valuables. They'll 'ave to move on or stay in the stable. There's an empty stall."

"It's cold in the stable," she said.

"Not with all 'em extra 'orses," the innkeeper said. "It's there or nowhere, Letty." He picked up his jug and turned determinedly to the quiet gentleman. "They comes 'ere expectin' a body to snap 'is fingers and make new rooms appear." His voice was aggrieved. "And they probly don't 'ave two 'a'pennies to rub together."

The quiet gentleman merely smiled at him. Poor devils, the marquess thought, having to sleep in the stable. But it was probably preferable to the muddy road. He would not think of it. It was not as if the inn itself offered luxury or even basic comfort. The dinner they had just eaten was disgusting, to put the matter into plain English.

"Poor people," Lady Birkin said quietly to her husband. "Imagine having to sleep in a stable, Henry. And she is with child."

"They will probably be thankful even for that," he said. "They will be out of the rain at least, and the animals will keep them warm."

She stared at him from her dark eyes with an expression that never failed to turn his insides over. She had a tender heart and carried out numerous works of charity though she always fretted that she could do so little. She was going to worry now about the two poor travelers who had arrived at safety only to find that there was no room at the inn. He wanted to reach across the table to take her hand. He did not do so, only partly because they were in a public place.

"Will they?" she said. "Be warm, I mean? The landlord was not just saying that? But it will smell in there, Henry, and be dirty."

"There is no alternative," he said, "except for them to move on. They will be all right, Sally. They will be safe and dry, at least. They will be able to keep each other warm."

Her cheeks flushed slightly, and he felt a stabbing of desire for her—the sort of feeling that usually sent him off in search of his mistress and an acceptable outlet for his lust.

"I am going back upstairs," she said, getting to her feet. He walked around the table to pull back her chair. "Are you coming?"

And impose his company on her for the rest of the evening? "I'll escort you up," he said, "and return to the taproom for a while."

She nodded coolly, indifferently.

Her movement was the signal for everyone to get up except the quiet gentleman, who continued to sit and sip on the bad ale. But Lord Birkin did not wait for everyone else. He escorted his wife to their room and looked about it with a frown.

"You will be all right here, Sally?" he asked. "There is not much to do except lie down and sleep, is there?"

"I am tired after the journey," she said.

He looked at the bed. It did not look as if it were going to be comfortable. He was to share it with her that night. For the first time in over three years they were to sleep together, literally sleep together. The thought brought another tightening to his groin. He should have slept with her from the start, he thought. He should have made it the pattern of their marriage. Perhaps the physical side of their marriage and every other aspect of it would have developed more satisfactorily if he had. Perhaps they would not have drifted apart.

He did not know quite why they had done so, or even if drifted were the right word. Somehow their

marriage had never got properly started. He did not
know whose fault it was. Perhaps neither of them was
to blame. Perhaps both of them were. Perhaps she had
really been as fond of him as he was of her at the
beginning. Perhaps they should have put their feelings
into words. Perhaps he should not have given in to the
fear that she found him dull and his touch distasteful.
Perhaps he should not have treated her with sexual restraint as his father and other men had advised because
she was a lady and ladies were supposed to find sex
distasteful. Perhaps he should have taken her with the
desire he felt—surely it was not disrespectful to show
pleasure in one's wife's body.

Perhaps. Perhaps and perhaps.

"I'll be up later," he told her. "Don't wait up for me."
You may sleep. I'll not be demanding my conjugal rights. He
might as well have said those words too.

She nodded and turned away to the window, waiting
for the sound of the door closing behind her and the
feeling of emptiness it would bring. And the familiar
urge to cry. It was Christmas, and he preferred to be
downstairs drinking with strangers to being alone with
her.

She looked down into wet darkness and shivered.
Those poor people—trying to get warm and comfortable in a dirty and drafty stable, trying to sleep there.
She wondered if the man loved his wife, if she loved
him. If he would hold her close to keep her warm. If
he would offer his arm as her pillow. If he would kiss
her before she slept so that she would feel warm and
loved even in such appalling surroundings.

She wiped impatiently at a tear. She did not normally
give in to the urge to weep. She did not usually give
in to self-pity.

The Misses Horn were busy agreeing with Mrs. Forbes that indeed it was dreadful that those poor people had to find shelter in a stable on such a wet and chilly night. But what could the husband be thinking of, dragging his poor wife off in search of work when she was in a, ah, delicate situation? There was a deal of embarrassed coughing over the expression of this idea and furtive glances at the gentlemen to make sure that none of them were listening. She would give the man a piece of her mind if she had a chance, Miss Amelia Horn declared.

The Marquess of Lytton got to his feet.

"Allow me to escort you to your room, Miss Wilder," he said, offering her his arm and noting with approval that the top of her head reached his chin. She was taller than she had appeared when she entered the dining room.

She looked calmly and steadily at him. At least she was not going to throw a fit of the vapors at the very idea of being conducted to her bedchamber by a rake. He wondered if she knew enough about the world to recognize him as a rake and if she realized that all through dinner he had been compensating for the appallingly unappetizing meal by mentally unclothing her and putting her to bed, with himself.

"Thank you," she said and rested her hand on his arm, a narrow, long-fingered hand. An artist's hand. Either she was a total innocent or she had accepted the first step of seduction. He hoped for the latter. He hoped she was not an innocent. It was Christmas for God's sake. A man was entitled to his pleasures at that season of the year above all others.

"This is an annoyance and a discomfort that none of us could have foreseen this morning," he said.

"Yes." Her voice was low and sweet. Seductive, though whether intentionally so or not he had not yet decided. "Do you suppose they are dreadfully cold out there? Was there anything we could have done?"

"The couple in the stable?" he said. "Very little, I suppose, unless one of us were willing to give up his room and share with someone else."

She looked up into his eyes. Hers had a greenish hue though they had looked entirely gray from a farther distance. "I suppose that was a possibility," she said. "Alas, none of us thought of it."

He had, though he did not say so. Of course, if they did share a room that night, they could hardly go and advertise the fact to the Palmers. The poor devils were doomed to their night in the stables regardless. A governess. A quiet, grave girl instead of Lady Frazer. A poor exchange, perhaps, though not necessarily so. The quiet ones were often the hottest in bed. And this one was definitely stirring his blood.

She knew that he had offered his escort not out of motives of chivalry, but for other reasons. Her employers entertained a great deal. She had learned something about men during the year of her service. She might have had half a dozen lovers during that time. She had never been tempted.

She was tempted now. She was twenty-three years old, eldest daughter of an impoverished clergyman, a governess. In all probability she was headed for a life of drudgery and humiliation and spinsterhood. She did not believe in her heart that Wesley would ever feel himself in a secure enough position to take her as a wife. Or perhaps he used insecurity as an excuse to avoid a final commitment. The hope of marriage with him was just the frail dream with which she sustained her spirits. It was in truth a dreary life to which she looked forward.

And now even the promised brief joy of this Christmas was to be taken away from her. Except that she could spend it with this incredibly attractive man. She did not doubt that he wanted her and that he would waste no time in sounding out her availability. She had even less doubt that he knew well how to give pleasure to a woman. She could have a Christmas of unimagined pleasure, a Christmas to look back upon with nostalgia for the rest of her life. Now, within the next few minutes, without any chance for her mind and her conscience to brood upon the decision, she could discover what it was like to be with a man, what it was like to be desired and pleasured.

She was tempted. The realization amazed her—she did not even know him. She did not know his name. But she was tempted.

She stopped outside her door and looked up at him. "Thank you, sir," she said. "The innkeeper called you 'my lord'?"

"Lytton," he said. "The marquess of. Green eyes, gray—which are they?"

"A little of both, my lord," she said. A marquess. Oh, goodness. He was tall, broad-shouldered. "Thank you," she said again.

He opened the door for her, but when she stepped inside he followed her in and closed the door behind his back. She had been expecting it, she realized. And she realized at the same instant that this was the moment of decision. She did not have any time in which to think, not even a minute.

"It is likely to be a lonely Christmas," he said. "You away from your family, me from my friends."

"Yes." One of his hands had come up so that he could touch her cheek with light fingertips. She felt his touch all the way to her toes. His eyes—yes, they were blue—were keen beneath the lazy lids. She looked into them.

"Perhaps," he said, "we can make it less lonely together."

"Yes." But no sound came out with the word.

She had been kissed before—twice, both times by Wesley. But the experience had not prepared her at all for the Marquess of Lytton's kiss. It was not that it was hard or demanding. Quite the opposite, in fact. His lips rested as lightly against hers as his fingertips had against her cheek a few moments before. But they were parted, warm and moist, and they moved over hers, feeling them, caressing them, softening them, even licking at them. When his hands came to her waist to bring her against him, she allowed herself to be embraced and rested her body against his—against this hard, muscled, warm male.

He felt wonderful. He smelled wonderful. And he was doing wonderful things to her body though his hands were still at her waist and his lips still light on hers. Then his hands moved up to her breasts and she knew that now—now, not one moment later—was the point of no return. Now she must stop it or move on to new experiences, to a new state of being.

She would be a fallen woman.

She was incredibly sweet. He had never known innocence, had never imagined how arousing it could be. She was yielding without being in any way aggressive. She held still to his touch without being in any way cringing. She was his, he knew, with a little skill and a little care. And yet he knew equally that she was an innocent despite having allowed him inside her room and having allowed his kiss without any hesitation or coyness.

Her waist was soft, warm, small, with the promise of feminine hips below. He slid his hands up to her breasts. They were not large, but they were firm and soft all at the same time. Her nipples, he found when he tested them with his thumbs, were already peaked. She was his, he knew, despite the almost imperceptible stiffening he felt when his hands moved. He felt her indecision, but knew what that decision would be. He raised his head and looked down at her. She gazed back, wide-eyed.

"I had better say good night," he said, "before I go too far and get my face slapped. Yes, perhaps we can make each other less lonely for Christmas, Miss Wilder. I look forward to conversing with you tomorrow."

"Yes," she said, but he could not tell from her expression if she had been fooled. Did she really believe that he had meant nothing more than pleasant conversation and almost chaste good-night kisses as the means of soothing their loneliness at Christmas? Did she believe that he had not entered this room to bed her?

"Good night," he said, inclining his head to her and letting himself out of her room. Fortunately there was no one to witness his leaving it.

Fool! he thought, his lip curling into a cynical half smile. He had been issued the sort of invitation he had never before in his life refused, and yet he had done just that. He had wanted her. He still did. And yet he had put her from him and pretended that he had meant nothing more than a good-night kiss. He did not believe he had ever kissed a woman good night and not expected more.

She would have had him, too. And she would have been sweet despite her innocence and inexperience. Of course, there would have been her virginity to take—he would wager his fortune that she was a virgin. Perhaps that had been the problem, he thought, shrugging and turning in the direction of the staircase and the taproom. The thought of taking someone's virginity frankly terrified him. He might be a rake, but he was not a corrupter of innocence. Especially when the girl was lonely and unhappy and incapable of making a rational decision.

All the men were in the taproom, though it seemed likely that they were seeking out one another's company rather than their landlord's ale, the marquess thought, grimacing as he tasted it again. Christmas would be beginning now at the Whittakers' with all its rich and tasty foods and drinks and with all its congenial company. He pictured Lady Frazer and put the image from his mind with a mental sigh.

Lord Birkin did not stay long. He could not concentrate on the conversation. It was true that she did not seem to find his company of any interest, and equally true that she must be horrified at the thought of sharing a bed with him all night. But even so it seemed somehow wrong to sit belowstairs, making conversation with the other gentlemen guests while she was forced to be alone in their small and shabby bedchamber.

A candle still burned in their room though she was lying far to one side of the bed with her eyes closed. He could not tell if she slept or not. He undressed, wondering if she would open her eyes, finding it strange to think that they had never allowed themselves to become familiar with each other physically. They had never seen each other unclothed. He wished again that it were possible to go back to the beginning of their marriage. He would do so many things differently. Now it seemed too late. How did one change things when patterns had been set and habits had become ingrained?

He blew out the candle and climbed into bed, keeping close to the edge. But it was impossible to sleep and impossible to believe that she slept. She was too still, too quiet. He almost laughed out loud. They had been married for longer than three years and yet were behaving like a couple of strangers thrown together in embarrassing proximity. But he did not laugh, he was not really amused.

"Sally?" He spoke softly and reached out a hand to touch her arm.

"Yes?"

But what was there to say when one had been married to a woman for so long and had never spoken from the heart? Patterns could not so easily be broken. Instead of speaking he moved closer and began the familiar and dispassionate ritual of raising her nightgown and positioning himself on top of her.

All their actions, hers and his, were as they always were. There were never variations. She allowed him to spread her legs though she did not do it for him, and she lifted herself slightly for his hands to slide beneath. He put himself firmly inside her, settled his face in her hair, felt her hands come to his shoulders, and worked in her with firm, rhythmic strokes until his seed sprang. He was always careful not to indulge himself by prolonging the intercourse. She never gave the slightest sign of either pleasure or distaste. She was a dutiful wife.

And yet he wondered after he had disengaged himself

from her and settled at her side why he carried out the ritual at all since it brought neither of them any great pleasure and was not performed frequently enough for there to be any realistic expectation that she would conceive. Why did he do it at all when his desires and energies could be worked out on women who were well paid to suffer the indignity?

Perhaps because he needed her? Because he loved her? But of what use was his love when he had never been able to tell her and when he had never taken the opportunity to cultivate her love at the beginning when she had perhaps been fond of him?

Lady Birkin lay still, willing sleep to come. Were they reasonably warm and comfortable in the stable? she wondered. Did the man care for his wife? Was she lying in his arms? Was he murmuring words of love to her to put her to sleep? Did her pregnancy bring her discomfort? What did it feel like to be heavy with child—with one's husband's child? She burrowed her head into the hard pillow, imagining as she often did at night to put herself to sleep that it was an arm, that there was a warm chest against her forehead and the steady beat of a heart against her ear. Her hand, moving up to pull the pillow against her face, brushed a real arm and moved hastily away from it.

Breakfast was late. It was not that the night before had been busy and exciting enough to necessitate their sleeping on in the morning. And it was certainly not that the beds were comfortable enough or the rooms warm and cozy enough to invite late sleeping. It was more, perhaps, lethargy, and the knowledge that there was not a great deal to get up for. Even if the rain had stopped, travel would have been impossible. But the rain had not stopped. Each guest awoke to the sound of it beating against the windows, only marginally lighter than it had been the day before.

And so breakfast was late. When the guests emerged from their rooms and gathered in the dining room, it seemed that only the quiet gentleman had been sitting there for some time, patiently awaiting the arrival of his meal.

Greasy eggs and burnt toast accompanied complaints about other matters. Eugenia was sure to have taken a chill, Miss Amelia Horn declared, having been forced to sleep between damp sheets. Miss Eugenia Horn flushed at the indecorous mention of sleep and sheets in the hearing of gentlemen. Colonel Forbes complained about the lumps in his bed and swore there were coals in the mattress. Mrs. Forbes nodded her agreement. The Marquess of Lytton lamented the fact that the coal fire in his room had been allowed to die a natural death the night before and had not been resuscitated in the morning. Lord Birkin wondered if they would be expected to make up their own beds. Lady Birkin declared that the ladies could not possibly be expected to sit in their rooms all day long. In the absence of any private parlors, the gentlemen must expect their company in the taproom and the dining room. The other ladies agreed. Even Pamela Wilder nodded her head.

"That is the most sensible suggestion anyone has made yet this morning," the Marquess of Lytton said, nodding his approval to Lady Birkin and fixing his eyes on Pamela.

The innkeeper's wife was pouring muddy coffee for those foolish enough or bored enough to require a second cup. The innkeeper appeared in the doorway.

"You'd best come, Letty," he said. "I told yer we

should 'ave nothing to do with 'em. Now look at what's gone and 'appened."

"What 'as 'appened?" The coffee urn paused over the quiet gentleman's cup as Mrs. Palmer looked up at her husband. " 'Ave they gone and stole an 'orse, Joe?"

"I wish they 'ad," Mr. Palmer said fervently. "I wish they 'ad, Letty. But no such luck. 'E's in the taproom." He jerked a thumb over his shoulder. "She's 'aving 'er pains. In our stable, mind."

"Oh, Lord love us," Mrs. Palmer said. The quiet gentleman was still waiting for his coffee. "She can't 'ave it there, Joe. Who ever 'eard of anyone 'aving a baby in a stable?"

The quiet gentleman smiled and appeared to resign himself to going without his coffee.

"Oh." Lady Birkin was on her feet. "The poor woman. How dreadful." She looked at her husband in some distress. "She must be taken extra blankets."

"There ain't no extra blankets," Mrs. Palmer said tartly. "We 'ave a full 'ouse, my lady."

Lady Birkin looked appealingly at her husband. "Then she must have the blankets from our bed," she said. "We will manage without, won't we, Henry?" She reached out a hand to him and he took it.

"Perhaps one from your bed and one from ours, Lady Birkin," Mrs. Forbes said. "Then we will both have something left."

"I have a shawl," Miss Eugenia Horn said. "A warm woollen one that I knitted myself. I shall send it out. Perhaps it will do for wrapping the baby when it is, ah, born." She flushed.

"And I will send out my smelling salts," Miss Amelia Horn said. "The poor woman will probably need them."

"I have a room," Pamela said quietly. "She must be carried up there."

"We don't 'ave no other room to put you in, Miss," Mrs. Palmer said.

"And I won't 'ave no one in the taproom," Mr. Palmer added firmly.

"Then I shall sleep in the stable tonight," Pamela said.

The Marquess of Lytton got to his feet. "Is the husband large and strong?" he asked the innkeeper. "If not, I shall carry the woman in from the stable myself. To *my* room. Miss Wilder may keep hers. And you will, my good man, have someone in the taproom. Tonight. Me."

Mr. Palmer did not argue.

"I'll lend a hand," Lord Birkin said, and the two gentlemen left the room together, followed by Mr. Palmer.

"Perhaps," Lady Birkin said, looking at the innkeeper's wife, who appeared to have been struck with paralysis, "you should have coals sent up to Lord Lytton's room to warm it."

"Lord love us," Mrs. Palmer said, "I 'ave breakfast to clear away, my lady, and dishes to wash before I gets to the rooms."

Colonel Forbes puffed to his feet. "I have never heard the like," he said. "I never have. An inn with no help. Where are the coals, ma'am? I shall carry some up myself."

Mrs. Forbes nodded her approval as her husband strode from the room.

"I shall go up and get the bed ready," Pamela said, "if you will tell me which room is Lord Lytton's, ma'am." She flushed rosily.

"That would be improper, dear," Miss Eugenia Horn said. "Though of course it is not his lordship's room any longer, is it? I shall come with you nevertheless."

"Thank you," Pamela said.

"And I shall go and fetch your shawl, Eugenia, and my smelling salts," Miss Amelia Horn said.

"You will send for a midwife?" Lady Birkin said to Mrs. Palmer.

"Oh, Lord, my lady," Mrs. Palmer said. "There is no midwife for five miles and she wouldn't come 'ere anyhow for no woman what can't pay as like as not."

"I see," Lady Birkin said. "So we are on our own. Have you ever assisted at a birth, Mrs. Palmer?"

The woman's eyes widened. "Not me, my lady," she said. "Nor never 'ad none of my own neither."

Lady Birkin's eyes moved past the Misses Horn and Pamela to Mrs. Forbes. "Ma'am?" she said hopefully.

Mrs. Forbes ceased her nodding in order to shake her head. "I was forty when I married Mr. Forbes," she said. "There was no issue of our marriage."

"Oh," Lady Birkin said. She looked around at the other ladies rather helplessly. "Then I suppose we will have to proceed according to common sense. Will it be enough, I wonder?"

Pamela smiled at her ruefully and left the dining room so that Lord Lytton's former room would be ready by the time he carried up the woman from the stable. Pamela had been surprised by his offer both to give up his room and to carry the woman up to it. She would not have expected compassion of him.

The quiet gentleman picked up the urn, which Mrs. Palmer had abandoned on his table, and poured himself a second cup of coffee.

*   *   *

Lisa Curtis's baby did not come quickly. It was her first and it was large and it appeared determined both to take its time in coming into the world and to give its mother as much grief as possible while doing so. Tom Suffield, the father, was beside himself with anxiety and was no help to anyone. Big strapping young man as he was, he made no objection to the marquess's carrying his woman into the inn and up the stairs, Lord Birkin hovering close to share the load if necessary. Tom was rather incoherent, accounting perhaps for his lack of wisdom in admitting to his unwed state.

"We was going to get married," he said, hurrying along behind the two gentlemen while Lisa moaned, having had the misfortune to suffer a contraction after the marquess had picked her up. "But we couldn't afford to."

And yet, Lord Lytton thought, wincing at the girl's obvious agony, they could afford a child. An unfair judgment, perhaps. Even the poor were entitled to their pleasures, and children had a habit of not waiting for a convenient moment to get themselves conceived.

A strange scene greeted them at the entrance to his former inn room—had he really given it up in a chivalrous gesture to counter Miss Wilder's brave offer to sleep in the stable? Miss Amelia Horn was hovering at one side of the doorway, a woolen shawl of hideous and multicolored stripes clutched in one hand and a vinaigrette in the other. Mrs. Forbes was hovering and nodding at the other side. The room itself was crowded. He had not realized that it was large enough to accommodate so many persons.

Colonel Forbes was kneeling before the grate, blowing on some freshly laid coals and coaxing a fire into life. Both his hands and his face were liberally daubed

with coal dust. He was looking as angry and out of
sorts as he always did. Miss Eugenia Horn was at the
window, closing the curtains to keep out some draft
and a great deal of gloom. Lady Birkin was in the act
of setting down a large bowl of steaming water on the
washstand. Pamela Wilder was bent over the tidied bed,
plumping up lumpy pillows and turning back the sheets
to receive its new occupant. Lord Lytton, despite the
weight of his burden, which he had just carried from
the stable into the inn and up the stairs, pursed his lips
at the sight of a slim but well-rounded derrière nicely
outlined against the wool of her dress.

What a fool and an idiot he had been the night before! He might by now be well familiar with the feel
of that derrière. She turned and smiled warmly at the
woman in his arms. He found himself wishing that her
eyes were focused a little higher.

"The bed is ready for you," she said. "In a moment
we will have you comfortable and warm. The fire will
be giving off some heat soon. How are you feeling?"

"Oh, thank you," Lisa said, her voice weak and
weary as the marquess set her gently down. "Where's
Tom?"

"Here I am, Leez," the young man said from the
doorway. His face was chalky white. "How are you?"

"It's so wonderfully warm in here," the girl said
plaintively, but then she gasped and clasped a hand
over her swollen abdomen. She opened her mouth and
panted loudly, moaning with each outward breath so
that all the occupants of the room froze.

"Who is in charge?" the marquess asked when it appeared that the pain was subsiding again. He had felt
his own color draining away. "Who is going to deliver
the child?"

The one Miss Horn, he noticed, had disappeared from the doorway while the other had turned firmly to face the curtained window. Obviously not them, and obviously not Miss Wilder. He must take her downstairs away from there. But it was she who answered him.

"There is no one with any experience," she said. She flushed. "And no one who has given birth. We will have to do the best we can."

Hell, he thought. Hell and damnation! No one with any experience. A thousand devils!

"Sally," Lord Birkin said, "let me take you back to our room. Mrs. Palmer is doubtless the best qualified to cope."

"Mrs. Palmer," she said, her eyes flashing briefly at him, "has the breakfast to clear away and the dishes to wash and the rooms to see to. I'll stay here, Henry." She turned to the girl, who was sitting awkwardly on the side of the bed, and her expression softened. "The stable must have been dreadfully dirty," she said. "I have brought up some warm water. I will help you wash yourself and change into something clean. I have a loose fitting nightgown that I believe will fit you." She looked up. "Will you fetch it, Henry? It is the one with the lace at the throat and cuffs."

He looked at her, speechless. She, the Baroness Birkin, was going to wash a young girl of low birth who at present smelled of rankly uncleaned stable? She was going to give the girl one of her costly nightgowns? But yes, of course she was going to. It was just like Sally to do such things and with such kindness in her face. He turned to leave the room.

"I'll help you, my lady," Pamela said. She stooped over the girl on the bed. "Here, I'll help you off with your dress once the gentlemen have withdrawn. What is your name?"

"Lisa," the girl said. "Lisa Curtis, miss."

"We will make you comfortable as soon as we possibly can, Lisa," Pamela said.

Miss Eugenia Horn coughed. "You must come with me away from this room, my dear Miss Wilder," she said. "It is not fitting that we be here. We will leave Lisa to the care of Lady Birkin and Mrs. Forbes, who are married ladies."

The Marquess of Lytton watched Pamela's face with keen interest from beneath drooped eyelids. She smiled. "I grew up at a rectory, ma'am," she said. "I learned at an early age to help my fellow human beings under even the most difficult of circumstances if my assistance could be of some value."

It was a do-gooder sentiment that might have made him want to vomit, the marquess thought, if it had not been uttered so matter-of-factly and if her tone had not been so totally devoid of piety and sentiment.

"I think it will survive without your further help, Forbes," the marquess said, looking critically at the crackling fire. "Let us see if our landlord can supply us with some of that superior ale we had last night, shall we? Join us, Suffield."

He was rewarded with a grateful smile from Pamela Wilder. Lady Birkin was squeezing out a cloth over the bowl of water and rubbing soap on it. Miss Eugenia Horn was preparing to leave the room and sights so unbecoming to maiden eyes.

It was strange, perhaps, that for the rest of the day all the guests at the White Hart Inn could not keep their minds away from the room upstairs in which a girl of a social class far beneath their own, and a girl moreover who was about to bear a bastard child, labored painfully though relatively quietly. Her moans could be heard only when one of them went upstairs to his own room.

"They should have stayed at home," Colonel Forbes said gruffly. "Damn fool thing to be wandering about the countryside at this time of year and with the girl in this condition."

"Perhaps they could not afford to stay at home," Lord Birkin said.

Tom could not answer for himself. He had returned to the stable despite the offer of ale and a share of the fire in the taproom. He was pacing.

"The poor child," Miss Eugenia Horn said, having decided that it was unexceptionable to talk about the child provided she ignored all reference to its birth. She was sitting in the taproom, knitting a pair of baby boots. "One cannot help but wonder what will become of it."

"Tom will doubtless find employment and make an honest woman of Lisa, and they and the child will live happily ever after," the marquess said.

Mrs. Forbes nodded her agreement.

"It would be comforting to think so," Lord Birkin said.

Mrs. Palmer, looking harried, was emerging from the kitchen, where she had given the guests' servants their breakfast and washed the dishes, and was making her way upstairs to tidy rooms.

They were all increasingly aware as the day dragged on that it was Christmas Eve and that they were beginning to live through the strangest Christmas they had ever experienced.

"We might decorate the inn with some greenery," Miss Amelia Horn said at one point, "but who would be foolhardy enough to go outside to gather any? Besides, even if some were brought inside, it would be dripping wet."

"As far as I am concerned," Colonel Forbes said, "there is enough rain outside. We do not need to admit any to the indoors." No one argued with him.

They all began to think of what they would have been doing on that day if only they had had the fortune or wisdom to travel earlier and had reached their destinations. But the images of elegant and comfortable homes and of relatives and friends and all the sights and sounds and smells of Christmas did not bear dwelling upon.

Lord Birkin went back upstairs with his wife when she appeared briefly early in the afternoon to fetch more water from the kitchen. She had reported to all the gathered guests that there was no further progress upstairs. Poor Lisa was suffering cruelly, but appeared no nearer to being delivered than she had done that morning.

Lord Birkin took his wife by the arm when they reached the top of the stairs and steered her past Lisa's room and into their own.

"Sally," he said, "you are going to tire yourself out. Do you not think you have done enough? Should it not be Mrs. Palmer's turn? Or Mrs. Forbes's?"

She sat down on the edge of the bed and he seated himself beside her.

"Mrs. Palmer is frightened by the very thought of becoming involved," she said. "I can tell. That is why she is keeping so busy with other things. And Mrs. Forbes is quite inept. Well meaning but inept. The few times she has come inside the room she has stood close to the door and nodded sweetly and clearly not knowing what she should do."

"And you *do* know?" he said.

She smiled. "Some things come by instinct," she said. "Don't worry about me, Henry."

"But I do worry," he said, taking her hand and holding it in both of his. "And I blame myself for not bringing you from London sooner than I did. This is Christmas Eve, Sally. Have you realized that? You should be with Lady Middleton and all your friends and acquaintances now. You should be in comfort. The partying should have begun—the feasting and caroling and dancing. Instead we are stuck here. Not only stuck, but somehow involved with a girl who is giving birth. This is no Christmas for you."

"Or for you," she said. "It really does not seem like Christmas at all, does it? But we cannot do anything about it. Here we are and here Lisa is. I must return to her."

"What is going to happen when it comes time for her to deliver?" he asked.

He had struck a nerve. There was fear in her eyes for a brief unguarded moment. "We will jump that hurdle when we come to it," she said.

"You are afraid, Sally?" he asked.

"No, of course not," she said briskly. But then she looked down at their clasped hands and nodded quickly. Her voice was breathless when she spoke again. "I am afraid that in my ignorance I will cause her death or the baby's."

He released her hand, set an arm about her shoulders, and drew her toward him. She sagged against him in grateful surprise and set her head on his shoulder.

"Without you and Miss Wilder," he said, "she would be alone in the stable with the hysterical Tom. You are being very good to her, Sally. You must remember that, whatever happens. I wish I could take you away from here. I wish I had not got you into this predicament."

She nestled her head on his shoulder and felt wonderfully comforted. If this had not happened, they would be caught up in the gaiety of Christmas at this very moment, surrounded by friends. Except that they would not be together. As like as not, he would be off somewhere with some of the other gentlemen, playing billiards, probably, since the weather would not permit shooting.

"Don't blame yourself," she said. "Besides it is not so very bad, is it? If we were not here, I fear that Pamela would have to cope alone. That would be too heavy a burden on her shoulders. She is wonderful, Henry. So calm and brave, so kind to Lisa. Just as if she knew exactly what she was doing."

"You sound like two of a kind, then," he said.

She looked up at him in further surprise. His face was very close. "Do you think so?" she said. "What a lovely thing to say—and very reassuring. I feel quite inadequate, you see."

He dipped his head and kissed her—swiftly and firmly and almost fiercely. And then raised his head and looked into her eyes as she nestled her head against his shoulder again. He very rarely kissed her. She ached with a sudden longing and put it from her.

"I must go back," she said. "Pamela will be alone with Lisa."

"If there is anything I can do," he said, "call me. Will you?"

Her eyes sparkled with amusement suddenly. "You

will spend the rest of the day in fear and trembling that perhaps I will take you at your word," she said.

He chuckled and she realized how rarely he did so these days. She had almost forgotten that it was his smile and the way his eyes crinkled at the corners when he laughed that had first attracted her to him. "You are probably right," he said.

He escorted her back to Lisa's room though he did not go inside with her. She felt refreshed, almost as if she had lain down and slept for a few hours. Pamela was leaning over a moaning Lisa, dabbing at her brow with a cool damp cloth. She looked around at Lady Birkin.

"Two minutes," she said. "The pains have been two minutes apart for more than an hour now. It must be close, don't you think, Sally?"

But it was not really close at all. There were several more hours of closely paced contractions and pain to live through.

Everyone moved from the taproom into the dining room for afternoon tea, just so that they might have a welcome change of scenery, Colonel Forbes said with a short bark of laughter. Lord Birkin, strolling to the window, announced that the rain appeared to be easing and that he hesitated to say it aloud but the western horizon looked almost bright.

"But it is happening too late, my lord," Miss Amelia Horn said. "Christmas has been ruined already."

Mrs. Forbes sighed and nodded her agreement.

And yet they were all making an effort to put aside their own personal disappointments over a lost Christmas. They were all thinking of the baby who was about to be born and of the child's destitute parents. Miss

Eugenia Horn was still busy knitting baby boots. Mrs. Forbes, having recalled that she had no fewer than eight flannel nightgowns in her trunk, flannel being the only sensible fabric to be worn during winter nights, declared that she did not need near as many. She was cutting up four of them into squares and hemming them so that the baby would have warm and comfortable nappies to wear. Miss Amelia Horn was cutting up a fifth to make into small nightshirts. She had already painstakingly unpicked the lace from one of her favorite caps to trim the tiny garments.

Even the gentlemen were not unaffected by the impending event. Colonel Forbes was thinking of a certain shirt of which he had never been overly fond. It would surely fit Tom and keep him warm, too. By good fortune the garment was in the trunk upstairs—for the simple reason that it was one of his wife's favorites. Lord Birkin thought of the staff at his London house and on his country estate. There really was no room for an extra worker. His wife had already foisted some strays upon him. He was definitely overstaffed. Perhaps some banknotes would help, though giving money in charity always seemed rather too easy. The Marquess of Lytton turned a gold signet ring on his little finger. It was no heirloom. He had bought it himself in Madrid. But it had some sentimental value. Not that he was a sentimentalist, of course. He drew it slowly from his finger and dropped it into a pocket. Sold or pawned, it would provide a family of three with a goodly number of meals. The quiet gentleman withdrew to the stable after tea to stretch his legs and breathe some fresh air into his lungs.

Pamela Wilder appeared in the dining room doorway when tea was over and immediately became the focus of attention. But she could give no news other than that Lisa was very tired and finding it harder to bear the pains. Miss Wilder looked tired, too, the Marquess of Lytton thought, gazing at her pale and lovely face and her rather untidy hair. Lady Birkin had sent her downstairs for a half-hour break, having had one herself earlier.

"The tea is cold, dear," Miss Eugenia Horn said. "Let me get you a fresh pot. There is no point in ringing for service. One might wait all day and all night too if one did that."

But Pamela would not hear of anyone else's waiting on her. She went to the kitchen herself. The marquess was sitting in the taproom when she came out again, carrying a tray.

"Come and sit down," he said, indicating the chair next to his own, between him and the fire, which he had just built up himself. "It is quieter in here."

She hesitated, but he got to his feet and took the tray from her hands. She sighed as she sat down and then looked at him in some surprise as he picked up the teapot and poured her cup of tea.

"Is she going to deliver?" he asked. "Or is there some complication?"

He liked watching her blush. Color added vibrancy to her face. "I hope not," she said. "Oh, I do hope not."

"Do you have any idea what to do?" he asked. "Or does Lady Birkin?"

"No," she said, and she closed her eyes briefly. "None at all. We can only hope that nature will take care of itself."

Oh, Lord. There was a faint buzzing in his head.

"You are a clergyman's daughter," he said. "You were never involved with such, er, acts of nature?"

"No," she said. "my mother made sure that I had a very proper upbringing. I wish I knew more." She looked down at her hands. "I hope she does not die. Or the baby. I will always blame myself if they die."

A thousand hells and a million damnations! He reached out and took one of her hands in his. "If they die—and probably they will not," he said, "they will die in a warm and reasonably comfortable inn room instead of in a stable, and tended by two ladies who have given them unfailingly diligent and gentle care instead of by a hysterical boy."

She smiled at him rather wanly. "You are kind," she said.

He looked down at her hand and spread her fingers along his. "You have artists' hands," he said. "You must play the pianoforte. Do you?"

"Whenever I can." She looked wistful. "We always had a pianoforte at the rectory. I played it constantly, even when I should have been doing other things. I was often scolded."

"But there is no instrument at your place of employment?" he asked.

"Oh, yes," she said. "A beautiful one with the loveliest tone I have ever heard. I give my pupil lessons and try to steal a few minutes for myself whenever I can."

He felt angry suddenly. "They have to be stolen?" he asked. "They are not granted?"

She smiled. "Mrs. Raven, my employer, suffers from migraine headaches," she said. "She cannot stand the sound of the pianoforte."

His jaw tightened. "It is not a good life, is it," he said, "being a governess?"

She stiffened and withdrew her hand from his. She reached out to pick up her cup and raised it to her lips.

"It is a living, my lord," she said, "and a reasonably comfortable one. There are many women, and men too, far worse off than I. We cannot all choose the life we would live. You do not need to pity me."

He looked at her broodingly. Her hand was shaking slightly though she drank determinedly on. Did he pity her? He was not in the habit of pitying other mortals. No, he did not think it was pity. It was more admiration for her and anger against employers who evidently did not appreciate her. It was more the desire to protect her and see happiness replace the quiet discipline in her face—the desire to give her a pianoforte for Christmas, all wrapped about with red ribbons. His lip curled in self-derision. Was this unspeakably dull Christmas making him sentimental over a governess?

"What would you be doing now," he asked her, "if it had not rained?"

She set her cup down in its saucer and smiled down into it, her eyes dreamy. "Decorating the house with the children," she said. "Helping my mother and our cook with the baking. Finishing making gifts. Delivering baskets to the poor. Helping my father arrange the Nativity scene in the church. Getting ready to go caroling. Looking forward to the church service. Running around in circles wishing I could divide myself into about twelve pieces. Christmas is always very busy and very special at home. The coming of Christ—it is a wonderful festival."

He took her hand again, almost absently and smoothed his fingers over hers. He was the Marquess of Lytton, she reminded herself, and she a mere clergyman's daughter and a governess. Last night he had held her and kissed her, and she had almost gone to bed with him. She was still not sure if she would have allowed the ultimate intimacy or if she would have drawn back at the last moment. But he had drawn back, and now they were sitting together in the taproom, talking, her hand in his. This was a strange, unreal Christmas.

"What would *you* be doing?" she asked. "If it had not rained, I mean."

He raised his gaze from their hands, and she was struck again by the keenness of his blue eyes beneath the lazy lids. They caused a strange somersaulting feeling in her stomach. "Stuffing myself with rich foods," he said. "Getting myself inebriated. Preparing to make merry and to drink even more. Flirting with a lady I have had my eye on for some time past and wondering if I would be spending tonight with her or if she would keep me waiting until tomorrow night." One corner of his mouth lifted in an expression that was not quite a smile. "A wonderful way to celebrate the coming of Christ, would you not agree?"

Pamela found herself wondering irrelevantly what the lady looked like. "I cannot judge," she said. "We all have our own way of enjoying ourselves."

"Yours is a large family?" he asked.

"I have three brothers and four sisters," she said, "all younger than myself. It is a very noisy household and frequently an untidy one, I'm afraid."

"I envy you," he said. "I have no one except a few aunts and uncles and cousins with whom I have never been close." He raised one hand and touched the back of a finger to her cheek. "I am sorry you have not been able to get home for Christmas."

"I believe that everything that happens does so for a purpose," she said. "Perhaps I was meant to be trapped here for Lisa's sake."

"And perhaps I was meant to be trapped here with you for . . . for what purpose?" he asked.

His eyes were looking very intently into hers. She could not withdraw her own. "I don't know," she said.

"Perhaps," he said, and his voice was very soft, "to discover that innocence can be more enticing than experience. And far more warming to the heart."

He raised her hand while she watched him with widening eyes and warming cheeks, and set his lips to it.

"I must be going back upstairs," she said.

"Yes." He lowered her hand. "You must."

But the next moment they were both on their feet. Lady Birkin had appeared at the top of the stairs. She was looking distraught and was beckoning urgently.

"Pamela," she called. "Oh, thank heaven you are there. Something is happening. Oh, please come." And she turned and hurried out of sight again.

Pamela could feel the color draining from her head as she rushed across the room toward the staircase. She scarcely heard the quite improper expletive that was the marquess's sole comment.

"Bloody hell!" he said.

The bed was soaked. Fortunately Mrs. Palmer had given them a pile of old rags and told them to spread some over the sheets. There was something about waters breaking, she had mumbled before scurrying away about some real or imagined chore. Pamela and Lady Birkin stripped away the wet rags and replaced them with dry ones. But Lisa was in severe distress. She was panting loudly and threshing about on the bed. Her moans were threatening to turn into screams.

"Hot water," Lady Birkin said, trying to keep her voice calm. "I have heard that hot water is needed."

"Lisa." Pamela had a cool cloth to the girl's brow. "What may we do for you? How may we help?"

But there was a feeling of dreadful helplessness, an almost overpowering urge to become hysterical or simply to rush from the room.

And then the door opened. Both Lady Birkin and Pamela looked in some surprise at the Marquess of Lytton, who stood in the doorway, his face pale. Perhaps they would have felt consternation, too, if they had not been feeling so frightened and helpless.

"I think I can help," he surprised them both by saying. And he grimaced and turned even paler as Lisa began to moan and thresh again. He strode over to the bed. "I think she should be pushing," he said. "The pain will subside soon, will it not? Next time we must have her in position and she must push down. Perhaps the two of you can help her by lifting her shoulders as she pushes."

The two ladies merely stared at him. Lisa screamed.

"The Peninsula," he said. "I was a cavalry officer. There was a peasant woman. There was a surgeon, too, but he had just been shot through the right hand. He instructed a private soldier and me. The private held her and I delivered."

Lisa was quiet again, and the marquess turned grimly back to the bed. "Raise your knees," he told her, "and brace your feet wide apart on the bed. The next time the pain comes, I want you to bear down against it with all your strength. This little fellow wants to come out. Do you understand me?"

Through the fog of weakness and pain, the girl seemed to turn instinctively to the note of authority and assurance in his voice. She looked up at him and nodded, positioning herself according to his instructions.

And then the fright came back into her eyes and she began to pant again.

"Now!" he commanded, and he pushed his hands forward against her knees through the sheet that still covered her to the waist while Lady Birkin and Pamela, one on each side of her, lifted her shoulders from the bed and pushed forward. Lisa drew a giant breath and bore down with all her might, pausing only to gasp in more air before the pain subsided again.

"Send down for hot water," Lord Lytton said while Lisa relaxed for a few moments. "Go and give the instruction yourself, Pamela, but come right back. Someone else can bring it. But wait a moment. She needs us again."

He was going to forget something, he thought as he pushed upward on the girl's knees. He would forget something and either she or the child was going to bleed to death. Or there was going to be a complication as there had not been with the Spanish peasant girl. This girl was already weak from a long and hard labor. Soon—perhaps after the next contraction—he was going to have to take a look and pray fervently that it was the child's head he would see. He could recall the surgeon's talking about breech births, though he had given no details.

And then between contractions, as he was about to draw the sheet back, there was a quiet voice from the doorway. It almost did not register on his mind, but he looked over his shoulder. He had not mistaken. The quiet gentleman was standing there.

"I am a physician," he repeated. "I will be happy to deliver the child and tend the mother."

Anger was the Marquess of Lytton's first reaction. "You are a physician," he said. "Why the hell have you waited this long to admit the fact? Do you realize what terrors your silence has caused Lady Birkin and Miss Wilder in the course of the day?"

"And you, too, my lord?" The quiet gentleman was smiling. He had strolled into the room and taken one of Lisa's limp hands in his. He spoke very gently. "It will soon be over, my dear, I promise. Then the joy you will have in your child will make you forget all this."

She looked calmly back at him. There was even a suggestion of a smile in her eyes.

But the marquess was not mollified. Relief—overwhelming, knee-weakening relief—was whipping his anger into fury. "What the hell do you mean," he said, "putting us through all this?" He remembered too late the presence in the room of three women, two of them gently born.

The quiet gentleman smiled and touched a cool hand to Lisa's brow as she began to gasp again. "How could I spoil a Christmas that had promised to be so dismal for everyone?" he asked, and he moved to draw the sheet down over the girl's knees. "The blood will probably return to your head faster, my lord, if you remove yourself. The ladies will assist me. Have some hot water brought up to us if you will be so good."

Lord Lytton removed himself, frowning over the physician's strange answer to his question. Lady Birkin and Pamela, moving back to their posts, puzzled over it, too. What had he meant? Christmas might have been dismal but was not? Because of what was happening?

"Set an arm each about her back to support her as you lift her," the quiet gentleman said. "Your labors too will soon be at an end, ladies, and you will experience all the wonder of being present at a birth. Ah. I can see the head, my dear. With plenty of dark hair."

"Ohhh!" Lisa was almost crying with excitement and exhaustion and pain.

But all sense of panic had gone from the room. Both Lady Birkin and Pamela were aware of that as the physician went quietly and efficiently about his work and Lisa responded to his gentleness. Her son was born, large and healthy and perfect—and crying lustily—early in the evening. They were all crying, in fact. All except the doctor, who smiled sweetly at each of them in turn and made them feel as if it were not at all the most foolish thing in the world to cry just because one more mouth to be fed had been born into it.

Lisa was exhausted and could scarcely raise her arms to Tom when he came into the room several minutes later, wide-eyed and awed, while Lady Birkin was washing the baby and Pamela was disposing of blood-stained rags. Lisa accepted the baby from Lady Birkin and looked up with shining eyes into Tom's face while he reached out one trembling finger to touch his son. But she had no energy left.

"I'll take him," Lady Birkin said, "while you get some sleep, Lisa. You have earned it."

"Thank you, mum." Lisa looked up at her wearily. "I'll always remember you, mum, and the other lady." Her eyes found Pamela and smiled. "Thank you, miss."

And so Lady Birkin found herself holding the child and feeling a welling of happiness and tenderness and . . . and longing. Ah, how wonderful, she thought. How very wonderful. She acted from instinct. She must find Henry. She must show him. Oh, if only the child were hers. Theirs.

Word had spread. Everyone was hovering in the hallway outside Lisa's room. The birth of a little bastard baby was the focus of attention on this Christmas Eve. The ladies oohed and aahed at the mere sight of the bright stripes of the shawl in which it was wrapped. But Lady Birkin had eyes for no one except her husband, standing at the top of the stairs close to the Marquess of Lytton and gazing anxiously at her.

"Henry," she said. "Oh, look at him. Have you ever seen anything so perfect?" She could hear herself laughing and yet his face had blurred before her vision. "Look at him, Henry."

He looked and smiled back up at her. "Sally," he whispered.

"He weighs nothing at all," she said. "How could any human being be so small and so light and so perfect and still live and breathe? What a miracle life is. Hold him, Henry."

She gave him no choice. She laid the bundle in his arms and watched the fear in his eyes soften to wonder as he smiled down at the baby. The child was not quite sleeping. He was looking quietly about him with unfocused eyes.

Lord Birkin smiled. What would it be like, he wondered, to look down like this at his own child? To have the baby placed in his arms by its mother? By his wife?

"Sally," he said, "you must be so tired." She was pale and disheveled. He had a sudden image of how she should be looking now, early in the evening of Christmas Eve, immaculate and fashionable and sparkling with jewels and excitement and ready to mingle with their friends far into the night. And yet he saw happiness now in her tired eyes—and breathtaking beauty.

The ladies wanted to hold the baby. And so he was

passed from one to another, quiet and unprotesting. He was cooed over and clucked over and even sung to, by Miss Amelia Horn. The occasion had made even the Palmers magnanimous.

"Well," Mr. Palmer said, rubbing his hands together and looking not unpleased. "I never did in all my born days."

"I mean to tell Mr. Suffield," Mrs. Palmer said in a voice loud enough for all to hear, "that we are not even going to charge 'im for the room."

No one saw fit to comment on this outpouring of incredible generosity.

The Marquess of Lytton reached out both hands to Pamela when she came from the room. She set her own in them without thought and smiled at him. "Have you seen him?" she asked. "Is he not the most beautiful child you have ever set eyes on?"

"I'm sorry," he said to her, squeezing her hands until they hurt. "I ripped up at the physician for keeping quiet so long, and yet that is exactly what I had been doing all day. You and Lady Birkin were wonderfully brave. I am sorry my own cowardice made me hide a fact that might have made your day less anxious."

"I don't think," she said, gazing up into his eyes, her own filling with sudden tears, "that I would change one detail of this day even if I could. How glad I am that it rained!"

His eyes searched hers. "And so am I," he said, raising both hands to his lips and continuing to regard her over them. "More glad than I have been of anything else in my life."

"Anyway," Colonel Forbes's voice was declaring gruffly over the babble of voices in the hallway; it seemed that Mrs. Forbes had been trying to force him to hold the baby. "Anyway, this was a damned inconvenient thing to happen. What would have been the outcome if one of our number had not turned out to be a doctor, eh? Whoever heard of any woman having a baby at Christmas?"

The babble of voices stopped entirely.

The Marquess of Lytton's eyes smiled slowly into Pamela's. "Good Lord," he said, and everyone kept quiet to listen to his words, "a crowd of marvelous Christians we all are. Did any of us realize before this moment, I wonder? We have, in fact, been presented with the perfect Christmas, have we not? Almost a re-enactment of the original."

" 'How could I spoil a Christmas that had promised to be so dismal for everyone?' " Pamela said quietly. "I think someone realized, my lord."

"The child was very nearly born in a stable," Lady Birkin said.

"It is uncanny enough to send shivers up one's spine," Miss Eugenia Horn said.

"I hope you have not caught a chill from the damp sheets, Eugenia," Miss Amelia Horn said.

"I wonder," Lord Birkin said, "if above the heavy rain clouds a star is shining brightly."

"Fanciful nonsense," Colonel Forbes said. "I am ready for my dinner. When will it be ready, landlord, eh? Don't just stand there, man. I would like to eat before midnight—if it is all the same to you, of course."

Lady Birkin took the baby from Mrs. Forbes's arms. "I'll take him back to his mother," she said, tenderness and wistfulness mingled in her voice.

"Back to his manger," Lord Birkin said, laughing softly.

*   *   *

"Well, anyway," Mrs. Palmer said to the gathered company as she cleared away the plates after dinner, "we didn't keep 'em in the stable like them innkeepers did in the Bible. We gave 'em one of our best rooms and aren't charging 'em for it neither."

"For which deeds you will surely find a place awaiting you in heaven," the Marquess of Lytton said.

"And yet it give me quite a turn it did when the colonel said what 'e did and we all thought of that other babe what was born at Christmas," Mr. Palmer said. He was standing in the doorway of the dining room, busy about nothing in particular. "I was all over shivers for a minute."

"I am sure in Bethlehem there was not all this infernal rain," Colonel Forbes commented.

"The kings would have arrived in horribly soggy robes and dripping crowns," the marquess said. "And the heavenly host would have had drooping wings."

"I am quite sure their wings were more sturdy than to be weakened by rain, my lord," Miss Amelia Horn said. "They were angels after all."

Mrs. Forbes nodded her agreement.

"I think it would be altogether fitting to the occasion," Miss Eugenia Horn said, "if we read the Bible story together this evening."

"And perhaps sang some carols afterward," Lady Birkin said. "Does everyone feel Christmas as strongly as I do tonight despite all the usual trappings being absent?"

There were murmurings of assent. Mrs. Forbes nodded. The quiet gentleman smiled.

"Does anyone have a Bible?" Lord Birkin asked.

There was a lengthy pause. No one, it seemed, was in the habit of traveling about with a Bible in a trunk.

"I do," the quiet gentleman said at last, and he got to his feet to fetch it from his room.

And so they all spent a further hour in the dining room, far away from friends and families and parties, far from any church, far away from Christmas as any of them had ever known it. There were no decorations, no fruit cake or mince pies, no cider or punch or wassail. Nothing except a plain and shabby inn and the company of strangers become acquaintances. Nothing except a newborn baby and his mother asleep upstairs, cozy and warm because they had been taken from the stable and given a room and showered with care and with gifts.

The quiet gentleman himself read the story of the birth of another baby in Bethlehem, and they all listened to words they had heard so many times before that the wonder of it all had ceased to mean a great deal. They listened with a new understanding, with a new recognition of the joy of birth. Even the one man who rarely entered a church, Lord Lytton, was touched by the story and realized that perhaps Christmas had not been meant to be an orgy of personal gratification.

Singing that might have been self-conscious since there was no instrument to provide accompaniment was, in fact, not self-conscious at all. Lady Birkin, Pamela Wilder, Colonel Forbes and, surprisingly, Miss Amelia Horn, all had good voices and could hold a tune. Everyone else joined in lustily, even the tone-deaf Mrs. Forbes.

Lord Birkin left the room after a while. He found Tom Suffield in the kitchen, where he had been eating with the guests' coachmen. Lisa and the baby were asleep, Tom explained, scrambling to his feet, and he did not want to disturb them. Lord Birkin took Tom through into the taproom.

"I don't know what you are good at, Tom," he said. "I can't offer much in the way of employment, I'm afraid, but I can send you to my estate in Kent and instruct my housekeeper to find you work in the stables or in the gardens. I doubt there will be an empty cottage, but we will find somewhere where you and Lisa can stay for a while at least."

Tom shifted his weight awkwardly from one foot to the other. "That be awf'ly good of ye, sir," he said, "but Mr. Cornwallis needs a cook and a handyman and have offered the jobs to me and Lisa."

"Mr. Cornwallis?" Lord Birkin raised his eyebrows.

"The doctor, sir," Tom said.

"Ah." It was strange, Lord Birkin thought, that even though they had all introduced themselves the evening before, he had thought of Mr. Cornwallis ever since only as the quiet gentleman. "I am glad, Tom. I hated to think of your taking Lisa and your baby to one of the industrial towns with no job waiting for you there."

"Aye, sir," Tom said. "Everyone is right kind. Thanks again for the money, sir. We will buy new clothes for the baby with it."

Lord Birkin nodded and returned to the dining room.

The Marquess of Lytton found Tom just ten minutes later. "Having a woman and child and no home or employment is a burdensome situation to find yourself in, Tom," he said.

"Aye, that it is, sir," Tom said. "But I feels like a wealthy man, sir, with all the gifts. And with your gold ring, sir. And a home and a job from Mr. Cornwallis." He told his tale again.

"Ah," the marquess said. "I am glad to hear it, Tom.

I was prepared to give you a letter of introduction to a friend of mine, but now I see you will not need it. I would like to give you a small sum of money, though. Call it a Christmas gift to you personally if you will. It is the price of a license. You must marry her, Tom. Such things are important to women, you know. And you would not wish to hear anyone calling your son a bastard."

"Bless you, sir," Tom said, flushing, "but Mr. Cornwallis is to marry us, sir, as soon as we gets to his home."

"The physician?" The marquess raised his eyebrows.

"He's a clergyman, sir," Tom said.

"Ah." The marquess nodded pleasantly to him and returned to the dining room. The quiet gentleman, he thought, was becoming more intriguing by the moment. Was he a physician or a clergyman? Or both? Or neither?

Lord Lytton seated himself beside the quiet gentleman and spoke to him while everyone else was singing. "You are a clergyman, sir?" he asked.

The quiet gentleman smiled. "I am, my lord," he said.

"And a physician, too?" The marquess frowned.

"It is possible to be both," the quiet gentleman said. "I am a clergyman, but not of a large and fashionable parish, you see. My time is not taken up by the sometimes tedious and meaningless duties I would have if I belonged to a large parish, and certainly not by the social commitments I would have if I had a wealthy patron. I am fortunate. My time is free to be devoted to the service of others. I am not distracted by the trappings of the established faith." He chuckled. "I have learned to deliver babies. It is the greatest delight and the greatest privilege a man could experience. You discovered that once upon a time, I believe."

"And the greatest terror," the marquess said fervently. "I dreaded facing it again today. There was the terror of becoming the instrument of death rather than of life."

"Ah," the quiet gentleman said, "but we must learn to accept our limitations as part of the human condition. It is Our Lord who controls life and death."

The marquess was quiet for a while. "Yes," he said. "We are all of us too busy, aren't we? Especially at Christmastime. Too busy enjoying ourselves and surrounding ourselves with the perfect atmosphere to remember what it is all about. This unexpected rainstorm has forced us to remember. And you have helped too, sir, by sitting back and allowing us to face all the terror of imminent birth."

"Without suffering there can never be the fullness of joy," the quiet gentleman said.

The Misses Horn were rising to retire for the night, and everyone else followed suit. But they did not part to go to their separate rooms without a great deal of handshaking and hugging first.

"Happy Christmas," they each said a dozen times to one another. But the words were not the automatic greeting they had all uttered during all their previous Christmases, but heartfelt wishes for one another's joy. Suddenly this Christmas—this dull, rainy disaster of a Christmas—seemed very happy indeed. Perhaps the happiest any of them had ever known.

And so Christmas Eve drew to an end. A baby had been born.

It was a little different when they were alone together in their room. Some of the magic went from the evening. It was all right for her, Lady Birkin thought. She had been busy all day and directly involved in the won-

der of the baby's birth. Men were not so concerned
about such matters. It must have been a dreadfully dull
day for him.

"Henry," she said, looking at him apologetically, as
if everything were her fault, "I am so sorry that this is
such a dull Christmas for you."

"Dull?" He looked at her intently and took a step
toward her so that he was very close. "I don't think I
have ever celebrated Christmas until this year, Sally. I
am very proud of you, you know."

Her eyes widened. "You are?" He so rarely paid her
compliments.

"You worked tirelessly all day to help that girl," he
said. "You and Miss Wilder. I don't know how Lisa
would have managed without you."

"But there was a physician in the house, after all,"
she said. "What we did was nothing."

He framed her face with his hands. "What you did
was everything," he said. "The doctor gave his skills.
You gave yourself, Sally, despite being frightened and
inexperienced."

"Oh," she said. She felt like crying. She had tried so
hard to impress him since their marriage, dressing to
please him, talking and smiling to please him. And los-
ing him with every day that passed. And yet now he was
looking at her with unmistakable admiration and . . . love?

"Henry," she said, and on impulse she put her arms
up about his neck. "What is it about this Christmas? It
is not just me, is it? Everyone has been feeling it. You
too? What is so wonderful about it? This inn is not *the*
inn, after all, and the baby is not Jesus, not even born
in the stable."

He slipped his hands to her waist. "We have all seen
to the core of Christmas this year," he said. "We are

very fortunate, Sally. We might so easily have never had the chance. We have no gifts for each other. They are somewhere with our baggage coach. And this inn has provided us with nothing that is usually associated with the season. We had all come to believe that Christmas could not possibly be celebrated without those things. But this year we have been forced to see that Christmas is about birth and life and love and giving of whatever one has to give, even if it is only one's time and compassion."

She should not say it, she thought. She might spoil everything. They never said such things to each other. There seemed to be a great embarrassment between them where personal matters were concerned. But she was going to say it. She was going to take a chance. That was what the whole day seemed to have been about.

"Henry," she said. She was whispering, she found. "I love you so very much."

He gazed into her eyes, a look of hunger in his own. He drew breath but seemed to change his mind. Instead of speaking he lowered his head and kissed her—an openmouthed kiss of raw need that drew an instant response of surprise and desire. She tightened her arms and arched herself to him. There was shock for a moment as she felt his hands working at the buttons down the back of her dress, and then a surge of happiness.

"I always have," she said against his mouth. "Since the first moment I saw you. I have always worshiped you."

She gasped when he lowered her bodice and her chemise to her waist, and her naked breasts came back against his coat. And then his hands were on them, cupping them and stroking them, and his thumbs and forefingers were squeezing her nipples, rolling them lightly until she felt such a sharp stab of desire that she moaned into his mouth.

"Henry," she begged him, her eyes tightly closed, her mouth still against his, "make love to me. I have always wanted you to make love to me. Please, for this special day. Make love to me."

She would die, she thought if he merely coupled with her as he had the night before and all those other nights since their marriage. She should not have said what she just had. She should not have given in to the temptation to hope. She should not have begged for what he had never freely given.

But she was on the bed before she could get her thoughts straight, before she could feel shame for her wanton words. She was flat on her back, and he was stripping away her clothes from the waist down, looking at her from eyes heavy with desire as he straightened up and began to remove his own clothes. She was surprised to find that she felt no embarrassment though the candles burned and those passion-heavy eyes were devouring her nakedness. She lifted her arms to him.

She had asked for it, begged for it, wanted it. He would not feel guilt. This was not the way a gentleman used his wife, but they both wanted it. They both needed it. He resisted the urge to douse the candles so that she would be saved from embarrassment. And as he joined her naked on the bed, he rejected the idea of somehow restraining his passion. She wanted him as much as he wanted her. For this one occasion, she had said. So be it, then.

He worked on her mouth with his lips and his tongue and on her breasts with his hands and his fingers. She fenced his tongue with her own and sucked on it. She pushed her breasts up against his hands and gasped when he pinched her nipples, hardening them before rubbing his palms lightly over them. Her own hands explored his back and his shoulders. She wanted him. He felt a fierce exultation. She wanted him. This was not a mistress. This was his wife. This was Sally. And she wanted him.

He moved one hand down to caress her and ready her for penetration. She was hot and wet to his touch, something she had never been before. His temperature soared and his arousal became almost painful.

"Please," she was moaning into his mouth. "Please. Henry, please."

And so he moved on top of her, felt her legs twine tightly about his, lifted his head to look down into her face—her eyes were wide open and gazing back—and mounted her, sliding deeply into wet heat. God. Oh, my God. Sally.

"Love me," she whispered to him. "Oh, please, Henry. There is such an ache."

She was going to come to him, he thought, the realization hammering through his temples with the blood. She was going to climax. He had heard that it was possible with some women.

"Tell me when." He lowered himself on his elbows until his mouth was an inch from hers and he began to move slowly and deeply in her. "I'll wait as long as you need."

But she did not have to tell him. He felt the gradual clenching of her inner muscles, the building tension of her whole body. He heard her deep breaths gradually turn to gasps. And he watched the concentration in her face as her eyes closed and her mouth opened in the agony of the final moments before she looked up at him, stillness and wonder in her eyes, and began to tremble.

He lowered himself onto her, held her tightly, held himself still and deep in her, and let himself experience the marvel of his woman shuddering into release beneath him and crying out his name. Only when he was sure that she had experienced the full joy of the moment did he move again to his own climax.

It was the most wonderful night of her life. She did not care if it was never repeated. She had this to hug to herself in memory for the rest of her days, the most wonderful Christmas that anyone could hope to have. She was nestled in his arms, watching him sleep. After more than three years of marriage she felt like a new bride. She felt . . . oh, she felt wonderful. And she would be satisfied, she swore to herself. She would not demand the moon and the stars. She had the Christmas star, the brightest and best of them all. She would be satisfied with that. Things could never be quite as bad between them now that they had had this night—or this part of a night.

He had opened his eyes and was looking at her. She smiled. *Don't remove your arm*, she begged him with her eyes. *Let's lie like this, just for tonight.*

"You said it," he said. "It seemed to come so easily, though I know it did not. You have not been able to say it in three years, have you? Why have we found it so hard? Why is it so difficult to talk from the heart with those closest to us?"

"Because with them there is most fear of rejection?" she said. "Because we have to protect our hearts from those who have the power to break them every day for the rest of our lives?"

"I do not have your courage," he said, one hand

stroking lightly over her cheek. "I still don't. Sally, my love . . . Ah, just that. My love. Did I hurt you? Did I disgust you?"

"Say it again," she said, smiling at him. "Again and again. And do it again and again. I want to be as close to you as I can be, Henry. Close to your body, close to your heart, close to your mind. Not just for tonight. I am greedy."

"My love." He drew her closer to him, set his lips against hers. "It is what I have always wanted, what I have always yearned for. But I have wanted to treat you with respect. Foolish, wasn't I?"

"To think that being respectful meant holding me at arm's length?" she said. "And giving much of what I have longed for to mistresses? Have I made you flush? Did you think I did not know? Yes, you have been foolish, Henry. And I have been foolish not to fight for your love and not to put you straight on this ridiculous notion that gentlemen seem to have about women."

"Would this be happening if we had reached the Middletons' before the rain came?" he asked her.

"No," she said. "No, it would not. Perhaps it never would have happened. We would have kept drifting until perhaps we would have lived apart. Henry . . ." There was pain in her voice.

He rubbed his lips against hers and drew back his head to smile at her. "But it did happen," he said. "Christmas happened almost two thousand years ago, and it has happened this year for us. Love always seems to blossom at the most unexpected times and in the most unexpected places. This was meant to happen, Sally. We must not shudder at the thought of how nearly it did not happen. It was meant to be."

"Do you think we will ever have a child?" she asked

him wistfully, snuggling closer to the warmth and safety of him. "I wanted so much today for that baby to be mine, Henry. Ours. Do you think we ever will?"

"If we don't," he said, and he chuckled as he drew her closer still, "it won't be for lack of trying."

"Oh," she said.

"Shall we try now?" he said to her. "And perhaps again later?"

"And again later still?" she asked.

He laughed. "After all," he said, "dawn comes late in December. And there does not seem to be a great deal to get up early for at this apology for an inn, does there? Especially not on Christmas morning."

"Christmas morning is for babies," she said.

"The making of them as well as the birthing of them," he said, turning her onto her back and moving over her.

She smiled up at him.

"Sally," he said, serious again as he lowered his mouth and his body to hers, "my most wonderful Christmas gift. I love you."

It did not seem quite the same once everyone had gone to bed and he was left alone in the taproom. Even though he built up the fire and sat on a settle close to the heat, the place felt cheerless again. Christmas had fled again.

He thought of the Whittakers' large and fashionable mansion and of Lady Frazer's enticing beauty. He felt a moment's pang of regret but no more. He did not want to be there, he realized with a wry smile directed at the fire. He wanted to be exactly where he was. Well, not exactly, perhaps. There was a room upstairs and a bed where he would rather be. But perhaps not.

He could no longer think of her in terms of simple lust. There was a warmer feeling and a nameless yearning when he thought of her. Also a regret for wasted years, for years of senseless debauchery that had brought no real happiness with them.

They would not be able to travel during the coming day, Christmas Day. Probably they would the day after. The rain had finally stopped, and the sky had cleared before darkness fell. He would have one more day in which to enjoy looking at her and in which to maneuver to engage her in conversation. One day—a Christmas to remember.

And then he looked up from his contemplation of the flames in the hearth to find her standing before him, looking at him gravely. She held a blanket and a pillow in her arms.

"I thought you might be cold and uncomfortable," she said, holding them out to him. "It was very kind of you to give up your room for Lisa. You are a kind man."

"I gave up my room," he said, taking the pillow and blanket from her and setting them down beside him, "because you had tried to give up yours and I wanted to impress you with a show of chivalry. Kindness had nothing to do with it. I am not renowned for my kindness."

"Perhaps because you sometimes try not to show it," she said. "But I have seen it in other ways. You came to help Lisa give birth though it terrified you to do so."

He shrugged. "I came for your sake," he said. "And I did not help all day long, while you were exhausting yourself. In the event I did not help at all."

"But you would have," she said. "The intention was there. Tom showed me the ring you gave as a gift for the baby."

He shrugged again. "I am very wealthy," he said. "It was nothing."

"No," she said, still looking at him with her grave eyes, "it was something."

"Ah," he said, "then I have impressed you. I have achieved my goal."

She stared at him silently. He expected her to turn to leave, but she did not do so.

"Do you know how you have affected me?" he asked. "I do not believe I have ever before refused an invitation to bed. That *was* an invitation you were issuing last night?"

She lowered her eyes for a moment, but she lifted them again and looked at him calmly. "Yes," she said. "I suppose so."

"Why?" he asked. "You are not in the habit of issuing such invitations, are you?"

She shook her head. "Sometimes," she said, "I grow tired of the grayness of life. It was so full of color until a little more than a year ago, but there has been nothing but grayness since and nothing but grayness to look forward to. It is wrong of me to be dissatisfied with my lot, and normally I am not. But I thought this was going to be a disappointing Christmas."

"And it has not been?" he asked.

"No." She smiled slowly. "It has been the most wonderful Christmas of all."

"Because of the baby," he said.

"Yes," she said, "because of him. And for other reasons, too."

He reached out a hand. "Come and sit beside me," he said.

She looked at his hand and set her own in it. She sat down beside him and set her head on his shoulder when he put an arm about her.

"I wanted you last night," he said. "You know that, don't you? And why I left you, the deed undone?"

"Because you knew I was inexperienced," she said. "Because you knew me to be incapable of giving you the pleasure you are accustomed to. I understood. It is all right."

"Because I realized the immensity of the gift you were offering," he said. "Because I knew I could not take momentary pleasure from you. Because any greater commitment than that terrified me."

"I expected no more," she said.

"I know," he said. "That was the greatness of your gift."

She sighed and set an arm across his waist. "I am going to remember this Christmas for the rest of my life," she said. "It will seem quite unreal when I get back to my post, but I will remember that it really did happen."

He turned his head, found her lips with his own, and kissed her long and lingeringly. Her lips were soft and warm and willing to part for him. He nibbled at them, licked them, stroked them with his tongue. But he would not allow passion to grow. It was neither the time nor the place for passion.

"I am a dreadful rake, Pamela," he said. "My debauched behavior has been notorious for several years. Decent women give me a wide berth."

She raised one hand and touched her fingertips to his cheek.

"But I have never debauched a married woman," he said. "I have always held marriage sacred. I have always known that if I ever married, it would have to be to a woman I loved more than life itself, for I could never be unfaithful to her."

Her finger touched his lips and he kissed it.

"Would you find such a man trustworthy?" he asked her.

"Such a man?" she said. "I don't know. You? Yes. I have seen today, and last night, too, that you are a man of conscience and compassion."

He took her hand in his and brought her palm against his mouth. "How do you think your father would react," he asked, "to the idea of his daughter marrying a rake? Would my title and fortune dazzle his judgment?"

Her eyes grew luminous. "No," she said. "But he would be swayed by kindness and compassion—and by his daughter's happiness."

"Would you be happy, Pamela?" he asked. "Would you take a chance on me?"

She closed her eyes and turned her face in to his shoulder.

"It is absurd, isn't it?" he said. "How long have we known each other? Forever, is it? I have known you forever, Pamela. I have just been waiting for you to appear in my life. I have loved you forever."

Her face appeared again, smiling. "I would be happy," she said. "I would take a chance, my lord."

"Edward," he said.

"Edward."

"Will you marry me, my love?" he asked her.

She laughed softly and buried her face again. She hugged his waist tightly. "Yes," she said.

He held her wordless for a while. Then he slid one hand beneath her knees and lifted her legs across his. He reached beside him, shook out the blanket, and spread it over both of them. He settled the pillow behind his head, against the high wooden backrest of the settle.

"Stay with me tonight?" he murmured into her ear. "Just like this, Pamela? It is not the most comfortable of beds, but I will not suggest taking you to your room. I would want to stay with you, you see, and if we were there, I would want to possess you. I want that to wait until our wedding night. I want our bodies to unite for the first time as a marriage commitment. Are these words coming from my mouth?" He chuckled softly. "Are these the words of a rake?"

"No." She turned her face up to his, her eyes bright with merriment. "They are the words of a former rake, Edward—and never-to-be again. Does that sound dreadfully dull to you?"

He grinned down at her. "It sounds dazzlingly wonderful actually," he said. "Pamela and only Pamela forever after. Are you comfortable?"

"Mm," she said and snuggled against him. "And you?"

"A feather bed could not compete with this settle for softness and ease," he said. He kissed her again, his lips lingering on hers. "Happy Christmas, my love."

"Happy Christmas, Edward," she said, closing her eyes and sighing with warm contentment.

Upstairs, in the room the Marquess of Lytton had occupied the night before, Tom kept watch over the mother of his child, who slept peacefully, and over his newborn son, who fussed in his sleep but did not wake. Tom stood at the window, gazing upward.

A single star almost directly overhead bathed the inn with soft light and glistened off acres of mud. It was not a pretty scene. Not a noticeably Christmas-like scene. The inn, somewhere in Wiltshire, was neither large nor picturesque nor thriving. No one has ever mapped its exact location.